"Quiet!" the Russian shouted. It didn't take an Enhancement to see that the guy was agitated as all hell. "Get on the ground! Now! Both of you!"

Sighing, Frank did as he was told. "I'm telling you, Comrade, this is gonna really blow up in your face. I mean, we have diplomatic immunity." Frank kept talking, stalling for time while trying to come up with a way out of this. Without the breadth and depth of expertise available to him through his Enhancement, he was left only with memories of past accomplishments and his own instincts—just like normal people.

But as he got on his belly, he saw that the goon next to him—the one who now just had one eye and was now out cold—had a small device clipped to his belt. It wasn't a gun or a radio, and there was no sign of the Russian Variant who naturally generated null fields. So that meant, just possibly . . .

"Hey, honey pie, it's gonna be okay," Frank called out to Maggie, using the pet name he knew would annoy her the most. "It'll be over in an instant. Like flipping a switch. It's gonna be fine."

"I'm so scared, Frankie," Maggie fake-sobbed. "How you gonna make this okay? How?"

"Shut up!" the Russian yelled toward Maggie, then began shouting in Russian. There was no time left.

Frank reached for the device quickly, feeling for a switch. It was a toggle. Whatever. He flipped it and prayed.

The scream behind him was like a Beethoven symphony.

Praise for the MAJESTIC-12 Series

"A smart look at a Cold War in many ways even colder and scarier and deadlier than the one we barely survived."—*New York Times* bestselling author Harry Turtledove

"A heady blend of super-spies and superpowers, *MJ-12: Inception* is Cold War-era science fiction done right. A taut thriller, and skillfully evocative."—*New York Times* best-selling author Chris Roberson

"*X-Men* meets *Mission: Impossible*. Martinez takes a concept as simple as 'Super spies that are actually super' and comes away with a hit. Filled with compelling, well-rounded characters, *MJ-12* is my new favorite spy series."—Michael R. Underwood, author of *Geekomancy* and the Genrenauts series

"The Cold War becomes even more chilling as super-powered Americans are trained to become super-spies in Martinez's new alternate-history thriller. It's morally complex, intense, and so steeped in the 1940s, you can smell the cigarette smoke."—Beth Cato, author of *Breath of Earth* and *The Clockwork Dagger*

"*MJ-12: Inception* is a thriller that blends the best elements of Cold War-era spy stories, supernatural fantasy, and splashy pulp comics."—*B&N Sci-Fi & Fantasy Blog*

"*MJ-12: Inception* is Michael J. Martinez doing what he does best: taking a selection of great genres and mashing them up into something fresh and exciting, and quite unlike anything you've read before. . . . Or to put it another way, it's like the *X-Files* and *Heroes* went back in time, dressed up in dinner jackets, lit a fuse, and jumped through a window to the theme from *Mission: Impossible*. Absolutely loved it."—*Fantasy Faction*

"Martinez made a point to recognize the sacrifices made by those in the intelligence community to protect their nation. . . . the characters were all well-developed, their powers were imaginative, the twists weren't obvious, and Martinez did a good job capturing the setting. . . . *MJ-12: Inception* was an enjoyable twist on the superhero genre and I look forward to seeing what happens next."—*Amazing Stories*

"With *MJ-12: Inception*, Martinez weaves an intense tale of patriotism, Cold War politics, the U.S. spy network, and the nuances of human relationships which I simply couldn't put down."—*The Qwillery*

"Martinez has me hooked, and I'm anxiously awaiting the next book in the trilogy; I imagine more Variants, more subterfuge, and more world-ending risks are to be revealed. It's good stuff."—*GeekDad*

"*MJ-12: Inception* is both a complete stand-alone adventure and a thrilling introduction to a richly reimagined Cold War spy-fi series. I eagerly await Michael J. Martinez's next novel featuring the Majestic 12."—*Mutt Café*

"So good, in fact, that it makes you wonder why all sequels can't be this good . . . a fun, inventive, action-packed exploration of super spies operating in the shadows of history, and an almost perfect sequel."—*Fantasy Faction*, 10/10

"A satisfying sequel to *Inception* . . . If you like superhuman operatives fighting the weird fight in the shadow of nuclear war, then go check out the Majestic-12 series."—*Amazing Stories Magazine*

"Martinez is just really good at hitting the ball out of the park when he writes a sequel. . . . A great spy novel. . . . may well rank as his best work."—*InfiniteFreeTime.com*

MJ-12

Books by Michael J. Martinez

The Daedalus Series
The Daedalus Incident
The Enceladus Crisis
The Venusian Gambit
The Gravity of the Affair (novella)

MAJESTIC-12
MJ-12: Inception
MJ-12: Shadows
MJ-12: Endgame

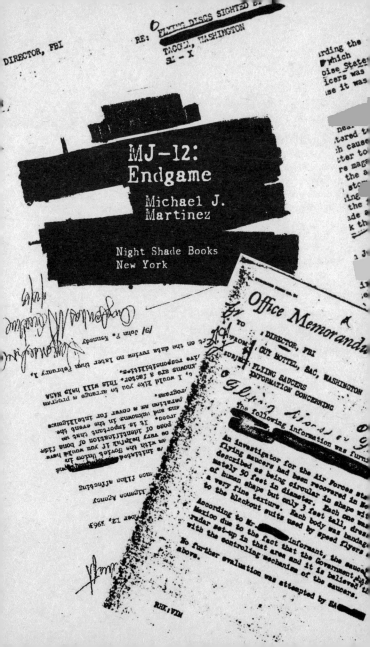

MJ—12: Endgame

Michael J. Martinez

Night Shade Books
New York

Night Shade books may be purchased in bulk at special discounts for sales promotion, corporate gifts, fund-raising, or educational purposes. Special editions can also be created to specifications. For details, contact the Special Sales Department, Night Shade Books, 307 West 36th Street, 11th Floor, New York, NY 10018 or info@ skyhorsepublishing.com.

Night Shade Books™ is a trademark of Skyhorse Publishing, Inc.®, a Delaware corporation.

Visit our website at www.nightshadebooks.com.

10 9 8 7 6 5 4 3 2 1

Library of Congress Cataloging-in-Publication Data

Names: Martinez, Michael J., author.
Title: MJ-12: endgame: a Majestic-12 thriller / by Michael J. Martinez.
Other titles: MJ-twelve | Endgame
Description: New York: Night Shade Books, [2018]
Identifiers: LCCN 2018016048 (print) | LCCN 2018019371 (ebook) | ISBN 9781597809719 (Ebook) | ISBN 9781597809702 (pbk.: alk. paper)
Subjects: LCSH: Paranormal fiction. | GSAFD: Suspense fiction.
Classification: LCC PS3613.A78647 (ebook) | LCC PS3613.A78647 M545 2018 (print) | DDC 813/.6—dc23
LC record available at https://lccn.loc.gov/2018016048

Cover design by Lesley Worrell

Printed in Canada

This one's for Sara.
Thanks for believing.

Author's Note

As with the other books in the MAJESTIC-12 series, this novel includes viewpoints and commentary in keeping with the early Cold War era of the setting. Thus, you'll find characters dealing with casual sexism and racism here that may, at times, seem disquieting to the modern reader. This isn't meant to endorse such views in any way—quite the opposite. These views are included to honor those who suffered through such shortsighted times, and to remind ourselves today of where we've been, and perhaps how far we have yet to go.

Likewise, you'll encounter historical figures who may hold different views than they did in reality. Given that these figures are reacting to the presence of superhumans in their lives—or in one case, that they themselves are superhuman—some departure from the norm should be respected. This is not in any way designed to malign those all-too-human figures, nor to justify their behaviors in real life. Dwight Eisenhower was a good president but had his failings. Nikita Khrushchev was the head of an anti-democratic Soviet regime, and he signed off on a variety of policies we would deem criminal today. And yet he wasn't as bad as, say, Lavrentiy Beria, who does not need to possess superhuman abilities to earn history's condemnation.

Long story short, this is a work of fiction. Please enjoy it as such, and if it gives you things to think about afterward, so much the better.

MJ-12
ENDGAME

February 28, 1953

Three limousines sped down the two-lane road in the cold night, headlights illuminating the piles of dirty snow on either side, the work of the plows creating a canyon for the cars to slalom. Dark trees loomed on either side, but to one of the limos' occupants, the destination loomed larger.

For Nikita Khrushchev, dinner with Josef Stalin was always a fraught affair. No matter how many times he went—and it was indeed a terrifying privilege he was granted with increasing regularity—he would never get used to the high-wire act they were all forced to perform.

When Stalin said dance, you danced. And for his four most trusted advisers, there was a great deal of dancing to do at these things. Khrushchev glanced at his watch, noting it was half past eleven at night. They wouldn't eat before midnight, undoubtedly, and would be expected to drink for hours afterward. And even as they drank, they would somehow need to be in full control of their faculties—one misstatement could mean demotion. Or worse.

Khrushchev looked over at his companion in the limo, Nikolai Bulganin, the new defense minister, who was dozing in his seat, his head propped against the glass of the window beside him. Khrushchev wished he could sleep so easily; he imagined it would do well for his fortitude during the night ahead. But no, the head of the Communist Party for Moscow and one of the top advisors to Stalin himself had to settle for a solid afternoon nap, one that kept him from his wife and daughter more often than he liked.

Was this, then, what the October Revolution had wrought? Grown men performing for a puppet master in the middle of the night, their livelihoods and lives on the line, all for . . . what? A chance to succeed Stalin as the puppet master? Or maybe, just maybe, a chance to do what could be done to fulfill the goals of the Revolution, to improve the lot of the workers and peasants. Perhaps to preserve them as much as possible from the increasingly erratic dictates of their glorious leader.

Khrushchev's silent musings—a death sentence if spoken aloud—were interrupted as the ZiS limousine ground to a halt in the snow outside a beautiful, ornate house. They were in Kuntsevo, at the Old Man's dacha. It was a rare thing for Stalin himself to enter Moscow except to entertain himself, so the business of government was handled here now, awash in wine and vodka, rich sauces and obsequiousness.

Khrushchev poked Bulganin in the arm. "We're here."

The other man stirred and stretched. "Time to play the game, then." With a yawn, Bulganin opened the door and braved the cold outside. Khrushchev followed suit. Behind them, the third limo was just coming to a halt. The doors opened and out came Georgy Malenkov, deputy chairman of the U.S.S.R.'s Council of Ministers, and Lavrentiy Beria, the first deputy premier and, many believed, the next supreme leader of the Soviet Union.

There was, of course, no finer mind for it, Khrushchev thought. Beria had the mind of an academician and the guts of a back-alley brawler. He looked like nothing more than a shopkeeper, with his balding pate and spectacles; only his piercing eyes betrayed this facade. Beria was, in Khrushchev's opinion, the most ruthless man in the Soviet Union. Even more so than Stalin himself.

It was a good thing, then, that most of the Politburo was scared of what Beria might do should he take such power. If Khrushchev had anything to do with it, he would ensure that the cost of such power would be too high for Beria to bear.

"Where is Comrade Stalin?" Bulganin asked.

Khrushchev turned to see the limo in front of him had already sped off, and he caught a glimpse of the supreme leader already inside the foyer of his dacha. The Old Man could still move at a decent clip, at least when it came to getting out of the cold.

"He's hungry," Beria said. "Perhaps he'll be easily sated tonight."

"Wishful thinking," Khrushchev said with a smile. "Come, let us see what he has for us."

The four men entered, their coats taken by Stalin's servants, a relic of the bourgeoisie that still troubled Khrushchev. Were they all not capable of managing their own coats? Or having their own wives cook their food? An army of servants, even for those of the proletariat honored with the heavy mantle of leadership, seemed counterrevolutionary.

Of course, Khrushchev wouldn't say no to them, either, should he eventually ascend to Stalin's position. Human nature would remain what it was.

The four—sometimes even referred to as "The Four" in the halls of the Kremlin, signifying their importance to the Soviet State—knew their way through the house and proceeded to the dining room. At least Stalin had opted to take in the picture show in Moscow, rather than here at the dacha, where the sound quality was bad and the movies were often Westerns smuggled in via diplomatic pouch from America. For some reason, Stalin loved Westerns. But since they weren't subtitled, the Old Man would ask someone in the room to make up the translation as the movie played. It was, of course, another test. Stalin could easily have employed a translator, but he wanted to see how his protégés handled the duties. A fine story would bring toasts to your health and playful banter. A poor one would earn a stream of profane invective if you were lucky. The unlucky might be frozen out of the Soviet Union's political structure for weeks at a time, and the other vultures would move in quickly.

But tonight was just dinner and drinking. Stalin's dining room was a relatively modest affair—a table for twenty, another along one side for the buffet, couches on the other side for relaxation, a warm fire, wood-paneled walls, and fine carpets. Tonight was Georgian food, which Khrushchev didn't particularly care for. He heaped food on his plate regardless.

Then he felt a jab in his stomach from a thick finger. "You eat too much, Nichik."

Khrushchev allowed himself to close his eyes for a moment before turning to address Josef Stalin with a smile. "You provide us with such food, Comrade Stalin, how can I not? You shall make all of us expand with your generosity."

At this, the Old Man laughed, and Khrushchev sighed with relief. Stalin was aged now, his hair and iconic mustache well grayed and heading for white, and his frame under his military fatigues had grown somewhat over the years. But he was still a commanding presence, and the worst part was that Stalin knew it—and knew he had the power to back up any commands he gave.

Soon the plates were filled, the wine was poured, the toasts to Stalin's health were duly made by each man present. While the supreme leader was arthritic and had slowed, each one of The Four remained disappointed in Stalin's continued good health, despite their toasts. They all knew that the Soviet Union was stagnating. The global post-war economy was booming, but the Soviet economy was well behind. This was, of course, largely due to the staggering losses suffered by the Motherland during the war, both in lives and resources. But it was also leadership, for how can an economy truly grow if one's economic solutions are to simply send managers and foremen to the gulag? Khrushchev had grand ideas, and had begun to slowly—so very *carefully*—implement them. But it was a drop in the bucket, and the bucket was vast and full only of need.

Khrushchev listened as Bulganin discussed the stalemate in Korea between the Chinese Communists and the

U.S.-led United Nations forces. The heady successes of late 1950 were a distant memory; the fighting had largely bogged down as the Americans and their allies flowed additional men and materiel to the front.

"Advise Chairmans Mao and Kim . . . oh, what Kim is this? Korea is full of Kims!" Stalin said, laughing at his own joke. "Anyway, tell them to negotiate. Communism will be happy to settle for half a country rather than none. When the Koreans in the south see the workers' paradise we will create in the north, they will knock down the borders and send the Americans home. Now, Comrade Beria, tell me of the doctors."

The Doctors' Plot was one of Stalin's pet peeves, one that Khrushchev felt had been concocted by Beria simply to keep the Old Man distracted. In short, it was an alleged plot by counterrevolutionary elements within Moscow's medical community—largely Jewish as well, which was convenient—to spread lies about Stalin's health—or even assassinate Party leaders—in an attempt to destabilize the Soviet Union.

"It fares well, Comrade," Beria replied smoothly. "Comrade Ignatiev has been doing fine work, and several will soon crack. And I have it on good authority that Dr. Vinogradov has quite the long tongue, and has been reported spreading scurrilous rumors about your fainting spells. Such nonsense, of course."

"Right, what do you propose to do now?" Stalin asked crossly after downing a shot of vodka. "Have the doctors confessed? Tell Ignatiev if he doesn't get full confessions out of them, we'll shorten him by a head."

"They'll confess," Beria replied. "With the help of other patriots like Timashuk, we'll complete the investigation and come to you for permission to arrange a public trial."

"Arrange it," Stalin said. He then paused to look around the table. "You are my most loyal and effective comrades. Some of you have done fine work and continue to do fine work on behalf of the State." Stalin's face grew redder and he stood from the table. "But there are those in the leadership of the Party and the State who think they can somehow get by on past merits! To sit in fine offices and enjoy their apartments in Moscow and their country dachas without continuing to do fine work! They are mistaken."

At this, Stalin strode from the room, and The Four were left to look at each other awkwardly, and to make small talk for the benefit of anyone else surely listening in. These sudden outbursts were becoming more common, as were the abrupt departures. Sometimes, Stalin would come back into the room after just a few moments, likely having gone to take a piss, and would either continue on his rant or change the subject entirely. Sometimes, The Four would be left to their own devices for hours, only to be told by a servant that Stalin had gone to sleep. Unfortunately, Stalin never really slept until just before dawn, so they would have to wait until he either came back to join them or was off to bed.

Khrushchev eyed the couch along the far wall longingly. Being caught napping would not perhaps be best, but tonight had already been long, and the morning too close by half. Instead, he joined the others in discussing the Korean question, which allowed them all to enjoy debating a topic that had little overall relevance for their careers.

Stalin joined them an hour later and was in far better spirits—and had better spirits with him as well, in the form of top-shelf bottles of Stolichnaya. Drinks were poured, toasts were made again. Someone produced a phonograph so that Stalin could play Ukrainian folk songs, and he tried to get Khrushchev to dance, repeatedly poking him in the stomach and singing, "Nichik! Nichik!" over and over. Finally, Khrushchev rose from his seat and—once the room stopped its alcohol-fueled spinning—tried a few moves from his youth. Stalin was pleased, the others laughed along, likely enjoying his embarrassment. But then it was done, and Stalin moved on to pick on someone else. Khrushchev slumped down upon the sofa and tried to stay awake.

Finally, at four in the morning, Stalin arose and wobbled toward his rooms, bidding his compatriots good night. With a sigh, Khrushchev hauled himself up off the couch and staggered toward the door. It was early, for once, and he might catch a couple hours of sleep in his own bed before tomorrow's meetings. A luxury, to be sure.

Within minutes of driving off in the limo with Bulganin, Khrushchev's head was up against the glass of the window. He wouldn't even remember dozing off.

He most certainly did not remember Lavrentiy Beria staying behind at Stalin's dacha.

But he clearly remembered the call that shook him out of his afternoon nap the following day. He'd remember it for the rest of his life.

2.

March 6, 1953

"So, Uncle Joe is dead, and good riddance. First order of business, who's got their nukes?"

The President of the United States folded his tall frame into the leather chair in the Oval Office and looked expectantly at Air Force General Hoyt Vandenberg, who felt that, at best, the nukes were the second-biggest open question facing the United States.

The first, well . . . most of the other men in the room weren't cleared for that. And even Dwight Eisenhower was still not a hundred percent sure of all the things he'd heard about the MAJESTIC-12 program. But Vandenberg was—he'd seen it. And Russian nukes were absolutely a secondary concern.

Yet there remained a game to play. "Right now, Mr. President, the Soviet nuclear arsenal, such as it is, remains in the hands of the military. Marshal Vasilevsky remains defense minister for now."

Eisenhower nodded thoughtfully. Vandenberg couldn't help but smile a bit, reminded of a time less than a decade ago when he was side by side with Ike, planning Normandy. Vandenberg had been responsible for the air cover for the invasion, and had the job of telling Eisenhower that the Germans were too entrenched to decimate via air power. The beaches of Normandy were a fortress, and there was only so much the Army Air Force could do. All Eisenhower did was nod gravely and go ahead with the invasion, hellish meat grinder that it was.

Being president was a cake walk compared to overseeing D-Day, it seemed.

"I know Vasilevsky a little bit," Eisenhower said. "Good man. Sober. Won't let anybody get too crazy. John, what news on the diplomatic front?"

Secretary of State John Foster Dulles sat up a little straighter in his chair. "There is, of course, a period of mourning, and then we're looking at a big state funeral. So far, it looks like the speakers will be Georgy Malenkov, Vyacheslav Molotov, and Lavrentiy Beria. We're invited to send dignitaries, of course. Any thoughts, sir?"

Eisenhower waved his hand dismissively. "Don't care, so long as I don't have to go to that bastard's funeral. Let the chargé d'affaires go if that'll be enough. Worse comes to worse, send Dick Nixon. Put him to good use for once." A chuckle arose around the room; there was no love lost in the political marriage between Eisenhower and Richard Nixon. "What I really care about is who's next. There's going to be a lot of instability and a lot of infighting over there. I see *opportunity*, gentlemen. Not just to contain the Soviets, but to roll 'em back. Buy space for Eastern Europe to breathe, maybe get back some of their independence. Reunify Germany under a democracy? Maybe. But I want to press. Hard. Wring everything we can out of them."

John Dulles shook his head sadly. "Mr. President, there are very, very few men in the Politburo with whom we could reasonably deal. Maybe Khrushchev, Bulganin . . . just *maybe* Mikoyan if we're lucky. But that's it. And they're all pretty junior compared to Beria and Malenkov."

Next to the Secretary of State, Director of Central Intelligence Allen Dulles—the secretary's brother—spoke up. "Probably not Mikoyan. And even if we like Khrushchev or Bulganin, it's not like we can prop 'em up or anything. This isn't Iran or Syria. Soviet Russia's a hard nut to crack. There's more political capital to be gained from hanging our men out to dry than doing a deal with us."

"Well, it's not like we'll show up with a briefcase full of cash or anything," Eisenhower joked, and there was another murmur of laughter around the room. "But gentlemen, let me reiterate, I want to take maximum advantage of this. We have a chance to defuse this Cold War before it gets hot again. We can wrap up Korea and not get caught up in proxy battles all over the world. Let the Soviets see what we can accomplish with peace."

Vandenberg couldn't hold his tongue any longer. "If their people see what we're doing here in the West, they'll want it back home. The Reds can't afford to let that happen."

"Depends how they handle it," Eisenhower said, his hands wide. "We need to try, don't we? John, Allen: How do we start?"

John Dulles shuffled his papers around until he found the right one. "First, we have to see how it all shakes out. You've got eight or nine men splitting up the government right now. Malenkov appears to have the top seat, but we think that's a consensus move, and everyone's gonna try to pull his strings. Beria, Molotov, Bulganin, and Kaganovich are the deputy premiers, and that's the real competition. Beria has state security again, and that'll make him first among equals. I'd also say Khrushchev has an outside shot—they're having him work to recentralize and refocus the Party committees. He's a sharp guy. He'll wheel and deal his way up."

Eisenhower looked squarely at Allen Dulles and Vandenberg. "Beria?"

The two men traded a look before Allen spoke. "Yes, sir."

The President's mood changed abruptly. "John, everyone. I have to talk with Allen and Hoyt here alone. Let's get everything written up and get our act together on the funeral, then start with the outreach to the individual satellite nations. Let's get 'em thinking that there's enough of a change going on in Russia that they can start taking chances—and we'll be right there for them when the time comes. Thank you, everyone."

John Dulles shot his brother a look, which was returned with an arched eyebrow. Vandenberg figured the DCI and the Secretary of State probably talked a lot more than their predecessors, but it seemed Allen Dulles could still keep secrets from his brother. The Secretary of State and the assorted aides and deputies filed dutifully out of the Oval Office, leaving just Allen Dulles and Vandenberg sitting across from the President.

Eisenhower didn't waste any time. "So you're saying that Lavrentiy Beria, a man who can literally shoot flames out of his hands, is head of state security and has the inside track on leading the Soviet Union, yes?"

Dulles gave a grave nod. "I've seen the reports, Mr. President. I've personally interviewed every single American who survived the Kazakhstan incident. I've seen every single aspect of the MAJESTIC-12 program, both here and out at Mountain Home. I even had a chat with Admiral Hillenkoetter about it last month. This is very, very real."

The President turned to Vandenberg. "Hoyt?"

"I've seen it firsthand, Mr. President. I've worked along-side our own Variants. They're good, patriotic Americans. I believe them when they say that Beria's a Variant as well. And we've seen enough intel on his private training camps, the Bekhterev Institute in Leningrad, all of it, to know that he's been running a Variant program of his own. He calls them 'the Champions of the Proletariat.' We think he's very much capable of grabbing power, for starters, and maybe even putting other Variants in top positions of power in the Soviet Union."

Eisenhower leaned back in his seat and ran a hand across his face. "I need to get out to Mountain Home. I need to see these things myself. Talk to these people. I mean, what's keeping our own Variants from trying to do exactly what Beria's doing over in Russia?"

Dulles sat up a little straighter. "I trust Hoyt, and if he's vouching for them, that's a start. But we're conducting our own security review as well. I don't want to say Harry Truman played fast and loose with these Variants, but they were given a wide degree of latitude in operating as covert agents on behalf of the United States government."

"And they've done an amazing job," Vandenberg said quickly. "Never had one wander off the reservation while on assignment. Time and again, they've proven their loyalty as well as their abilities. Honestly, they're the best covert agents we have right now."

"That true, Allen?" the President asked.

Dulles grimaced a bit, but nodded. "They have an excellent track record, sir."

Eisenhower pondered this a moment before shaking his head. "Either way, we have a situation in Russia. Variant or not, Beria's a bastard. He was Stalin's hatchet man. Hundreds of thousands of people killed or imprisoned—his orders. And if he really is a Variant, and believes in this Champions of the Proletariat nonsense, we need to do something about it. Options?"

There was a deep silence for several long moments before Vandenberg spoke. "We need a fresh assessment now that Stalin's gone. We need to figure out just how powerful Beria will get in the new order over there. And if need be, we need to take steps to—"

"That's enough, Hoyt," Eisenhower said, his hand raised. "I get the rest. First, assess. We need the lay of the land. And I really want to know if he's placing other Variants into government. How do we do that?"

Vandenberg smiled slightly and looked over at Dulles, whose grimace got deeper. There was only one way anybody knew of to ferret out Variants around Beria.

"Subject-1," Dulles said finally.

Eisenhower leaned forward, his face registering surprise. "From what I've read, Allen, Beria *knows* Subject-1. Beria knows *several* of our Variants. That's not exactly covert."

"Actually, I like it," Vandenberg said. "I think it sends a message."

"Being what, exactly?" Dulles asked peevishly.

"That we know what Beria is. That we're not afraid of him. That if he tries something with Variants, we'll return the favor," Vandenberg said.

"Deterrence," Eisenhower said. "Just like with the H-bomb."

"Exactly."

Eisenhower clasped his hands in front of him on the desk and looked down a moment. Vandenberg didn't envy him one bit. The President had only been told about the MAJESTIC-12 program the day after the inauguration, and it had taken him weeks to wrap his head around the entire concept of superpowered humans, everyday people given abilities by some kind of intelligence via an inter-dimensional portal that defied all known physics. There were a lot of meetings and a lot of talks, and Eisenhower remained skeptical of the whole thing—especially since they were being particularly cautious with the transition from Truman's administration. With Hillenkoetter out as DCI—and seemingly grateful to be back at sea after nav-igating political waters—Vandenberg was one of the very few men left in the MAJESTIC-12 program who had been there since the beginning. He'd come to appreciate the tal-ents of the American Variants—and their patriotism. But Eisenhower had his doubts—and had not yet had the time, nor the inclination it seemed, to actually meet some of the Variants or head out to Mountain Home himself. Thus, Beria's ascension would only confirm the President's worst fears about Variant ambitions.

Finally, the President looked up. "Okay, do it. Send them in."

3.

March 9, 1953

Russians in dark suits and coats shuffled by the bier at the front of the Hall of Columns, where the body of Josef Stalin lay in state, the ornate hall within the House of the Unions belying the drabness of the mourners' clothes. Attitudes, too, were drab and colorless; emotions were muted. Frank Lodge had been expecting more from the death of the Soviet Union's supreme leader, given the emotions he knew Russians could display when properly motivated. Maybe there just wasn't enough vodka in 'em yet—it was half past nine in the morning, after all.

There is too much uncertainty. And Stalin was feared more than loved, even by the Georgians, came the voice of the late Grigory Yushchenko, a colonel in the MGB who attempted to capture Frank and his fellow American Variants in '48. Like all who died around Frank, Yushchenko's memories and personality were embedded in Frank's mind—the ability granted by his Variance. Since 1945, Frank had absorbed the memories, abilities, and talents of dozens of individuals; he now spoke north of twenty languages, and in any given moment could be a doctor, mechanic, soldier, acrobat, thief, military strategist, or academic in half a dozen fields.

It made Frank the perfect covert agent. It also made his mind buzz with conversations and opinions at any given time. Only tight mental discipline—along with more and more time alone with minimal outside stimuli—kept Frank sane.

But Yushchenko and the handful of other Soviets he'd absorbed were handy at times like these. There was general agreement in his head that Stalin's death would be a relief to many Russians, even with the uncertainty sure to unfold at the top of the Soviet power structure.

The man beside him, a thin, nebbish, bespectacled diplomat, shook his head sadly. "I went to Pershing's funeral in 1948, and there was more pomp than this," he said. "This is sedate by comparison."

Frank turned to face Jacob Beam, the current chargé d'affaires at the American Embassy. The position of ambassador was open—the previous one had been kicked out of the U.S.S.R. last year for daring to speak out against the regime. Frank figured the guy was lucky he wasn't arrested, even with diplomatic immunity. So Beam, a career State Department man, was the one who ended up representing the United States at the funeral. "You think they're already distancing themselves from Stalin?" Frank asked.

Beam smirked. "Absolutely. The cult of personality around Stalin was strong—though not as strong as they believed. But they still need the distance. It'll be interesting to see how the speeches go, see who gets propped up as next in line. The chess game on this is gonna last months."

Frank turned to the woman beside him and leaned in close. "What are you getting?" he whispered so that Beam wouldn't hear.

Maggie Dubinsky narrowed her eyes and scanned the room. She was a fellow Variant; she could both sense and affect the emotions of those around her. The latter could be particularly brutal if she put her mind to it—Frank had seen her reduce grown men to abject fear, lust, or catatonia. And in the five years he'd know her, he'd seen her grow colder, more distant, her eyes taking in other people like a scientist examining a newt.

"Going through the motions," she whispered. "Resignation, mostly. A few of them seem happy to be here. That guy there," she added, nodding toward a civil servant in a gray suit leaning over Stalin's coffin, "he's thrilled. Good riddance. A few others are afraid. But mostly, just another day at the office."

It's in the Russian soul, said Kirill Suleimenov, a Kazakh soldier in the Soviet Army whom Frank had absorbed in 1949, on a mission that went so sideways he and some others ended up prisoners of the Soviets—and of Lavrentiy Beria. Suleimenov was just a farm boy, but Frank had found that of all the voices in his head, the Kazakh was one of the more even-keeled. *The Russians, unlike my people, are used to seeing regimes change. First there is one boss, then another. Lenin and Stalin were tsars like any other. And so they wait to see who is the next tsar.*

Yushchenko couldn't resist then adding his own opinion. *So long as the next tsar isn't Beria. The Soviet Union would fall and take the rest of the world down with it.*

Frank would never tell anyone this, but sometimes he would just sit and listen to the voices converse with one another. It was eerie and yet somehow soothing at the same time. He had no idea how it worked, and realized that his . . . *relationship* . . . to the voices was evolving over time. It was less about calling on skills or memories, more about juggling personalities.

With a supreme act of concentration, eyes screwed shut and brow furrowed, Frank silenced the voices. As much as the conversations provided comfort—he was never truly alone, after all—it would sometimes feel like he lived in a giant dormitory where nobody slept.

"Here and now," Maggie whispered, breaking Frank's concentration. "Look sharp. We got new faces."

Frank turned to see several groups of somber-looking men enter the room. First in line was a delegation from China, led by none other than Zhou Enlai, the premier of the relatively new People's Republic of China. Then the rest of the satellite states came in, most of whom had sent their top leaders along. It wouldn't do for Communist countries, after all, to place such an important event in the hands of a mere ambassador, even though the vast majority of Western nations had done just that.

"This is a big deal for them, too," Beam said, following Frank's gaze. "With Stalin gone, they'll be lobbying for

more support, more freedoms, whatever. They'll be working the system just as much as the internal folks."

Frank smirked a bit. "So who do you like, Mr. Beam? If
you had to slap a sawbuck down, who's your pick to win
the derby?"

The diplomat smiled broadly. "I know who I *want*, Mr.
Lodge. Someone safe and sane, like Kaganovich, who has
a real sense of what's possible and necessary, rather than
someone like Beria, who couldn't give a rat's ass about getting things done, so long as he has all the marbles."

"What about Malenkov?" Frank asked.

"Bah. Puppet. The deputy premiers have the power, and
they'll be working to pull his strings," Beam said.

Any further conversation was cut short as the somber ceremonial music changed to a slightly louder, more
up-tempo melody when the current leadership of the Soviet
Union entered the hall, led by Georgy Malenkov, the new
premier—a round-faced, pudgy bureaucrat who looked for
all the world like a harried accountant. Behind him was
Molotov, Malenkov's recently reappointed foreign minister, whose spectacles and mustache gave him the air of a
college professor or cartoon supervillain, depending on
your point of view, and whose idea of "diplomacy" boiled
down to repeating what he wanted until he either got it or
called off the talks. Stern-faced Nicolai Bulganin came in
full Soviet Army regalia, which to Frank's eye made him
look like a tin-pot dictator of a banana republic somewhere. Lazar Kaganovich was a balding, mustachioed man
with a sturdy frame who, frankly, was the only one who
looked like any of the workers or peasants supposedly in
charge of the Soviet Union.

And finally, there was Lavrentiy Beria—head of State
Security and the infamous MGB and, apparently unbe-
knownst to the rest of the Soviet leadership, a Variant.

Frank's eyes followed Beria as he proceeded down the
hall, hoping that the man would catch a glimpse of him.
It was unlikely—there were several hundred people in
the hall, after all, and the American delegation had been

exiled to a back corner of the room along with the other non-Communist officials, cordoned off from the rest by a wall of anonymous, stone-faced handlers.

They'd have to send their message later, then.

* * *

U.S. Navy Commander Danny Wallace pulled the collar of the woolen coat up around his face and adjusted the pageboy cap on his head to ward off the morning chill in Red Square. He was wearing the simple clothes of a factory worker—heavy overalls and a work shirt, steel-toed leather boots—and kept his gloves on lest someone discover the hands of an officer and desk worker rather than those of a laborer. Danny paused to look at his left hand briefly, flexing it. Nearly four years ago, that hand had been severely damaged in an experiment with a vortex phenomenon created by the bombing at Hiroshima and transported to a secret American facility—a kind of dimensional anomaly that was somehow connected to the advent of Variants worldwide. The Russians had stumbled upon and quarantined a vortex of their own as well, of course, because nothing was ever easy. The hand had gotten better, thanks to another Variant's Enhancement, but Danny swore he could feel it still ache some days, a phantom pain that would never quite go away.

Shaking off the memory, Danny turned and opened his mind, stretching out with his senses for the unmistakable mental pull of other Variants. In addition to being the day-to-day commanding officer of the MAJESTIC-12 program, Danny himself was a Variant too. His only Enhancement was the ability to detect other Variants—a tool that proved extremely useful for the U.S. government as it was finding and collecting Enhanced individuals to recruit for the MJ-12 program.

It also made discovering Soviet Variants a hell of a lot easier. And today, Moscow was full of them.

Danny couldn't see any Variants right now, but he felt no fewer than a dozen in the immediate area around Red

Square. Three of them were well known to him—Frank and Maggie, of course, would be part of the procession from the House of the Unions to Red Square, where Stalin would take his place next to the body of Lenin. Then there was Tim Sorensen, a middle-aged Minnesota electrician who could turn invisible at will—one of the absolute best Enhancements a covert agent could have, frankly, even if a condition of his ability was that he had to remain silent, not touch anything, and make sure to dodge whoever was coming his way. Crowds made Sorensen's job especially tough, which was why he was wandering the halls of the largely empty Kremlin now—a robust opportunity to gather intelligence straight from the source while nearly everyone else in Moscow was at the funeral. Danny smiled slightly at the thought of Sorensen invisibly rifling through filing cabinets in Beria's office while the man himself was only a few hundred yards away.

Of course, there was Beria himself, whom Danny had met before on a plain in Kazakhstan, part of the mission to rescue Variants who'd been captured during a crapshoot of a mission in Syria in '49. The Soviet spymaster was slowly entering Red Square now, among Stalin's pallbearers. Frank and Maggie were trailing behind him—along with two others who were likely Beria's own agents.

Yet another Variant seemed to flicker in and out of Danny's senses; he figured it was another Russian he'd met before, one who could send a shadowy projection of himself to almost anywhere else in the world. It made sense that this other Variant would be checking out the funeral—running interference for Beria and keeping an eye on the crowds.

Danny pulled his coat collar up a little higher. Just in case.

The rest of the Variants Danny sensed were spread around the city. He felt the vague pull of others leading off toward Leningrad, home of the Bekhterev Institute—a front for Beria's Soviet version of the MAJESTIC-12 program. Over the coming days, Danny would need to track down and visually identify the other Variants in the city. The palm-sized camera in his hand would help with that, and give the American Embassy and its staff of full-time spooks new persons of interest to track and tail.

As the first speaker of the day—Malenkov, the one who had taken Stalin's place at the top of the Party—began his oration, someone bumped into Danny's shoulder hard, prompting him to turn quickly and defensively. It was only a "fellow" worker, straining for a better view. "*Izvini, tovarishch*," the man said absently. *Sorry, Comrade.*

"*Ya v poryadeke*," Danny replied. *I'm fine.* Unlike Frank's facility with languages, Danny's Russian skills had been earned the hard way, through intensive classes at the Army's language school in Monterey, California. But he was getting pretty good, and Frank humored him enough to practice regularly at their base in Mountain Home.

The man next to him then bent down and picked something up off the ground. "*Dumayu, ty uronil eto, tovarishch*," the man said to Danny, handing him his wallet.

Danny immediately reached for his back pocket, and found that his wallet was indeed missing. "*Oy! Spasibo!*" Danny said, taking the wallet from the smiling "comrade" next to him, amazed at the skill that must have been used to lift the wallet from a deep pants pocket. The MGB wasn't taking any chances today, it seemed—but neither was Danny, which was why his wallet contained perfectly doctored papers identifying him as Dmitry Alekandrovich Vavilov, late of the village of Gornyy, near Irkutsk in the far western part of Russia.

Really, it should've been Frank pulling crowd duty— his usefulness with language and culture was, of course, built on lifetimes of other people's experiences. But Danny wanted the freedom to pursue other Variants, if necessary, whereas Frank's insights into the new politics of the Soviet Union would be handier if he had a front-row seat.

The MGB man who had lifted Danny's wallet smiled at him and then continued to push his way through the crowd. Another test passed, one of dozens through the years—though never here, in the very heart of Communism. Danny and his fellow Variants had been to Istanbul, Prague, Vienna, Damascus, Beirut, Kazakhstan, East Germany, Guatemala, Honduras, Argentina, Korea, and China—so many countries—since the MAJESTIC-12 program started up in 1947, but they'd never been sent to the U.S.S.R. itself until now. The power vacuum after Stalin's death—and the unspoken but very real fear in Washington of Beria's ascension—had paved the way for MAJESTIC-12's position in the vanguard of this particular op.

That had Danny excited. He'd been working for years to prove to the powers that be that the Variants were normal, patriotic Americans, despite their uncanny abilities, and that they deserved the full faith and trust of the United States government. But even MAJESTIC-12's biggest supporters—Vandenberg and Truman foremost among them—never seemed a hundred percent comfortable with people who could kill with a touch or twist emotions like Silly Putty. Someday, maybe.

Danny's attention was drawn back to the present by thunderous applause—Malenkov had finished speaking, and now Beria was heading to the podium. He stood there, watching the crowd and accepting their applause, appearing to soak it in, until he raised his hands and the noise immediately died down.

What if he just shot flames from his hands, right here and now? Danny wondered. *Is he that confident? Would he push the world that far?*

"Dear Comrades! Friends!" Beria began. "It is difficult to express in words the feeling of profound grief that is being experienced during these days by our party and the peoples of our country, as well as all progressive mankind. Stalin, the great comrade-in-arms and inspired continuer of Lenin's work, is no more. We have lost a man who is near and dear to all Soviet peoples, to millions of working peoples of the whole world."

Danny looked around at the rest of the dignitaries up on the dais, pinpointing the other Variants. He could immediately make out Frank and Maggie—their patterns, for want of a better word, were intimately familiar to Danny by now. The two others that had been trailing them were now behind the dais, making it tough for Danny to make them out. He thought about going around to try to catch a glimpse, but the stone-faced Red Army soldiers in their greatcoats, armed with Kalashnikovs, held a very firm line all around the VIP area.

The flickering shadow was no longer around, and most of the other Variants in the city weren't moving around much—probably listening to the funeral proceedings on the radio.

"Comrades!" Beria continued, warming up as he went; Danny had glossed over a bit, admittedly, as he scanned the crowd and the city. "The grief in our hearts is unquenchable, the loss is immeasurably heavy, but even under this burden the steel will of the Communist Party will not bend; its unity and its firm will in the struggle for Communism will not waver.

"Our party, armed with the revolutionary theory of Marx-Engels-Lenin-Stalin, taught by the half-century-long struggle for the interests of the working class and all the working people, knows how to lead the cause in order to secure the building of a Communist society. The Central Committee of our party and the Soviet government have been trained in the great school of Lenin and Stalin to direct the country."

Laying it on thick, Danny thought as Beria continued to give a history lesson about the leadership of the Communist Party through Russia's long history of troubles. Even the most caustic critic of Communism had to admit that Russia had experienced its share of woes during the past fifty years, even if much of it was caused by Stalin's own ineptitude.

"The enemies of the Soviet state calculate that the heavy loss we have borne will lead to disorder and confusion in our ranks," Beria said, his finger raised high. "But their expectations are in vain: harsh disillusionment awaits them. He who is not blind sees that our party, during its difficult days, is closing its ranks still more closely, that it is united and unshakable. He who is not blind sees that during these grievous days all the peoples of the Soviet Union, in fraternal unity with the great Russian people, have rallied still more closely around the Soviet government and the Central Committee of the Communist Party.

"The Soviet people unanimously support both the domestic and the foreign policy of the Soviet state," Beria said. "And let it be known that the Champions of the Proletariat stand ready to defend the Soviet people against the enemies of our great, multinational state—the Union of Soviet Socialist Republics!"

Danny froze in his tracks, and not simply at the mention of the Champions of the Proletariat—Beria's glorifying nickname for his own Variants.

In that moment, Danny saw the glimmer of a shadow both behind and *within* Beria, a shadow in the shape of a person, mimicking Beria's movements and yet also seeming to pull away from him as well.

Or pull *at* him.

Danny shook his head and shut his eyes; the shadow was gone when he opened them again. Beria thundered on in his speech, seemingly unaffected by whatever just happened.

This was new—*really* new—and Danny didn't like it one bit. He'd seen shadows like that before, though. Once, within the depths of the strange vortex that had, at the time, been housed at Area 51 in Nevada, and was now hidden away at Mountain Home in Idaho. The second time was when Danny had been within range of the Soviet Union's first atomic test—Beria's vain attempt at killing American Variants that had only barely been thwarted.

Those shadows had remained an official mystery, but Danny feared them all the same. They were, he was sure of it, some kind of intelligence. Some kind of sentient beings responsible for the Enhancement of Variants. And deep down, somehow, Danny knew they weren't friendly.

* * *

For the umpteenth time, Maggie found herself compressed into some slinky dress for some party so she could fuck with people's heads and get information for the good old U.S. of A. To be fair, the dress was more conservative than usual—it was a funeral, after all—and the ubiquitous champagne was nowhere to be found. But still, it was getting rote. The conversations, the people, the secrets—all of it.

Maggie smiled and laughed at the joke made by Molotov, the foreign minister, even though she really didn't find it funny. But then she felt a slight pull on her arm, which was entwined with Frank's. *Tone it down a bit.*

"Sorry. A bit too much wine," she said reflexively, nodding to the red in her glass. It was either wine or vodka, and while Maggie could hold her liquor as well as any man, it was still barely lunchtime.

Molotov smiled as the interpreter translated, and then replied in Russian—a language Maggie had studied, but still had yet to master. "Mr. Molotov says it is good to hear laughter in these dark times," the interpreter said. "The great Stalin himself was fond of laughter, so it is right that there should be some here now."

Frank nodded and said something presumably nice and diplomatic in Russian, and Molotov left them alone a few moments after that. Maggie felt her smile evaporate—her cheeks were hurting from the effort—and she resumed scanning the room, seeking out the threads of extreme emotion amongst the otherwise sedate crowd in the Hall of Columns, where they had returned for the reception.

"You know, for someone who reads emotions every day, your acting is getting worse, not better," Frank said quietly, radiating a quiet amusement.

"But that's what you people do, isn't it?" Maggie responded, allowing him a smirk. "Someone makes a joke, you laugh."

"It was a shitty joke," Frank replied. "And this whole detachment thing . . . You still seeing your shrink, Mags?"

Maggie sighed. "Three times a week while I'm home. You still seeing yours, or are you relying on the one in your head?"

"As a matter of fact, Dr. Mills is telling me right now that he'd like you to stop projecting," Frank said. Maggie knew enough about the people inhabiting Frank's skull to know that there was indeed a psychiatrist named Mills in there with him. "He says your disassociation is getting worse every day. You know what he suggests?"

"Enlighten me," Maggie said, eyes rolling.

"Go visit a hospital. See the newborns. See the kids in the critical wards. See the folks dying there. See all the visitors and feel all that emotion. Maybe that'll hot-wire your brain again."

Maggie frowned. "You can both keep your ideas to yourself. In fact—" She was interrupted by four quick buzzes in her clutch; a small radio disguised as a makeup case was there, and someone had keyed in a silent, vibrating code. *Beria is in the room.*

Both Maggie and Frank looked toward the back door of the room, where Danny was lounging by the bar, having traded in his fake proletariat clothing for his own real U.S. Navy uniform, even though he was still acting, this time as America's fake deputy naval attaché to the U.S.S.R. Danny nodded forward, and they turned to see Beria enter the room, now wearing a Western-style suit. Maggie was amazed at how much the Georgian had gained weight and lost hair in the less than four short years since they'd met on the battlefield, and wondered just how much juggling Stalin's declining health had taken a toll on the man.

One way to find out.

"I'm gonna go say hi," she said to Frank. "Coming?"

"Wouldn't miss it," he replied, tightness and tension softly radiating from him. Frank was coiled, ready for anything. She'd felt it a hundred times before from him; it was an emotional state peculiar to only a handful of people—people who took life-and-death risks for a living.

They walked across the hall, drinks in hand, and then waited their turn as Beria made his way through the crowd, glad-handing the diplomats and party officials present, his face seamlessly shifting from practiced smile to practiced somberness. His emotional state was one of impatience and, depending on his conversation partner, boredom or contempt, with barely a few sparks of interest or favor.

Then Beria laid eyes on them, and she felt a tendril of fear from him that was quickly quashed down. *Good.*

Beria walked over and extended his hand to Frank. "Ah! Mr. Lodge, if I recall? So kind of you to come. I am pleased America sent individuals so ... accomplished ... as your-selves to pay your country's respects to our great leader."

Frank took Beria's hand and shook it perfunctorily. "It's been a while, Comrade Deputy Premier," he said quietly. "I haven't forgotten your hospitality from before."

Beria smiled; the "hospitality" Frank mentioned was imprisonment and a battery of tests at Beria's secret base in Kazakhstan, where the Georgian had tried to turn Frank and two other Variants against the United States—then attempted to drop an A-bomb on them when that had failed.

"I should hope you would be my guest again very soon, Mr. Lodge," Beria said before turning to Maggie. "And ... my dear, I'm sorry, we met but only briefly, and I do not remember your name. Though you certainly made an impression then."

Maggie smiled—a genuine smile this time. She was part of the rescue mission to get Frank and the others back, and her "impression" on Beria had been putting the holy fear of God in him, prompting him to flee in terror. "Maggie Lodge, Comrade," she replied, using her false married name, "and as you said, I hope for the opportunity to make an impression again soon. Perhaps even now?"

She thrilled at the new thread of terror that whipped around Beria's head, but resisted the urge to seize it, to pull, to send nightmares into Beria's mind and turn him into a puddle of terror, spit, and piss on the floor. For his part, the Russian took a little longer to clamp down on the fear again. "Are you now part of the embassy here, Mr. and Mrs. Lodge? Shall we be seeing more of you in the future?"

Frank smiled. "I think that depends on how things go here," he replied, venom just barely concealed under the gentle cadence of his voice. "Obviously, the United States is keenly interested in a peaceful transition within the Soviet Union, now under new leadership, with whom we might work toward more peaceful coexistence. Should that occur, our talents would be better used elsewhere, no doubt."

In other words, we're onto you, asshole, Maggie thought.

"I see," Beria said, his facade slipping slightly. "Well, then. We can only hope for such fine goals. Until then." And with that, Beria turned his back and started working the rest of the crowd—pausing only to whisper something to an aide, who shot both Frank and Maggie a brief but hardened look.

"And now we're tailed," Frank said simply. "Time to go."

Maggie reached into her clutch and tapped her makeup case three times—*we're tailed, we're leaving*. The two of them then sauntered slowly toward the exit, making sure they talked to as many diplomats and Party officials as possible—but not Danny or any other Americans in the room. It took them an hour just to get to the coat check.

* * *

After that, they got in a cab, which was dutifully followed. So they went to an early afternoon tea at the Hotel Budapest, then took another cab to the Hermitage Garden, where they took a stroll and made a point to interact with as many people as possible. Frank felt bad about that—the old pensioner, the young couple with a couple of cherub-faced kids, the vendor selling hot tea from a cart—they'd all be taken to one of the MGB's many offices hidden around Moscow, to be interrogated as to what the Americans said and did. Their backgrounds would be checked for subversions; God forbid any of them had any actual opinions that differed from the Communist Party line. Frank's stomach sank as he thought of those kids never seeing their parents again because their grandpa was the old tsar's gardener or something. It was a necessary evil, one he would add to the litany he'd committed over the past five years.

"Don't feel bad," Maggie said, her breath fogging in the cold. "They'll be fine."

Frank tamped down on the surge of anger that rose inside him. She didn't *know* that, and it was getting hard to tell just how much her detachment had grown. It had started as a defense mechanism against all the emotions thrown at her, but maybe she genuinely didn't care anymore. And while he felt spied on, he also knew she was using her Enhancement to keep a sharp lookout for their tails—ten yards behind them, sauntering slowly through the gardens, only the evergreen topiaries offering anything to really look at. The fact that she had picked up on his state of mind was part of the package.

But still. "I'm gonna start using more null generators on you," Frank groused. The null generators were a refinement of an Enhancement displayed by a Russian Variant early in their careers: creating a field in which no other Enhancement worked. Rose Stevens, MAJESTIC-12's resident genius and technology expert—a Variant herself, with an Enhanced intellect—had taken that one person's ability and concocted a way to transfer the power into devices. The gadgets weren't perfect; after years of tinkering, they still had a deleterious effect on Variants—aside from stripping them of their abilities, they also contributed to cancer if used long enough. But there was no better way for mere mortals to keep Variants in check.

Maggie, however, was having none of it. "Don't you fucking dare," she hissed between gritted teeth. "I'll gut you in your sleep."

Maggie was one of the most effective combatants MAJESTIC-12 had. If it weren't for the lifetimes of combat experience in Frank's head, she could probably take him wide awake if she worked hard enough. But the anger was surprising. "Easy, champ. It was a joke. Don't you shut it off now and then? I do. If the voices are particularly rambunctious, I'll flip on a generator for a few hours just to get some peace and quiet."

"You do that?" Maggie asked, eyebrows raised. "Don't you feel strange without them?"

Frank just shrugged. "It's nice. There's no running commentary in my head. No analysis of every little thing I do. No opinions on how to cook a goddamned egg, or whether I'm doing enough weights at the gym, or arguments between voices on what's the most authentic way to eat caviar with tea."

"That happened?"

"Yeah, just now at the hotel. Apparently, you can either serve it on half a boiled egg, or on bread with butter. If they weren't just disembodied voices attached to random memories, I'd swear the people in my head would've ended up in a fist fight."

Frank thought that would make Maggie laugh, but she just shook her head. "All that company with you, all the time. You're never lonely. That's something."

"Wish I were sometimes," Frank said. "That's why I use the null generator, just to get some alone time. You don't ever use one?"

"Hell, no," she said, looking alarmed. "I'd feel . . . blind. Scared. I wouldn't know how people were feeling, what they'd be likely to do."

"You mean exactly how the rest of us live our lives?" Frank asked. "I have no idea how people are feeling except for what they say or how they look."

"Most people hide it well," Maggie replied, clutching Frank's hand a little tighter as they walked, part of their married couple ruse, an old tradecraft habit. Their Russian tails likely already had a brief on them anyway. "But under the surface, they carry around so much anger. Disappointment. Lust. Sadness. All of it. That shit builds up and you never know when one of 'em is just gonna pop. The average person is just a stupid, instinctual, emotional powder keg ready to blow. All they need is the right push. And I don't wanna be around when that happens."

"You sound like you really don't like people anymore," Frank said quietly.

"People are shit, Frank. They really are. In the end, they're just fight or flight, pleasure and pain. Everything else is just window dressing to cover up the fact that they're animals."

"Including me?" Frank challenged. "Danny? Cal?"

Maggie smiled slightly at hearing Cal Hooks's name. Frank knew Maggie was fond of the old Negro man who could absorb life force to get younger and stronger, or spend it to heal others at the expense of his own health and age. Lately, Cal had taken to appearing as his actual age, pushing sixty, though with a strength and spryness of a man half as old. Cal was a good man, a religious fellow who, thankfully, knew better than to try to Jesus everyone up. He had an almost paternal thing with Maggie. Frank figured Cal felt sorry for her, somehow.

"Cal's okay," Maggie said. "I mean, he gets angry and sad and scared like everyone else. But he has such a handle on it. Better than you or Danny or anyone I've ever met. Honestly, I don't know how he does it. He—wait." Maggie's walk slowed as she looked off into the distance; Frank knew that look. She sensed something. "Anger and fear coming for us. Six o'clock. And . . . ten o'clock. And . . . fuck, three o'clock."

Pincer move. Multiple directions. Capture or kill, came the voice of U.S. Army General Mark Davis. *If it's more than five, you need to leave.*

"How many?" Frank asked quietly.

You should've brought a gun, added Gunnery Sergeant William Collins, one of the best shots to come out of World War I. *Even one of Mrs. Stevens's pea-shooters would've helped.*

"I'm sensing six," Maggie replied, her body tensing. "Three

pairs. Thirty seconds out, give or take." She opened her clutch casually and pulled out her makeup case, clicking the side two times, then two times again, while she ostensibly checked her rouge. It was the signal for immediate danger and enemy contact. She then pulled out a cigarette case. "Rose specials," she said. "One for each of us. Got your lighter?"

Frank smiled. He'd forgotten about the lighter in his pants pocket, and hadn't thought to pack any of Mrs. Stevens's "special" butts. "I do," he said quietly. "You aim right, I'll take left, and the lighter will handle the guys behind us. Ready?"

Maggie put her cigarette case away and leaned toward Frank with a slight smile. "Always, *darling*," she said, putting the cigarette between her lips. "Light me up."

Frank flicked the lighter and lit her cigarette, then his. He turned to his left just in time to see two men in dark suits and coats striding toward him purposefully, grim looks on their faces. *One on the right looks like the bruiser,* said James O'Keefe, a two-bit boxer and bouncer who died back in '51. *Take him out with the cig and—*

The voices suddenly went silent, like a door slamming shut between them and Frank. "Null field," he whispered.

"Fuckers," Maggie spat. "Let's go."

Frank smiled at the approaching goons. "*Privet tovarishchi. Chto ya mogu sdelat' dlya vas?*" Then he pointed his cigarette at the bigger one just in time for the tip to explode, launching a sleeper dart that plunged itself straight into the man's left eye.

Wasting no time, Frank flicked his lighter again and threw it to his left, where the two suits behind them had rushed to catch up. By the time Frank had turned to punch dart-guy's friend in the face, the lighter exploded, spraying the Russians with concentrated oil that immediately caught fire—and engulfed the two in flame. The guy who took the dart to the eye—unlucky bastard—was on the ground writhing in pain, but Frank's punch didn't seem to faze the last Russian much, and Frank had to duck awkwardly to avoid the man's roundhouse.

Frank kicked a leg out and caught the Russian's knee from behind, staggering him as the missed roundhouse sent him twisting off balance, exposing the back of the man's head to Frank. Immediately, he remembered one of O'Keefe's signature moves and jammed a fist into the back of the man's neck, just under his skull, likely sending a shockwave of pain and disorientation through his body. The man staggered as he turned around, but Frank was ready with an uppercut that caught him right under the chin and sent him sprawling down onto the gravel pathway of the garden.

"Enough!"

Frank whirled around to see the last Russian standing— holding a gun to Maggie's head. She stood at arm's length from him, staring at the barrel from just a few inches away. She looked incredibly pissed.

"Easy there, friend," Frank said, his hands instinctively up. "Let's not get anybody killed today."

The Russian nodded to the two men who had taken the brunt of Frank's lighter grenade. They were crumpled on the ground, completely on fire. "It is too late for that, I think. We have more coming. You will hang for this, American."

Frank smiled his best, most diplomatic smile. "Look, we're with the American Embassy, and honestly, I thought we were getting mugged. I mean, I'm from New York. That happens, you know? My uncle Tony, he was walking on 42nd Street, right near Times Square of all places, and out of nowhere three guys came up and just—"

"Quiet!" the Russian shouted. It didn't take an Enhancement to see that the guy was agitated as all hell. "Get on the ground! Now! Both of you!"

Sighing, Frank did as he was told. "I'm telling you, Comrade, this is gonna really blow up in your face. I mean, we have diplomatic immunity." Frank kept talking, stalling for time while trying to come up with a way out of this. Without the breadth and depth of expertise available to him through his Enhancement, he was left only with memories of past accomplishments and his own instincts—just like normal people.

But as he got on his belly, he saw that the goon next to him—the one who now just had one eye and was now out cold—had a small device clipped to his belt. It wasn't a gun or a radio, and there was no sign of the Russian Variant who naturally generated null fields. So that meant, just possibly . . .

"Hey, honey pie, it's gonna be okay," Frank called out to Maggie, using the pet name he knew would annoy her the most. "It'll be over in an instant. Like flipping a switch. It's gonna be fine."

"I'm so scared, Frankie," Maggie fake-sobbed. "How you gonna make this okay? How?"

"Shut up!" the Russian yelled toward Maggie, then began shouting in Russian. There was no time left.

Frank reached for the device quickly, feeling for a switch. It was a toggle. Whatever. He flipped it and prayed.

The scream behind him was like a Beethoven symphony.

He called for reinforcements on the radio, Suleimenov said in his head. *Your friend has him, though.*

Frank turned to see the Russian sink to his knees, his eyes wide, his scream having turned into a kind of soft gurgling sound. A wet stain spread from between his legs and down his pants, and he grew so pale, Frank could see the stressed-out veins under the man's skin. He clutched aimlessly at his chest as he stared up at his tormentor.

Maggie Dubinsky was not pulling punches. At all.

Frank scrambled to his feet, pocketing the null generator, just as the man fell over unconscious. "Is he alive?"

Maggie shrugged, then took his gun from him—and shot him in the head.

"Nope."

"Jesus Christ, Mags!" Frank said, looking around to see if there were witnesses. Thankfully, the locals had likely dutifully scurried away at the first sign of trouble, and the weapon had a silencer on it. "He was out of the game!"

She turned and shot the other three Russians who weren't on fire, then, after pausing a moment, shot the two guys still burning as well. "*Now* they're out of the game. Give me the generator," she said, steel in her voice.

Before he could respond, Frank's mind was besieged. Memories, names, skills, knowledge—the sum total of the dead men on the ground—flowed into him, a tsunami of information. He sank to his knees, his hands reflexively going to the sides of his head as he screwed his eyes shut to concentrate. *Boris Mikhailovich. Ivan Vladimirovich. Vasily Vasiliovich. Grigory Karlinovich. Andrei Borissovich. Josef Antoninovich.* Their names came at Frank as if they were being shouted in his face. Images of wives, mothers, fathers, children. Memories of youth. Hopes for old age. Joys of life. Sorrows and indignities.

And information. The orders transmitted by some mid-level flunky to capture the "dangerous Americans" on behalf of the Deputy Premier. The null generators, given to them without explanation. The offices and safe houses in Moscow run by the MGB. Command and control. Contingency plans.

Frank grabbed as much as he could of the latter, which felt like grabbing at schools of fish in a rapid stream with his bare hands. In all his years, he'd never had so many die at once around him. It buffeted his mind, sent his senses reeling.

And then it passed. All was silent.

He opened his eyes to see Maggie standing above him, for once looking concerned and altogether humane. She still held the silenced gun. "Frank?"

"Get rid of that gun," Frank whispered as he slowly staggered to his feet. "Can't be seen."

"Give me the device," Maggie said, challenge returning to her voice and face.

"No. We're taking it in for analysis. Didn't know they had their own generators, need to know if they got it from us. Drop the gun. We're leaving."

Maggie looked as though she was going to argue, but Frank focused his own emotions into an angry "do not fuck with me" thought, and a moment later, the gun hit the gravel.

"You get anything?" Maggie asked.

I already called for backup. They will be coming in from the north. You must head east, said Boris Mikhailovich Kirov, the officer in charge of the men sent to capture them. His voice echoed in Frank's head and, for a moment, he wondered if Boris would mislead him. That never happened before, in all the years of absorbing memories and knowledge, but Frank couldn't help but wonder. He then shook his head to clear it. That wouldn't happen.

"Some MGB stuff. Nothing big. Come on. This way."

The two quickly ran into the topiary gardens and, a few minutes later, came out onto Upensky Street, where they quickly hailed a cab and headed for Red Square. From there, they'd take two more cabs before finally heading back to the Embassy.

"Jesus, Maggie," Frank breathed once they were safely in the cab. "You gotta get a handle on it."

She turned to him, confused. "I'm fine, honey," she said, then gave him a saccharine smile.

She's really not, Dr. Mills said in Frank's head. *Her sociopathy is reaching dangerous levels.*

"Yep," he replied aloud. To both of them.

41

Action
SS

Info

OFFICIAL USE ONLY

FROM: MOSCOW

TO: **Secretary of State**

NO: 2663, MARCH 9, 6 P.M.

Control: 1275
Rec'd: MARCH 9, 1953
6 P.M.

1

To be read only with the permission of the Director of S/S.

CONFIDENTIAL

PRIORITY

IN ACCORDANCE SECRETARY'S INSTRUCTIONS DEPARTMENT TELEGRAM 707, I ATTENDED STALIN FUNERAL CEREMONIES AS SPECIAL US REPRESENTATIVE, ACCOMPANIED BY SPECIAL REPRESENTATIVES LODGE AND DUBINKSY. IN COMPARISON OTHER STATE FUNERALS I HAVE WITNESSED, NAMELY GENERAL PERSHING'S IN 1948 AND THAT OF GENERAL VON FRITSCH IN BERLIN IN 1939, ARRANGEMENTS WERE CASUAL BUT CEREMONY COULD NOT HELP BUT BE IMPRESSIVE AGAINST BACKGROUND RED SQUARE. CHIEF EMPHASIS WAS ON SATELLITE PARTICIPATION, PARTICULARLY THAT OF CHINESE.

WITHOUT ANY ACTIVE DISCOURTESY BEING SHOWN, NON-COMMUNIST DELEGATIONS AND MISSIONS WERE DEFINITELY LESS FAVORED. OUR PRESENCE WAS REQUIRED AT HALL OF COLUMNS 8:50 WHEN WE WERE LEFT STANDING FOR MORE THAN HOUR AT ONE SIDE WHILE LAST DESERVING RUSSIAN PUBLIC SERVANTS FILED PAST STALIN BIER. AT 10:00 THE LARGE SATELLITE DELEGATIONS WERE BROUGHT IN AND PLACED IN FRONT OF US, FOLLOWED BY TOP RUSSIAN GENERALS IN FRONT OF THEM. FINALLY AT 10:15 NEW SOVIET GOVERNMENT LEADERS ENTERED TAKING THEIR PLACE IN FOREFRONT. AFTER A FEW

xg

A /MES

OFFICIAL USE ONLY

53

Action
EUR
Info
RMR

P
IES
UOP
E
OLI
DCL

OCB
USIA
CIA

MINUTES FURTHER PLAYING CEREMONIAL MUSIC, LID WAS PLACED ON STALIN'S COFFIN WITH BEARERS LED BY MALENKOV AND INCLUDING CHOU EN-LAI BORE BRIGHT RED CHIFFON PALL AND STRAINING HEAVILY TOOK IT FROM HALL. AFTER SATELLITES WE TOOK OUR PLACE IN PROCESSION BEHIND COFFIN ON GUN CARRIAGE AT DEAD MARCH, PROCEEDING TO RED SQUARE WITHIN HALF BLOCK PAST OUR EMBASSY WHERE OUR FLAG AT HALF MAST WAS IN SIGHT OF EVERYBODY. WE WERE FLANKED BY TWO MOVING COLUMNS OF SOLDIERS AND WERE COURTEOUSLY ATTENDED BY FOREIGN OFFICE AND/OR SECRET POLICE OFFICIALS IN PLAIN CLOTHES IN OUR RANKS WHO SHOWED US TO PLACES ON ABUTMENTS LENIN'S TOMB. LATTER QUIETLY INTERPOSED THEMSELVES BETWEEN US AND LEADING SOVIET AND SATELLITE GROUPS EACH TIME THEY ASCENDED AND DESCENDED FROM TOP OF MAUSOLEUM. SOLE NAME OF LENIN HAD BEEN ERASED AND TWO NAMES LENIN AND STALIN SUBSTITUTED IN SMALLER LETTERS OVER ENTRANCE.

AFTER EXACTLY ONE HOUR OF SPEECHES BY MALENKOV, BERIA AND MOLOTOV3 COFFIN BORNE BY SAME PALLBEARERS INTO TOMB SHORTLY BEFORE NOON WHEN SALUTES FIRED AND FACTORY WHISTLES BLOWN. FOLLOWING RETURN PALLBEARERS WHO RESUMED THEIR PLACES ON TOP OF MAUSOLEUM STRIKING BREAK OCCURRED WITH PLAYING NATIONAL ANTHEM AND INTRODUCTION LIVELY MARTIAL MUSIC FOR MILITARY MARCH-PAST WHICH FINALLY ENDED WITH OVER-FLIGHT MILITARY AIRPLANES. RELAXATION FOLLOWED WHEN TOP GROUP BEGAN CHATTING WITH EACH OTHER AND CEREMONY ENDED WITH FINAL DESCENT INTO TOMB BY LEADING COMMUNIST SPECTATORS FOLLOWED BY DIPLOMATIC CORPS.

TO SAY THE LEAST, WHILE ALL PROPRIETIES OBSERVED, STALIN LAST RITES COMPARATIVELY

53

Action

EUR

Info
RMR

P
IES
UOP
E
OLI
DCL

OCB
USIA
CIA

UNAESTHETIC, CONSIDERING MAGNIFICENT
FACILITIES WHICH COULD HAVE BEEN MADE
AVAILABLE IN KREMLIN IN KEEPING WITH HIS
STATURE AS GREAT SOVIET LEADER. (UNDER
COMMUNISTS KREMLIN OF COURSE NO LONGER
POPULAR PROPERTY.) PECULIARLY INCONGRUOUS
THAT STALIN IS PLACED EVEN TEMPORARILY AS
DARKENED CORPSE IN NARROW AISLE ON SIDE
LENIN'S LIGHTED BIER.

WITH GRADUAL REMOVAL POLICE LINES GROUPS
OF THE CURIOUS FREQUENT RED SQUARE BUT LIFE
OUTWARDLY RETURNING TO NORMAL INDICATING
THAT WHATEVER CHECK WAS PRODUCED BY FIRST
ANNOUNCEMENT STALIN'S ILLNESS IS WEARING OFF.

BEAM

741.11/10-357

PA

FIELD REPORT
AGENCY: Central Intelligence Agency
PROJECT: MAJESTIC-12
CLASSIFICATION: TOP SECRET-MAJIC EYES-ONLY
TO: POTUS, DCI DULLES, GEN VANDENBERG USAF
FROM: CMDR WALLACE USN, MAJ LODGE USA, AGENT
DUBINSKY, AGENT SORENSEN
DATE: 12 MAR 1953

The assault on MAJ Lodge and Agent Dubinsky was a
successful diversion from the activities of Subject-1 and
Agent Sorensen. As planned, their visible presence during
Stalin's funeral and subsequent events focused USSR
Deputy Premier Beria's attention on them, and away from
other matters.

Agent Sorensen was able to penetrate elaborate security
inside the Kremlin and obtain several dozen photographs
of sensitive documents pertaining to MGB activities both
within the USSR and throughout the world. The information
in those documents should be disseminated—under appropriate cover and with care to not reveal source documentation—to the relevant military and civilian intelligence agencies in the US and among allied governments.
(See report under separate US Naval Intelligence cover
this date from CMDR Wallace.) However, Agent Sorensen
was unable to find any documentation regarding Soviet
Variant activities or organization. It is assumed Beria
keeps the Soviet Variant program well compartmentalized,

and possible that among the current Soviet leadership, he alone knows of its existence.

Subject—1 was able to identify ten Variants within the greater Moscow area. Among these are the following known Soviet Variants:

- Lavrentiy Beria, who has the ability to create flames and project them from his hands;

- Maria Savrova, who can mentally track an individual to their exact location anywhere in the world after touching them;

- Mikhail Tsakhia, a Mongolian—Russian man who can generate fields of null—Enhancement organically; our devices were mirrored after his ability;

- Boris Illyanov, who retains his ability to move at extreme speeds despite his age;

- Unknown name, an individual who can project a semi-solid shadow figure of himself anywhere in the world.

There were five others identified by Subject—1, all of whom were successfully tracked down and photographed—three women and two men. Two of the men and one woman wore MGB and/or Red Army uniforms, while the other two were seen in the kind of high-end civilian dress reserved for Communist Party functionaries—suit and tie, nice dress, greatcoats, etc. Likewise, none of the new

targets identified as Variants displayed any Enhancements
while under observation. While this has kept us from
better identifying their potential threat, it is also continued assurance that the Variants under Beria continue
to keep their presence a secret from the larger Soviet
population.

These Soviet Variants were observed entering and leaving
several nondescript buildings scattered throughout Moscow.
None of the buildings carried signage consistent with
Soviet government or Communist Party facilities, though
two addresses are consistent with intelligence obtained by
MAJ Lodge via his Enhancement regarding MGB safe houses
in Moscow. It appears at least some unmarked MGB facilities have begun to overlap with Beria's Variant program.

It is also worth noting that the MGB appears to have
successfully replicated the null generator devices first
perfected by the MJ-12 program. Since they have encountered them before, it is possible they have simply developed the technology on their own. Recommend, however,
that all null devices be accounted for, and also conduct
additional security screening for those with access to
any part of the development process.

CONCLUSION AND RECOMMENDATIONS

None of the new Variant targets are known MGB or
Red Army personnel in Moscow, and we are working with
Station Leningrad to perhaps identify them there, as

Leningrad remains a center of Variant program activity
through the Bekhterev Institute. We are also cross-ref-
erencing other stations to further help identify these
new individuals.

We believe Beria, as part of his ascension to the Deputy
Premiership, has brought several Variants to Moscow as part
of an effort to centralize his authority over MGB and, possibly, over the rest of the Soviet governmental apparatus. We
believe the other Deputy Premiers and high-level officials
within the Soviet government remain unaware of the Variant
program and Beria's own Enhancement, given Stalin's pen-
chant for secrecy and compartmentalization. (Whether Stalin
himself was aware of Beria's Enhancement or the program is,
at this point, moot.)

Given Beria's secretive nature and the power of the
MGB in both government and in Soviet life, it is
entirely possible that Beria could move to consolidate
power while keeping his Enhancement and the Variant
program a secret, placing his Variant allies into positions of authority as he works against the other elements within government. This would, of course, not
only give him the upper hand in most political con-
frontations, but could lead to a situation in which the
Soviet Union itself is led by a Variant—one who has
demonstrated a callous disregard for normal people in
his quest for power.

·············
· TOP SECRET ·

We firmly believe that a Variant—led USSR is an exis-
tential danger to the United States, to the people of
the Soviet Union, and to Variants around the world.
Beria's ascension to unquestioned leadership within the
Soviet Union—on a par with Stalin or Lenin—would lead
to worsening relations with the United States, greater
crimes against the Soviet people, and the possibility that
Variants themselves could be made public knowledge as
"Champions of the Proletariat."

While we recognize that interfering with the internal politics of the Soviet Union is unlike any other operation
heretofore attempted by CIA or MJ-12, we believe the lessons learned from operations in Syria, Eastern Europe, Iran,
and South America could be useful here, and that a limited operation may prove beneficial in securing American
interests.

We propose to undermine Beria by taking covert action
against the MGB and Soviet Variants within the Soviet
Union and Eastern Bloc states. This operation would serve
to discredit and undermine Beria's leadership, authority
and resources, prompting other competing elements within
the USSR to remove him from power as the struggle to
replace Stalin continues.

We furthermore propose that this operation should not
seek to back, in any way, any other candidate for power
within the Soviet Union. For one, none of the other candidates present the same threat as Beria, and can be

dealt with through normal diplomatic and covert means
as necessary. We also believe that such a move would be
far too dangerous for both MJ-12 agents as well as any
Soviet official we would choose to back.

The limited scope of this operation—discredit and remove
Beria from power—ensures a greater degree of plausible deniability for the United States Government and
more opportunity for reformist elements within the Soviet
Union to achieve victories without seeming to be unduly
influenced by outside activity.

-END-

March 14, 1953

MEMORANDUM FOR THE DIRECTOR OF CENTRAL INTELLIGENCE

Dear Director Dulles:

As per our conversation yesterday on this matter, you are hereby directed to initiate Operation TALISMAN as suggested in the Majestic Twelve Field Report dated 12 March 53. With all due haste and consideration, you are to deploy your assets as discussed.

Any changes to plans or procedures around Operation TALISMAN must be approved by the Office of the President after consultation with yourself and General Vandenberg.

I must reiterate the sensitive nature of both Operation TALISMAN and the Majestic Twelve program. If either are compromised in any way, this office will disavow both programs entirely. This will be the only written record of either operation from this office, only one copy of which will be preserved. Destroy this memorandum upon receipt.

Dwight Eisenhower

March 15, 1953

"Calvin Hooks, what do you mean, you aren't coming to church?"

Cal slipped on a white dress shirt from the closet and began buttoning it, praying that he could find a reasonable excuse for not going with his wife, Sally, to services. It was, of course, bad enough that they had to drive fifty miles into Boise to find a decent Baptist church with a preacher who could truly make the Word sing. And in winter, of course, when the roads were bad, they'd have to make do with the chaplain's services right there at Mountain Home Air Force Base—and that chaplain, a bespectacled white boy who looked outright scared whenever proper black people were in the congregation, did not so much sing the Word as stutter through it.

But not going at all was worse. And that was what Cal had to do.

"I'm sorry, Sally. Truly I am. But this is how it goes. I don't know when I get called up. Just do," Cal said as he slipped on a pair of gray pants. "You just gonna have to pray extra hard for me today."

Finally, Sally came around into the bedroom, her hat and veil already on and looking perfect. She was in her late fifties and, truth be told, ever so slightly starting to look her age—a little gray in her hair, a few more wrinkles around the eyes. Cal knew many Negro women were blessed with the ability to defy age for the longest time—they had to have *some* blessings for all the Lord put 'em through—but nobody could truly outrun time.

Except for Cal, of course. But Cal and Sally didn't talk about that. They had, once, about three years ago, when Cal had offered to bring back some of Sally's youth if she liked. He'd ended up spending the healing energy on the welt on his head instead. Sally was deft with a fry pan. The topic hadn't been broached since, and Cal worked to slough off as much of the youth he gathered during assignments before he got home, preferring to stay at a healthy, robust midfifties when he was around Sally or their boy, Winston, who was now off in his first year of law school.

"There just ain't nothing sacred anymore," Sally said. "You can't tell them no? After all this time? You've been working for them now for seven, eight years. They put you through the wringer every time. You can't tell them you'll be along after church?"

Cal shook his head sadly. "You know how it is, Sally. This job, this thing I do, this is what pays for Winston's schooling. Pays for our house here on base, all the things we've been able to do since I left the Firestone factory. Ain't no more third shift, getting all dirty and sweaty. You ain't gotta work a job and take in laundry to make ends meet."

Sally walked over and started helping Cal button his shirt. "I know all that, and I'm proud of you, really I am. You've done right by us, and you're doing right by your country, too. But even when you come back looking like that rough-and-tumble teenager I met back in the day, I see what's going on, Cal. Your eyes. How long you think you can last doing what you do for them?" She held up her hand to forestall the forthcoming protest. "I know. I don't know what they have you do. But I know enough. And I know that making sure you're right with Jesus is more important than ever because of that. You know it well as I do."

Cal sighed and smiled and let Sally tie his necktie for him. "How many years is law school again?"

"Three. Two to go after this year."

"All right. Two more. And I got two more after that on my ten years here. After that, maybe it's time to see about moving on. Maybe I get a pension or something. Or we can just find a nice quiet place to work and live, without any of that stuff that's happening down South right now."

Sally's face brightened. "You mean it?"

Cal gave her a quick kiss as she finished tying his tie. "You bet I do. Winston will be out of school, probably being some hot-shot lawyer somewhere. We've been able to save up quite a bit, too. But right now, baby, I have to go work."

Sally stepped back and nodded. "You gonna be back when I get home from church?"

Cal shrugged on his dark suit jacket. "I don't know. Depends if this just a meeting or if we're heading out. I'll try to be here either way, but if not, I'll be sure to leave word."

"I know the drill," Sally said with a sigh. "I best get going if I'm going to make it to Saint Paul's on time. I'll tell everyone you're on duty again, and try to keep those church ladies from being too nosy."

Cal chuckled and kissed her again, feeling her body stiffen slightly. She was upset, of course. He wasn't pleased either—what was with all the decisions and meetings coming down on Sundays anyway? Didn't anybody in Washington ever take a weekend? Maybe go play some golf like good white people do?

Sally offered to drive Cal into the base proper—they lived in a little cluster of homes for officers and high-ranking enlisted men just inside the outer perimeter—but he waved her on to Boise and started walking, pulling his coat around him as he went. It was warm for that time of year—a relative term when the temperature was maybe forty degrees and the wind off the mountains cut like a knife. But it had been more than three years since they moved, and he was getting used to the mercurial Idaho weather. Honestly, he was getting to like the cold. The South he knew as a child was always hot and sticky and unpleasant. And full of crackers all too eager to send calls of "nigger" and "boy" his way. Maybe some of the folk in

Idaho stared a bit too long, maybe they were a little too short with their words, but it was a damn sight better than Memphis. Cal had heard some good things about Seattle and San Francisco from some of the young black men at the air base. Maybe they'd move there.

Cal's attention was pierced by a car horn, and he turned to see Frank Lodge rolling up in his latest car—a 1952 Buick with enough chrome to blind a man. Frank did like his cars. "Jesus, Cal, it's freezing. Get in!" Frank called.

With a smile, Cal jumped into the passenger seat and rubbed his hands vigorously. "Thanks, Frank. How was Moscow?"

"Colder than this," Frank said, pulling away toward the base proper. "I imagine we're about to find out what's next with all that. We missed you there."

"Well, a black man gonna stand out pretty good in the middle of Red Square," Cal said with a chuckle. "Only so many times I can play an ambassador to some African country nobody ever heard of. Did much better down in Guatemala, Caribbean, Egypt. Places like that."

"It's getting tougher for all of us," Frank said. "Spent five hours in the airport before they allowed us to board. Lots of questioning. Thought they'd snag us then and there."

"Why you think they didn't?"

Frank could only shrug, but Cal knew the worry lines on his face all too well after what they'd been through together. "We were traveling with some other folks from State and Defense, heading home for leave. They probably knew they'd create a ruckus. And I don't think Beria wants to do that quite yet. His to-do list has a lot more on it before it gets to us."

Cal nodded. "He wants the whole country, doesn't he?"

"Yep, near as we can tell. Figure Danny's gonna tell us all about it. How's Sally?"

"Oh, she's fine. Upset I'm missing church again. It's a good life here, but it's hard for her when I'm off on assignment. Wondering just how much more I'll have to do before I can hang it up."

This earned Cal a raised eyebrow from Frank. "I'll be real interested to see what they say to that, too. We haven't been around long enough for anyone to retire from the program. I sure as hell hope they let you."

"Me too," Cal said, grimacing as Frank pulled into one of the base's nondescript office buildings that served as MAJESTIC-12's headquarters. "It's gonna be prickly, I imagine, when it comes time. I ain't told Sally that, but I gotta wonder if they're really gonna let any of us just leave."

Frank parked and turned to put a hand on Cal's shoulder. "You know we're behind you, Cal. All of us."

Cal smiled sadly and nodded. "Hope it don't come to that."

The two men got out and hustled toward the entrance, where a pair of M.P.s stood sentry. Both Variants flashed their identification, and while one of the airmen gave Cal a quizzical look—the boy seemed new to Mountain Home— they entered without difficulty. The new ones always wondered why a black man would be allowed into sensitive areas of the base, something Cal was used to, even if he never quite accepted it. At least this time nobody had to give anybody a dressing down just to get in the damn door.

Inside, down two flights of stairs into a subbasement, past another pair of sentries and down a harshly lit corridor, the rest of the Variants had begun to gather in a small lecture room. Danny was up front, going through notes, but paused to give Cal a hearty hello and handshake. Maggie rose from her seat up front to give him a hug; he returned it gratefully, but noticed she was looking worse for wear, pale and sleepless. He imagined something had gone down in Moscow, and made a mental note to have her over for dinner if and when he could. Cal always worried after Maggie, what with her ability and its side effects and all. In the years he'd known her, she'd become more and more distant. Detached. Alone. His heart ached for the poor girl, but Maggie remained stubborn as a mule about it, only going to see the assigned MJ-12 shrink because they made her.

Mrs. Stevens was there too, and Cal got a hug from her as well. Lovely lady, Rose Stevens. Still sort of on the back foot after her divorce three years ago, but seemed to be recovering. Still kind, sort of like the program's mother hen, always looking after the others. She was also a certified, one hundred percent genius—that was her Enhancement. She'd been a housewife prior to 1946. Now, she could make Einstein dizzy. She'd become the group's quartermaster and chief researcher, creating spy gadgets and gear for missions, but also leading the research on the strange vortex of white light created after Hiroshima that had somehow given them all their Enhancements.

Another Variant, Tim Sorensen, the invisible man, greeted Cal with a wave as he made his way to a seat. None of Tim's clothes made the transition with him when he went invisible, so Mrs. Stevens had made him clothes that would. He'd started with something that looked to Cal like a pair of tight-fitting long johns, but Mrs. Stevens had been able to improve her designs so that he could wear normal-looking clothes and shoes that would disappear along with the rest of him.

Next to Sorensen was Rick Yamato, a Japanese American who'd spent his teenage years in the internment camps out West. Yamato could create electricity out of thin air, and could shoot bolts of lightning out of his hands or short-circuit a city block with a touch. The boy was with Cal down in Guatemala in '51. Steady man, if a little too quick to fry first and ask questions later. Cal remembered the impetuousness of his own youth, of course, and could relate sometimes, Lord help him.

Ekaterina Illyanova sat up front without really acknowledging Cal, which was okay, as it seemed they'd never really get along. They first met in Czechoslovakia in '48, when she was about ten. A year later she'd defected to the U.S. and MAJESTIC-12 when Lavrentiy Beria left her for dead during a mission in Kazakhstan. Now fifteen and called Katie by her new compatriots, she had become a sullen teenager—understandable, given the circumstances.

She could also punch through walls and lift a jeep over her head, so most folks knew to tread carefully around her. Cal knew her enmity toward him ran pretty deep; Cal had aged the hell out of her brother, a Soviet Variant who could run fast as hell, when they'd met back in that Czech forest. Cal hadn't meant to, but there was nothing for it now, and even a good Christian man could only ask forgiveness so many times.

Frank settled down next to Cal. "Where's Zippy?" he asked.

"Think she told me she was leading a team out in Iran," Cal replied. "Apparently CIA got something going on there with their Shah, trying to get him back on the throne."

Frank shook his head. "God, we don't learn, do we?"

Cal knew what he was thinking about: the horrible events out in Syria in '49, where the CIA had overthrown a democratically elected leader only to install a strongman who ended up deranged as hell. "We're human," Cal said simply.

Cal thought back to the young boy whose Enhancement, they had ultimately discovered, had driven Husni al-Za'im mad. The boy could possess a person, just like the fire-and-brimstone preachers of Cal's youth warned Satan himself could do. The third Syrian government to seize power in that horrible year had handed the boy off to the Americans, and warned the Variants not to return to the country—ever. That boy disappeared soon afterward, and Cal sometimes wondered just what had happened to him. He probably wasn't cleared for finding out, and Lord help him, he figured he wouldn't want to know.

"All right, let's get started," Danny announced, and the talking in the room quickly died down. "Yes, this is every-body. Most of your fellow Variants are off on assignment in places you aren't cleared for, and the rest are still train-ing. For the record, there's twenty-seven of us now in the program. I'm real pleased about that."

There were a few nods in the room, but otherwise silence reigned. Like Cal, most everyone—even Danny—had mixed feelings about MAJESTIC-12. It was nice to get trained up on Enhancements, and good to be valued by your country. It would've been nicer to get an actual choice in the matter, though. After all this time in the program, folks were starting to wonder whether getting out was even an option anymore.

"The President has just approved a new op for us, code-name TALISMAN," Danny continued. "Most everyone here is going to play a role at some point or other. It's pretty big. In fact, it's going to make everything else we've done seem like the minor leagues.

"We're going to undermine and ultimately depose Lavrentiy Beria from power within the Soviet Union."

There were a few gasps in the room, and wide eyes throughout. Cal bowed his head and said a short prayer, because he knew this one was going to be bad.

"Now, unlike what we've tried to do elsewhere, we're not going to actually support anybody else in the fight to replace Stalin," Danny said. "That's way too dangerous and, if you think about Syria and our first effort in Guatemala, we're just not good at it. Plus, if anybody catches a whiff of us supporting, say, Molotov or Malenkov, those guys are dead and that strengthens Beria's hand. So we're neutral toward anybody else in the fight, and frankly, collateral damage against other interests in the Soviet Union is perfectly acceptable so long as Beria suffers the most damage.

"Our goal is to neutralize Beria's power base within the MGB and state security apparatus. We're also authorized to capture or eliminate any Soviet Variants working for him as part of his Bekhterev program. Now, I know some of you are uncomfortable with this—striking out against your fellow Variants—but I need to make this crystal clear. Beria is nothing short of a monster. He was ready to drop an A-bomb on some of the people in this very room, just to see if he could create another vortex or Enhance more Variants. We believe that if he seizes power in the Soviet Union, he will seek to create a Variant-led nation and reveal Variants to the world as his 'Champions of the

Proletariat.' If you think it through, this is a spectacularly bad idea. Normal people aren't going to be understanding and accepting of us. They're going to be scared. And if the first group of public Variants are Communists aligned against America, well . . . we're all gonna find ourselves in a lot of trouble."

There were nods around the room, Cal included. Maggie, however, wasn't one of them. Instead, Cal caught a glimpse of her turning around to look, gauging the room, and grimacing. *Definitely need to have her over for a talk.*

"TALISMAN is an all-hands-on-deck operation inside the Soviet Union. Every one of you will have a part to play. I'm serving as overall ops commander, and Frank is number two and commander on the ground when I'm not around. Mrs. Stevens will be with us in Moscow to serve as our strategist and analyst. Katie, Maggie, and Tim will round out the first-wave team. We've had contingency insertion plans in place for a while now, so we're ready to get you in there.

"Tim, since nobody really saw you, you and Mrs. Stevens are going in under official cover with State and will be our liaison with the embassy. Frank, you're going in through Crimea and up, covered as a minor Party functionary attached to one of the industrial committees. We'll also give you a couple of other covers you can switch out of. Maggie and Katie, you're a widowed academic and her daughter, moving to Moscow from Murmansk. We'll insert you up north and you can make your way down. Since Beria knows my face as well, I'm taking the long way—I'll be in from Vladivostok and make my way across as a migrant from Siberia, which means I'll have the worst ride." There were some chuckles around the room at this. "Rick and Cal, you're heading with me for a bit, then out to Helsinki to be our on-deck hitters."

Cal frowned. This was easily a six-month assignment. Sally wouldn't be pleased, though at least Helsinki would be a fine enough place to hang his hat for a while. He wouldn't be in the thick of it. It would have to do, all things considered, but it was still too far and too long to be away from his wife. Maybe she could come out for a vacation, though. He wondered just what Finland was like. Cold, probably.

"We ship out tomorrow," Danny concluded. "Aside from Cal and Rick, we should all be together in Moscow in three weeks' time. By then, Tim will have worked with the CIA station chief in Moscow to get us a safe house, and Mrs. Stevens should have some preliminary plans on how to proceed. Come on up and get your briefing papers. Study them tonight and commit them to memory—we'll be burning them in the morning. Good luck, everyone. See you in Moscow."

Cal let everyone get up to get their files first, figuring they had the harder task ahead. But when he got to the lectern, Danny and Rick were waiting for him. "Got a little something else for you to do before you head to Helsinki, Cal," Danny said with an apologetic smile. "Sorry to do this to you, but we're making a pit stop on the way."

Of course, Cal should've known nothing would be so easy. He took the folder Danny offered him. "Do I wanna know where?" he asked.

"Korea," Danny replied. "We have a new Variant we need to find and collect."

Grimacing, Cal looked down at his shoes for a moment, mustering some patience and peace before replying. "I hope you mean to say somewhere way in the south part, right? Away from the lines?"

Danny didn't reply.

5.

March 23, 1953

The ground shook constantly as the skies rained metal and the angry shouts of God and Satan pummeled the ears. Miguel Padilla would have given anything for a respite, anything for two minutes of quiet and safety in order to pray and put his soul in God's hands before rising from his trench again to face the bullets of the Chinese Army.

That wasn't going to happen, of course. He turned to look at his compatriot, Hugo Contreras, a fellow private in the 2nd Platoon, Company B of the 31st Infantry's famed Colombia Battalion. Two years ago, they were aimless boys in the poor neighborhoods of Bogotá, resigned to scraping together a meager existence on odd jobs and petty theft. They had volunteered together, gone to Korea together, sent the Chinese fleeing in Operation Thunderbolt.

And now Miguel was sure they would die here on Hill 266, a scrap of a hill called Old Baldy that wasn't worth a damn to anybody except as something to fight over.

"Come on," Miguel told Hugo, trying to regain courage. "Let's show these bastards how Colombians fight."

Hugo, wide-eyed and covered in mud and sweat and the blood of the dead men around them, nodded nervously, clutching his rifle. "I'm with you. But I'm not a good shot like you."

This was true. Miguel was the best shot in the squad. In the company. The battalion. Possibly on the entire Korean Peninsula. He pointed to a now vacant machine gun emplacement ten yards off. "When I start shooting, run over there and start firing," Miguel said. "You don't have to be a good shot to kill Chinese with a machine gun, yes?"

Hugo smiled this time and nodded quickly, then crouched down and prepared to run. Miguel, meanwhile, set his rifle down and pulled two pistols from his belt—one from his now deceased sergeant, the other from a wounded lieutenant who was in a bunker that would probably not last another hour. The shells rocked the ground around them, the flashes pierced the cold, wet night. He could hear the screams of men on both sides and the barrage of gunfire popping like the sounds coming from the Devil's own drums.

Miguel had thirteen rounds between his two weapons.

Time to go.

He stood quickly and immediately saw a Chinese face thirty yards away. A second later, the face erupted in a crimson splash from Miguel's first bullet. The second hit the hand of a Chinese soldier from forty yards out, one gripping a hand grenade. The explosion robbed him of two more targets, but he found three others on his right, another forty-five yards off. Three bullets later they were dead and he ducked back down into the trench.

Hugo was still there. "What the hell, you bastard?" Miguel hissed. "That was your chance!"

But Hugo had no words. He merely stared, on the verge of tears, trembling.

"*Mierda*," Miguel sighed. "Let's try again, okay? I'm going to—"

A gout of flame erupted overhead, prompting both men to duck.

The Chinese had a flamethrower.

"That fucker!" Miguel growled. "Hang on."

He popped up again, one pistol already extended, and took his shot from just twenty yards out. The bullet went right through the nozzle of the flamethrower, through the Chinese soldier's right lung and into the tank of fuel behind his body.

The explosion bathed the valley in unholy light—revealing

more targets. In the space of five seconds, Miguel took seven more shots. Seven more men died, the last one from nearly a hundred yards away.

A moment later, he was back down in the trench, but Hugo was not there. Ten feet away, Hugo's body was crumpled on the ground, just short of the machine gun emplacement.

Miguel wanted nothing more than to stop and cry and scream and mourn and take his friend's body away from this meat grinder. He could do none of those things.

A radio nearby, in the hand of another dead man, sparked to life. *"Attention all forces! Retreat! Retreat! We're about to be overrun! Retreat! Retreat!"*

Miguel took one last look at Hugo's body. "Go with God," he whispered. Then he ran.

Bullets tore after him as he leaped across the open space and grabbed Hugo's rifle, crouching behind the machine gun. There were only about fifty rounds left on the machine gun, but Miguel decided to put them to good use. Closing his eyes and reaching out with his mind's eye, he remembered the terrain in front of him, thinking where the Chinese might try to come next.

He put his finger on the trigger and opened fire, swinging the gun around and targeting the Chinese with short bursts. When the rounds were spent, he took up Hugo's rifle again and ran, knowing there were fifty less Chinese behind him who could shoot him in the back.

Indeed, he had just gotten his two seconds of silence, and he used it to run like hell for the bottom of the hill.

* * *

"Commander, I genuinely don't give a damn whose order this is, but right now Pork Chop Hill and Old Baldy are being overrun by the Reds, and if you go even one mile north, you're gonna get dead real fast."

Colonel William Kern, U.S. Army, stared hard at Danny, as if willing him to make better choices in life, and honestly, Danny couldn't blame him. It wasn't like he *wanted* to drive up into a hellstorm, but there wasn't much of a choice. Danny could sense the new Variant ahead of him, toward the fighting, and he was afraid that spark of Enhancement in his mind's eye might wink out at any moment. There wasn't any time.

"Colonel, I appreciate that, and believe me, I'm not looking forward to going. But I have to. These orders are straight from General Vandenberg himself, and I don't think anybody here is in a position to countermand them. All I need is a jeep. That's it," Danny said.

Kern shook his head sadly. "Jeeps don't grow on trees, son. I've half a mind to make you walk. But—" The colonel raised his hand to cut off Danny's retort. "You got one. If you don't bring it back, at least do me a favor and crash it into the Chinese, okay? But really, bring it the hell back in one piece."

Danny walked out of the farmhouse serving as Kern's office in some village outside Yeoncheon and made his way to the impromptu motor pool in a nearby barn, where Cal and Rick were already waiting. Both were covered as Marine-enlisted—Cal as a gunnery sergeant, Rick as a lance corporal. Danny had given some thought to covering them all as U.S. Army, since the Army was in charge of the front here, but the customs and nuances would likely escape them all. Their orders would cause them to stick out anyway, so they might as well stick out all the way.

Cal whacked Rick on the arm and both of them saluted Danny, who returned the gesture crisply. Three days in Korea and Rick still hadn't caught on to the military saluting thing yet, but Cal was an old hand; Danny figured Cal had pretended to be every serviceman except a Coastie by now. "Lance Corporal, go get us a jeep," Danny said, handing off Kern's written order. "Make sure we get extra gas."

Rick ducked inside the barn, leaving Cal and Danny outside. To the north, they could hear the rumble of shelling in the distance, like a gathering storm. A moment later, several Air Force fighters screamed overhead.

"Don't seem like a good direction to go," Cal said.

Danny closed his eyes a moment to concentrate, finding the target again in his mind. "I think he's heading south, away from the fighting. Colonel says they've abandoned the hill and the Air Force is bombing it to hell behind them. Should be okay, just . . . wait."

Then suddenly there was a second Variant there.

Danny saw the new target in his mind, probably no more than two miles away from the one that had blazed into his consciousness just after they'd returned from Moscow. A second Variant coming south.

Coming from North Korea.

Danny opened his eyes and looked right at Cal. "Gunny, get in there and set a fire under them. I want that jeep *now*."

Poor Cal nearly jumped out of his skin, but immediately dashed inside the barn and started raising hell. And Danny began to wonder if they could end up getting two for the price of one there in the middle of the Korean War. If they survived.

* * *

Miguel staggered down the road with the rest of his company, as dawn broke over Korea. His squad was all but gone, and all he could do was think of poor Hugo, whose body was probably bombed to hell and back by the U.S. Air Force. Even though he was just a private, Miguel understood the bombing all too well—if the U.N. forces couldn't keep Old Baldy, they'd make damn sure nobody else could either.

So there would be no body to bring home. Miguel hadn't even stopped to take any token from Hugo's body, no dog tags or photos. He would someday go to Hugo's mother and have nothing to offer other than that her son died in battle, and while Hugo had been scared, he'd died moving toward a gun, moving to help.

It was a small comfort, but it was something. Hugo had not been the bravest of men, but when he'd fought, he'd fought well. What was more, he'd kept everyone's spirits up with his jokes and his singing and his outsized stories of his exploits back in Bogotá. Miguel, of course, had known full well that Hugo had not, in fact, courted the daughter of a banker or beaten eight men in a row playing darts, but it had been fun all the same.

Miguel, of course, wouldn't have had any trouble beating eight men in darts. Or eighty, for that matter.

Two weeks earlier, Miguel had woken up from a sound sleep and felt . . . different. He hadn't been able to explain it, but it was as though his reflexes and his mind had grown sharper, his hands and eyes acting as one. That day, they had engaged in target practice, and Miguel's sergeant had been furious to find that Miguel had only registered one shot on target, in the very center.

In fact, all of Miguel's shots had been on target—they had all gone through the same hole as the first. The second round of practice had gone better, as Miguel had clustered his shots neatly around the center bullseye. This, too, had brought unwanted attention, but in a different way, and by the third round, Miguel had known to place his shots carefully, to make them *look* random, even though every bullet had landed exactly where he'd wanted.

That night, Miguel had gotten an idea. He'd taken a knife from the mess hall, as well as an old football one of the Americans had lying around. He'd thrown the knife—something he had never done before with any seriousness—using a tree for target practice. Twenty-seven throws had landed in the exact same spot, even when he'd backed up as far as he possibly could and just heaved the knife away from him.

It had been the same with the football. Miguel was strong but untrained, yet he'd been able to land the football right into an empty oil drum from seventy-five yards out without even trying. Without even *looking*.

Before putting the knife back, he'd sat down at a wooden table in the mess hall and stabbed at the wood in rapid succession. The little experiment had been worthwhile indeed, because Miguel had found he could not place the

tip of the knife in the same place every time—he'd almost
stabbed himself in the hand, in fact. It was only with fire-
arms or thrown objects that he'd been perfect. It was . . .
odd, to say the least.

But by the time they were deployed to Old Baldy in relief
of A Company, Miguel had known it was a blessing. The
hill had been under constant attack and bombardment,
and the Chinese had spent three horrible days trying to
take their position. At one point, one of the sergeants had
chided Miguel for not using up his ammunition in defense
of the hill, but Hugo and some others had been quick to his
defense, having seen Miguel's newfound ability in action.
Every bullet had found a home in the body of an enemy.
One of the others, a farm boy named Paco, had counted
Miguel's kills and was up to 173 on the afternoon of the
second day. Paco was still on Old Baldy, along with Hugo.
Together in death and honor.

Well, at least in death. Honor seemed trivial now. There
were only twenty-three men with Miguel now, the rem-
nants of his company who were still able to walk and fight.
All of them had the faces of ghosts, men who had seen far
more than they would ever be able to take in, knowing that
whatever they couldn't process now would revisit them
again in nightmares, over and over, for the rest of their
lives.

A shot rang out. And the sergeant next to Miguel fell.

Ambush, he thought as he reflexively hit the dirt, bringing up his weapon and firing into the distance. A Chinese
soldier screamed from the ridge above the road, falling
down the hill as he died.

"Down! Down!" the officer in charge cried out before
he, too, was silenced by a bullet.

The men scattered into ditches and behind the scrubby
trees and bushes. The road was shit for cover, but from
the sound of it, there seemed to be maybe only twenty or
thirty Chinese firing on them—a couple of squads caught
behind the lines when the Air Force bombing sealed off
their way home.

Miguel crawled over to the fallen officer and grabbed his sidearm. The M1911 only held seven rounds, but Miguel knew he could fire faster and more efficiently than with the M1 rifle he'd been carrying. Using the officer's body as cover, Miguel looked up and saw movement. Six shots later, six more Chinese were down.

There was more shouting in Chinese, more movement. Miguel caught a glimpse of something on his left flank, fired again, and watched as a Chinese soldier rolled down the side of the hill toward the road. That led to more shouting and shuffling around while Miguel scrambled on his belly to another fallen comrade, grabbing his rifle before diving into a ditch with three other terrified soldiers—two Americans and a fellow Colombian he hadn't met before. One of the Americans was shouting into his radio in a panic, and Miguel knew just enough English to know he was practically begging for backup.

What was more surprising was the response—someone was coming. That was a rare bit of good news.

"Five minutes," the American said, holding up five fingers, panic now mingled with hope. "*Cinco minutos.*"

Thanks for the translation, Miguel thought. He'd been serving long enough to know the basics. The big question was how long they could realistically last. And that meant protecting their flanks, keeping the Chinese in front of them. Miguel pointed toward the right. "Watch there," he told the soldiers around him in English. "Keep in front."

The American looked like he wanted to argue, but instead just nodded and tapped his compatriot on the shoulder, speaking in too-rapid English with a horrible accent Miguel couldn't follow. Miguel turned to his countryman. "What's your name?" he said in Spanish.

"Pablo," the man said, eyes wide as saucers. Miguel automatically assumed the man wouldn't make it out alive, and felt bad for thinking it immediately after.

"Cover the left flank. If it moves, fire. We can't let them get on top of the ridge on either side of the road, you hear me?"

Pablo nodded and brought his weapon to bear once more, while Miguel took stock. They had two extra rifle cartridges between them. He hoped the Chinese were merely scouts, rather than a vanguard of a larger assault. Otherwise, they would all die.

The Americans started firing to the right, and Miguel saw one man fall—and two others scurry between the trees. He turned, waited patiently, and within the space of ten seconds, found his targets. Hearing Pablo fire, he turned back to his left, finding another target and another victim.

"Damn, son, you're a fine shot," the American with the radio said. "How'd you do that?"

"*Suerte*. Luck," Miguel said, hunkering down again. "Watch. Careful."

Ahead, more shots were fired. There were a couple other clusters of still-living U.N. troops ahead, but the shots grew less frequent. Miguel imagined they were being winnowed down. This wasn't some kind of scouting mission; this was an assault. The Reds were going around Old Baldy to strike at their underbelly—and Miguel was nestled right in that underbelly.

"What the hell?" the other American said in wonder. The man was staring forward, not toward the right flank where he should have been. Miguel turned and dropped two more Chinese where the American had been slacking.

"American! You watch right!" he yelled in English, but the man kept staring forward. Miguel followed his gaze, and then saw why.

An entire squad of Chinese were walking up the road, out in the open, about seventy-five yards ahead. They were alert and ready, but just walking. No cover. Nothing. A stroll down the street.

"*Tu funeral*," Miguel muttered, bringing his rifle up and focusing on the point man of the group, a very serious-looking Chinese man with a baby face. Miguel fired.

The Chinese waved a hand. The shot . . . *missed*.

"*Qué es esto?*" Miguel breathed. He took another shot. Another miss.

The radioman also opened fire, squeezing off three shots. All misses.

Then Miguel saw chips of bark and tree flying away off either side of the road. Ricochets.

Miguel's mind raced, and he quickly came to an impossible conclusion. If he was somehow lucky enough to land every shot, it stood to reason that someone else might be lucky enough to cause them to miss.

From up ahead, he heard a man yell "Down!" in English, and saw another American lob a grenade at the oncoming Chinese. The enemy point man lazily moved his hand toward the grenade while it was still ten yards out—and it changed course in mid-flight, heading right back to the ditch it had been thrown from.

Miguel ducked just in time. Dirt and pebbles rained down on them as the grenade exploded. The debris was sticky, but he didn't have time to think about that too much, because his problems in that moment were so much bigger.

"Run!" the American radioman screamed. He and his compatriot took off quickly down the road. Miguel didn't even have time to call out to them before they were shot in the back and fell. Miguel rose up with his rifle and fired again, this time landing a shot against one of the Chinese in the rear of the squad. His second shot whistled past his ear before he hit the deck again—had he not moved ever so slightly after firing, he'd be dead.

Pablo turned to him, tears in his eyes. "What do we do?"

Miguel weighed his options. Retreat, whether straight back or up the hills on either side, would get them killed quickly. They needed a distraction.

Suddenly, he heard a jeep motor coming up from behind them. Their reinforcements. But they didn't know what they were up against. All those bullets ricocheting around. . . . Miguel looked around for the radio, but the now dead American had taken it with him.

"Don't come!" he yelled, turning behind him. "Retreat! Retreat!"

The jeep rounded the corner and was greeted with a steady staccato of Chinese rifle fire. They were all going to die.

But a blinding white light and a massive explosion suddenly filled the air.

"The Air Force!" Miguel shouted, grabbing Pablo by the shirt. "Move!"

They immediately started running back down the road to the jeep, which had stopped. There were three men inside—two Americans, one of them a black man, and what looked to be a Korean. "Go! Go! We go now!" Miguel yelled. The white American stood up and motioned them to hurry, while the Korean . . .

Another blinding white light and explosion sent Miguel and Pablo to the dirt. For a moment, Miguel could've sworn the light had come from the jeep itself. From the Korean man. But it had to be a trick of the light or something. So he got up and kept moving.

Pablo was right there with him—until the Chinese started firing again. Miguel's countryman went down without a sound. Miguel kept running.

A third flash and explosion silenced the rifle fire, and several strong hands lifted Miguel into the back of the jeep. "Others," Miguel panted. "There are others. Friendlies."

"Go!" the white man yelled.

Miguel struggled to sit up. "No! Others! Reinforcements!"

The black man sat down next to him and put a hand on his shoulder. "Ain't no reinforcements. We gotta go." He then closed his eyes a moment. "He's fine, Danny."

The jeep tore back down the road at high speed, the futile pops of Chinese fire fading in the distance. "Why? Why do that?"

The white man—an officer from the leaf on his collar— turned back to face Miguel and, to his surprise, responded in Spanish. "I'm sorry, soldier. But we had to get you out of there. You're more important than you realize."

Miguel took several long seconds to process this, then ventured a guess. "Because I have good aim?"

"How good?" the officer asked.

"I never miss. Ever."

"Yes. Probably that."

"Except there was a man back there, I couldn't hit him. He sent my shots flying back at me," Miguel said. "He stopped a grenade in mid-air and sent it back to the American who threw it."

The officer frowned. "Let's get you back. You have a lot to tell us."

TOP SECRET / MAJIC
EYES ONLY
NATIONAL SECURITY INFORMATION

．．．．．．．．．．．．．．．
• TOP SECRET •
．．．．．．．．．．．．．．．

FIELD REPORT

AGENCY: Central Intelligence Agency

PROJECT: MAJESTIC-12

CLASSIFICATION: TOP SECRET-MAJIC EYES-ONLY

TO: POTUS, DCI Dulles, GEN Vandenberg USAF, DR Bronk
MJ-12

FROM: CMDR Wallace USN

DATE: 25 Mar 1953

Agents Hooks, Yamato and I have successfully recovered the new Variant previously uncovered by Subject-1
on the Korean peninsula. He is PFC Miguel Padilla of
the Colombian Battalion, 31st Regiment, 7th Division, and
was successfully extracted from Hill 266 as the Chinese
entered the area in force. No Variants suffered injuries
during the extraction.

Padilla (DOB 2/17/30) is a native of Bogota, Colombia, and
a Colombian national. At this time, he has elected to
continue service to his Battalion, which remains under
U.S. Army command. MG Smith, CINC 7th Division, has agreed
to my request that PFC Padilla be placed on temporary
detached duty under my command for the duration, though
may follow up with GEN Vandenberg as to the particulars.

After preliminary experiments it appears Padilla's
Enhancement allows for limited control of kinetic energy,
along with enhanced hand-eye coordination. As a result,

he is a superlative marksman with any firearm or thrown object. The upper end of his range is limited only by the weapon or object in question. His Enhancement does not seem to extend to any other applications other than marksmanship, broadly defined.

At this time, neither I nor Padilla has identified any particular side effects. However, his Enhancement seems to have occurred only a few weeks ago, and the circumstances in which a side effect may manifest might have yet to occur.

While I do not have the capacity or facilities necessary to conduct a full psychological profile, Padilla seems to be a well-adjusted individual under the circumstances. He has expressed a desire to continue fighting the Chinese on behalf of fallen compatriots, and while this is an admirable goal, I have convinced him that, for now, his newfound abilities may be better utilized as part of the MAJESTIC-12 program. Nonetheless, he remains a foreign national and, thus, I have given him very few details as to the nature of the program, other than the fact that there are others out there with various preternatural abilities. (He had already seen Agent Yamato's Enhancement during his extraction under combat conditions, so shielding him completely from the existence of other Variants was not an option.)

I recommend he undergo further testing and evaluation prior to full indoctrination into MAJESTIC-12. However,

* TOP SECRET *
****

I believe current circumstances require us to make use
of Padilla on a probationary basis, and I recommend the
following new operation, tentatively codenamed FLAPJACK.

OPERATION FLAPJACK PROPOSAL

At the time of Padilla's combat extraction, Padilla
encountered an individual in the uniform of a Chinese
Army sergeant who exhibited abilities consistent with
Enhancement. According to Padilla, this individual
appeared to be able to redirect kinetic energy, to the
point where he was able to deflect and redirect bullets
and, in one case, a hand grenade.

Up until now, MAJESTIC–12 and its associated agencies had
not discovered evidence of Variants in the employ of the
Chinese government or military, but given the size of the
Chinese population—over 500 million according to current estimates—it is likely that several Variants exist
there. A program similar to MJ–12 or Bekhterev may or
may not exist; we should find out the truth as quickly
as possible.

I propose that PFC Padilla accompany Agents Hooks and
Yamato and myself in an attempt to locate and capture
this potential Chinese Variant. Doing so would give us
critical intelligence into any Chinese effort to collect
Variants, and whether any such program is being run in

cooperation with Beria's Bekhterev Institute, thus also furthering Operation TALISMAN.

Please advise on approvals for Operation FLAPJACK, as Subject—1 is continuing to track this potential Chinese Variant to the north of the front lines.

GET A TELEX TO WALLACE. FLAPJACK APPROVED WITH HOOKS, YAMATO AND PADILLA. WALLACE IS ORDERED TO STAY WITH TALISMAN AND PROCEED AS PLANNED.

—VANDENBERG

6.

March 29, 1953

Frank gratefully sat amid the hustle and bustle of Moscow, resting on a park bench and smoking a horrible, acrid Russian cigarette with unabashed enjoyment as he waited for the next leg of his journey—a very long, boring, occasionally harrowing trip that was leaving him as tired as he'd been since his Army days.

His trip started, of course, at Mountain Home two weeks ago. He wished Danny would've let him commandeer a plane—he could fly damn near anything thanks to his brain full of memories—but the boss wanted to go as deep into cover as possible. So Frank played the traveling businessman. He hopped a bus from Boise to Denver, which was a horrible idea, then it was good old Delta Air Lines from Denver to Chicago and Chicago to New York. Two full days after the briefing and he hadn't even left the United States, but from there he walked right onto the Pan Am headed for London—with stops in Newfoundland, Reykjavik, and Shannon, of course, which meant a twenty-hour commitment. Frank gave himself a day and a night in London to hit some pubs and sleep—on the CIA's dime, of course—before taking off the next morning for Paris, then Rome, and finally Istanbul. One final evening of luxury awaited him in a decadent hotel in Sultanahmet. Frank couldn't help remembering his misadventures in the cisterns below that venerable district five years prior, but this time he took the opportunity to see the Hagia Sofia and Blue Mosque like any old tourist. He avoided the Topkapi

Palace, however . . . just in case someone there had a long memory. That diplomatic reception in 1948 didn't quite go as planned for anyone, after all.

The next day, Frank grabbed the package he'd sent ahead at the hotel's front desk, and carefully laid his freshly laundered, Russian-tailored, and horribly ill-fitting business suits in his suitcase, along with some more proletarian options, should the need for them arise. He chose a simple jacket, shirt, and khakis for the next leg of his trip, and had the front desk send his American clothes back to the States. He was going native now.

Frank crossed the Bosphorus by ferry and caught a bus for Ereğli, a small Black Sea port town on Turkey's northern coast. It was mostly a steel town, though the bus passed a few little beach resorts as well, all of which looked ghostly and abandoned, out of season. The town was otherwise pretty much working class, like Pittsburgh with fezzes. He arrived just as first shift was heading home, and he grabbed dinner at a little tea house with a friendly waitress who complimented him on his Turkish.

At least language wasn't a problem. He couldn't imagine trying to do all this without all the languages at his disposal.

After dinner, it was time to make contact. He walked down to the docks, where most of the commercial vessels were brightly lit as crews conducted maintenance under the evening stars. There was some singing and laughter, and Frank felt a twinge of something at that—simple lives, lived well. No politics, no need to be constantly looking over your shoulder. He thought back to Cal, hoping that MAJESTIC-12 would indeed let the man have a retirement of some kind somewhere down the line. Because if Cal could, maybe he could too.

Frank stopped at a beat-up trawler near the end of the dock, owned by a man who once helped ferry supplies to the Red Army during the war, part of an O.S.S. program to help the besieged Soviets fighting the Nazis. Naturally, the CIA kept their contacts after the war, and from what

Frank read in his briefing papers, the fisherman was more than willing to continue earning a few bucks on the side.

"Mehmet! Permission to come aboard!" he called out in Turkish.

A bearded man in a battered fez poked his head out from the small quarters near the bow of the trawler. "Who is it? What do you want?" the man demanded, sounding put out.

"I've come from Bezapan seeking work," Frank replied, just as his brief spelled out. "The crops have been poor, and my uncle Baki says the sea will do me some good. He says you might have a job for me."

Mehmet stood staring for several long moments before he could bring himself to reply. "I might, but only if you know how to fish and you don't get seasick."

Frank smiled and completed the sequence. "Uncle Baki used to take me out in his sailboat, years ago. I won't make a mess on your deck, I promise."

The man sighed and nodded, waving Frank inside. Clambering aboard and ducking into the cabin, Frank came face to face with a young, strapping Turk looking at him with deep suspicion. "This is my son, Alif," Mehmet said. "We were going to spend a few days on shore. The fishing is terrible right now."

Mehmet sounded tired, and Frank felt bad that he was putting the old man in a spot. Nonetheless, he put his suitcase down, opened it, and withdrew an envelope filled with lira. "I'm sorry. This will help, I hope."

Mehmet reached out and took the envelope in his weathered, calloused hand, weighing it. "It will," he said, eyes wider now. "Where?"

"Three miles off Foros. I'll swim the rest."

Alif and Mehmet traded looks. "You're going to swim the Black Sea in winter?" Alif asked.

Frank smiled. "Technically, it's spring. But yes. We don't want to get you in trouble. Three miles is enough. I'll be fine."

Actually, Frank was pretty pissed he had to do it, but at least his suitcase was a Mrs. Stevens special, totally

waterproof and buoyant. That, combined with a special wetsuit she'd developed, would get him to shore.
Thankfully, Mehmet and Alif simply shrugged and showed
him to a bunk, promising to set off in the morning. Frank
settled in and within a half hour was sound asleep.

He awoke to the sounds of seagulls and a battered diesel
engine, and saw that someone had left him some bread,
sardines, and cheese on the table. It wasn't flapjacks and
bacon, but there was tea on the small stove as well, and it
filled his stomach. They spent the day heading north-north-
east, Frank acting as lookout and checking their position
on Mehmet's battered maps. Thankfully, most Black Sea
traffic was well to the west, between Istanbul and the ports
of Odessa and Sevastopol, and there were no sightings
other than a few large commercial barges.

By nightfall, they were about fifty kilometers out, and
Frank went around the boat to douse the lights, unscrew-
ing lightbulbs in a few cases. Alif seemed as though he
would complain, but all it took was a look to silence him.
He was young and strong, sure, but Frank had faced a lot
more in life than a fisherman's son could imagine. He also
asked Mehmet to cut his speed, to muffle any noise that
would carry across the water, and calculated their position
by the flame of a cigarette lighter.

Finally, at 2 a.m., Frank could see a very faint light off
in the distance. His navigation told him it was Foros, a
small resort town about thirty miles away from the bustling Crimean port of Sevastopol. There would be security there, certainly—many Party higher-ups had dachas
in and around the town. But there was also a small army
of proletarian workers and peasants who supplied those
same dachas and lived around Sevastopol in decidedly less
luxurious accommodation.

The fisherman and his son, they could blow your cover,
one of the late MGB men said inside Frank's head—he
was still sorting out who was who and couldn't place it.
Eliminate them and send the boat off on a random course.

"What?" Frank muttered quietly.

Concur. Operational security is paramount. If Beria gets a whiff of you in Russia, no one will be safe, General Mark Davis, U.S. Army, added. *No loose ends.*

Frank's brow furrowed and he thought for several long moments about the advice he was getting—unsolicited advice, which in and of itself had been unusual but was becoming more common. Rare enough that a U.S. military expert and a Soviet goon would agree on anything, but this . . . ?

Shaking his head, Frank put the voices aside, changed into his wetsuit—a stretchy thing that made him suddenly aware of a growing middle-age paunch despite his P.T. regimen—and stuffed everything into his suitcase, tightly sealing it. There would be no "eliminations" today.

"Head back due south and keep your lights doused and your speed low for at least an hour," Frank warned Mahmet. "Let's get you home in one piece."

The old man nodded and, to Frank's surprise, extended his hand. "Go with God." Frank shook and turned to Alif, but the younger Turk simply scowled. Shrugging, Frank left the little cabin, lowered his suitcase gently into the water, and then clambered down the side of the boat until he could slip in without making a splash.

For a moment, Frank watched the fishing boat turn and head back while he clung to his suitcase, wondering for the millionth time in his life how he'd gotten himself to that particular moment, this time as a mote of a person bobbing in the Black Sea. But then a chill struck him; the wetsuit was doing its job, but the sea was cold regardless. He started swimming for a point just to the right of Foros, hoping it would take him to the secluded bit of shoreline he'd identified earlier from surveillance photos in his briefing packet.

The suitcase made for easy going, to Frank's surprise. He flung his body over it and used his legs to kick, and managed to make good time. There was one nerve-racking point when Frank saw a light leaving Foros and heading out to sea—a fishing boat getting an early start or a patrol boat, he couldn't tell—but thankfully it headed east instead of west, and Frank waited in the water until it was well out of sight. By then, he could see the hills of the Crimean peninsula rising over the horizon, and could pick his spots better. Sadly, he was further west than he'd expected, but was able to change course without too much difficulty. The coastline was rocky and, to his annoyance, covered only in short trees and scrub. Nonetheless, he found his tiny cove and slowly hauled his suitcase to shore at around 4:30 a.m. More than anything, he wanted to build a fire and warm up, but had to settle for dry clothes out of the suitcase instead. He stashed the wetsuit under a large rock in an out-of-the way corner, then slowly trudged his way up the hill toward the main road, passing within sight of a handful of large houses. No lights, though, which was a very good sign.

By dawn, he was walking into Foros itself, a pretty little town with a beautiful old hillside church that had, somehow, managed not to get bulldozed by the Soviets. Instead, it had been turned into a tourist trap and snack bar. Frank wished it had been open—he was hungry as hell—but instead made his way to the nearest bus stop without being observed. Soon, he was joined by a handful of other workers, most of whom seemed to know each other. Nobody remarked on his presence, though. Frank hoped it was because Foros was used to tourists, rather than someone making note of him so they could snitch later.

An old diesel bus rumbled up the road toward the bus stop, screeching to a halt with a symphony of squealing and grinding. Frank paid the fare—*Look bored and tired*, one of his voices whispered in the background—and settled into a seat in the back third of the bus, near a window. He wanted to drift off to sleep, which would've been a good look for a tired worker on an early bus, but the need to watch his back kept him somewhat alert.

Any one of these people could be an MGB agent. Develop an attack plan to take out this entire bus if need be, the voice of U.S. General Mark Davis said. *All of them.*

Frank sat up sharply, causing the man next to him to start. "Sorry," Frank said in Russian, recovering quickly. "Thought I forgot something." His fellow passenger scowled, but settled back into his two-day-old copy of *Pravda* as the bus rolled out of Foros, leaving Frank to his business, just like his voices.

The problem was, those voices had never really been in *conversation* with him before. They responded to what Frank saw, or a problem he faced, but never engaged with his idle thoughts, like simply reminding himself to stay awake. Outside stimuli had been needed, like an imminent attack or a problem that demanded his full attention. This was new, to some degree, wasn't it? But then, Frank tried to reason, they did offer up opinions at times, and those opinions would sometimes contradict one another. There certainly were times when it seemed as though the voices had some sort of thought behind them, especially as the years wore on. They argued, even, or at least seemed to.

Frank thought back to when he first started accessing the knowledge and abilities of the recently deceased, nearly eight years prior. At first, he'd had to focus and mentally search for the information he wanted. Over time, that information became easier to find and, if he thought about it now, was practically volunteered.

He had always thought he was accessing echoes of memory, not necessarily leveraging the minds of still-active, still-sentient people. Now . . . Davis's comment had startled him, but it seemed more of a natural progression. And he wasn't sure he liked it. He felt *watched* now.

Heads up, Davis's voice came again. *Company. I told you*.

Frank looked up and saw the bus was coming to an achingly slow halt at a checkpoint outside Foros. That made sense; with so many *apparatchiks* with dachas in the area, security would be tight. Frank had contingency plans in place and quickly ran through the list in his head as three uniformed MVD men got into the bus. The Ministry of Internal Affairs was under Beria's control, and there was some intel out of Moscow that MVD and the spy-focused

MGB might merge into a single secret police/covert action ministry. Yet another reason why America might want Beria out of the picture—even if the bastard wasn't also a Variant.

The MVD man went seat by seat, checking papers. Frank waited until the man next to him reached for his own before doing a slow, quiet three-count and removing them from his coat pocket as well.

"Papers," the head MVD man, a lieutenant, said. Frank handed them over with a practiced look of attentive compliance. But not too attentive.

The lieutenant scanned the documents and looked up at Frank again. "What is your business in Foros, Comrade?"

"Agricultural inspection," Frank replied simply. *Never give them more than the minimum*, Ivan Vladimirovich said in Frank's mind. *Let him ask the follow-up questions. That's what Russians do. Don't be friendly.* Frank considered this good advice, as Ivan Vladimirovich had, until a few weeks ago, been one of Beria's men.

"What is it that they grow in Foros at this time of year, Comrade?" the lieutenant asked. "It's not even spring yet."

Frank looked at the man dully. "Dairies produce milk throughout the year, do they not, Comrade? And there was a question among the Party leaders who visit Foros as to the quality of the milk and butter. I was sent to give them answers."

The lieutenant scowled slightly, his eyes returning to Frank's papers. Frank had a second set of papers on him as well—an MGB identification and forged letter of passage that would serve as a get-out-of-jail-free card if needed. But it felt too early to play that hand, and Frank knew he'd be marked and watched for the remainder of his trip to Moscow.

Stay calm, Ivan said. *There is nothing there for which to detain you, and there will be other buses coming soon.*

"Thank you, Comrade," the lieutenant said, handing back Frank's papers, which he took with only a slight nod. The MVD man continued on, and Frank simply put the

documents back in his coat and looked out the window
again, silently thanking Ivan for his input.

You're welcome.

Shit. This was gonna get ugly if it kept up.

But it didn't. The bus was waved on, and Frank settled
in for the long ride to Sevastopol. The trip was unevent-
ful from that point on, and without additional commentary from the people in his head. He arrived in time for
lunch, which meant a big bowl of borscht and a half dozen
varenyky dumplings filled with mushrooms and mashed
potatoes. The waitress at the bus station café chided him
for his appetite, but Frank just smiled and thanked her. He
was tired, and his capacity for small talk was waning.

After that, Frank killed time walking around the port
city, making mental notes about what was where. He didn't
have an eidetic memory, but training and some help from
his voices would do the trick. Not many Americans made
it down to Sevastopol, so he figured a little lay-of-the-
land might be handy to have for other operatives at some
point down the road. Finally, he boarded the 5 p.m. bus to
Donetsk, mentally bracing himself for the fourteen-hour
ride through the Crimean darkness. Thankfully, and to
his great surprise, Frank was out like a light by sunset, and
didn't wake up until about 4 a.m. local time. He still felt
folded up like a Japanese paper sculpture—*It's called ori-
gami*, came one of the voices, almost chiding—but he still
felt marginally better rested than before.

Another papers check in Donetsk went without incident, and Frank was able to hustle to catch the 9 a.m.
train to Kursk, crossing the border between the Ukrainian
Soviet Socialist Republic and the Russian Soviet Socialist
Republics. Frank expected a sign, maybe, or even a little
announcement by the conductor, but the passage went
by without so much as a peep. In Kursk, Frank tried to
get an overnight to Moscow, but found it was booked up.
That was perfectly fine by him, however, because it meant
a hearty Russian supper of beet-and-potato salad, roasted
chicken with mashed potatoes and more beets, and a pile

of sliced rye bread at least six inches high. And, of course, the vodka. Frank was asleep by 9 p.m., and just managed to wake up in time to make a mad dash for the train station to catch the 7 a.m. train for Moscow.

The train pulled into Kazanskaya Station after 1 p.m., and immediately Frank went to the newsstand to purchase his cigarettes, one of the keys to identifying him at the park so that the rest of the team would know he was all right and unfollowed. In the men's room, he took a thick black string and tied it to the handle of his suitcase in an easy-to-loosen knot—the other sign. If either the cigarette or the string was missing, the team would avoid him like the plague.

Finally, three different subway trains later, Frank was sitting in the park—a glorified median between two lanes of a busy boulevard—next to a statue of some Russian from the tsarist era who had, inexplicably, managed to stay ahead of the cycles of purges and erasures that condemned so much history to the trash bin.

Thirty minutes and three cigarettes later, a man sat down next to Frank, slumping against the back of the bench, his hands in the pockets of his factory worker overalls. Frank knew without looking that it was Tim Sorensen, doing an excellent job of playing the tired early-shift worker. The two sat in silence for about five minutes before Tim turned to him and spoke. "Do you have a spare cigarette, Comrade? I'm dying for a smoke," he said in Russian.

Frank gave him a weak smile and reached for his cigarettes, shuffling one halfway out of the pack and extending it to Tim, who took it gratefully. Without being asked, Frank also offered his lighter. Tim took it with a tired smile and lit his cigarette, then handed it back to Frank—with a small slip of paper tucked in next to it. It was a smooth move, but then Frank expected no less at this point. Tim's Russian, however . . . well, they'd have a chat about accents when they caught up later. Frank originally had thought to just have Tim tuck the note in his suitcase at some point, but Danny wanted Tim to practice some old-fashioned tradecraft now and then, for those times when invisibility wasn't an option or particularly desirable.

Tim took a few drags on the cigarette and, to Frank's great amusement, turned a little pale as he fought the desire to cough. Frank really didn't know if Tim was a smoker, but Russian butts would catch up to anyone fast, smoker or not. After a few more minutes, Frank got up and headed for the nearest subway. In the station's men's room, Frank entered a stall, dropped trow, and took the slip of paper from his pocket, noting the address: 25 Bolshaya Spasskaya. Frank concentrated a moment to try to place it on the map he'd studied back in Idaho but was interrupted by Boris, another of the Russians he had encountered in the park after Stalin's funeral. *It's not far. I will guide you.*

Frank scowled as he pulled up his pants and wadded up the note in some toilet paper before flushing it down the can. The help was nice, but Frank was used to being in control. Of course, maybe that was an illusion, and he wasn't in control at all. Maybe the folks in his head were more directly guiding his hands when he shot, or drove, or piloted.

He shook his head and washed his hands before he left the restroom. There was no time for this. Maybe when he got back to Mountain Home he'd have a sit down with Danny about it. It *felt* like his relationship to the voices was changing, but honestly, it could have just as easily been the travel and lack of real sleep.

At Boris's urging, Frank took the subway three stops, switched trains, and went another two stops to the Komsomolskaya stop—right back to the Kazanskaya train station, in fact. From there, it was a tram and a decently long walk to get to the little two-story townhouse at 25 Bolshaya Spasskaya. Frank gave it a good look as he approached, and approved of the choice—detached on one side with a driveway heading into the back, good sight-lines up and down the street, a roof that looked easy to access, but without any windows overlooking it directly, and the featureless brick wall of a factory on the other side of the small back garden. Mrs. Stevens had done a fine job of finding a safe house.

Frank walked up and knocked on the door. A few moments later, Mrs. Stevens herself opened the door. "Dimitri, my brother!" she exclaimed, wrapping him in a hug. "Come in! So good to see you! Are you hungry?"

Frank laughed and allowed her to lead him inside, closing the door behind him. Mrs. Stevens turned toward him, her smile instantly gone. "Oh, Frank. We have a problem."

"Shit," Frank said, dropping his suitcase. "What's wrong?"

Tim and Ekaterina entered the small reception room from what Frank assumed was a dining area. Both looked worried, particularly Ekaterina. "We had problems coming here," the girl said quietly.

Frank looked past them into the other room, then turned back to Mrs. Stevens.

"Where's Maggie?"

March 30, 1953

On Liteyny Prospekt in Leningrad, a mere block from the Neva River, a gray-and-beige building sat towering over the thoroughfare, casting shadows over the streets nearby. Leningraders hustled past its thick wooden doors with their heads down. Conversations ceased for the block between Shpalernaya and Zakharyevskaya streets. No eye contact was made with the uniformed MBG guards at the doors, nor with the three or four men loitering on the street near the bus stop or at the entrance across the street.

The shadow of the Bolshoy Dom—literally, "the Big House"—wasn't just cast over the streets. Its imposing shade was infectious.

And it was worse inside.

Maggie Dubinsky sat in a single cell no more than eight feet by four feet. A narrow barred window, high up on the wall, overlooked an internal courtyard that housed a handful of black sedans and a couple of large black trucks. MGB soldiers drilled there in the morning. The afternoons were for outdoor torture and firing squads. She saw one of the executions and heard four others. Blessedly, her captors kept her cell firmly in a null zone; the emotional roller coaster of people facing death—sudden, painful, bloody death, full of terror and sorrow and rage—was too much even for her, detached as she was from her own emotional state.

Or, perhaps, detached as she *once* was. Four days of deprivation and torture had reacquainted Maggie with emotions she'd long thought she'd left behind. Not that she showed it, of course. She was still Maggie Dubinsky, and she wouldn't be giving the bastards the pleasure any time soon. The cold cell, the waterboarding, the strip searches by rough, calloused hands, the electroshock, and the beatings—they'd all been taken without a word. Oh, she'd cried out. She'd screamed and tore at them when they came. She'd fought with every ounce of her being. Over the course of four days, three men had been carried out of her cell due to their injuries. She'd paid for it, of course. She figured she'd suffered at least three cracked ribs, a sprained ankle, and a dislocated shoulder that she'd slammed back into place against the concrete block wall. But she gave as good as she got, if not more, and dammit, that was a source of pride.

But there was fear. There were many more violations male guards could yet inflict upon a woman, and aside from one set of wandering hands—hands attached to quickly broken fingers—the Soviets hadn't gone there. Yet. She had no doubt that she'd seen her last days of freedom, and that whatever life left to her would be short and painful, unless the MGB fucked up.

So far, they didn't seem to be the fuck-up types, though. The null field was always on, the guards always at attention, weapons drawn and trained. She understood the rhythms of the prison now, the shift changes, the meal times, the questioning and torture sessions. She always looked for flaws or inconsistencies, listening for them whenever they decided to throw a bag on her head when they moved her from place to place. Even as the fists rained down on her, she looked through swollen eyes for an unsecured weapon, a briefly opened avenue of attack or escape.

Nothing.

Maggie hated being scared. She hated the weakness of it, the taste it left in her mouth. So she did everything she could to not think about it. She jogged in place, watching the torture in the courtyard. She'd even managed twenty push-ups that morning, despite having just fixed her shoulder the night before. She screamed through the second set of ten, and it felt like absolution. Purification.

If nothing else, she knew Ekaterina had escaped, because by now they would've thrown it in her face if she hadn't. "We have your traveling companion, of course," they'd told her the first night. "We will do things to her you can't imagine." Maggie had spat at the interrogator and told him to show her the prisoner or be called a coward. An hour later, another interrogator had asked her who she was traveling with. To think, the very least they could have done was to trade notes before heading in to see her. She felt professionally insulted, and told them so. The first of her cracked ribs was worth the look on the MGB man's face.

She knew Katie had escaped, at least temporarily, but only due to a quirk of timing. They'd arrived outside Primorsk via a Finnish fishing boat, using the early spring darkness as cover. Like Frank, they'd been given the floating suitcases and wetsuits from Mrs. Stevens, and had managed to find easy shelter in the deep pine forests lining the water. They'd changed into filthy peasant clothes and had walked into Primorsk to catch a creaky old bus into Leningrad without issue. Katie had made some noises about wanting to storm the Bekhterev Institute—the girl was strong enough now to throw a car into the second story of the building—but they were under strict orders to avoid the Soviet Variant headquarters at all costs. So they'd made a beeline for the Moskovsky train station and had booked shit-class tickets to Moscow.

All their false papers had checked out fine, and Maggie had just been starting to relax inside the train to Moscow when she'd looked out the window to see at least four dozen MGB officers with rifles swarming the station, headed straight for the train.

There were contingencies for this, of course. "You should go to the bathroom before we depart," Maggie had said in Russian. Katie had nodded quickly and nervously, then gotten up and headed for the toilet, her papers in hand. The contingency plan was to rendezvous in twelve hours at Leningrad's Summer Garden—ironically, just a few blocks from the Big House where she was now. Maggie'd watched nervously out the window, finally spotting Katie well behind the column of guards that were now busy boarding the train. Katie, of course, was just a teenager, and had been easily overlooked by officials. And even if they had been looking specifically for her, they only had photos from when she was a baby-faced ten-year-old. Plus, she'd had her own MGB training to fall back on. Maggie hadn't felt very guilty about letting her be on her own for a while; hell, she'd have pitied anyone who might have tried laying a hand on the girl. She would have removed said hand at the wrist with only the slightest of tugs.

Once Maggie had been certain Katie was in the clear, she'd decided to make her move as well, getting up and heading for the toilet. She'd left the suitcases in place—they'd only have called attention to herself when she eventually left the train—and had headed down the aisle, only to see four guards enter the car in front of her. She hadn't even needed to turn around to hear the door at the other end of the car open behind her.

That had been fine. She could have taken 'em.

But when she'd reached for the mental threads that would have activated her Enhancement, she'd found nothing there.

Null zone.

The sting at the base of her neck had barely registered, and she'd been knocked out cold by the time she hit the floor of the train car.

She'd awoken in the cell she found herself in now. She'd been briefed on all known MGB and police facilities in Leningrad and Moscow, and she'd guessed she was in the Big House long before she ever heard a guard say the words *Bolshoy Dom*. She had to assume that, despite the null-zone generators around her at all times, she'd been tagged by Maria Suvovra, the Soviet Variant with the tracking ability. Even if she hadn't been, it was wise to assume so anyway. That meant that even if Maggie managed to escape, her mission was effectively over. She didn't know the range of Suvovra's abilities, and so she had to further assume they were global. Her only real option for survival now was getting back to the United States before the MGB put a knife in her back.

Of course, escape remained a pipe dream. But it kept her going. No matter what they did to her, she wanted to be ready. Hope, she found, was a weird thing. When her Enhancement *was* available to her—which was nearly always now—she found hope to be particularly debilitating. It made people do stupid things, she thought. But maybe she was wrong. Right now, she figured hope and alertness were the two best things she had going.

It was late afternoon when her cell opened and eight MGB men, all armed with rifles, swarmed into the room, barrels trained on her head. She decided to hold off this time, let them perhaps get a little complacent before she decided to strike, so she allowed them to shackle her wrists and ankles and lead her, shuffling in chains, wearing nothing but a prison gown, down the hallway and onto an elevator.

The courtyard again. She closed her eyes briefly to prepare herself. That's where she'd been beaten the day before. It would hurt, but at least they were getting repetitive. There was pride in that, too. When torture becomes rote, it becomes less torturous.

The lift descended past the ground floor, past the basement, and into a sub-basement. This was . . . new. She wasn't sure how to feel about that, and she tamped down on the rising fear that had wormed its way into her chest, squeezing her heart and empty stomach. Adrenaline was running through her now, and her eyes went from the dull glaze of a beaten prisoner to the shining alertness of someone looking for an edge.

The guards led her down a long dark hallway, past several closed wooden doors. Finally, they opened one and thrust her inside a small room with stone walls, a dirt floor, and a flickering fluorescent light humming loudly from the ceiling. The only furniture was a couple of hard points on one of the walls, to which they affixed her chains, leaving her to kneel awkwardly on the floor, her arms not quite at her sides. She watched carefully as they unshackled and shackled her again, and maybe, just maybe saw an opening in the process. A lot would have to go right, of course, including snapping the neck of the guy with the keys in such a way that he fell *toward* her, and not away, but . . .

"Thank you; that will be all."

The MGB men ducked out of the room quickly, only to be replaced by a small, balding, bespectacled man in a nice suit. Of course, Maggie had met Lavrentiy Beria before, but she couldn't help but register surprise at seeing him in front of her now.

"Don't you have a country to take over?" she said quietly. "Or am I just that special?"

Beria chuckled. "You have no idea how special you are, Miss Dubinsky. May I call you Maggie?"

"Can't stop you," she said, moving her chained arms slightly. "May I call you Baldy, Comrade Deputy Premier?"

A flicker of annoyance crossed Beria's face—ah, *so* good to see—before his smiling, placid countenance returned. "I can't stop you either, Maggie, though I would hope we might dispense with such ploys. They're so very *typical*, and we are anything but."

Maggie shrugged calmly, but her mind was going a mile a minute. MAJESTIC-12 had indeed planned for every contingency—there were three or four options she could play with here—but she was still rather surprised this particular contingency had come to pass. "So what can I do for you, Baldy?"

Beria began to slowly walk around the room. "Do you know what I am trying to build here, Maggie? Here in the Soviet Union?"

"Dictatorship of the proletariat," she replied. "Funny, though, how some members of the proletariat have dachas in the country and some still have to travel fourth class on the train."

Beria shrugged. "We have an embarrassment of choices in the Soviet Union. Some of our comrades may choose to spend their money on other things, should they decide to travel without certain comforts. Or they may forego theater tickets or a bottle of Georgian wine, should they want to mitigate the rigors of travel."

Maggie shook her head. "I thought we were gonna dispense with the typical bullshit."

This earned her the short bark of a laugh. "Ah, you are as every bit delightful as your file suggested. Very well. Are you going to tell me anything at all about your American colleagues? It is highly likely that your MAJESTIC-12 program has already initiated an operation to stop me."

"Yeah, not telling you squat," Maggie said. "But you know that already, too. Come on."

Beria nodded. "Yes, indeed. Did you know that roughly seventy-eight percent of prisoners here capitulate after the third day of our interrogation program? And ninety-eight percent of women? Even without your Empowerment, you are truly remarkable."

"Yes, I am. Your point being?"

"The Soviet Union needs remarkable people. We need you, Maggie Dubinsky. Step out of the shadows. Come into the light and assume the rights and responsibilities your so-called friends wish to keep from you."

Are we really going down this road? Maggie thought, her heart racing. "Bullshit. You just want another puppet."

Beria simply walked over to the door and pounded on it. A moment later, a muffled voice said something she couldn't quite make out.

Then Beria's hand burst into flame, just as Maggie's mind suddenly awakened to its full potential, and she could see the threads of fear, desire, and confidence coming off Beria.

"I am trusting you, Maggie Dubinsky, because I believe in you. And because I really don't want to hurt you. I want to offer you something the Americans wouldn't dream of giving you."

Finally. "All right," she said, staring at Beria's flaming hand as he slowly moved it around in front of him. "I'm listening."

8.

April 2, 1953

"What the hell do you mean, 'We lost one'?"

President Eisenhower glared at his CIA director and Air Force Chief of Staff as only a five-star general could, a look that mixed worry and disciplined rage in equal measure. Vandenberg thought his days of suffering such stares were over, but then, they'd never lost a MAJESTIC-12 agent like this before. Even in Syria, they'd had a trail to pick up, and Wallace had turned a near catastrophe into a successful rescue and intelligence coup.

Maybe Wallace—who had finally arrived in Moscow last night and reported in—could pull another rabbit from the hat. If not, Vandenberg figured he'd be out of a job in short order. Honestly, the thought of spending more time on the golf course seemed pretty good right about now, despite the growing pains and aches he suffered with age.

"We're working to figure out where she's been taken," Allen Dulles replied, suitably chagrined yet still meeting the President's gaze. "Sorensen's infiltrated the MGB and NKVD several times to try to find records that could help, even as they plan the next operation."

Eisenhower threw his briefing folder onto the mahogany Theodore Roosevelt desk with disgust. "And of course, you lose the one the psych boys are worried about the most. The one who just might listen to Beria and whatever cockamamie Übermensch fantasy he's working on."

Dulles and Vandenberg traded a look. "We do have a contingency in place, Mr. President," Vandenberg said. "It's a risk, but it could be a real win if it pans out."

"Yeah, I read about it. It's more than just a risk. And if it doesn't pan out, it's a catastrophe for this entire plan of yours," Eisenhower said. "What if she turns? She's the most powerful Variant we have. Paralyze a room in fear, create a riot with a thought—and now the Reds have her. I'm not convinced there's anything to do other than a full sanction."

Full sanction. For such a new president, Eisenhower certainly had the clinical lingo down pat. His position was clear: he would rather have Margaret Dubinsky dead than in the hands of the Soviets.

"The problem is, we can't locate her. Soon as we do, we'll work on a rescue plan. If that doesn't work, our people know to exercise that option," Dulles said assuredly.

"They'd better. Meantime, Allen, if this scheme to get the Soviets to turn on Beria doesn't work, I want you to come up with a new plan to ensure his tenure as Premier is short," the President said.

"Sir?" Dulles asked, before shooting Vandenberg another look.

Eisenhower just stared, and the message was clear. Reach into the bag of dirty tricks for the dirtiest, trickiest plan of all—the elimination of a Soviet Premier. To the President's credit, he at least looked pained at the prospect.

"Let's give the MAJESTIC team a little more time," Vandenberg said. "Allen can work up the contingency op, but the latest from Beam and the Moscow station chief is that the Russians are still running things by committee— Malenkov on top, Beria right behind, and Molotov rounding it out."

"There's also a new Central Committee," Dulles added. "It looks like Nikita Khrushchev is consolidating power in the Party while Malenkov, Beria, and Molotov duke it out in government."

"Which weakens Malenkov and gives Beria an opening," Eisenhower countered. "Beria owns the secret police. How long before Malenkov or Khrushchev gets that knock on the door in the middle of the night?"

"He's not ready yet, Mr. President," Dulles countered.

"Beria just took over the secret police again. It'll be months before he's in full control. Until then, the *apparatchiks* still hold the cards, and they'll get word to the other contenders if Beria tries to pull any funny business before he's consolidated his power."

"Which is why it's critical for Wallace and our people to get in there and create headaches for him as soon as possible," Vandenberg added. "If Malenkov or Khrushchev see him having problems, it'll be easier to freeze him out."

Eisenhower sat back in his chair and steepled his fingers. "There's always a chance Beria could just unleash his Variants. Blow it all up at once."

"It's possible, but it immediately creates too many enemies for him to handle," Dulles said. "We think there are some higher-ups in the Red Army who know about Beria's program. If they're smart—and we have no reason to think otherwise—they already have some contingencies in place. Nobody wants a country run by Beria and his supermen."

The President sighed and seemed to weigh everything in his mind for several long moments. "All right. We're committed at this point. Give Wallace the green light to begin operations. I want Beria hit hard, from every side, just so long as nobody figures out it's us. If they can find Miss Dubinsky, so much the better, but as of right now, getting her back is secondary to getting Beria out of the picture."

Wallace won't like that, Vandenberg thought. The Navy man had spent the war in intelligence analysis, and had become Roscoe Hillenkoetter's golden boy when the latter took over CIA and the MAJESTIC-12 program. Vandenberg thought Wallace was a little too independent-minded for his own good, and didn't spend nearly enough time cultivating allies in the Pentagon or CIA to keep his program secured. And given what Vandenberg's doctors were telling him, the Air Force general wasn't going to be around too much longer to give MAJESTIC-12 the cover it needed.

Vandenberg just hoped Wallace delivered for the President, no matter how closely he followed orders.

9.

April 9, 1953

It was an unusually warm night in Moscow, which meant that it was actually above freezing, and the breeze was keeping most of the smoke and smog well above ground level. The Russians were embracing these first signs of spring, walking through Red Square at a leisurely pace and enjoying the sights and sounds. A small band played traditional music in one corner, and several carts offered steaming cups of tea from battered samovars. Most of these Russians were among the nation's elites—government workers, midlevel military officers, minor Party functionaries, factory foremen and the like. A few less-fortunate citizens mingled with the rest, mostly cutting through the square to get wherever they needed to be, whether it was work or home. The luxury of a stroll on a clear night with a cup of tea wasn't theirs to have, despite living in a worker's paradise. A few of these souls, clad in the woolen coats and trousers of the proletariat, were noticeably drunk. Most everyone else paid these unfortunates little mind.

That suited Danny Wallace just fine. He pulled a small bottle out of his coat pocket and gave it a long pull. The label said Stolichnaya, but the contents were simply water. Admittedly, he'd always had a taste for Russian vodka, but tonight wasn't the night. He replaced the bottle in his coat and picked up the broom and long-handled dustpan from where they leaned against the side of a garbage bin before continuing his slow, leisurely patrol of Red Square, on the hunt for cigarette butts and candy wrappers.

Join the CIA and see the world, he thought. *What a great idea.*

To be fair, it was a great cover. The actual street cleaners only worked from nine in the morning until six in the evening, but nobody seemed to notice or care that someone was working late, nor would they bother to question it. It was his fourth night on the job, and the NKVD men posted around the square were already ignoring him. The first night, one came up and questioned him, but his cover story—that one of the Party men wanted an extra shift to cover the square to improve cleanliness and prevent vagrancy—passed muster, as did the work order and papers Sorensen had lifted from the Kremlin's maintenance offices the week prior. The NKVD man let him be, and he'd been free to roam ever since, complete with limited access to the bowels of the Kremlin itself, thanks to a stolen key to the janitorial department.

It was all going according to plan, including Sorensen's nightly forays into the most secure, secretive parts of the Kremlin itself. For the past week, MAJESTIC-12's very own Invisible Man had gained access to the entire building, thanks to momentary lapses in security, unlocked doors, and, of course, his Enhancement. He'd been able to rifle through Beria's desk drawers, take photos of Malenkov's personal diary, listen in on phone calls between high officials, and lift hundreds of forms and papers that would help MAJESTIC-12 wreak havoc on the Soviet Union.

Danny wondered if the Soviet Variants had gained similar access to the White House. Their shadow Variant—a man who could project a shadow image of himself anywhere in the world—could very well have gotten into the White House or Defense Department with ease, but he wasn't invisible, and more importantly, it didn't seem like he could actually move material objects without becoming material himself. If he was the best Beria had, Danny felt pretty good about keeping American secrets safe.

"Shouldn't you be cleaning, Comrade?" came a voice from behind him, speaking Russian.

Danny smiled and didn't bother turning around, but he did pick up the pace a little. "Your accent needs work, Tim," he muttered in English. "Any problems?"

"None whatsoever," the voice replied. Danny could *feel* Sorensen standing next to him, but saw nothing. "Thank God it's a warm night. Mrs. Stevens says she can't insulate this suit. Gonna get the flu or something."

"How'd the bag work out?"

"Halloween is on. See you back at the house, Comrade Colonel."

Danny chuckled and went back to his cleaning. "The bag" was a new innovation from Mrs. Stevens. Sorensen's Enhancement allowed him to be invisible—but in the beginning, only when he was buck naked. MAJESTIC-12's resident genius had created a kind of mesh suit for Sorensen to wear, which gave him some limited protection from the elements and certainly helped with modesty. She was able to create small pockets in the suit so he could squirrel away papers and keys, even a small pistol when warranted. But bigger items still eluded them, resulting in the sight of a satchel or bag being carried around by invisible hands—which was hardly covert by any measure.

After another half hour spent sweeping up, Danny carried his garbage bin back inside and locked up for the evening, then took his usual roundabout way home, using two separate subway lines and three buses that took him an hour out of his way. At least he got to sit—Sorensen would walk the entire way home, invisibly.

By the time Danny arrived back at the safe house, Mrs. Stevens had a dinner of chicken, potatoes, beets, and carrots ready. Danny had offered to create a rotation to cover meal prep, but Mrs. Stevens insisted on cooking—though she was happy to surrender dish duty in the process. Sorensen had already arrived and unpacked his bag, judging from the pile of documents on the table next to the food. There were also three NVKD uniforms thrown over one of the chairs—a key resource for any future operations that they'd been itching to get their hands on.

Danny immediately shucked his coat and took a seat at the table, while Mrs. Stevens gathered some documents and stood at the head to give her now-nightly briefing. "All right, couple things," she began. "Let's start with the back-burner stuff. Tim here found a number of communiqués from Eastern Europe, complaining to other members of the Politboro that Beria's MGB has been, for want of a better word, slacking off in keeping their people in line."

"How so?" Danny asked.

"Diplomatic relations are handled through Molotov, but Beria is charged with working directly with the secret police in the Eastern Bloc countries, like the Stasi in East Germany," Mrs. Stevens said. "Most of them are afraid to take any initiative without consulting with Beria first, and he hasn't been keeping up with their requests for guidance lately. So they're worried that they're going to see some dissent. With Stalin gone, some are even wondering if that's permissible. Of course, the Politburo says it's counterrevolutionary, so no."

"Why does this matter?" Ekaterina asked. "We're in Moscow, not other countries."

"If we want to undermine Beria, encouraging dissent elsewhere could be a possibility," Danny said. "Any good candidates, Rose?"

She shuffled through several papers. "I like East Germany for that, maybe Hungary. Both have economic issues that could light a fuse if things get worse. But they're not quite ready yet."

"Okay, keep an eye on it," Danny said. "What else?"

"This is the good one," Mrs. Stevens said. "Obviously, Beria keeps his most sensitive stuff at the Lubyanka, MGB headquarters, not at the Kremlin. But he's also first deputy premier, so his office at the Kremlin handles some things for him. Tim found a request for the transportation minister to add an additional train car on a Leningrad-to-Moscow route three days from now to accommodate a 'special NKVD project' based in Leningrad."

Frank shrugged as he helped himself to more potatoes. "That could be anything."

"Except there's a roster that includes twenty names. Any of them look familiar?" Mrs. Stevens asked, handing Frank a sheet of paper.

"Yeah, there's a Variant in there, Victor Smirnov," Frank said, handing the list to Katie. "Our old friend Yushchenko says the swimmer's there. Maybe two others, not sure. If so, unknown abilities."

"Here is another," Katie said. "Alexei Ivanovich Rustov. He can create water out of thin air. Lots of water. Like Beria does with fire."

Frank and Danny traded a look. "Our old friend from Istanbul," Frank said. "It'll be nice, punching him in the face."

Danny nodded. "Best as I can tell, there's only a few Variants left in Leningrad. Seems like he's cleaning the place out, consolidating them here." There were looks around the table, and Danny knew that this was their best chance yet to hit Beria where it hurt. "Rose, we're gonna need a plan."

She smiled and opened another folder. "Already thought of that. It'll take some doing, but I think we can grab 'em. Or if not, well . . . we can at least deny them to Beria."

"I'd much rather capture them," Danny said. "I think we can all agree there. What are the variables?"

Mrs. Stevens scanned the list of names and pulled out a railway map. "Obviously, unknown powers is a big one, but worse comes to worse, we can use null generators to even our odds. There's a lot of rural space in Russia, even right outside the city, so time and place isn't an issue. But there's a lot of MGB people here. We'll have to figure out what to do with them. If we have to use Enhancements, well, they're going to run straight to Beria to tell him what they saw."

Danny nodded quietly. "Frank and I will take care of it. Let's get to work."

10.

April 10, 1953

There are times when the Lord decides to try men's hearts, and Calvin Hooks was sure that getting rained on in a muddy trench on some Korean hillside was one of them. His olive drab fatigues were soaked through, and while his helmet provided some cover, the metal was cold, chilling him to the bone. At least they had a sputtering fire, courtesy of a subtle spark from Tim Yamato's Enhancement, which had only led the Colombian fellow to stare and ask more questions.

Of course, while Miguel's English was pretty good, the whole concept of Variants was a tough one to manage. Yamato had leaned on a shared knowledge of comic books to get the point across, which had apparently led Miguel to wonder whether he could learn how to fly.

Wouldn't that be nice, Cal thought. *Maybe we could get a nice aerial view of things, track this Chinese boy down fast and easy.*

But there was nothing fast nor easy about their mission. Without Danny to point them in the right direction, they ended up having to go from unit to unit, muscling in on interrogations of Chinese prisoners for any inkling of intel on the superpowered soldier who could change the direction of bullets. And always—still, now, even with Truman having desegregated the armed forces—Cal and Yamato had to put up with all kinds of white-boy grief. Never mind that Cal now wore the double-bars of a U.S. Army captain. Never mind that he had orders drawn up by Colonel Kern himself—or, rather, orders Kern reluctantly signed under orders from Washington. They were still questioned and hassled and given all kinds of static about how some "nigger officer" and his "gook sergeant" and "that wetback spic" were tying things up with prisoner transfers.

It took all of Cal's God-given patience not to punch some of those crackers into next year. A couple times, he hadn't even bothered to ask Jesus for forgiveness after getting short-tempered. Some of those boys deserved a good old-fashioned chewing out, and Cal had been around enough Army boys over the past five years to dish it out pretty well.

But finally, after a couple weeks of going from unit to unit, from POW camps to MASH units to rear-guard intel units and turf freshly retaken at the front line, they'd finally found a Chinese Red with something useful. Their initial chat under the watchful eye of Army Intelligence had led Cal to believe the boy—and he was a boy, probably no older than seventeen—had known something. He shifted in his seat uncomfortably when Cal started talking about "unusual soldiers" who seemed "blessed." It had taken some doing to kick the intelligence officer out of the building, but once they had, Cal had asked Yamato to produce a little parlor trick, and a second later the Japanese American's hand had been covered in flickering arcs of lightning.

The translator had nearly had a heart attack. The Chinese boy had spilled everything shortly after.

They still didn't know the Chinese Variant's name, but the soldiers had taken to calling him Black Wind—a rather impressive nickname, Cal thought. Black Wind had apparently kept his ability secret from the officers around him, but had nonetheless risen through the ranks because of his success on the front lines, going from conscripted private to full lieutenant in just six months. The men, of course, loved him, because all they had to do was come up behind him and fire away, knowing damn well that Black Wind would keep them from getting shot.

The interrogated soldier even said that he personally believed that Black Wind was secretly one of the *xian*—the

Immortals of ancient Taoist belief, even though Black Wind himself said he didn't really know and generally doubted it.

Then the soldier asked Yamato if he was an Immortal.

Yamato just smiled. "Maybe."

That idea hadn't sat too well with Cal, but from that point, it had been easy enough to get a unit name from the Chinese boy, including where he thought the unit had last been seen. Naturally, they were in the thick of it, right where the fighting was worst, but it wasn't as though they had a choice. So Cal had taken Yamato and Miguel, thrown them in the jeep and, to Army Intelligence's chagrin, commandeered the translator as well, a Korean fellow named Kim Park Song, who had been too damned scared to question anything they asked after having seen Yamato's arm light up like a Jacob's ladder.

And now here they were, at the very front lines, stuck in the rain, trying to keep a fire going and wondering just how to get across to the Chinese side of the line without getting killed. The best plan they figured on was, in Cal's estimation, outright horrible.

"It'll work, I swear," Yamato said, huddling under his rain poncho. "I look Korean enough, don't I?"

Kim looked him over. "Maybe so, if it is dark outside, but you do not actually speak Korean. Or Chinese."

"But you do, Kim. So you'll take the lead, I'll stay back and stay quiet. I'll even put a bandage around my throat so they think I can't talk no more. We cuff Cal and Miguel here, tell 'em we took 'em prisoner, and that they have special information for Black Wind."

Cal shook his head sadly, with a grim smile on his face. "What if that Chinese fellow made your face couple weeks ago? You were throwing the lightning around pretty good."

Yamato smiled. "Well, that's the best part. When I let loose, I tend to blind people. I figure he really didn't get a good look at any of us. Plus, he was concentrating on not getting shot. Face it, it's the best plan we got."

"This is a horrible plan," Miguel chimed in. "Just get me

close enough. If I can see him, I can shoot him, and we can go home."

"No can do, Miguel," Cal said. "Those ain't our orders, and it's not something I'm interested in doing unless we got no other choice. We gotta try to capture him before we pull the trigger."

Looking nervously at each of his new compatriots in turn, Kim piped up again. "So let us say that we get behind enemy lines and the Communists decide that we are telling the truth, which they will not. Let us say we meet this Black Wind. And even though he can do what you say he can do, that he can move bullets with his mind? Let us say we capture him. Somehow. We do not know how yet. But we do. How do we bring him back to the U.N. side of the lines? If they think he is a *xian*, then they will come and try to rescue him, yes?"

Cal shrugged. "We gotta give him a chance to defect to our side first. Folks like us—like Rick and Miguel and me—we're pretty special. And I'd like to think we look out for each other. Plus, compared to what I know of how the Commies treat folks like us, I think Mister Black Wind may want to take his chance with us."

"Hei Feng," Kim corrected.

"What?"

"His name in Chinese. We should all know it, so we know who to ask for."

Cal nodded. Honestly, it really *was* a horrible plan, and it was predicated on no fewer than three big strokes of luck even before Kim and Yamato marched into a Chinese camp with Cal and Miguel held "captive."

Cal took some small comfort that, even if Danny was there, he wouldn't have magically had better options for them, though his tracking ability sure would have come in handy.

"All right," Cal said. "We're gonna go across, hopefully find some uniforms for Rick and Kim here. Now, I would much rather sneak around and try to spot Hei Feng before we try to march into a camp. Ideally, he's gonna go take a leak or something away from everyone else and we can grab him then. This little play-act you got going, that's our last resort. And since we got no time limit, I suggest we load up on rations here, because I'd rather wait a week to get him quietly than give ourselves over to the Chinese."

There were grim nods all around the guttering fire, which Rick hit again with an arc of lightning to keep going under the deluge. Cal stood and felt his back protest—it'd been a few weeks since he'd been able to grab a bit of life from some livestock, and his body was getting older. No matter how much life force he gathered to make himself strong and young, or how much healing he did to age himself, Cal's body was like a slow-motion rubber band, eventually heading back to his late fifties. He'd arrived in Korea the equivalent of a hale, hearty twenty-eight-year-old, but was feeling easily ten years older than that now.

"Are you okay?" Miguel asked quietly.

Cal smiled at him. "I ain't no good sleeping on the ground like you young boys."

"You're aging."

"It's what I do, Miguel," Cal said with a nod. "I heal folks, and I get older. I take life from people or animals, I get younger. If I do neither, I fall back to my regular age."

"How old are you?"

"Old enough to be your daddy, and that's as specific as I care to be right now," Cal said with a smile. "Now, I suggest you get yourself some rations and ammo and whatever else you need. We're gonna be out there a while."

Miguel nodded and headed down the hill toward the bulk of the battalion covering this part of the front. They had free rein to grab whatever they needed, within reason, and Cal was sorely tempted to grab a jeep and just drive. But that was suicide. Here, in the dark and the rain, they had the best chance of sneaking across the lines and settling into Chinese territory. It was the perfect weather for—

Cal heard a large branch snap in the woods off to his left and, even through the rain, some sort of muffled whisper.

Perfect weather for an ambush.

"*Down!*" Cal shouted, diving for the mud.

Muzzle flashes lit up the woods from both sides of their little encampment, and the ground was sprayed with bullets and mud. Cal heard more shots from back down the hill, and figured Miguel was being kept busy as well. Hopefully he'd run out of Chinese before he ran out of bullets.

A blinding light erupted next to Cal as he huddled down behind a rock; Yamato was going to work with the lightning again, but stopped after a few seconds or so.

"I can't see for shit," Yamato yelled. "Don't know what I'm hitting!"

About a hundred yards away, Cal could hear excited shouting from multiple people. "*Shi tāmen! Shi tāmen!*" "*Tāmen zai zhe'er!*" "*Gàosù Hei Feng!*" "*Gàosù bùxiŭ!*" "*Wŏmen bă tāmen bāowéile!*"

"Kim? What they saying?" Cal called out.

Cal looked around for the Korean translator, but Kim was nowhere to be seen from Cal's admittedly horrible vantage point. The fact that all that chatter was happening after Yamato lit up the place couldn't be good, though. Cal was used to people running *away* from Yamato's lightning. These boys weren't.

The rain stopped.

But it didn't just peter out, nor did any sort of wind push through. The rain just stopped dead. Cal looked up at the clouds, but they were low and black and seemed like they were still ready to open up. And the *sound* of rain was still all around them. About twenty yards away, Cal could still see the mud splashing up from the ground where the rain was landing.

Oh, this ain't good.

"Move! Back down the hill!" Cal cried out. "Let's go!"

Cal grabbed Yamato by the scruff of his poncho and dragged the young man to his feet, but before they could get going, a metal canister landed at Cal's feet, a thick cloud of white gas spewing forth from it. Cal tried to kick it away, but the gas was already doing its work, and his foot missed the target as his world suddenly became very dizzy.

As Cal fell back onto the mud, he began to nod. He understood it now.

Just as they were hunting the Immortal Black Wind, no doubt Hei Feng was doing the same, looking for the lightning thrower and his friends.

Then Cal's world went black, his last conscious thought being how disappointed Sally was gonna be that he wasn't coming home.

11.

April 12, 1953

L ight bathed the grand hall of Leningrad's Moskovsky Station, a welcome respite from the concrete-and-brick gray of more recent Soviet architecture. A bust of Lenin, stern and visionary, welcomed Danny into the building, but the authorities somehow deemed the station's mid-nineteenth-century facade and interiors worthy of preservation, even after a recent renovation that somehow failed to overshadow the building's grandeur. It reminded Danny of Grand Central in New York, or Union Station in Washington—a temple to the idea that everyday people could escape their place of origin and see more of the world than their parents and grandparents could ever imagine.

Of course, this was the Soviet Union, and travel was still highly regulated and monitored. Thankfully, a different shift was working security today than had been on duty last night when Danny arrived. This was intentional, of course, but there was a risk that there would be someone putting in some overtime or covering for a sick comrade. Danny had different papers today, ones that said he'd arrived in Leningrad two weeks prior to provide assistance to the Ministry of Agriculture as a student of the Moscow Agricultural Institute. Yesterday, he'd been a dockworker newly assigned to one of the shipyards.

The student papers at least got him into a slightly better berth on the return train to Moscow, which he looked forward to greatly after yesterday's journey on a hard wooden bench, pushed against the window by a couple of pensioners who took up generous amounts of pine. But Danny lingered over a cup of tea near the track, carefully watching the train through the reflection of a distant window, an old tradecraft trick, while pretending to read today's *Izvestia* newspaper. *Izvestia* meant "News" in Russian, and was paired with *Pravda* ("Truth") at most newsstands. He was reminded of the phrase heard constantly all over the Soviet Union: *V novostyakh net pravdy, i nikakikh novosti v pravde net.* "There is no news in *Truth*, and no truth in *News*."

For all the rallies and slogans spouted off at every corner, it felt good to know that most of the Russians still weren't buying the Party line wholesale. Most of the people milling around him were just regular Joes and Janes—well, Ivans and Ioannas—trying to get through the day. That gave him hope. Maybe, one day, even Variants would be accepted with that sort of collective shrug. But not if Beria had his way. Danny knew, as surely as he knew his own name, the Joes and Janes and Ivans and Ioannas would quickly turn on Variants around the world if they believed they were trying to seize power, no matter how careful they were. The best Variant paradise would be one in which they could live like everyone else, drinking tea and reading newspapers and catching trains to wherever they needed to be.

The sounds of heavy bootsteps echoed down the track, and Danny looked up at the window to see a squad of uniformed men walking behind him toward his train. He couldn't see the uniforms in the dim reflection, but he concentrated a moment and felt the presence of three Variants very close by. Turning to throw his newspaper in a rubbish bin, Danny looked up to see that, yes, the men were wearing NKVD uniforms, and were boarding the fifth car of the train. Danny was in the seventh car. *Perfect.*

Slowly, in the slightly tired manner of your typical Soviet Russian, Danny trudged toward his assigned car, papers in hand. He looked up idly at the cars as he passed, referring back to his ticket as if he were trying to find the right car, but instead peering through the windows to ensure that his targets were indeed where he thought they'd be.

As he passed the fifth car, an unfamiliar face stared blankly out the window, and Danny felt his presence in his mind—a Variant, one he'd never seen before. There was no sign of the man's Enhancement, not that he expected him to be on fire or anything, but a physical cue might have helped. Regardless, Danny made note of the man's appearance—brown hair, lean, midthirties, captain's rank.

Then something began to stare back.

Danny nearly froze in his tracks as a ghostly face seemed to somehow *detach* from the NKVD officer's head to look right at Danny. It was only for a split second, but Danny could've sworn that the face of a woman was looking at him, one with Asian features and a poisonous look of malice.

Then it was gone.

"Problem, Comrade?"

Danny jumped and turned around to find one of the station's security men standing behind him. Apparently, Danny had stopped dead in his tracks, a goddamn rookie move. "No, Comrade, I'm sorry," Danny stammered in Russian. "I am very tired and misplaced my car."

"Papers."

Handing over his papers and ticket, Danny looked up to see that the man requesting them was familiar—one of the guards working late the night before. It wasn't one that had dealt with Danny personally, but he was around. A supervisor, maybe. Shit luck, for sure.

Yet the man simply handed the papers back. "You are in the seventh car. Two down. You can—wait a moment."

Shit. "Yes, Comrade?"

The man—a dark-haired, burly fellow filling out his uniform to good effect—gave Danny a disconcerting once-over. "When did you arrive in Leningrad, Comrade?"

"Two weeks ago," he replied. "I was helping Oblast Collective Farm Number Twelve with planning for the planting season, soil testing, that sort of thing." Danny put

down his suitcase. "I can show you some of the soil sam-
ples if you like, Comrade."

The man stared intently at him. "I could swear I've seen
you sooner than that. Let me see your hands."

"My hands?" Danny asked, heart fluttering.

"Hands." It was nothing short of an order, and an imper-
ative one at that.

Danny held his hands out in front of him, and the
security man took his right one and held it up to his face.
"Hmmm. Yes. All right." The guard dropped Danny's
hand and gave back his ticket and papers. "Seventh car.
Hurry up."

Trying not to seem horribly relieved, Danny grabbed his
suitcase and, with a quick *spasiba*, hustled for his car. Only
when he found his seat—padded this time—did Danny
look down at his fingers.

At the time, it had seemed like an unnecessary bit of
theatrics, but now, Danny was immensely grateful he'd
had the foresight to jam his hands into the dirt of a freshly
planted flowerbed at his hotel that morning. The dirt
under his nails may have just saved his life.

This spy shit is gonna give me a heart attack.

* * *

The police station on Pervomayskaya Street in the little town of Skhodnya was tucked into a brick apartment
block, across the street from another brick apartment
block and about six blocks up from the local train station—perfect for commuters into Moscow. It was a sleepy
little burg that, as Frank and Ekaterina got out of their car,
would soon wake up in a big way.

"This is stupid," Katie said as they walked up to the front
door. "I am too young to be an NKVD cadet or assistant or
whatever you say I am."

Frank just smiled. "You look older than you are," he said
quietly, noting that the uniform Tim had stolen fit her
perfectly, as did the colonel's uniform he now wore. "And
quit with the English. *Pa Ruskiy, pozhalsta.*"

Katie frowned, but kept quiet as Frank unceremoniously barged into the station. "Where is the chief of police? I need to speak to him now," he demanded in perfect Russian.

The desk officer looked up lazily, then launched to his feet as if he had a rocket strapped to his ass and gave a salute that wouldn't have passed muster in basic training anywhere in the world. "Hello, Comrade Colonel! The chief is on patrol with another officer now!"

Frank put on his best senior officer glare. "You have a radio, do you not, Comrade?"

The officer, a pudgy man in his midthirties, swallowed hard. "Yes, Comrade Colonel. We have a radio."

"Then pick it up and call him in immediately. And do not, for the love of the Motherland, tell him who is here!"

The officer practically dove for the radio and made the call, greeted at the other end by a peevish older voice. It took some doing—the chief wanted to know why he had to come all the way back to the station—but the officer held fast, and soon the officer looked up with a sycophantic smile. "The chief will be here in five minutes."

"If you wish to make yourself truly useful, you will call in every single officer from this town for a briefing. Every shift. I want them here and ready in thirty minutes," Frank said. "Where is the chief's office?"

The officer quickly paled. "Everyone?"

Frank leaned in menacingly. "Is there a problem with your hearing, Comrade?"

"No, Comrade Colonel. Every officer. Thirty minutes. The chief's office is the second door down the hall to the left."

Frank immediately marched off, Katie in tow, and let himself into the shabby, wood-paneled office, closing the door behind them. The desk was stacked high with papers, covering every square inch not occupied by a small blotter, a typewriter, or a telephone. "What a shithole," he muttered in English, looking at the photos on the wall showing a corpulent man in a policeman's uniform next to several other corpulent men in suits, shaking hands and smiling.

"What is it about the locals that they all have 'love-me' walls like this?"

Ekaterina plopped down in a chair in front of the desk. "It is for when people like us come in, so we can see he is a proud member of the local Party, and loyal."

Frank took the chief's chair behind the desk. "Nice to know ass-kissing knows no borders. Timmy? How you doing?"

A voice came from the corner of the room. "The cleaning staff here needs to be fired."

"They use inmates from the local jail," Ekaterina said. "The drunks and the wife-beaters. You expect them to work hard for a man like this?"

Frank heard Tim chuckle, and let the matter drop as they waited. Four minutes later, the door opened and the chief himself—grayer and fatter than most of the pictures—barged in. "What is the meaning of—Oh."

Frank rose stiffly. "Comrade, I am Colonel Pavel Andreyovich Petrov of the Ministry of State Security. And you are?"

The chief hustled over with a broad smile and a meaty hand extended. "I am Chief Mikhail Mikhailovich Mikhailov. It is an honor, Comrade Colonel."

Most unoriginal parents ever, Frank thought as he shook the man's hand and waved him to the seat next to Katie, which he took without argument. *Like calling someone Michael Michaelson Michaels.* "Understand, Mikhail Mikhailovich, the conversation we are about to have is of the utmost sensitivity. What I am going to ask of you is a critical matter of state security, and goes to the very heart of the Party and the Motherland."

Frank could practically see the chief's heartbeat increase before his eyes. "I am your man, Comrade Colonel. You may rely on my discretion fully."

One of Frank's voices entered his head—Andrei, one of Beria's men from the park. *This one is an opportunist. He will call to confirm your orders. Tread carefully.*

"I am not sure you understand, Mikhail. I need your

help. There are counterrevolutionary forces within the Party that wish to see the legacy of our beloved Stalin dismantled. There is talk of socialism's failings—if there was ever such a thing!—and even a broadening of political discourse beyond the path shown us by Vladimir Ilych himself. So when I say I need your discretion, Comrade, I need to know that you will follow my orders to the letter over the next twelve hours. This is a critical point in my investigation and, I should note, a critical point in your career. Succeed, and you will be honored greatly for your contribution. But if word gets out and we fail, lives will be at risk. Possibly including both of ours. The enemies of the State cannot know we are about to score a decisive victory over them! Have I made myself clear?"

The chief nodded vigorously, his smile gone, replaced by the most serious—and worried—mien he could muster. "I understand, Comrade Colonel. What can I do to help you preserve our great Party and Motherland?"

"How many officers do you have in total?"

"Two dozen, Comrade Colonel."

Frank smiled. "That will do, Mikhail Mikhailovich. I have your man up front bringing them all in. I have very precise instructions for them. I expect you to help me carry them out."

"What will we be doing?" the chief finally asked. *Took him long enough*, Andrei noted.

"Stopping a train and capturing counterrevolutionaries," Frank said simply. "And we cannot fail."

Mikhail Mikhailovich Mikhailov nodded vigorously. "I swear to you, we will not, Comrade!"

Frank caught Katie giving the man a piteous look, and gave her a swift kick under the desk. She whipped her head around to glare at him, but quickly fell back into character, pulling out a sheaf of paper. "Comrade, we will need to gather the following materials in the next three hours, and do so without alerting anyone as to why. Can you make this happen?"

Mikhailov took the paper and scanned it, his eyebrows shooting upward several times. "This is . . . extensive."

"We were told we could rely upon you," Frank said, an edge to his voice.

The chief looked up and nodded again; Frank thought the man's head would pop off at any moment. "It will be done, I promise you, Comrade!"

* * *

Ekaterina stood stock still, in a military at-ease, and watched as Frank and Mikhailov positioned the portable barrier across the train tracks, electric lights already blinking. She had to admit, the spot Mrs. Stevens had chosen was perfect—flat and lightly forested, with well over a mile of straight track and line of sight ahead. Even if the train didn't have a working radio—always possible, given the Soviet Union's notorious lack of efficiency—the train had plenty of time to stop before plowing into them. The dirt road that crossed the tracks there was well away from most everything else nearby—just a couple farms on either side, with farmhouses well away from the tracks themselves.

Of course, if it had been her on the train, she would've set a watch among the NKVD men there, ensuring that they'd have plenty of warning against such an ambush. But it wasn't a bad gamble on Mrs. Stevens's part, thinking they'd be caught off guard on such a common route, in the heart of the Soviet Union and barely twelve miles from central Moscow.

That said, she figured they'd have twelve minutes, at most, before someone would come rolling up. Grab the Variants, deal with the rest of the NKVD, get the local police moving and get the train moving again—all in twelve minutes.

To think that most American girls her age were just sitting around their phonographs at home, listening to Eddie Fisher or the Four Aces and scribbling unsent love letters to high school crushes. More and more, Ekaterina found herself wanting to join them, to embrace being Katie the

American Teen-Ager. To go to high school, whatever that was. It seemed . . . nice.

All that said, she figured she'd last maybe a week before getting frustrated with all the simplistic, ineffectual nonsense involved and punching someone into a coma.

Danny warned her that theirs wasn't meant to be a normal life, at least not yet and not any time soon. He was right, but there were times she mourned a life never to be lived.

Mikhailov rushed up to where she and Frank were standing, Handie-Talkie at the ready. "I have reached the conductor! The train will stop for us!"

Frank nodded. "Position your men. Remember, I want every paper checked. Every passenger. They could be hiding anywhere. Every single potential counterrevolutionary must be detained. Understand, Mikhail Mikhailovich?"

"Yes, Comrade Colonel! It will be done!"

The chief rushed off and Frank turned to Ekaterina. "Twelve minutes, huh?"

She nodded. "Someone heard that radio call. They will look into it."

Frank turned around and saw Tim Sorensen, now in an MGB uniform, by the truck he'd stolen from the local Red Army barracks. With a nod and a salute, Tim ducked into the back of the truck to shed his uniform and get to work.

The sound of screeching brakes and a growing bright light heralded the arrival of the train, slowly gaining volume and luminance as it ground to a halt. "Remember, Comrades!" Frank shouted. "Wait until I give the word to board the train! We do not want these traitors jumping out beforehand!"

The police—twenty-two in total, given the chief's near-groveling request for someone to stay behind and man the phones, and another to patrol his town—took positions on either side of the tracks, pistols and war-vintage SKS carbines pointed toward the train.

With a gasp of steam and a final long, piercing grind, the train stopped just two feet away from the temporary

barriers. Frank dashed forward, Ekaterina easily following, to come up beside the chief. "I have a man inside. He
should be toward the back. My assistant will go to see him
now. Have your men remain at their stations."

The chief assented, and Ekaterina ran toward the back
of the train as quickly as she could—which was pretty fast,
considering her strength had her covering five or six yards
at a stride once she was away from all the lights. She saw
Danny clambering off the train, pinning a badge to his
otherwise shabby suit.

"Well?" she demanded.

"Fifth car. Three of them," Danny said. "Where's Tim?"

The sound of footsteps came from behind them.
"Dammit, Katie, I can't run as fast as you!" Tim huffed
from the darkness.

"Fifth car. You ready?" Danny asked him.

"Yeah. Just . . . yeah. Okay."

Ekaterina turned to the direction of his voice. "Go!"

Sorensen's footsteps retreated and, a moment later,
the door leading to the back of the fifth train opened.
Ekaterina and Danny watched closely and, a few seconds
later, the car began to fill up with noxious smoke. There
was suddenly a great deal of movement in the car, and
some shouts, and the door in the back slammed shut.
Sorensen appeared a second later out of thin air, coughing
up a lung.

"Jesus, Tim," Danny said, rushing over. "What
happened?"

"Someone . . . some . . . someone bumped into me," he
said between outbursts. "Couldn't . . . hold . . . breath."

Before they could do anything more, the side of the train
ahead of them erupted.

A huge gout of water at least thirty feet long burst out
half the windows on their side of the train, spraying them
with liquid and, more importantly, ventilating the car. A
second later, gas began pouring from the now-broken windows, and the sounds of shouting and swearing were far
more clear.

"Dammit," Ekaterina swore in Russian. It was her turn.

Grabbing Danny by the scruff of his uniform, she jumped up—at least ten feet—and grabbed the edge of one of the broken windows. Leaving Danny hanging from the edge of the window beside her, she tore open a gaping hole in the metal hull of the train car and proceeded inside, punching the first uniformed man she saw. He didn't get up.

Then she was hit by a fierce wave of water, one that actually staggered her back a few steps. *That was impressive*, she thought. She couldn't remember the last time she'd been pushed back by anything.

The water abated, and Ekaterina surged forward, wiping her eyes. She saw a thin man in the uniform of an NKVD major, and recognized him immediately, despite the five years since she'd defected. He was Alexei Ivanovich Rustov, a Variant like her, one of the first found by Beria's Behkterev Institute. And his Enhancement seemed to have improved considerably over the years.

"Ekaterina, is that you?" Rustov asked, a flash of recognition in his eyes. "Ekaterina?"

Grimacing, Ekaterina tromped toward her former comrade, shoving a would-be tackler into the wall of the train. She grabbed Rustov by his necktie and threw him back toward Danny, who managed to crawl into the car behind her. Many of the other men were still coughing, dazed but not unconscious as planned. Moving determinedly down the car, Ekaterina pummeled and slammed her way through the officers, trying not to take a grim sort of pleasure from it. They were Beria's men, yes, but most of them were simply doing their jobs and trying to feed their families. That was, perhaps, not a very good excuse, but for her, it was enough to show relative restraint.

That is, of course, until a wave of vertigo washed over her, one so profound that it dropped her to her knees and brought her latest meal up onto the floor of the train.

"What?" she gasped, looking around. Most of the people in the train, including Danny and Rustov and the NKVD men still conscious, were similarly indisposed.

Except for one.

A woman three rows ahead of Ekaterina simply sat there, smiling, an eyebrow raised. She was young, though older than Ekaterina—perhaps in her twenties. Ekaterina had never seen her before, but the captain's rank on her uniform—far too high a rank for the woman's age—was enough to tell her that this new woman had to be one of Beria's special recruits.

Suddenly, the woman's head jerked to the side as her eyes widened, and she collapsed into the aisle, unconscious. At that moment, the nausea and vertigo evaporated like a mist, and Ekaterina shot to her feet once more, dashing forward to grab the woman and heave her bodily through the gash in the car's side.

"Thanks, Timoveyish," she muttered in Russian, using her pet name for Tim Sorensen. She'd seen enough of his handiwork to know when he was around.

"Guess she can't target what she can't see," the invisible man whispered in English in her ear. "Let's go."

Ekaterina shouted over to Danny, in Russian. "Where's the third? The swimmer?"

"Outside, heading toward Frank," he replied. "Let's move."

Jumping through the hole in the side of the train, Ekaterina took off at a dead run, passing each car in just a few strides and quickly catching up to the man ahead. She took a great leap and landed right on top of him from a height of about fifteen feet. He didn't get up.

Tough being a Variant whose Enhancement requires being submerged in water.

"Secure!" she shouted ahead.

The stolen Red Army truck surged forward from the temporary barrier, Frank Lodge at the wheel. "Let's go," he called out. "We need them all in there."

"All of them?" Ekaterina asked. *That's not the plan.*

"All of them," Frank replied.

Ekaterina took the runaway she'd landed on and hurled him into the back of the truck, then jumped on the tailgate as Frank sped back toward Danny and the other NKVD officers. Danny had already secured the two other Soviet Variants, hands tied behind their backs as they lay unconscious on the ground.

"Frank wants them all," Ekaterina muttered as she fetched Rustov and the vertigo woman.

Danny looked over to Frank, waiting impatiently in the truck. "There's twenty men in there. Some of them won't stay down for long," Danny said. He then walked over to the truck and got in next to Frank. Ekaterina couldn't hear what was said, but she could see the two of them getting pretty animated. After a couple minutes, Danny got out again and, looking angry and pained, walked over to Ekaterina. "Let's get them in the truck. We'll need to gas them when they're inside."

With a sigh, Ekaterina jumped back into the train car and started gathering unconscious NKVD men. Well, mostly unconscious—there were a couple groggy ones who needed a bit of reinforcement, but again, she restrained herself from being too rough with them.

Ten long minutes later, Ekaterina put the last officer in the back of the truck, and Danny followed suit with a second canister of gas, quickly closing and securing the canvas flap around the top. It wasn't ideal—Ekaterina could see gas starting to flow out from around the edges of the truck bed—but those inside wouldn't be in a position to complain much about their destination, wherever that was.

"Tim, you and I are in the truck. Katie, you go back with Frank. Rendezvous at Point B in an hour," Danny said tersely.

Again, not the plan, Ekaterina thought as she followed Frank back toward Mikhailov's policemen. There would be glad-handing and Frank acting imperious and commanding, more scraping and bowing by the police chief . . .

. . . and then what?

What the hell are we going to do with two squads of NKVD officers?

* * *

Danny rode silently in the truck while Tim navigated through the darkness of the Russian countryside outside Moscow. Their operation was, technically, one of the greatest successes MAJESTIC-12 had scored to date—the capture of *three* Soviet Variants in the middle of the Soviet Union itself.

But the other twenty guys presented one hell of a complication. And there were no good solutions.

Tim pulled onto a dirt road that led through a thick stand of trees. Pulling to a stop, Tim shut down the truck's headlights and waited a moment for his eyes to adjust to the dim moonlight, then started down the rutted road again, the truck bouncing and straining in protest.

"The Ruskies don't really believe in shock absorbers, do they?" Tim said quietly. "This thing handles like a goddamn battleship. And we're low on gas."

Danny sighed. "Gas won't be an issue. Truck's staying here."

Tim nodded and kept silent for the next several miles, finally pulling into a small clearing where a couple of burned-out farm buildings—likely casualties of the Nazi invasion during World War II—sat squat and dark in front of the trees. They were easily forty miles outside Moscow now, and a good half hour from anything remotely civilized.

It would do.

Danny got out of the truck and reached back with his senses to check on their captives. All three were unconscious. He'd seen the water Variant's work firsthand, and felt the woman's vertigo, of course, but he still didn't know what the third could do, though apparently the man decided running was a better option than using his Enhancement. Maybe his abilities weren't particularly combat-effective, or maybe he was just a rookie. Or a coward?

Still, Danny didn't feel like finding out suddenly, so he rifled through his rucksack for a null-field generator. Mrs. Stevens had managed to get the device down to the size of a smallish ashtray without sacrificing too much range.

Before he could turn it on, though, he felt a . . . rustling . . . in his senses. He looked toward the truck, and for a moment saw three pale swirling mists and, God help him, one of them formed an enraged face for a split second.

Watching carefully, Danny flipped on the null-field generator. The mists seemed to speed up and flail around before dissipating entirely.

They know? Dear God, do these . . . things . . . know when we're about to cut them off? Have they . . . learned . . . about the generators?

Relatively early on, in 1949, Danny and the scientists working at Area 51 had discovered that there were indeed intelligences on the other side of the strange vortex created by the Hiroshima bombings. They had come to believe that Variants were created when one of these intelligences *escaped* the vortex and attached itself to a normal person. Each time the vortex surged with radiation, Danny believed, a new Variant was Enhanced. The correlation was too strong to ignore, even if they hadn't always been able to locate every single Variant. Maybe the intelligences didn't find a good "host" in time, or the Enhancement was too minor to pick up.

But it seemed the Variants were indeed hosts to these entities. Thus far, no Variant had ever showed signs of being controlled by these intelligences, or of being in contact or communion with them in any way. The entities just sort of tagged themselves to a person, and that person would manifest an Enhancement, along with a side effect or two.

The only two Variants known to the MAJESTIC-12 program who didn't exhibit any side effects at all were Frank Lodge and Danny himself. Frank, of course, did seem to be in some sort of communion with the memories of the dead folks he'd absorbed, but no one was sure if that really counted or not. And as for Danny, his sole Enhancement seemed to simply be the ability to detect other Variants, sometimes at great distances.

Though Danny sometimes wondered if his ability was changing, evolving. Ever since the Russian nuclear test in Kazakhstan in 1949, it seemed Danny was sensing more about these intelligences. Just glimpses, really, and they didn't make much sense.

"I hate it when we use those," Tim said, startling Danny slightly.

"Yeah, well, we don't want our guests getting ideas," Danny replied. "But I know how you feel."

Tim nodded. "It's like . . . being cut off from a part of yourself. There's a comfort to having that ability there. It's like a companion, almost. Weird, I know."

"Not weird. Well . . . not weirder than things already are."

"True that, son. There are days when I just want to go back to Minnesota and screw around with electronics for a living again," Tim said. "I mean, I'm in the middle of god-damn Russia, in the middle of the night, wearing a secret police uniform with like twenty-plus Soviet officers in my truck, which I hot-wired and stole from the Red Army."

Danny laughed at this, feeling a little better about things in general. "Well, when you put it like *that*. At least it'll be something you can tell your grandkids about."

Tim's good humor waned as he dug around for a cig-arette. "Dan, I ain't gonna see my grandkids. And if you don't have kids by now, you won't have any either."

"Kids were never in the cards for me," Danny replied. "I'm not wired like that."

Tim lit up and drew in deeply. "Married to MAJESTIC?"

"No. Just . . . not a family kind of guy."

"Confirmed bachelor. Or . . . *confirmed* bachelor?"

The difference in Tim's question was telling, but while Danny liked him just fine—there were some secrets Danny wasn't prepared to tell anyone. There was a reason he was good at his job. Secrets came naturally.

"Never mind, you dirty bastard," Danny replied jokingly. "Go keep watch down the road. I'll keep an eye on our guests."

Tim gave Danny a clasp on the shoulder before heading off back down the road, pistol in hand, while Danny cracked open the back of the truck. The gas had finally dissipated, but the canvas and enclosed space had kept it circulating in there for a while. Nobody was getting up any time soon. Mrs. Stevens had designed the gas to last three hours, and they were barely a third of the way there.

Still, Danny kept the null-field generator going. It was hard to battle Variants when you didn't know their abilities, and the geyser guy threw things out of whack. The program had Rustov in its files since '47, so they should've taken him and the others into account. Danny thought back to the close call they'd had in the cisterns under old Istanbul back then, and figured Rustov had to have been in on it. Only natural that his abilities might evolve during that time. Others certainly had.

Frank had confided to Danny that his dead-man memories were becoming more conversational in his head, and seemed to interact with him and one another in very self-aware ways. Cal could still glean life energy from living things to keep young and strong, or use that energy to heal others in exchange for aging himself back to normal, or beyond into old age. But the continued testing at Mountain Home showed that, over time, he had to take in and expend more and more energy to get the job done. In 1948, Cal could kill a steer and age himself twenty years younger. Now, it was maybe fifteen years. Where would it be a year from now?

Yamato had more difficulty with random sparks and arcs when he slept lately. Sorensen would occasionally phase in and out of sight—sometimes just a hand or leg, sometimes all of him—unless he kept a conscious grip on his ability. And Maggie . . . well, Maggie had just become more reserved, more cold and distant over time, even as she honed her emotional control over others into the most potent weapon MAJESTIC-12 had.

If he was being honest with himself—and being alone in the woods with a truckful of Russians that needed to be dealt with was a surprisingly good opportunity for introspection—it was clear to him that the Variants within MAJESTIC-12 would likely have a short shelf life for government work. Maybe ten years, maybe less. After that, Danny feared that Cal would require downright disturbing amounts of life energy to function; Frank would be overwhelmed by the voices in his head; Sorensen and Yamato would likely have to be hidden away from everyone as their Enhancements became uncontrollable. And Maggie . . .

Danny didn't want to think about what Maggie might become.

A whistle from Sorensen—it was supposed to be a whippoor-will call, but he never mastered it—dragged Danny's attention to the road. There was a car coming, lights off. It should be Frank and Katie, but . . .

Danny drew his pistol and aimed it at the road just as the car pulled up. Katie and Frank were inside, but both Danny and Sorensen had their weapons drawn.

"Lovely evening," Tim said in Russian, the first part of the password.

"*Yob t'vyu mat*," Frank replied as he got out. It was one of the vilest curses in Russian, and still not really used in polite company, and not so immediately in conversation. So oddly enough, it was a good rejoinder for the second part of the password.

Danny and Sorensen holstered their weapons. "Any problems?" Danny asked as he walked over to the car.

"Just an overeager police chief excited about his Order of Lenin medal, sure to come in the mail any day now," Frank replied. "I told him to keep off the phones and radios for forty-eight hours, until I could 'secure the NKVD and remove all the traitors to the Motherland.'"

"Will he do it?" Danny asked.

"So long as he doesn't call tonight, we're good, right?"

Danny nodded. *Here we go.* "Been thinking about the solution for these guys, Frank. I think there's another option."

"Dan, I'm sorry. Really. But you gotta expect at least one of these guys made Katie on that train. She says one of the Variants there recognized her and called her *by name* while there were still guys standing. So if even one says, 'I got beat to shit by a teenage girl,' and another says, 'I heard someone say Ekaterina,' then Katie's been made as active here in the Soviet Union. Right here and now. She doesn't leave. These guys can't be allowed to go back."

"And what if Maggie's already told Beria about all of us?" Danny shot back. "What if Katie's already been made? Killing these guys isn't going make that better, Frank."

Ekaterina quickly moved herself between the two men, facing Frank. "Wait. You want to *kill* all these men? There are twenty of them!"

Frank put a gentle hand on her shoulder. "Katie, honey, I'm sorry, but Beria really can't know you're around. Do you know what he'd do to get you back?"

"I don't care!" Ekaterina said, shoving Frank's hand off her hard enough to stagger him backward. "You're so worried about 'Katie, honey,' so why am I here then? I will not have these men die just because they may tell Beria something about me he likely already knows!"

Danny stepped forward again and looked Frank squarely in the eye, even though the latter had a couple inches on him. "Frank, get the Russian Variants secured. Decision's been made. Time to move out."

Frank stared hard at Danny for what seemed like an eternity, but Danny stood his ground, relying on their shared history and, yes, the privileges of rank. Finally, Frank stalked off toward the truck, and everyone else relaxed.

"What was that about?" Sorensen asked.

"Stress, probably. Let's go," Danny replied, hoping it was true.

Five minutes later, the unconscious Variants were piled into the car—two pretzeled in the trunk, one propped up in the back seat—and the keys to the Red Army truck were flung deep into the woods. Frank took the wheel and, with everyone else piled in tight, sped off into the night, headlights still doused.

Two minutes later, Danny saw a flash of light in the rearview, accompanied by a loud boom a second later.

He quickly turned to Frank, who just stared straight ahead on the unlit road. "What the hell did you do?"

There was an excruciating moment of silence before Frank replied. "I did what I had to."

From the back seat, Ekaterina screamed and lunged forward, her hands going for Frank's throat. Thinking quickly, Danny flipped on the null-generator before she could snap Frank's neck and send the car careening off the road.

"You killed them! Those men! Murderer!" she shouted as Sorensen held her back—successfully, now that her strength was gone.

Frank said nothing. He kept driving.

When Ekaterina's shrieks had died down to mere sobbing, Danny turned to Frank. "Why?"

"Because you were wrong, Dan. Every single expert jammed in my head agreed—they couldn't live. We need the extra time, and we need to keep our covers secure. Simple as that."

"Because of your voices? I outrank those voices!" Danny shouted. "You killed twenty men!"

"Don't you think I know that?" Frank snapped. "You think I like doing this shit? But if we're gonna get Maggie back and win this thing, we have to do it right."

Danny turned toward the darkness outside again and mulled it over for a few minutes. Finally, he made a decision.

"Major Lodge, for violating a direct order from a superior, you're hereby relieved and confined to quarters until further notice," he said calmly. "At the earliest possible date, you will be transferred back to the United States to face disciplinary charges. Now get us the hell home and don't say another goddamn word."

Frank said nothing. He just kept driving.

CLASSIFICATION: TOP SECRET-MAJIK

DATE: 14 Apr 53

FROM: DCI Dulles

TO: CMDR Wallace USN

CC: GEN Vandenberg USAF, DR Bronk MJ-12

RE: Operation Report of 13 Apr

National Command Authority commends you and your team on your successful operation. Extraction of Soviet Variants not advised at this time. Border controls around USSR have been upgraded as of 13 Apr. Shelter captives in place.

Extracting MAJ Lodge for disciplinary action is likewise not advised at this time. Maintain confinement at safe house until Lodge is required in an operational capacity. Further disobedience should be remedied in the field, up to and including elimination, at your command discretion.

Request for Operation SATCHMO clearance granted. Proceed with all due caution.

Per your information request, Agents Hooks and Yamato failed to make check-in and, at the moment, are unaccounted for in Korean theater. Search continues. You and your team are to remain in place and continue operations.

/s/ Dulles

April 15, 1953

Five days can seem like an awful long time when you're a prisoner of war. Especially in Korea. Especially during a cold and wet spring. Especially when they took your shoes and coats and rain gear.

Calvin Hooks marched up the muddy track, shivering and hugging himself to conserve what little warmth was left in his bones. His body ached all over—from the ten miles of daily marching, from the cold and the damp, from the old age that was catching up to him rapidly now that he was expending life energy just to stave off total exhaustion.

Along with Kim, Padilla, and Yamato, Cal was one of fifty or so prisoners of war rounded up after the North Korean and Chinese offensive that horrible night up on the hill. They were shoved around, punched, kicked—standard fare, he figured, Geneva Conventions be damned—then stripped of everything valuable. Coats and boots and ponchos were handed out by the Chinese to their North Korean allies, who would occasionally fight over who got what. *So much for the glories of socialism,* Cal thought. Of course, he kept that thought to himself. *Keep walking.*

Kim and the South Koreans were quickly separated from the Americans and other U.N. forces; Kim looked back plaintively as they marched him away, and Cal figured it wasn't going to go well for the poor fellow. In his briefing papers, Cal had read that captured South Koreans weren't considered prisoners of war, but rather "liberated soldiers" rescued from oppression, or some damn fool crap like that. So the South Koreans would be put to work in mines, or construction, or other hard labor jobs, and forced to undergo all kinds of Communist indoctrination.

The Americans, of course, were bargaining chips. But since nobody really had a clear picture of just how many were captured, they could afford to lose a few along the way.

So there were twenty-two U.S. and U.N. troops that started marching three days ago. They were already down to eighteen. The four that died—dysentery, exposure, whatever got 'em—were left on the side of the road. Everyone else was told to keep walking. *Keep walking.*

To Cal's surprise, he and Padilla were treated a little bit better than the rest—fewer beatings, a little extra food here and there. Nobody really told them why, but then, nobody really spoke English either. A couple times, some Chinese fellow tried to talk to Cal in Chinese, and apparently in French, but Cal couldn't get his meaning. All he got was a nod and a small smile from the guy, followed by a shove in the back from another, less pleasant one. *Keep walking.*

Yamato, though, was treated *far* worse. The Japanese hadn't been kind to the Koreans or Chinese during World War II, and it seemed like the North Koreans and Chinese were more than willing to take it out on Yamato, despite the American uniform. Either that, or they saw what Yamato could do with the lightning and didn't want a repeat. Either way, they beat the poor kid so badly right off the bat that he was completely out of it, totally incoherent, and Padilla had to help him walk.

Keep walking.

At least it wasn't raining today, though the sun was having a devil of a time cutting through the clouds hanging over the hills and forests. Fog clung to the higher trees and hills, and the buds of spring were just starting to emerge from the bare trees. It would've been pretty, almost, under other circumstances. Then again, any kind of sign of life, of the world at large, of hope . . . any of it would've seemed pretty.

A Chinese jeep honked behind them—jeep, truck, whatever they called 'em here—and Cal moved to the side of the road as quickly as possible. The traffic today was getting more frequent, and all heading in the same direction they were marching. At this point, that seemed like a good thing, since there might actually be a destination in store.

Back on the road, he found himself next to Padilla and Yamato. "How's he doing?" Cal whispered. Speaking out loud wasn't in the cards, not unless they all wanted a good, solid beating.

"No good," Padilla replied. "They beat him bad last night."

Cal frowned, nodded, and went back to walking. If he could just get some juice, he could fix up Yamato and, at that point, they could easily head for the hills. Cal had healed far worse than what the kid had suffered, even to the point of brain damage. But there was nothing for it— the opportunities were just too scarce, and nobody really wanted to touch the prisoners, all caked with mud, soiled from the lack of bathroom breaks, cold and probably sick with the flu or whatever the hell was gonna get 'em.

Sally and Winston occupied a lot of Cal's thoughts. He had little whispered conversations with them, telling them all the things he wanted them to know. He prayed to Jesus that they'd somehow hear him, and dared to hope that his prayers would be answered, because faith was all he really had left going for him at this point. He thought of Frank and Danny, that poor girl Maggie, and whispered some thoughts to them, too. Just in case.

Cal wasn't planning on dying, of course. He was still looking for the escape route. But nobody gets to choose when they're called home, so best to make peace when you can.

Finally, around the next bend, Cal saw some better odds. They had arrived.

The camp was large—much larger than the little cluster of buildings he'd stayed at back at Area 51, but not so large as, say, Mountain Home. He figured it was maybe half a square mile, surrounded by a pair of barbed wire fences. There were wooden watch towers set up here and there, seemingly at random, and Cal immediately wondered if there was a blind spot in the sightlines. Something to check out later, if given the opportunity.

The POWs were marched through the gates and into a courtyard surrounded by tents, huts, and sheet metal buildings cobbled together from scrap. The nicer tents had Chinese and Korean labels on them—Cal was getting better at telling the two languages apart, if not actually understanding any of the characters—while the sheet metal buildings seemed to be for the actual prisoners. A few groups of POWs were being marched to and from some of the buildings, no more than four or five at a time.

And God, they looked horrible.

Most of them were skinny to the point of emaciated, practically rattling around inside the uniforms hanging off their bony bodies. Scraggly beards, sunken eyes, unkempt hair . . . Cal was aghast at the treatment, and couldn't help thinking it was likely a preview of what might be in store for him soon. He thought back to the American camps where they questioned the Korean and Chinese prisoners—was that just last week?—and seeing the difference in treatment was a real punch in the gut.

"Wha . . . .what . . . .?"

Cal turned and saw Yamato looking up, half-dazed but trying to figure out where he was, what was going on. Stepping over to him, Cal whispered, "Hey, buddy. Keep your head down. We're at a camp. We gotta try to stick together. Remember our capture plans from the briefing, okay? We're gonna be okay."

Anything further was cut off as something hard smashed into the back of Cal's head, sending him to the muddy ground, dazed. Looking up, his vision blurred, Cal saw a soldier standing over him, with something . . . yeah, a rifle . . . carrying a rifle. Probably had taken the butt to the head.

Without really thinking about it, Cal reached out and touched the man's ankle. *Just a little. Just enough.*

It was more than a little.

The man cried out as he aged suddenly, the scream piercing through Cal's haze just as surely as the life flowed out of the soldier and into him. Stronger and surer, Cal flipped onto his back, still grasping the Korean man, and grabbed Yamato's leg with his other hand.

"Give 'em hell, son," Cal muttered.

Rick Yamato needed no encouragement.

Cal's eyes were blinded by white-hot lightning, which seemed to erupt from all around Yamato's body. There were screams and shouts, quickly joined by the sound of gunfire. Cal rolled onto his stomach and saw lightning arc toward four soldiers, all with rifles pointed at them. They spasmed and fell immediately.

"Get your ass down, Rick!"

Yamato looked down at Cal and just smiled. "No."

More shots popped off, and Cal watched helplessly as Yamato took a hit to the shoulder. The Variant staggered, but turned and let rip a half dozen bolts of lightning, one of which caught a jeep and turned it into a fireball that sent everyone ducking for cover.

"Okay! We go! We go now!" Padilla shouted, hauling Cal up by the arm. "Come on!"

But the gates were closed now, and it seemed like every goddamn Chinese and Korean Red was running toward them with guns aimed, shouting. But Yamato's lightning was getting less impressive with each arc. The kid was nearly spent.

"Aw, no," Cal said, shrugging off Padilla. "No, we ain't going nowhere. Rick, let it go. Bad idea."

By this point, Yamato was on his knees, still trying to pull the lightning out of him, but getting weaker by the second. There were dozens of Reds on the ground, but the ones most recently hit were shaking off the shock and getting back up. Cal put his hands up, and Padilla followed suit. Finally, Yamato fell over on his side, spent, and the Chinese and Koreans approached slowly, still shouting, weapons raised.

This beating's gonna hurt, Cal thought. *This is what I get for getting angry, for not planning. Stupid. So stupid.*

"Tíngzhǐ!"

With a single shouted word from somewhere behind Cal, all the soldiers stopped shouting and advancing, holding their positions. They were still aiming their guns at the three Variants, but it was an awful lot of improvement for just one word. Cal turned to see who it was.

The first face he recognized was Kim, their translator, looking none the worse for wear. Did he turn? Was he a spy to begin with? He didn't look happy, but he wasn't doing a comic book villain smile, either. And he was standing next to—a step behind and to the left, really—a rather short, skinny Chinese fellow in a Red Army uniform with sergeant's stripes. And even though that fellow, who looked to be maybe twenty, was thoroughly outranked by half a dozen officers in the mix, they all immediately seemed to defer to him.

"Black Wind," Padilla whispered. "Is that him?"

Cal shrugged. "We're gonna find out, I guess."

The Chinese sergeant approached and started speaking in rapid-fire Chinese, which Kim began to translate. "The sergeant wishes to apologize for the inconvenience of the past several days. There was an error in sorting through the captives from the battle, and the sergeant was called away to attend to other matters before he could return to you. You will be treated with respect and comfort now and in the future."

Cal looked squarely at Kim. "That's nice. That who we think it is? Hei Feng?"

The sergeant scowled at this and immediately started in again before Kim could translate back. "The sergeant's name is Chen Li Jun. The name Hei Feng is one given to him by others, and he would prefer a simple address as Sergeant Chen," Kim said.

"And how you doing, Kim? They treating you well?" Cal asked, trying his best not to sound too suspicious.

Kim offered up a small smile. "I wish I were home, Captain Hooks, but I have been treated well. I have a skill, and the sergeant here thinks I will be useful in finding out more about you."

Yamato finally staggered to his feet again, prompting a wave of murmurs from the soldiers surrounding them. Cal held out his hand, motioning for the young man to save his strength, but it wasn't necessary. "It's okay, I'm out of it for a while," he said. "So, Kim, did you sell us out? Told 'em everything?"

The Korean translator grimaced and turned slightly red. "I have family in the North, Sergeant Yamato. I was assured their safety would be guaranteed if I cooperated."

Cal nodded. "What's done is done, Kim. Ask Sergeant Chen here what's gonna happen to us."

Kim and Chen had a brief conversation in Chinese before the translator responded: "The sergeant has brought with him your confiscated possessions, including the electric generator you possessed which keeps his . . . blessings? . . . his *ability* from him. You will now be housed along with this generator to keep your own abilities from you. You will be given coats and boots, and the opportunity to bathe and eat well. Then the sergeant wishes to talk to all of you about your own blessings. Abilities. What do you call them?"

"Enhancements," Cal said. "In America, we call ourselves Variants. We're different. But we're good together. Tell the sergeant we'd welcome all that. We'd like to talk to him, too."

There was more conversation in Chinese, a few quick queries in English, and then the party broke up when Chen turned on the backup null-generator Cal brought with him. Immediately, Cal felt the years begin to pile back onto his body, though it would still take about an hour to get him back to his early sixties, age-wise. It wasn't going to be pleasant.

But a shower and some food and some warmth was a good start, and if that Chen fellow wanted to have a chat, well . . .

Not every escape opportunity had to be a shoot-out, even if it might take a while longer to pull off.

13.

April 30, 1953

Three weeks can seem like an awfully long time when you're a prisoner of war, even a Cold War. Especially when you're cut off from the outside world and haven't seen the sun in all that time. Especially when your food is day-old at best and rarely hot, and your prison is the cellar of some ancient, decrepit building in the worst part of Moscow.

For all that, the three Soviet Variants captured by MAJESTIC-12 had remained stubbornly uncooperative since their capture on the train. Cut off from their abilities by no fewer than three different null-generators—redundancy being Mrs. Stevens's watchword of late—the Variants were effectively trapped by the cellar's stone walls and floor. The windows had been boarded up in several layers, and barred on the inside.

The old townhome was abandoned—it was considered too bourgeois for current tastes, and the Moscow authorities were concentrating on apartment blocks and infrastructure with the limited resources available to them—mostly the shortage of strong men, victims of the Great Patriotic War eight years prior. A trip to the Moscow city records repository showed the owner of the house to be deceased with no other claims on the property, and surveillance of the block indicated there were just enough people still living there so that new faces wouldn't be out of place, even though the side street had little in the way of traffic.

So twice each day, at staggered times, a pair of MAJESTIC-12 agents dressed as construction workers entered the home to take care of the captives, bringing them food and ensuring they hadn't gotten up to any trouble. The basement had just one electric bulb for light and, sadly, no heat, though Danny made sure the prisoners had plenty of blankets for their mattresses, which were on the floor. The captives used a bucket for a toilet, and others held water for washing and drinking, a system that the female Russian Variant found highly intolerable and vociferously complained about in the rare times when she did bother to speak. But that also meant shit-bucket duty twice a day for the Americans, who always went in pairs and with guns at the ready. Nobody was pleased with the situation, Soviet or American. But it was the best they could manage.

Despite repeated attempts at everything from good-natured interviewing to light torture, the captured Variants weren't talking, and knew well enough not to talk amongst themselves while left alone, either—the bugs Mrs. Stevens had placed in their makeshift prison perfectly captured their conversations about favorite foods and vacation spots, but nothing about Beria or the Behkterev Institute or the Soviet Empowered.

Despite Danny's doubts, Frank Lodge had to be pressed into service to help maintain the captives. Since Danny wasn't quite ready to give him weapons, he usually took feeding and shit-bucket duty. He didn't complain. In fact, he hadn't said much at all lately, accepting his house arrest with a kind of troubled stoicism. Danny had known him long enough to know when he was out of sorts, and this was bad. Did he feel remorse? Was he planning something? Hard to say.

Back at the safe house—well away from the townhouse used as a prison—more silence reigned. Frank mostly stayed in his room, emerging only for meals and the trips to see the captives. Ekaterina was even more sullen than usual, also confining herself to her room unless she was needed on a mission—and Danny purposefully excused both her and Mrs. Stevens from captive housekeeping duties at the other house. Ekaterina and Frank sat at opposite ends of the table during meals, neither speaking at all, which prompted Mrs. Stevens to talk at an exponentially higher and faster rate. Sorensen had taken to performing his invisible reconnaissance missions during meal times, likely just to get away from the awkward dynamics.

Honestly, for Danny, it was all getting exhausting. But there had been some progress, at least, and more intel coming in each day, largely due to Sorensen. The Party elite, it seemed, did their best work after the rest of the *apparatchiks* left for the day, which meant Sorensen had an easier time moving quietly around the Kremlin's halls of power. The ambush of Beria's NKVD men had not gone unnoticed, and he'd received a sound talking-to from Malenkov, Molotov, and Khrushchev—separately and together—about making sure that counterrevolutionaries were being rooted out. Beria had responded by offering veiled accusations that his cohorts and rivals had been the ones who set up the ambush, and that the MGB and NKVD—as well as the merged agency they would become in short order—might find reason to investigate them.

The quest for power in the Soviet Union was getting ugly, fast.

There were still very few hints about the state of the Soviet Variant program, but Danny was making headway. He could sense seventeen Variants in the city, not including the captives or the Americans themselves, which meant that two more of them had just come in over the past week. That had to be the bulk of the Variants in the entire Soviet Union, possibly even the Eastern Bloc. Danny was able to track down five different safe houses used by Beria's Variants, all duly noted for whatever operation might come next. It seemed there were only two or three individuals, at most, left in Leningrad—one of whom, he hoped, was Maggie.

The problem was that they didn't know what abilities these Soviet Variants had, or anything about their training and talents. Mrs. Stevens was working on a number of capture scenarios, but there were far too many unknowns to make for a clean operation. They were all pretty reluctant to risk a repeat of the large-scale battle that had occurred on the train. So Danny watched them carefully, from a distance, and had managed to get photos of fourteen Variants—six women and eight men, ranging in ages from about fifteen to seventy, with most in their twenties through forties.

Beria was working hard to consolidate his resources—and his power. Bringing the Variants to Moscow en masse, combining the NKVD and MGB into a single, powerful political police and spying operation . . . those were big bets. But the others were betting big too. Malenkov and Molotov seemed to be working together to consolidate influence over the Red Army and the diplomatic corps, the outward-facing pieces of the Soviet apparatus, while Khrushchev was acting swiftly and surely to consolidate his control over the Communist Party itself. Party and government in the Soviet Union were nigh inseparable under Lenin and Stalin, so the recent ongoing developments were all kinds of interesting.

And Mrs. Stevens finally seemed to have found a place to throw a wrench in the middle of it all.

"The satellite states in Eastern Europe," she began while ladling out mashed potatoes to everyone during the evening meal. "That's where we can really weaken Beria."

"I thought Molotov was the diplomat," Danny said, eagerly spooning some beets onto his plate. Oddly, he'd developed quite a taste for the vegetable during his sojourn in Russia, despite having hated it as a child.

"Molotov is the diplomat to the West, and Asia, but the Eastern European countries are special cases," she replied. "They're treated less as separate nations and more as colonies or states, like back home. The Party here in Moscow gives orders to the Party in Bucharest or East Berlin or wherever. The secret police here, under Beria, is responsible for ferreting out traitors and counterrevolutionaries in those nations through the secret police there. So the centers of influence in Moscow extend into the Eastern Bloc, too."

"So?" Sorensen said, his mouth full.

"So nobody's really paying *attention* to the Eastern Bloc nations here in Moscow," Mrs. Stevens said. "That's why Mr. Dulles—well, both Misters Dulles, at State and CIA—are reaching out to those countries to see about helping out, being better friends. And we're getting reports from Foggy Bottom that the lack of oversight from Moscow is leading to whispers of dissent here and there. East Germany is a big one, I think, a big opportunity."

"How so?" Danny asked.

"The East Germans are being ordered to spend a ton on their military, and the Soviets are still taking reparations from them for the war. That's something like twenty to twenty-five percent of their budget going to feeding the Soviets' demands," she explained. "Their economy isn't growing fast enough. Everything's being poured into industrial production, and industrial workers quotas are going up. Agricultural production is down because everyone's going to the factories, which means food is getting imported and it's getting expensive. But wages aren't going up with the quotas. That's a completely unsustainable scenario."

For the first time in days, Frank spoke up. "Uprising."

"Possibly!" Mrs. Stevens said with an encouraging smile; Danny could tell she was happy to hear him contribute. "The trade and labor unions there are pretty strong, and somewhat outside the Party apparatus. I have to see how things play out over the next several weeks—there's a big Party meeting there at the end of June that could be pivotal, and if it goes the way I think it'll go—more quotas, less help with costs and wages—we could really light the fuse on something."

"So what's that get for us?" Sorensen said. "I mean, great to help them out and all, but our target is Beria. He's gotta go."

Danny took this one. "Dissent is Beria's portfolio. Any

dissent here or in the Eastern Bloc reflects poorly on him. He's already a little under the gun because of the stunt we pulled. If we pull off some kind of ruckus in Germany, maybe combined with another op here—maybe we blow up an MGB barracks or get some convincing propaganda aired—that could really push him hard. Maybe it'd be enough for Malenkov and Khrushchev to team up and end him, or maybe he overplays his hand in response and it achieves the same effect."

"Or he goes all in, kills off his rivals and tells the world that the Variants are in charge now," Frank offered. "That's a possibility. Seems like we need another front to distract him, one more thing to take care of before he launches a coup. We need to hit him where it really hurts."

"A Variant problem," Mrs. Stevens said, nodding. "That's interesting. If he feels his Variants are threatened at the same time as he's dealing with political issues, he can't use one to defuse or destroy the other. That's not bad, Frank."

At this, Ekaterina noisily got up from her place, put her half-full dish in the sink, and stalked off to her room, leaving the rest of the team staring at each other.

"My fault," Frank said quietly. He, too, got up and cleared his plate, then headed off to his own room, leaving Danny, Sorensen, and Mrs. Stevens to quietly finish dinner, though not before Danny encouraged her to formulate some operational plans on three fronts—East Germany, Moscow secret police, and Variants.

As Danny dried the dishes—he and Sorensen had dish duty that evening—he figured it was time to sit down and try to hash it out with Frank. Admittedly, Danny had been putting it off, this reckoning, mostly due to sheer exhaustion. But they needed Frank's savvy and his operational abilities. They needed another body to help with surveillance of the Variants and to tail Party leaders, to make sense of intel reports and to do something other than shit-bucket duty.

Above all, Danny needed to know why Frank had unilaterally decided to kill those men. If it *was* the voices in his head, then that would raise a big alarm bell, given what Danny himself had seen on the train. Because those faces had almost seemed like . . . ghosts. What if Frank's voices were themselves ghosts of some kind, rather than just skill sets or memories? What if the voices and what Danny saw were related?

Danny headed upstairs to Frank's tiny bedroom. The door was closed, as usual. Yes, Frank was largely confined to quarters, but even with that, he had been quieter than normal. Danny hoped it was due to guilt and reflection, but Frank always played things close to the vest, and as the years wore on, it seemed he was spending an increasing amount of time just communing with the memories in his head.

Danny knocked. "Frank, can I come in?"

Nothing.

"Frank, we need to talk."

Nothing. No sense of movement.

On a hunch, Danny concentrated on his Enhancement.

Frank wasn't there. He wasn't in the house. He wasn't in the neighborhood.

"Shit."

Focusing, Danny stretched out his senses to try to find him. With Variants he knew well, like Frank or Maggie or Cal, Danny could sometimes pinpoint them if they were within a certain distance—a few miles, give or take. Any further and they were just another Variant milling about the city. Further than about five hundred miles, Danny simply got a sense of direction on the compass, nothing more—and no sense of how many, either.

The problem was, Danny had last seen Frank maybe a half hour ago. Maybe he took the car. Or maybe . . .

Danny opened the room to find everything neat and tidy—Frank's military background had never left the man. There was no sign of anything amiss. Dashing downstairs, Danny ordered everyone to assemble, and to account for every bit of equipment and intel they had.

Fifteen minutes after that, Danny and Sorensen were

out the door, heading for the car. He knew where Frank was going, and it was practically suicide.

* * *

The Lubyanka Building stood like a silent guard over its namesake square in the cold Moscow evening, poorly lit and imposing. Headquarters of the MGB and the seat of Beria's power, the running joke was that the massive yet squat structure was, in fact, the tallest building in Moscow—because so many people could see Siberia's prison camps from its basement cells. Its neo-Baroque facade, with pillars and all kinds of architectural flourishes, stood out amongst the brutalist buildings going up around Moscow, a grand old haunted house amid the city. Listen closely, and one could imagine the screams coming from the basement.

Frank would be the first to admit he wasn't the most imaginative guy, but as he flashed his falsified MGB papers and walked into the building, he couldn't help but feel a bit like Daniel in the lion's den. How'd that Bible story go again?

Daniel was condemned to die by being thrown into a pit of lions, but an angel came and saved him, came the voice of Ibrahim, a Turkish scholar who had been with Frank for several years now.

I thought the lions ate one of Daniel's accusers instead, said Jan, an Icelandic fisherman.

Doesn't matter. Nobody comes out of this den, added one of the Russians Maggie had killed in the park last month. Frank still hadn't sorted out all their names. *You're going to die. The office is on the third floor. And you really should've brought a null generator.*

"Everybody shut the fuck up," Frank muttered under his breath as he straightened his stolen MGB uniform and made his way up the main stairs, throwing back salutes from the minor officers stuck with night duty. Yes, he should've brought a null-field generator, but they were valuable and expensive and, frankly, he'd done enough damage to the team without risking one of their key operational advantages.

The Russian—Boris? Andrei?—led him to the end of a hallway and a corner office, the anteroom of which looked far too ornate. A rather attractive young woman in an MGB uniform looked up from her reading and regarded him with a cocked eyebrow. "Yes?"

"Here to see Comrade Beria," Frank said.

Her look grew more quizzical. "Is he expecting you?"

"No, Comrade," Frank replied with a smile. "You may tell him that the operative codenamed DOMIK is here."

The woman looked ready to send him packing, but eyed the insignia on his uniform and thought twice about it, instead picking up one of the three phones on her desk and pressing a button. "I am sorry . . . yes . . . there is an officer here to see you . . . he says he is an operative, code name DOMIK . . . yes, he is, in fact . . . yes . . . very well."

With a look of surprise, the woman hung up the phone. "Are you armed, Comrade?"

Frank held up his arms. "No, Comrade. Do you wish to check?"

The woman came around and efficiently frisked Frank, then nodded. "Go in."

Frank opened one of the two heavy wooden double doors behind the woman's desk and entered an even more ornate corner office, brimming with fancy moldings, gold-paint trim, heavy red curtains, and a glittering chandelier. A pair of couches—*late nineteenth century, very expensive*, came an unwanted critique—flanked a coffee table in the center of the room, and beyond that was a massive carved mahogany desk with a silver tea service on one side and four phones on the other.

Lavrentiy Beria looked up and smiled. "Comrade DOMIK. It took me a moment, but that is very clever," the man said in English.

Frank closed the door behind him and slowly walked toward the desk. "I was hoping you'd get the translation right. I don't really know how good your English is."

"Good enough to know what a 'lodge' is." Beria waved toward a crystal decanter on the coffee table. "Drink?"

"No, thanks. I'm not here to be social." Frank stopped about three feet from the desk, heeding several voices in his head telling him the right distance necessary to dodge one of Beria's fiery assaults, should things come to that.

Beria regarded him for a long moment, leaning back in his leather chair with his fingers pressed together—a perfect look for a matinee villain—before switching to Russian. "I did not know you had returned to the Soviet Union, Mr. Lodge. Am I to assume you are responsible for the recent attack on my NKVD men? And the loss of three of my Champions?"

Frank smirked, but replied in his perfect Russian. "That what you're calling them now? I thought you guys used 'Empowered' instead."

"Answer the question." Beria's expression didn't change, but his voice was quickly layered with icy menace.

A pair of voices rose out of the jumble in Frank's mind, both agreeing that Beria was just as much on edge as Frank was. Small comfort. "Your people are fine. They're taking a little break, getting away from it all. You know how it is. Stressful times."

"I was surprised at the fate of the others, Comrade Lodge. I didn't think you Americans had it in you," Beria said, slowly reaching over to pour himself a cup of tea from the small samovar on the desk. "Efficient. Cruel, but efficient. Of course, we knew you Americans had sent your 'Variants' here, but we had assumed your target would have been the Behkterev Institute. That is, of course, the heart of our operation, just as you once had yours at that base in the desert in . . . Nevada, I believe the province is called."

"State," Frank corrected.

"State. Of course. United States," Beria said with a smile. "And so we began to move our resources here to Moscow. That was our mistake, and my men paid for it. The murder of our men has accelerated our timetable. The Champions may introduce themselves to the Party ahead of schedule."

"That could happen even earlier than you'd like," Frank said, taking a seat on one of the couches. "They could end up parked in front of Malenkov's dacha tomorrow. Or Khrushchev's. With a little note explaining just who they are and what they can do—and who they answer to."

Beria chuckled. "Oh, Comrade Lodge. Do you think they are so poorly trained as that? They will keep their abilities to themselves, swear fealty to whomever they must, blend back into society, even go to Siberia and work in the camps until the time is right. None of my Politburo colleagues would even begin to entertain such a fanciful story."

"I'm not your comrade," Frank said, quietly but with a sharpness of his own. "I came to deal."

Beria stood with his teacup and walked around his desk toward Frank. "Ah, now I understand. Of course." He took a seat opposite Frank. "You want to trade."

"One for one," Frank said. "I'll even let you pick. Whichever 'Champion' you want in exchange for ours."

"I didn't know you were so sentimental," Beria said. "But then, Margaret has a certain proletarian beauty to her, rather like our beautiful Russian peasant women."

"We look after our own," Frank countered. "Do you?"

Beria shook his head and smiled, a serpent's grin merely in need of a forked tongue. "I very much care for my own, *Mister* Lodge. But I think we define things differently. Margaret is one of my own. You are one of my own. All of us, whether you call them Variants or Empowered or Champions of the Proletariat—we are one people. The sooner you realize this, the sooner you can embrace your gifts and take your proper place in the world."

Frank stood. "You're obviously not serious, *Comrade* Beria. I'll be in touch. Think about it."

You should join him. Maggie did.

A single voice in his head—Frank couldn't tell which one—was quickly followed by a chorus of others. *Join him. Think of what you could do. The world is crap. Join him. He may have a point. You trust Maggie; look at her now.*

JOIN HIM.

Frank stopped and looked around, wide-eyed. Out of the corner of his eye, he thought he saw movement—that shadow Variant of Beria's maybe? But there was nothing, except for the clamor in his mind.

Beria just smiled a little wider. "Things are different lately, aren't they?"

"Wh—what?"

"Your abilities. 'Enhancements.' It is a phenomenon we have seen over the past several weeks. Our abilities have begun to change. They are more insistent, *angrier* if you will. We both know there is something behind the phenomena that gave us these abilities—ours in Leningrad, yours in, oh, what is that place called where you moved it? Idaho?"

Frank shook his head to clear it. "You have good sources."

"Of course we do. And if your teams had been as diligent in their study of the phenomena as ours, you would've noticed some changes. Perhaps they have and you're not being told. But there is something coming, Lodge. It feels . . . like a storm. I intend to act before it strikes."

JOIN HIM.

"I . . . I really don't know what you're talking about, pal," Frank said. "Do you want to trade or not?"

The doors to the office opened again, and Frank's jaw nearly hit the floor.

"I don't think we're doing a trade, Frank," Maggie said in her passable Russian as she walked in, wearing the uniform of an MGB officer, then switched to English. "Heya, buddy."

You really should've brought the null generator, Boris said.

April 30, 1953

anny really wanted to tell Sorensen to floor it, drive faster, dodge traffic—anything to get to the Lubyanka—but getting pulled over by the local cops would delay them further, if not blow their covers entirely. But now that they were closer to the city center, Danny could feel Frank's presence in the general direction of MGB headquarters—and he could sense someone else as well.

"Are you sure it's Maggie?" Sorensen said as he cruised through a traffic circle. "I thought she was in Leningrad."

"I'd know her presence anywhere," Danny said. "She's there with Frank, and another Variant, too. I'm betting Beria. It's his office, after all."

"Any others?"

Danny closed his eyes and concentrated. "I think . . . yeah, there's a couple others heading toward the Lubyanka, like us. But I only get those three in the actual building right now."

Sorensen sped up. "So it's a race. Great."

Danny ran through the contingencies in his head. He'd left Katie and Mrs. Stevens behind, to prepare to bug out if everything went sideways. Their worst-case scenario—and this was looking more and more like it might very well become that—was to gather what they could carry, burn the entire safe house to the ground, and make for the U.S. embassy with all due haste. They all had code words that would get them past the Marine guards and safely onto U.S. territory.

The Soviet Variants were another story. Danny's orders were to try to get them to the embassy as well and, barring that, deny them to Beria—permanently. He honestly wasn't sure if he could do that.

"So is Frank really off the reservation here?" Sorensen asked. "I mean, do we have to take him down? Is he flipping to Beria? Or is this some kind of super-secret wrinkle in the plan?"

Danny shrugged and gave Sorensen a tired smile. "We'll find out in a few minutes, I guess. I really don't know. They don't always tell me everything."

Sorensen frowned, but said nothing and kept driving. Even with all of his experience in the field—four-plus years—the former mechanic from Minnesota still had problems adapting to changes in operational plans.

Granted, this was a doozy.

Sorensen sped past the Bolshoi Theatre and, within a few blocks, tore into Lubyanka Square, the MGB headquarters hulking over the place. "Now what?" he asked.

Danny pointed toward the left. "There—Ulitsa Bol'shaya Lubyanka. Pull over there and—oh, shit. Stop the car!"

Sorensen veered toward the curb and hit the brakes while Danny watched a glass window explode and shards fall from the corner of the building's third floor. A second later, he saw someone jump out, seemingly trying to rappel off the side of the building without a rope, almost bouncing off the wall and grabbing onto the building's ornamentation to momentarily arrest his fall. To his surprise, the man landed on his feet and began to run, off in the direction of the Bolshoi.

"Wrong way, Frank," Danny muttered, then turned to Sorensen. "Go dark and head back to the house. Prepare to bug out. Stay by the radio."

Sorensen vanished.

The driver's side door opened and the driver's seat relaxed outward as Sorensen invisibly left the car. Danny scooted over to the driver's seat and gunned the engine, taking off while keeping Frank's location firmly in his

mind's eye. Teatral'nyy Proyezd was one way, so Danny
swerved past the Lubyanka building in the opposite direction, then took a hard left onto Pushechnaya Ulitsa and
took off back in Frank's general direction.

There were flashing lights in the rearview mirror now,
and the sound of sirens. Beria apparently wanted Frank
back. Badly. As he drove, Danny concentrated a moment
on Maggie, but she was no longer in his mind's eye. He
hadn't traveled out of his usual range, so that meant one
thing—she was back in a null field of some kind.

And likely still in Beria's grasp.

Danny focused back on Frank, only to find that he'd
stopped moving, roughly four blocks north of the Bolshoi.
Danny immediately recognized the location as one of the
dozen or so caches that had been hidden around Moscow
in the first few days since the team arrived. In abandoned
alleys, damaged buildings, disused basements, and other
forgotten places, the MAJESTIC-12 agents had stored
spare clothes—nearly all were proletarian outfits designed
to blend in—and forged papers. To Frank's credit, he intu-
itively understood the need to get out of his MGB uniform.
He also likely knew to sit tight and let the dragnet spread
out well beyond the Lubyanka building.

Danny pulled over on a side street, killed the engine . . .
and waited. That was the worst part, sometimes. Just waiting. But it was necessary—patience was an unheralded but
critical part of espionage. So he sat and leaned back in his
chair, pretending to doze off while keeping an eye on his
mirrors. The police activity continued for a while, but then
died down. After about a half hour, Danny keyed on his
radio, cannily hidden inside his wallet, an innovation only
Mrs. Stevens could make possible. "Misha, this is Alexi,
did you make your delivery? Over," he said in Russian,
should there be other ears listening. *Sorensen, are you back
at the safe house?*

A moment later, the radio crackled to life. "Misha here,
Alexi. Yes, delivery made. Receipt is signed. Over." *I'm
back, and all is well here. No signs we've been made.*

"Thank you. I think that's it for tonight, but keep your radio at hand. Over and out." *Put the bug-out on hold. Stay sharp and await further orders.*

So that was one positive sign. Whatever Frank had done at MGB headquarters, the Soviets hadn't made a move on the safe house. Sorensen was trained to do a thorough, invisible surveillance of the immediate neighborhood to ensure the house wasn't being watched, and by now he was getting pretty good at identifying which "casual bystanders" were actually carrying concealed weapons and radios. Danny figured that they had at least tonight to figure out whether or not the op was truly busted. He wasn't worried about whether Maggie would flip on them—she didn't know the location of the safe house, wouldn't have been told until she made contact in Moscow.

Danny closed his eyes and shook his head tiredly as he realized he hadn't discounted the fact that Maggie really might've flipped on them. She'd been with MAJESTIC-12 since the beginning; Danny had personally recruited her out of a mental hospital near San Francisco. But she'd always been independent, and her emotional detachment—the biggest side effect of her Enhancement—had increased considerably over the years, to the point where the things she said and the choices she made seemed almost alien at times. But then she'd smile and end up doing the right thing. Was that genuine, or was she so accustomed to pulling emotional threads that she did it out of habit now? Would she ultimately see Beria's power play, centered on Variant supremacy, as the way to go? Or was she simply playing along until she could turn the tables?

Danny ran through the dozen or so contingencies in his head before finally giving up. He just didn't have enough information to figure out what to do next, and wouldn't until he talked to Frank.

And Frank was moving again.

Checking his watch and seeing seventy-four minutes had gone by since he pulled over, Danny started the car and slowly started driving again, heading toward Frank, who was now slowly walking northward toward the safe house. As he drove, Danny didn't see any great increase in police or military activity. On the one hand, that was a little surprising, as Frank would be an extremely high-value target, but on the other, it was possible Beria wouldn't want to create too much of a ruckus and show his hand politically. Just as Beria was sure to have informants in the Party and Red Army, his rivals likely would have their own people reporting on the First Deputy Premier as well.

Five minutes later, Danny spotted Frank on a side street, dressed in a factory worker's overalls and coat. Checking his mirrors and finding no other cars coming up behind him, Danny pulled over to the side and rolled down his window. "Dmitry! I haven't seen you in ages!" Danny called out. "Can I give you a ride, Comrade?" *Coast clear. Get in the car.*

Frank turned and gave a smile. "Alexi! How are you? How are Anna and the kids?" *What about the safe house?*

"They're well, thank you! I feel like I haven't seen much of them, though. I'm working hard these days." *So far so good, but can't say for certain.* "Come, let me take you home." *Seriously, get in the car.*

Frank walked over and opened the passenger door. "That's kind of you, Comrade. Thank you." The door slammed and Danny pulled out, leaving Frank to slump back in his seat. "They got to Maggie," he said, dropping the pretense.

"I know. I sensed her."

"No, they got *to* her, Dan. She's wearing an MGB uniform now." Frank's voice had a tinge of anguish in it, even as he tried to report matter-of-factly on his unauthorized excursion. "I went to talk trade, and to let Beria know we were behind the train job. And she just comes in and says 'Heya' and Beria's all smiles about it. It's bad."

Danny nodded. "Unless she's doubling. What do you think?"

"Possibly?" Frank said. "I mean, I could never read her very well, and the psych guy in my head can never make heads or tails of her. So who knows? She came in, Beria picks up his phone—probably to call the cavalry—and I decided to get the hell out of Dodge."

"Right. So what the hell were you thinking doing that?" Danny's voice remained calm, belying his burning desire to reach out and punch him in the face.

Frank just shrugged. "Beria was hunkering down, we're stretched thin babysitting the Commies we got. Figured I'd stir things up. But Dan—we got bigger problems."

"Bigger how?"

Frank rolled down the window a hair to let some cold, fresh air into the car, which smelled of spilled booze and cigarettes—one of the reasons they got it so cheap to begin with. "You know my memories, my voices, they've been growing more active lately, yeah?"

Danny's heart sank. He feared where this was going. "Yeah."

"Well . . . I killed those MGB men, from the train . . . I killed them based on their advice. Not just the Russians I took on the last time we were here. But from some of the guys who've been with me since the beginning, like Mark Davis. They were all insistent that those men had to die in order to keep our cover from being blown. I . . . I trusted them."

"You trusted them more than me," Danny replied.

Frank smirked. "Yeah, I guess I did. I mean, I feel like they know me and I know them, right? It's . . . I don't know . . . it's intimate in a way that nobody else would really get."

"I have a hard time thinking General Davis and all those military guys you've absorbed would have encouraged you to disobey direct orders." Danny tried not to sound peevish, and knew he was failing.

"But that's why I trusted them! Because you're right, there's a lot of respect for chain of command from some of those guys. But when I got the Americans and the MGB guys and the Red Army guys and even the academics and everyone else all on the same page? It's . . . well, that's the problem. Something else happened just now."

"What?"

Frank took several long moments to reply, and Danny turned to see him staring out the window as the city went past. "They all wanted me to join up with Beria. *All* of them. Just now."

Danny absorbed this for an equally long time.

"I have to ask," Danny said finally. "Did you feel like they were exerting any control over you? Like, you had to fight them off in order to *not* join up with Beria?"

Frank chuckled, surprisingly. "Am I possessed? No. I don't think it works like that. There was never any surrender of motor control or anything like that. Just a big fucking shout in my head from everybody there. 'Join him. Join him.' Honestly, it was spooky as hell. And apparently I'm not alone. Before Maggie came in, Beria told me that the Soviet's Enhancements were changing. Evolving. We seeing anything like that?"

Danny thought back to the angry faces he saw on the train, emerging like specters from the Variants themselves. "I don't know. I'm not sure the science team has reported anything like that. But we've been so busy with ops . . ."

The two men looked at each other for a long moment.

They don't always tell me everything.

15.

May 5, 1953

Hoyt Vandenberg grimaced with every jolt of the C-47 Skytrain as it cruised over the Northern Rockies. The transport wasn't particularly well suited for comfort—Vandenberg was traveling below the radar, hence a seat on one of the Air Force's mainstay troop and cargo transports. But each jostle sent a wave of pain through the lower core of his body, a reminder of the sentence he'd been given months ago.

Cancer.

And not just any cancer—prostate cancer, which he felt was the worst goddamn sentence he could've gotten. Every trip to the bathroom was an ordeal. Sitting down had to be managed very carefully, and standing up almost as much. He'd gotten good at wearing a poker face through the pain, but every now and then his body would come up with some new stab of agony, or some additional indignity that required him to change his habits or limit his activities. He missed golf like you wouldn't believe, but the last swing he took with his driver had him doubled over in pain for a good ten minutes.

He wasn't going to give up the Scotch, though, despite what the docs at Walter Reed said about mixing booze with meds. It was the only goddamn thing that let him sleep at night. He wished he had a flask with him now, but Vandenberg had spent thirty years in the military without taking a drink on duty, and he was going to hold on to that distinction until he retired.

That day was probably coming soon. He hated admitting

it, but the pain was getting unmanageable some days. The docs gave him maybe six months if he stayed in uniform and kept trying to do his job, maybe a year or two if he gave in and retired. But what the hell would happen then? Bedridden and drugged? Vandenberg had flown combat over Africa and Italy during the war. He wanted a better end than that. He probably wouldn't get it, though.

And the kid flying this bird seemed to have a natural affinity for finding turbulence. The pilot looked to be all of seventeen, blond-haired and freckled like the boys on the cover of *The Saturday Evening Post*. Sure, he was a first lieutenant and probably ten years older than that. But Vandenberg knew his appraisal was shaded by his own mortality.

With a sigh and a wince of pain, Vandenberg pulled a folder from his bag and began reading. The Russia op wasn't a bust, per se, but it sure as hell wasn't going according to plan. Wallace had reported on Frank Lodge's exploits as if they were all part of the plan, and suggested Maggie Dubinsky was playing double agent. How much of this was true, and how much of it was to help cover a massive snafu, Vandenberg couldn't say. But he knew Wallace was inherently cautious—a trait which made him an excellent field operative. What was going on now was far too cowboy for Wallace. Lodge, sure. Lodge could rely on the expertise, skills, and memories of, at last count, forty-three different people. But Wallace was the commander on the scene, and Lodge would have to go through him—unless he went off on his own.

What a mess. And now Wallace wanted to smuggle the three captured Soviet Variants out of the country and back to the U.S. for study, to see if Beria's assertion of changes in Variant abilities was indeed true. And since the NKVD and MGB were now on lockdown—the Lubyanka was completely off limits, as was the Kremlin—Wallace wanted to send Lodge and Sorensen to East Germany, of all places, on the recommendation of Rose Stevens, in order to drum up dissent and try to give Beria another black eye.

Oh, and to top it all off, three Variants were missing in action in the Korean theater.

President Eisenhower had been spitting bullets when they'd briefed him a few days ago. Publicly, Ike was a model of Midwestern restraint and moderation, but the President could deploy his rage like a tank column hitting the breach. Vandenberg and Dulles had gotten an earful yesterday, culminating in an ultimatum—figure out what's going on with the Variants, fix the Russia op and get Beria out of there, or else the MAJESTIC-12 program would be shut down for good.

Dulles was managing the Russia end of things, and seemed to be settling in for the long game. CIA would start drawing up plans to try to get the Soviet Variants out from behind the Iron Curtain, and the director was leaning toward approving the East German op, if only to get some of the Variants out of the Soviet Union for a while to let things cool down.

Vandenberg—the most senior official remaining in the MAJESTIC-12 program—had been tasked with getting to the bottom of the potential changes in Variant Enhancements, hence the trip to Idaho aboard a rustbucket cargo plane now on its final approach to Mountain Home Air Force Base, blessedly beyond the mountains.

Of course, the kid at the controls jostled the landing, causing Vandenberg to nearly cry out in pain as his body bounced off the seat. Sure, the crosswinds over the high prairie were pretty intense sometimes, but what the hell were they teaching those kids before giving them their wings? He hoped the new Air Force Academy, once it opened, would do a better job. And he hoped he'd get to see it opened some day.

Vandenberg packed up his things, got up, and headed for the hatch, pausing to shake the pilot's hand and give him a little advice on the wind. He was tempted to rip the kid's head off, but knew that wouldn't really teach him anything, so he opted for magnanimous paternal advice and hoped it would pay off. Heading down the stairs, he saw Detlev Bronk waiting for him next to a jeep, carrying a briefcase.

"How was the flight, General?" Bronk asked after a handshake.

"Bumpy. How do things look here?"

The lanky scientist just scowled. "Let's get you to a secure area."

Bronk took the general's duffel and threw it into the jeep, hopping into the driver's side. The biophysicist wasn't full-time at Mountain Home anymore, having accepted a position at Johns Hopkins. Rumor had it that he'd soon be running the Rockefeller Institute for Medical Research. Bronk was a smart guy, and cleared for everything related to MAJESTIC-12, so it was perfectly natural to bring him back for an audit.

Within minutes, the jeep pulled up to a large prefab hangar, notable only for the multiple layers of barbed wire around it and the squadron of MPs at the gate. Both men had their credentials reviewed three times, and were searched thoroughly enough to make Vandenberg wince again, before they finally entered the building itself. Inside was a cramped conference room, where Bronk flipped a switch on a small metal box on the table—an electronic jammer designed to confound listening devices.

"We have a problem," Bronk began. "I thought you said you'd have your best minds working on this project."

Vandenberg was taken aback. "We do. Or we did. We assigned Lloyd Berkner and Don Wenzel to the project after you left. What happened?"

Bronk snorted as he took a seat, leaning back and folding his arms across his body. "I've met them. Fine men, sure. But their background is in engineering and radiation, not biology or the kind of physics we need to really study this thing."

"Not everybody can get themselves a TOP SECRET clearance these days, what with McCarthy and all the paranoia," Vandenberg replied with a shrug. "So what did they miss?"

"A little too much. For one, the study of the Variants themselves is almost completely lacking now. Any new Variants are brought in and assessed for their Enhancements, then sent off to training. They're establishing a baseline, sure, but there's no further testing. And neither of those men trusts Rose Stevens enough to let her in on it, so the greatest mind we have available to us is being purposefully left out of the loop."

Vandenberg scowled. "I know. Same with Wallace. That's a direct order from Truman after what happened in '49, and Eisenhower agreed to keep it that way. The vortex study and Variant assessments aren't part of their purview now."

"Well, that's dumb, Hoyt. Between the two of them, they're the sum total of the institutional knowledge around this project, aside from me." Bronk opened his briefcase and started pulling out files. "I have them doing follow-ups on the Variants we have left here now, mostly new recruits, to see if there's any changes in their Enhancements, as well as their physical and psychological profiles. Probably won't have anything for a few more days yet, but already I'm starting to see evidence that some of their abilities have changed. Nothing big, but a few of them have taken on some new side effects, and we already have one—you know the Spanish girl who can fly? She can now go supersonic, whereas she couldn't before."

"That's handy," Vandenberg said.

"Not really. For one, she needs a special flight suit now, otherwise she'll hurt herself due to the pressure and friction. She still can't carry anything or anyone with her, and she'll really do a number on herself if she collides with anything. She can just fly really fast now."

"All right. So their Enhancements are changing. What else?"

Bronk pulled out a series of readouts and charts. "We're still using the same monitoring equipment that Kurt Schreiber put in place back in '48. There's better equipment out there now. I suppose, to their credit, Berkner and Wenzel tried to get better gear, but the Defense Department budget's been constrained over the past few years, what with Korea. They're in limbo. But I made a few calls to some friends at General Electric, and we got new monitors up and running yesterday. These are the results."

Vandenberg looked at the squiggly lines and series of numbers and immediately gave up. "What am I looking at?"

With a smile and a sigh, Bronk circled three similar-looking patterns of lines on one page, then found others on subsequent pages, followed by groupings of numbers throughout. "We know that the vortex simply churns out low levels of nonionized radiation as it sits there and spins and defies physics," Bronk said. "When it creates a new Variant, it sends out a huge pulse, directionally. Between that and Wallace, we're usually able to track down the new Variant and get them in here before too long."

"Right. So?"

"These patterns are similar in wavelength and frequency, but they're happening at the extreme ends of the electromagnetic spectrum, which is why our gear couldn't detect them. They're also happening a *lot*. These are just the instances we've had over the past twenty-four hours, since we got our new detectors up and running. Twenty-seven transmissions."

"And these are new?"

"Not entirely. There's a tiny bit of this pattern that could be picked up on our old gear, just a fraction. I had the boys here look back over the data to find spikes in that piece of the EM spectrum. We've had hits like that going back to '46, but it looks like background noise against everything else—except for this."

Bronk pulled out a hand-drawn bar chart, with each bar labelled annually. The bars were pretty small—until 1952, which rose considerably. The bar for 1953 was even larger—and it was only May. "So you think that this activity's increased," Vandenberg said. "Is it creating new Variants? Maybe different kinds of Variants?"

"We don't think so. If it were, then we just had twenty-seven new comic book superheroes created in the last day, and there's no way in hell you could cover that up," Bronk said with a smile. "Unless I'm not cleared for that sort of information."

Vandenberg wasn't laughing. "So what is it, then?"

"We don't know."

"Theories? Shot in the dark?"

"Dan Wallace confirmed that there's some kind of intelligence behind all this, but we've been unable to communicate with it," Bronk said. "What if these patterns are communication? What if the vortex is communicating with our Variants? Variants all over the world?"

Leaning back, Vandenberg closed his eyes and counted to three—a tic he used to calm himself when under stress. And this was a doozy. "What are they saying?"

"I don't even know if we have the gear to interpret it, if it's really communication at all," Bronk said. "It could be anything. We can't even say for certain if it's related to the variability we're seeing in Enhancements, and we're still trying to nail down the vectors, since the signals are so weak. But this," he added, stabbing the stack of papers with his finger for emphasis, "is a real, material change in this phenomenon, and we need to make it a priority to get to the bottom of it."

"Yes, you do," Vandenberg said. "What do you need from me?"

Bronk pulled another piece of paper from his briefcase and handed it over. Vandenberg scanned it and realized he'd have to do some serious budgetary and logistical maneuvering to get everything squared.

Then he got to the last item.

"Schreiber? Really?"

Kurt Schreiber was a former Nazi scientist who'd conducted early research into paranormal abilities as part of Hitler's Übermensch drive. He had been brought over as part of Operation PAPERCLIP after the war, and had been attached to MAJESTIC-12 until 1949—when he'd tried to

ally with a captured Soviet Variant and sell out the program to the Russians, but had gotten caught up in a sting
orchestrated by Wallace.

Schreiber'd spilled everything he knew, eventually,
thanks to Maggie Dubinsky's sometimes brutal emotional
manipulation. But the interrogations had left him a complete basket case, and the former Nazi had spent the last
four years in lockdown right there at Mountain Home,
monitored by the psych staff and generally ignored by
everyone else.

Until now.

"I know he's round the bend, Hoyt, and we wouldn't let
him anywhere near the vortex. But if he has some insights
into any of this, no matter how cracked, I think we need
to use him. I mean, if Danny's right about the changes he's
seeing and what Beria's telling them, this could spiral out
of control fast."

Vandenberg leaned back in his seat and winced through
the pain that shot through his body. *Do we use an insane
Nazi to figure out if some kind of alien intelligence is trying
to manipulate our agents through a freakish hole in the fab-
ric of space?*

Retirement was starting to look better by the second.
This was a horrible way to spend one's remaining days.

* * *

At first glance, the room looked normal, if Spartan. The
bed looked comfortable, with a homemade quilt giving it
a homey touch. The writing table didn't have drawers, but
it did have a radio and lamp, and the chair was padded
leather. There were shelves, though lacking in the usual
knickknacks beyond a handful of paperback books, copies
of the *Idaho Statesman*, and some old photographs—without frames, oddly enough. The bureau had the usual collection of men's clothing, all neatly folded, and the wooden
floor was covered by a knock-off Persian-style rug.

But the walls were completely bare, and if you looked
closely, you'd find the radio and lamp were bolted to the

table—which in turn was bolted to the floor, as was the chair. The bed, too, was firmly fixed to the floorboards. Open the drawers, and you'd see no belts or suspenders, and the corners of the furniture were all rounded.

The man in the room didn't seem to notice or care, busy as he was writing in pencil on a legal pad, covering the paper with mathematical formulae, sketches, notations, and a jumble of words in several languages. There were four other legal pads next to him, all filled. That was just yesterday's output.

There was a knock on the door, but the man didn't stop his work, only began to write faster, more frenetically and sloppier, a rush to finish his thought before the next thing happened. Already, his mind jumped ahead—it was not meal time, nor bathroom time, nor was he scheduled for an exam or evaluation. It was a Tuesday, and nothing was supposed to happen on a Tuesday. That and Sunday were the days he could truly be productive, so whatever was coming was going to be new.

New was in such short supply these days.

Finally, the man stopped writing and turned to see who interrupted him—and smiled. New, indeed.

"I can only imagine one plausible reason for your visit. Let's get to work, then, shall we?" Kurt Schreiber said.

Detlev Bronk just scowled.

16.

May 13, 1953

Getting up every morning was a little bit tougher. Old age did that to you—especially when you were aging a couple weeks every day. And sleeping on a thin mattress thrown onto a wooden floor hadn't been helping much either.

Nonetheless, Cal got his feet under him and went outside the building just as the sun was starting to peek up from over the mountains. The weather had improved considerably since he was captured. As long as you were going to be held captive somewhere, there were far worse places than a thousand-year-old temple.

Cal really didn't think highly of other religions, when he thought of them at all, but there was an undeniable serenity to the place. It was called Songbul-sa, a Buddhist temple tucked into an ancient fortress on the side of Mount Jongbang. He had no idea where he was on a map—and would've been stricken to know he was less than 150 kilometers from the front—but the place seemed like a slice of heaven compared to what had come before.

The Chinese and North Koreans were using the ruins of the fortress and the still-operating temple as a safe haven and operating base. Most of the soldiers were camped among the ruins, but Black Wind was held in such high regard that he was given quarters within the monastery itself, and tended to silently, almost reverently, by the robed, bald monks. They also gave the same treatment to Cal and Miguel, and Yamato as well, to Cal's surprise, allowing them the bedding and some decent food. Cal would've killed for some spare ribs, mind you, but the temple food was surprisingly good, even with the lack of meat. Those Buddhists really knew their way around some spice.

They'd been kept there for a couple weeks now, once the Koreans had figured out just how to keep them. After Yamato's outburst in the POW camp, they'd kept him fully sedated for days, waking him just enough to feed him. Even then, though, Cal could tell the young man was getting weaker and weaker. Cal had tried to slip him a little life energy whenever he could, but they'd been keeping Cal's hands chained up behind his back most of the time, having seen what he could do to a man when angry enough. He felt bad about what had happened to that soldier. Some folks could get used to really hurting people like that. Cal hoped he never would.

Ultimately, they were given a choice. Behave, or watch a bunch of American POWs get slaughtered—as many as they had on hand. Kim had translated the ultimatum with a pained look on his face, and even Black Wind himself had seemed uncomfortable with the idea. But it was incredibly effective. If the Reds so much as saw a spark out of Yamato, or Cal made someone feel even just a little sleepy, people would die. Lots of people.

Now, that didn't mean Yamato was always a hundred percent on board—Cal had to talk down the hothead a few times after he was allowed to wake up and had the situation explained to him. But Cal remained the senior commander on the scene and, with a great deal of patience, he'd managed to get Yamato in line every time. It was wiser, of course, to hold out for the right time. Their last attempt was ill-conceived. They'd been tired and angry and they hadn't been thinking right. They had to pick their spots better moving forward.

Mostly, though, Cal felt bad for all the people who died for nothing. Even the Reds had moms and dads. And he wasn't going to condemn a bunch of Americans to the same fate just so they could try and fail again.

Cal looked over to the guards on the other side of the

little room—each Variant had two men on him at all times, armed to the teeth. Today's pair looked young, maybe sixteen each, and that was generous. But they had fully loaded rifles with them, as usual—leftovers from World War II or even earlier, but rifles all the same. Cal nodded at them and waved, but was greeted with stoic, inscrutable staring, as always. They no doubt had orders to shoot on sight at the slightest hint of provocation, so Cal made damn sure not to give them any.

Instead, he pulled on his boots—they'd been given fresh clothes and real boots, another sign of favor—and stepped outside his room and onto the wooden building's porch, beautifully carved and tended to, with a tiled roof overhead and intricate columns supporting it. There was a mist hanging low over the trees this morning, obscuring some of the mountains, but it was a damn fine sight regardless. Toward the main temple building, Cal could hear woodblocks being struck—the Buddhist monks were at their morning prayers. That meant breakfast would be soon, with rice, some kind of salty soup, and pickles. It wasn't bacon and eggs, but there was definitely something to it, because Cal always felt nourished afterward, but not heavy. He figured he might look into that diet more when he got home, have Sally give it a try. . . .

If he ever got there again. A wave of sorrow and regret washed over Cal for a long moment as he thought of his beautiful wife and his son, Winston. He swore that if he ever got home again, he'd find a way to hang it up with MAJESTIC-12 and just go off with Sally and grow old together on Social Security. And they'd watch Winston, now in law school, become a lawyer and follow his dream of seeking justice and equality for his fellow Negroes.

Yes, Cal wanted to grow old. Theoretically, so long as he kept his life-energy levels up, he could live indefinitely. But how much life would he have to hoard as he got older? Back when he'd first discovered his ability to drain life—well after he found out he could heal people—he could slaughter a horse or a cow and be a hale and healthy twenty-five.

Now it took two or three head of cattle to take him from his real age to that peak again. So how much would he need when he turned eighty? Ninety? A hundred? It really didn't seem fair, after a while, living like a vampire to stay young. Sure, he could keep Sally young, too, but there would come a point when the price tag would be too high. Best to let it go sooner rather than later, before they got too used to the benefits and started justifying the drawbacks.

At least, that's where Cal stood now. He wondered if, when he was old and about to die, he might start thinking differently. What a test of faith and morality that would be . . . and Cal honestly couldn't say how he'd respond. That was a frightening thing to contemplate.

Cal's attention was drawn to the monastery gate, where shouts and movement could be heard on the other side. He didn't know Korean from Greek, but he could at least tell the ruckus was a positive one—there was no gunfire, for starters. Finally, the gates opened, and Cal saw Hei Feng stride into the courtyard, flanked by a bunch of grinning young soldiers, weapons held in triumph. They hadn't seen much of the Chinese Variant since they arrived—apparently, the young man was in high demand. Of course, the ability to deflect bullets and send people flying wasn't something you came across every day. Cal had picked up enough scientific lingo through the years to theorize that, like Miguel Padilla, Hei Feng had the ability to manipulate kinetic energy. Miguel's Enhancement allowed him to adjust a moving object's kinetic energy to make sure it went where he wanted, every single time. Hei Feng could do the same, but only *away* from him, and only if that object was already moving. Neither of them could so much as lift a pebble, but once that pebble was thrown, the two of them could probably have it bounce all over the damn place.

Cal turned to see that Miguel and Yamato, the latter looking particularly sleepy, had joined him out on the porch, along with their guards. At least three of the guards had weapons trained on them, but the frightening thing was, Cal was getting used to that.

A young soldier separated himself from Hei Feng's pack and ran toward the porch, shouting in Korean. Suddenly, there were rifle barrels in their backs and some shouted words Cal had grown to recognize, in a general sense, as "move it." They were shoved and prodded down the stairs and into the courtyard, and from there toward one of the nicer buildings in the complex, where the monks stayed and ate. It was also where Hei Feng himself was quartered, when he was around.

A few minutes later, they were seated on the floor around a low table, monks bringing them steaming bowls of soup, rice, pickles, that rotting cabbage crap they called kimchi, and some other less-identifiable stuff. There were four places—and just as many guards. A moment later, Hei Feng came in and bowed to them, followed by Kim, their old translator.

"Hei Feng welcomes you and apologizes for not having had the time to show you more hospitality," Kim said after Black Wind spoke a whole bunch of Chinese. "He remains very curious about you and hopes that you and he may speak freely. He would be most eager to keep the soldiers outside, so long as you continue to honor your word regarding the use of your abilities. Of course, an attack now on him, or anyone else, would result in the regrettable end of many of your countrymen. It would only take a single code word on the radio for that to happen. He urges you to join him for this meal in peace and comradeship."

Cal looked at Padilla and Yamato, who looked just as puzzled as Cal felt, and finally decided to speak for the group. "You tell him, Kim, that'd be just fine. Happy to sit down for a nice breakfast and a chat. Tell him we'll behave."

Kim related the information, and a moment later, Hei Feng dismissed the soldiers, leaving the four Variants—and one translator—in the room. Cal started to feel a little bad for Kim, frankly; he already knew way too much for any one side to want him around after all was said and done.

Tea was poured and plates filled, and Cal dug in with relish, his chopstick usage surprisingly deft for having just learned, while Padilla and Yamato still struggled with theirs. "So, can I ask what Hei Feng's been doing lately? Haven't seen him around."

"He has been away on missions, and also to consult with his superiors in the Red Army," Kim replied after some back and forth with Hei Feng. "He would like you to know that he has kept your existence secret from all but a few trusted officers and friends, which is why you are here and not with the other prisoners, or sent away. Hei Feng knows you would be of great interest to the government of China—or the Soviet Union."

Cal nodded and smiled. "Tell him thanks for that. He's right. I'm gonna assume, then, that the folks in Beijing and Moscow don't know about him, either. Otherwise, I figure they'd snap him up and ship him off to Beria or somebody. Does he know of anything like that? A program where they use people like us?"

Another flurry of translation and discussion followed. "There are rumors, yes, that the Communists gather people with strange abilities, and that some go to Moscow, some go to Beijing. It is Hei Feng's belief that he can be more effective and useful to his people here, than in such a situation."

Oh, boy. There's a Chinese Variant program too, Cal thought. It made sense, of course, given China's huge land and population. Enhancements didn't really seem to hold to a particular geography or race, so it made sense that China might have more than a few Variants around. And if Beria was poaching where he could, well . . . that'd be interesting too. How long before China would say enough to that?

"Hei Feng would like to know about the kind of program America has for its special people," Kim added. "He believes you to be soldiers and wishes to confirm this."

"Don't tell him shit," Yamato warned quietly. "He could already be working for Moscow. Or someone else."

Cal just smiled. "And if he's working for Beria, he already knows all about us. I mean, Beria himself saw you throwing lightning around pretty good in Kazakhstan, if I'm not mistaken." Yamato said nothing to that, just scowled into his meal, so Cal turned back to Kim.

"You can tell him that, yeah, we have a program. We're not just soldiers, though. We do a lot of different things to help our government and our people. And we're paid well and treated well."

"But you are a black man, Calvin Hooks," Kim replied after translating. "The Chinese and Koreans know that black people are still treated like slaves in America, and that capitalism will keep them as slaves forever."

Well, ain't that something. "Yeah, black folks aren't treated too well. We aren't slaves no more—my grandfather was born a slave, but he was freed after the Civil War. But yeah, especially in the South, we have to sit in the back of the bus, can't go where we like. It's called segregation. But that ain't gonna last forever. Every year goes by, black people like me, we're getting stronger. We're fighting back. My boy is studying law in order to try to help with that. And as for me, yeah, there's still some prejudice. But I live up North now, and for the most part, we're treated just fine. And my program, for folks with abilities, they really don't see color. Me and Yamato here, we're treated just the same as white folk. I mean, they really gonna treat us bad, knowing what we can do?"

Hei Feng laughed at this once translated, then continued to pepper them with questions. Each of them was asked about their abilities. Yamato remained sullen but Padilla offered a modest demonstration by using a grain of rice to strike a fly on the ceiling in the corner of the room, which delighted Hei Feng and even impressed Cal a bit.

As they talked, Cal got a sense that Hei Feng was sizing them up, putting rumor to fact and figuring out where his loyalties might truly lie. The Chinese Variant said he was a simple farmer's son, drafted into Mao's revolution not because he was a believer, but because his village had been on Mao's way to Beijing. Then he'd been sent to Korea and, about six months ago, his Enhancement had manifested. Cal was impressed that the boy had been able to keep the secret from so many people for so long, but at the same time, he couldn't help but wonder if Hei Feng had maybe trusted some people he shouldn't. It wasn't likely that a Chinese farmer's son would have anything more than an instinctual grasp of operational security—and the Devil's in the details.

Breakfast stretched onto lunch as they talked, and the monks cleared their plates and brought more food, including some of Cal's favorite spicy dishes. Cal told stories about his life in the States, and some heavily redacted tales of his work with MAJESTIC-12. Yamato kept shooting him warning glances, but when Hei Feng excused himself for a moment, Cal explained that this was as much a recruitment opportunity as an interrogation. That mollified him for the time being, and by the time Hei Feng returned, lunch was served, and Yamato offered a few reluctant details about his own upbringing. Hei Feng was particularly intrigued to hear about the Japanese internment during World War II, since the Chinese Variant had lost an older brother and an uncle to the Japanese invasion of China back in the late 1930s.

They finally wrapped things up by mid-afternoon, and Hei Feng thanked them profusely for their time and openness, which Cal was sure to return in kind. Cal figured he maybe needed three or four more sessions like these before Hei Feng would seriously consider defecting, and that outcome wasn't certain at all. Black Wind might be a *xian* and have all kinds of admiration and worship from the people around him, but in the end, he was just a kid pressed into service in a war he didn't really believe in. And like most folks—like Cal himself—he just wanted a better life. And in Cal's case, MAJESTIC-12 had largely delivered on that.

Except, of course, for him being a prisoner in Korea. But it wasn't the first time he was captured by someone. All he could do was hope it might be the last.

17.

May 29, 1953

It didn't take Frank Lodge long to see what everyone in East Berlin was grumbling about in the coffeehouse that morning. The front page of *Neues Deutschland* spelled it out perfectly. "Economic Reforms Approved by Council of Ministers," the headlines read. "Workers Will Achieve New Heights Under New Socialist Program."

Sounded great, of course, but as the newspapermen liked to say, the story buried the lead—the East German government had just increased work quotas by ten percent in order to help the country dig itself out of an economic slump. Any worker who didn't meet the quota would see their pay docked. Oh, and they were raising prices, too, which amused no fewer than three economists in Frank's head.

Frank closed his eyes and concentrated to silence the voices. He really, *really* wasn't interested in hearing from them. Not after what happened last month in Moscow. Instead, Frank used his own know-how, honed by the lessons received through the years from the memories of those who had died, to scan the room. It was a good exercise, using what he had already learned in the past rather than continuing to rely on the real-time expertise of those now-suspect personas in his mind. And he saw plenty of discontent, especially from the men—and a handful of women—dressed as factory workers. The guys in suits were less perturbed, but even they were talking intently, a few making reference to *Neues Deutschland* or its young persons' counterpart, *Junge Welt*.

They had good reason to be unhappy, even beyond the latest government indignity. The East German plan for postwar recovery was to turn the country into the preeminent industrial powerhouse of the Eastern Bloc. Problem was, however, that they had to import far more raw materials than they had before, since West Germany drew the lion's share during the post-War divorce. And because they kept busing in all the young men to work in those new factories, the agricultural sector was in sharp decline. So they had to import food, too, and so prices for even the basics were high. And now the government was going to raise prices again, while making the workers meet higher quotas.

So basically, work more to get less. Even without a PhD in economic theory, most folks could see how that would make zero sense. But then, Frank always felt that Communism was an exercise in hand-waving the details anyway.

Folding the newspaper, Frank paid his tab and, grabbing his hard hat and lunch pail, headed off to work. For the past two weeks, Frank had been working in construction in East Berlin's burgeoning building sector—probably the only part of the economy where supply and demand still worked, given the massive amount of reconstruction still necessary eight years after the war, combined with the drive to build all kinds of factories and warehouses. When he'd gone to the job site to ask about work, the foreman had barely scanned his forged work papers, instead eagerly asking him about his qualifications. Having kicked around Europe for a few years after the war while trying to get his voices straight in his head, Frank had plenty of construction experience. By noon, he'd been riveting girders together, and his cohorts seemed happy to have another hand.

Honestly, the work was a welcome distraction, a little oasis of calm amid all the other crap that had happened. Frank and Danny had spent a week smuggling themselves out of the Soviet Union, at one point walking two entire days just to avoid a popular train station. They'd bugged out near Leningrad, using a pair of Mrs. Stevens's body suits for the still-cold swim to Finnish territory. Frank had hoped to be welcomed by Cal and Rick Yamato in Helsinki—they'd been out of contact with Washington during their travels, and Frank thought they might have finally put Korea behind them—but there was no sign of them, and it turned out Washington was assuming the two were MIA. Frank had been in favor of heading to Korea to find them, but Danny was adamant that they continue with the approved East German op.

So, after a luxurious night at Helsinki's Hotel Seurahuone, they liaised with the CIA station there and wrangled passage aboard a Finnish trawler to Stralsund. Frank was covered as a farmhand seeking better work prospects, while Danny came in as a Russian academic. The Stasi, East Germany's answer to the MGB, didn't have much of a presence in Stralsund, so they were able to come ashore outside the town, walk to the train station, and buy tickets to East Berlin without anybody once checking their forged papers. Danny busied himself by hanging out in the beer halls and coffeehouses around Humboldt University, trying to gauge the level of academic resistance to Communist rule. There wasn't much thus far, as best he'd been able to tell, but Frank had found fertile ground among his fellow construction workers.

"Come on, Franz," one of his new colleagues said as he arrived at the work site. "Those quotas won't fulfill themselves."

Frank just smiled. "I heard the quotas may increase."

The other worker just grimaced. "The foreman is furious about it, but there's nothing he can do, so he takes it out on us," the other man whispered, in case there were unfriendly ears nearby. "Better get moving. I'd like to see my family before they go to bed tonight."

Once they climbed the superstructure and began riveting in earnest, the words flowed more freely; the men had known each other a while, and Frank had already let slip some of his own "discontent" with the working conditions. He enjoyed losing himself in the rough-and-tumble community of iron workers, and did his level best to subtly encourage their conversations. Most of them were young men—too young to have fought in the war, but old enough to remember the Nazis and their depredations. Nearly all of them had lost someone during the fighting, and remembered well how the Russians had treated them during the initial occupation. The current government was seen as a collection of Soviet stooges, selling out the German people to yet another dictatorship. Some had family in West Berlin or West Germany, and told stories of the largesse enjoyed by their relations on the other side of the Iron Curtain—easy access to food and jobs, good education, the freedom to travel and speak one's mind.

Frank felt for them. Sure, he remained under MAJESTIC-12's thumb, but America was still America, and he'd long ago resigned himself to his own circumstances, knowing that his work was helping his countrymen preserve their freedoms. Here, if anything, the East Germans suffered more than even the Soviet people. The Muscovites could at least enjoy some simple pleasures and, since Stalin's death, were even beginning to speak a little more freely. The East Berliners saw the shadows of Stasi informants nearly everywhere—except eight stories up, dangling from girders above the city.

The late spring sun was well on its way down when Frank and his coworkers descended to the ground again, their quotas met and their bodies exhausted. He wanted nothing more than to go back to the crappy flat he shared with Danny, eat some crappy food, and get some sleep on a crappy mattress. But instead, he accepted an invitation to drink beer at the flat of someone named Ernst, one of the older veterans of the iron workers' cohort. So he threw some money and ration stamps into the pool and went with another young man, Max, for the beer run. It took forty-five minutes, all their ration stamps, most of their money, and two bribes to get enough beer, but soon they were heading back to Max's flat with enough alcohol to drop a horse.

Max had a young wife and a baby boy, Lucas, who slept in his mother's arms as she hosted six burly, sweaty iron workers, sitting around the tiny apartment wherever they could find room—the little kitchen table, the ratty couch, the floor. Cigarette smoke filled the room, and Frank couldn't help but worry for the baby's lungs. Blessedly, Max's wife put the little one down for the night after about a half hour.

"So what do we do if they raise quotas again?" Max asked. "All of you heard the news. They are now talking about pay cuts if we don't meet quotas. I can barely afford to feed my family as it is."

There were nods around the table, and many swigs of Radeberger beer—a surprisingly good pilsner, despite the brewery being nationalized by the East German government shortly after the war. "What do you mean, 'what do we do?'" answered Ernst, one of the grizzled old hands in their work group. "We work harder to make sure we meet the quotas. There's nothing else to do."

Frank sized up the group—nobody was really happy with that answer, even Ernst. "Are we not the workers?" Frank said when nobody else spoke up. "All of this talk about Communism, where the workers are in charge of the means of production. Doesn't that mean we're in charge? That we're the ones they have to listen to?"

Ernst shook his head and took a long drag off his cigarette. "You look too old to be so stupid, Franz. The Party says the workers are in charge, but these are the same bureaucrats who ran the Nazi government. They answered to Hitler, then rolled over, and now they answer to Stalin— or whoever replaces Stalin in Moscow now. Those bureaucrats haven't worked a day in their lives. They sit in offices and write reports and have meetings and make all the decisions, and then hope and pray Moscow allows them to do what they planned. Or they figure out how to make Moscow's demands work. We don't matter."

"We *should* matter," replied another young man named Manfred, a wizard with rivets who almost singlehandedly boosted them over their quotas each day. "If they could just see how bad things are, maybe they would adjust the quotas, or increase pay, or fix things. Maybe they just don't know what it's like."

"So how do we show them?" Frank prodded. "We are the workers. We're the backbone of the State. 'From each according to his ability, to each according to his needs.' Our abilities are stretched to the limits, and our needs aren't being met!"

The youngest of their circle, a fresh-faced boy named Gunter, shifted in his chair uncomfortably. "Comrades, we know the Americans and their allies brought us low during the war. We had nothing after Hitler was removed. Don't we all have to make sacrifices in order to bring our Fatherland back? We are starting from nothing. And there are still those far worse off than we are, those who can't even afford beer!"

There were nods around the table at this, and Frank saw the power of propaganda at work. *Tighten your belts and work for each other, not for yourself. Work toward equality for the collective. Even if we're all starving, we'll be equal.* "The bureaucrats can afford beer. They get more ration stamps and better pay, and they skip the queues at the stores to get the best cuts of meat and the best produce for their families. How is this a sacrifice?"

There were more nods now, more grimaces and grumblings, and Frank knew he had them. He might not have had Maggie's emotional manipulations, but experience certainly counted for something. By the time the beer was gone and the men were stumbling out of Max's flat, their rage was well stoked. Frank walked old Ernst to his flat, then walked another mile to his temporary home. Danny was already there, and there was a plate of potatoes and a bit of sausage waiting for him.

"Actual meat?" Frank asked. "Where'd you get that?"

"The students sometimes use ration stamps when

they're playing *doppelkopf*. I had a good hand tonight,"
Danny said. "Where've you been?"

Frank plopped down at the tiny table and tucked into his
food. "Fomenting dissent. You saw the news this morning.
The workers are pissed. Quotas are going up, and they're
worried that the pay cuts are gonna follow soon. If that
happens, well . . . these people are strapped, Dan. I blew
most of my wad on beer to get them loose and talking.
They can barely feed their families, and if they get their
pay cut for failing to meet quota, I think that's our shot."

Danny nodded and cracked open a beer. "There's a lot
of sympathy for the workers among the students. They're
sitting in classes all day, getting an earful about the proletariat and the nobility of work and all that, then see all
the bureaucrats walking by in good clothes and full bellies.
They're starting to whisper, but I don't think they'll take
the lead. The Stasi is pretty well entrenched in the schools."

"But if it starts up elsewhere? You think they'll play
ball?" Frank asked between bites.

"Some of them, sure," Danny said. "Sure would be nice to
know the whens and wheres, though. Hard to plan a rebel-
lion when we don't have control over when it kicks off."

"Probably when they announce the pay cuts for not
meeting quotas," Frank replied. "That's the rumor, at least.
But there's no telling when that will be."

"Be nice to know. We could coordinate with Mrs. Stevens
and try to pull something in Moscow at the same time. A
revolt here and a black eye there would really whack Beria
good. Latest intel reports say he's struggling to keep up
with Malenkov and Khrushchev. Starting to look like he
might be outmaneuvered."

Frank leaned back and ran a hand over his tired face.
"If they're not careful, Beria will go for broke. Unleash his
Variants. Kill 'em all and just take over."

You should've killed him when you had the chance, said
one of the voices in Frank's head, and a few others echoed
the sentiment. Frank closed his eyes and willed them back
into the dark corner of his mind.

Danny noticed. "More voices?"

"Opinions," Frank said. "They're second-guessing now. I'm really not listening to them much anymore."

"Have your language abilities been affected?"

"Nope. Things like languages, skills that rely on muscle memory, that sort of thing—those kinds of natural, sub-conscious abilities, those aren't really affected. Just don't ask me to fix a car or perform surgery. I'd have to let them in to do that, and I honestly don't know at this point how they'd react."

"You think they'd refuse you?" Danny asked, eyebrows raised.

Frank just shrugged. "They never have, after nearly eight years of this. But then again, they've never really offered up opinions outside of a crisis situation. Now, though, it seems like they're restless. Pushing. It's really not fucking helpful at all."

Danny took another swig of beer and looked Frank in the eye. "I gotta tell you, Frank, I don't know what the powers that be will say to all this when we're done. They've been conspicuously silent on our reports around our Enhancements. I can't get any word on what the vortex in Idaho is doing. We're in the dark here."

"So what? You think they'll put us under arrest when we come back?" Frank asked. "I mean, me, sure. I bombed that truck and went to see Beria on my own. I figure I'm in trouble when everything settles out. But you? Rose? Katie?"

"I'm the deputy director of MAJESTIC-12. I'm the oper-ations guy. And they're telling me nothing about the other Variants, about the vortex, no word on any new studies based on what Beria told you. We have a new administra-tion now. We've been so busy, I've only met Eisenhower once, back in January, when we briefed him up. Can't hon-estly say how he feels about us."

"So what do we do?"

"We do the job," Danny replied. "We get Beria out of there. After that . . . we'll have to see how things go. But if you don't have contingency plans, maybe think about that."

Frank just smiled. "I'm forty-seven different people, Dan. I speak twenty languages. I'm not worried about me. I'm worried about Katie. And Cal. And Maggie, if we can ever get her back."

"So maybe those are your contingency plans, then."

Frank nodded and finished his food in silence, the wheels spinning in his head. He could feel opinions from the others bubbling up, but he quashed them before the thoughts were fully formed. This was something he had to figure out on his own.

And he knew, if nothing else, how to get started.

* * *

June 2, 1953

"How was your weekend, Franz?"

Frank smiled at Max as they walked toward the worksite. "Quiet. How is your little boy?"

Max just shook his head. "We can't sleep. He's up at all hours, always wanting to be fed."

"This is good! He'll grow up big and strong like his father!" Frank said, slapping Max on the back. "I hear they eventually sleep through the night. You'll get there."

Max just nodded wearily and trudged toward the ladders that would take him to the top of the building where they left off Friday. Excusing himself, Frank made for the latrine—which was right next to the shack the foreman used as an office. The foreman himself was by the ladders, checking people in and exhorting them, as always, to make their quotas and work hard for the glory of the proletariat.

Frank ducked behind the building, rather than using the door, and looked up to see if the men were on the beams yet. They weren't—but they'd be there in about three minutes, maybe less. Frank prayed the window at the back of the little shack was open—and it was. Deftly, he lifted himself through the window, diving into the office, landing on his hands and holding the position until he could safely place his feet back on the floor with a minimum of noise. It hurt—his arms protested greatly—but at least he retained a gymnast's sense of balance. That gymnast was named Alan Reeves, and he had died in 1950.

Frank made his way behind the desk and started flipping through papers and folders. There were work orders and personnel folders and delivery receipts, but nothing important. Frank checked the drawers and found the one that was locked. A paperclip and twenty seconds later, the drawer was opened and he found what he was looking for.

Frank dove through the window head-first again, executing a perfect flip and landing on his feet. The conversation up on the steel would be a fruitful one today.

CLASSIFICATION: TOP SECRET—MAJIK

DATE: 4 June 53

FROM: DCI Dulles

TO: AGENT Stevens CIA, AGENT Sorensen CIA

CC: CMDR Wallace USN, GEN Vandenberg USAF, DR Bronk MJ-12

RE: Operation AERIE

Intelligence indicates potential for disruption of East German political situation on 16 June. Begin planning for Operation AERIE immediately. Identify targets for maximum disruption and impact, particularly on primary target. Do not engage primary target.

On 16 June, AGENT Stevens is to report to Station Chief Moscow for direct updates from Station Chief West Berlin. Should East German disruptions meet minimum operational requirements—deployment of armed police or military, use of deadly force, or widespread protests—launch AERIE on 17 June, or no later than 19 June.

Extraction of Soviet Variants still not recommended. Continue holding until advised. Success of AERIE remains top priority.

Per continued information request, AGENTS Hooks and Yamato remain missing in action.

/s/ Dulles

18.

June 16, 1953

Danny watched with a deep and abiding satisfaction as a throng of workers marched toward Potsdamer Platz along Leipziger Strasse. There were hundreds of them—thousands—and they even somehow managed to find the time and materials to create banners. "Lower work quotas!" "Listen to the workers!" "Unity is Strength!" Some bold souls were hoisting a bed sheet tied to poles that read "We want free elections!"

This was, of course, far more impressive than Danny could've dreamed of, and he knew well enough that this wasn't entirely due to their meddling. At best, he and Frank had simply given it a nudge, and fueled the rumor mill that made the coordinated effort possible. Frank had discovered the date for new pay cuts and higher quotas, and he and Danny had simply spread the word amongst the workers and students. When the cuts and quotas were announced, the construction workers at Frank's site had rioted and began marching on the Free German Trade Union Federation, gathering workers from other worksites as they went. When the protests at the federation went unheeded, the throng then marched on the government itself at the Detlev-Rohwedder-Haus, just a handful of blocks from the East-West border.

From Danny's perch three stories above Potsdamer Platz, he could see both the protestors at the government building as well as a growing number of West Berliners gathering on the other side of the barbed wire and barricades that separated them from their former countrymen.

Would the East Berliners try to break through? Would the West Berliners join them? The Stasi and East German military were conscious of both possibilities, reinforcing the barricades while sending troops to Detlev-Rohwedder-Haus as well. But they were already spread thin—the protestors were growing in number by the minute, and Danny could hear the volume of their chanting increasing as well. Before Danny headed up to his lookout post—a disused corner office of a faceless government building—he saw some of his student cohorts joining the crowd.

It was exciting. It was freedom at work. He couldn't help but be happy for the East German people, and could only hope that their numbers would be too big to ignore or suppress.

Danny turned away from the protest to the other window, looking toward West Berlin. Off in the distance, he saw a window with an "X" taped on it. He backed away from the window toward the corner of the room and pulled a flashlight out of his satchel. He aimed it at the West Berlin "X" and began flicking it on and off.

A moment later, a series of dim lights answered from the same window.

Contact.

Danny began reporting in. He hoped Mrs. Stevens had everything lined up. It was time to make some noise.

* * *

"Ma'am, secure cable coming in."

Rose Stevens practically launched herself from the sofa outside the secure communications room at the American Embassy in Moscow. The Embassy had already received a handful of unconfirmed reports, mostly cribbed from radio and the wires, that *something* was going on in East Berlin. Mrs. Stevens knew full well that any spark Frank and Danny created might very well not catch. But her analysis of the economic and political environment in East Germany all pointed to opportunity.

She dashed past the communications clerk and into the

secure room, closing the door and flipping a switch. The teletype immediately burst into action, churning out line after line of encoded text. On the face of it, the string of letters and numbers meant nothing. But Mrs. Stevens had looked up the codes of the day and committed them to memory. The rest she did in her head, on the fly, which would've made the clerk faint dead away if he saw it.

"AEGIS is go," she muttered. "Situation optimal for immediate action. Revise timetable and execute ASAP."

She couldn't help but smile broadly. They wouldn't be asking her to speed things up if things were going badly, that's for sure. Something had caught fire in East Berlin, and it was her job to fan the flames all the way to Red Square.

Good thing she'd planned for this contingency.

Turning on her heel, Mrs. Stevens strode out of the communications room and headed to the embassy's secure conference room, home to every electronic countermeasure known to man. There, in the windowless room amidst the hum of signal jammers, Sorensen and Katie were waiting. "Good news and bad news," she said. "Things are going well in East Berlin. Looks like our boys lit the fuse on something big."

Sorensen nodded. "Heard a couple of the embassy guys talking. UPI is reporting a large protest at the East German government building. Thousands of people. Pretty amazing."

"So what is the bad news?" Katie asked, nonplussed.

"We've been asked to move things up. Tonight. As in right now."

Sorensen and Katie looked at each other in disbelief. "Right now? We only finished getting everything in place this morning."

Mrs. Stevens put her hands on her hips and gave them a tight-lipped smile. "Well, then we're ready, aren't we? Contingency plan Beta-Beta. Let's move it!"

Sorensen rolled his eyes and promptly disappeared, leaving only his civilian suit in place, which flopped to the floor seemingly of its own accord. Ekaterina, meanwhile, got up and dashed off to her embassy quarters to change into her outfit for the evening. Mrs. Stevens followed her to get into her own get-up, stopping by Jacob Beam's office along the way. The chargé d'affaires wasn't too pleased at being drafted into service with just two hours' notice, but reluctantly agreed to the change in plans.

"Espionage doesn't keep schedules," Mrs. Stevens said cheerily. "Get your tux on. We're out in twenty minutes."

* * *

Lavrentiy Beria put on a game face, for sure, but Maggie Dubinsky could feel the tension inside him, ready to boil over at a moment's provocation. She just needed to make damned sure she wasn't the source of the provocation.

Instead, she hooked her arm into his and leaned over in the back seat of the limousine as they rode through the early Moscow evening. "Hey, it's okay," she said quietly. "Not your fault that the damn Germans can't keep their own in check."

Beria turned to her and gave her a small smile. "I told Molotov. I told him. Their economic plan was completely unsustainable. One cannot create entire industries out of whole cloth in just a few years. But the Party overruled me and let the Germans try. And now those fools have an insurrection on their hands."

"Exactly," Maggie said, watching his tension build further. "Not your fault, right?"

The smile evaporated. "Tell that to those fools, Malenkov and Khrushchev. It's been less than twelve hours and they want heads to roll for this. Now I have my entire staff working through the night to determine the right levers to pull to quell the situation. I almost canceled tonight."

"You couldn't do that," Maggie said. "Preview night at the Bolshoi for the diplomatic corps—you have to be there. If they see you're missing, they'll read even more into what's going on. It'll undermine you further, and we're so close. So very close."

Maggie pulled in a little tighter and pulled a few emotional strings in Beria's head to bring his attention to the curves of her MGB uniform. "Yes, we are," Beria said. "Close indeed."

The car stopped before things progressed further, and Maggie waited for Comrade Illyanov to get out and open the rear door for them. Although he continued to look well past his prime, Boris Giorgievich Illyanov was as fast as ever when he needed to be, and Beria preferred to keep him close. The bodyguard's reaction times and speed would easily thwart most assassination attempts, while his elderly appearance made Beria look unprotected—and also helped with his public image, since many of those who saw Boris Giorgievich thought he was a pensioner from the Revolution, kept on as driver as an act of kindness.

Maggie got out and scanned the crowds heading into the Bolshoi, both visually and with her Enhancement. Most people looked on at Beria's arrival with mild curiosity, a little excitement, a few pangs of fear, but nothing she hadn't seen before. She nodded at Illyanov, who gave the all-clear to Beria. The First Deputy Premier emerged from the car to a smattering of applause and a few flashbulbs, and he waved to the crowd as he proceeded into the Bolshoi, Maggie and Illyanov on his heels.

It was only inside the lobby where Maggie got her first glimpse that something was up. In the corner of her mind, she felt a surge of surprise, recognition, anger, and fear. And when she turned, she saw Rose Stevens there, dressed to the nines in a conservative, dark-green gown alongside Jacob Beam, that embassy peon they'd been stuck with at the funeral back in March.

And they were approaching.

"First Deputy Premier," Beam said as he drew near, hand extended. "I wanted to thank you, on behalf of the United States Embassy, for hosting such a fine evening of culture. I hope it'll be yet another way our two nations can come together in appreciation and respect."

Beria smiled and shook his hand. "Of course, Mr. Beam.

I am most pleased to see you as well. Your Russian is improving. Have I met this lovely woman yet?" he said, turning to Mrs. Stevens and smiling.

Mrs. Stevens jumped a little bit, then extended her hand. "I'm Jacob's sister, Susan," she said in English, and Maggie couldn't help but smile at her enhanced Midwestern accent and volume. "This is such a lovely, lovely place, Mr. Beria. I must say, I've never been to the ballet before!"

Beria looked around blankly; his knowledge of English wasn't common knowledge, and he preferred to keep it that way. Maggie stepped in instead, quietly speaking in Russian. "The woman here says she is Mr. Beam's sister. She says the theater is lovely and she's never been to the ballet before. She is also a spy."

To her credit, Mrs. Stevens—who spoke decent Russian—barely flinched, and Maggie noticed it only because she was looking. Beria, meanwhile, spoke in rapid, sotto voce Russian. "Tell her I am pleased to meet her, and then we will talk, you and I."

Maggie turned to her former colleagues. "The First Deputy Premier is very pleased to meet you as well, Susan Beam," she said, trying on a Russian accent to go with her English. "If you'll excuse us?"

Mrs. Stevens wasn't having it. "Oh, darling, do you happen to know where the ladies' room is? I'd hate to have to get up during the show."

There was a time, not too long ago, when the prospect of field work terrified Mrs. Stevens. And now, here she was, brazen as all get out, right in front of the most powerful man in the Soviet Union. "Here, let me show you." She turned to Beria. "I will join you in a moment, after I've interrogated this one," she whispered in Russian.

Beria nodded and took his leave, while Maggie escorted Mrs. Stevens toward the ladies' room. Before they got there, though, Maggie took her arm and pulled her through a maintenance door. The corridor beyond was vacant and dim, the chatter of the crowd dulled by stone walls.

"What the hell are you up to, Rose?" Maggie demanded.

Mrs. Stevens's face was a mask of anger, and her emotional state was one of pure rage. To Maggie's surprise, she was beginning to feel a little remorse. Was that what it was? Regret? Sadness? She and Rose were friends. Weren't they?

"I could ask the same of you, Maggie Dubinsky," Mrs. Stevens replied. "Shame on you. Shame on you! Do you know how much Frank and Danny are worried about you? And we've lost poor Cal and Rick, too, somewhere in Korea. They're MIA! In a war zone! Your friends needed you, and you went and flipped on us. All of us!"

Maggie's eyes widened. "Cal's MIA? He never got out of Korea?"

"And if you were here, we would've bagged Beria by now and gone to Korea and got him back! Instead, Danny's off to . . . Danny's away. We're all busy trying to do our jobs, and now we have to contend with you, too! You're a traitor, Maggie! How could you!"

Maggie felt some genuine anger build inside her. "Shove it, Rose. You know why I'm here."

"Because you think this will be better?" Mrs. Stevens countered. "You think we're supposed to rule over people instead of help them? Because that's what this is all about. Once you start thinking you're better than everybody else, you're already far worse. You know better than this, Maggie!"

"Shut up!" Maggie hissed. "What's going on? What do you have planned? Are you behind the East German revolt? Spill it, Rose, or so help me, I'll—"

Mrs. Stevens actually shoved Maggie backward. "You'll what? Go ahead. Do it. Go ahead and turn me into a puppet or give me a heart attack or make me love you. Whatever you do, it's fake. It's not real. And don't think for a minute that I haven't accounted for this. Anything you drag out of me, it's already worthless. You can't stop what's coming. Nobody can. I'm too smart for that and you know it! So go ahead. DO IT!"

Maggie stared hard and long at Mrs. Stevens, who was beginning to tear up. As much as she wanted to plunge her former friend into the worst sort of nervous breakdown, she knew it would be useless. There was no doubt Rose Stevens had planned for every single possible contingency, including capture and interrogation by Maggie. And there was no point in drawing it out any longer.

"Goodbye, Rose," Maggie said quietly. "Take care of yourself. Next time we see each other, it's not going to go well. I promise."

Maggie walked back out into the lobby and stalked off toward Beria's box. The lights were dimming, and the performance was about to begin; she took the empty chair right next to his.

"Well?" Beria asked.

Maggie swiped a hand across her face to wipe away the surprising tears that had formed. "They're planning something. I think we need to get to Lubyanka as soon as possible."

"What are they planning?" Beria demanded. "Who was that woman?"

"Nobody," Maggie said. "A minor go-between with very little field experience. But because she's here, that means everyone else is very busy right about now. Which means we need to go."

Beria turned to her, anger in his eyes. "This is all you have? For all your abilities?"

Maggie just shrugged. "There was no time. But I do know that they lost two of their people in Korea. You may want to get in touch with the Chinese, see if they have them. It's Calvin Hooks and Richard Yamato. I told you about them."

That softened him up a bit. "Yes, they are powerful Champions indeed," Beria said. "Good. We'll exit after the opening number. Have Boris get the car and bring it to the service entrance. We don't want to make a scene leaving."

* * *

Ekaterina watched from the top of the Bolshoi Theater as her brother—her poor brother!—got into the limousine and began to drive to the back of the building. Another car followed; those would be the rest of Beria's security men. Ekaterina's radio already buzzed with chatter—the First Deputy Premier was leaving to go back to Lubyanka. Full security. Back entrance. All units on alert.

She turned off her radio and slid over to the side of the building where the service entrance was located. From above, she watched as the two cars settled into position.

Why did it have to be Boris? she pleaded with whoever would listen. But she got no response, so she waited for the right moment to get to work.

The second car pulled to a complete stop. She would have five seconds before the armed men inside got out.

The drop from the top of the building took three.

Ekaterina landed right on top of the black sedan, puncturing the metal hood and crushing the engine block under her feet. She lifted the rest of the car—with four shouting men inside—and hurled it back down the street. It traveled thirty-five yards and landed on its roof. The men inside were no longer shouting.

"Ekaterina!"

She turned to see her brother with a pistol pointed at her, his face anguished. She never wanted this confrontation, but knew when she arrived in Russia that it was possible. She knew she was going to hate it, but this was what she had chosen now.

"Hello, brother," she said quietly. "I am sorry they have not found a way to fix you yet."

The anguish turned to rage. "You traitor!" he shouted, his gun hand trembling. "How could you! You've betrayed our country! Our family! Me!"

"Beria betrayed us!" she shouted back. "He left us in Kazakhstan to die in fire! He says we are all his children, but we are disposable to him! You know this!"

The gun barked, and Ekaterina tensed. The bullet struck her in the shoulder, piercing her skin before bouncing off her muscles and down onto the pavement. The result hurt like a burn from a hot pan, but it was bearable. Boris's eyes grew wide—this was something he didn't know about her Enhancement. Even in the Soviet Union, nobody had thought to shoot a child to see if she survived, super-strength or not. She wasn't even a hundred percent sure it would happen, but was glad it did.

"You had better run, brother."

With a single leap, Ekaterina vaulted over her brother and onto Beria's limousine. She began tearing it apart with abandon, steel and glass flying everywhere. She let out a scream—and it felt good to let it all out. By the time she threw the engine block through the wall of the Bolshoi, she felt a whole lot better.

She turned to find Boris just staring at her, numbly, his mouth agape.

"Come with me," she said, pleading. "We can help. Get you out of here. We can have Cal heal you again, make you as you were. Please, big brother. Come with me!"

The service entrance burst open, and Maggie and Beria ran out into the alley, stopping suddenly when confronted with the wreckage of their cars and men.

"You!" Beria shouted. He raised his hand, and a gout of flame erupted toward Ekaterina.

Bullets were one thing, but flame—that would really hurt.

With a mighty leap, Ekaterina jumped four stories onto the building across from the Bolshoi and began running, leaping from rooftop to rooftop. Boris was fast, but she knew he couldn't run up the sides of buildings, and she changed direction a number of times to throw him off her trail as she headed to the next rendezvous point. Only then did she allow herself to cry—but only for a moment. There was still work to be done.

* * *

It had taken twenty minutes for a new limousine to come fetch Beria and Maggie, during which time the First Deputy Premier raged at Illyanov and commandeered a radio from a policeman to begin barking orders to secure the Lubyanka and the safe houses where his Champions of the Proletariat were hidden. Maggie knew it was a sure sign of his panic that he'd even mentioned the safe houses over a radio. Thankfully, he didn't broadcast any locations.

Now in the car on the way to his office, Beria laid into her—and used a null generator to keep her from calming him down. "This is happening now, in Moscow! An attack on me! You said this was not in your plans!"

"And it wasn't, Comrade," Maggie replied calmly. "But I told you those plans might change. They are willing to give their lives to ensure you do not take Comrade Stalin's place. So they expose themselves."

"But we still do not know where they are!" Beria shouted. "I will have that woman with Beam arrested! And you, Dubinsky, you will go to work on this woman immediately and make her tell me what they will do next, do you hear me?"

Maggie grimaced as she felt a surprising, unnerving pang of sadness. "Of course, Comrade Beria. But first we must secure our fellow Champions."

"We will do more than that," Beria said. "We must move up the timetable. When we return to the office, we will start gathering. The rest of the Politburo will see this as weakness. We must strike, now, before they decide to come for us. We must—"

Beria was interrupted by the sound of an explosion, and a bright red light flared a couple blocks ahead of the car.

The Lubyanka.

Illyanov pulled over to the side of the road by Lubyanka Square, well away from the building. The third-floor corner office—Beria's office—was now in flames, the facade crumbling to the ground even as they scrambled out of the car and looked on in horror.

Several uniformed NKVD officers rushed up to the car, forming a protective circle around Beria and Maggie, all shouting reports as to what happened. There was a power outage. There was the smell of gas. An electrical fire, perhaps.

Sorensen, Maggie thought. *He's an electrician. He fucks with the power, which kills any hardwired null generators around the building. He goes in, messes with the gas. Heads up to Beria's darkened office, and . . .*

She turned to Beria. "What did you have in your office?"

"What?" Beria said absently as he gazed up at the burning building.

"What did you have in your office?" she pressed, getting in front of his face. "Papers, documents, records, any of it. What did you have there?"

He finally focused on her, looking quizzical. "Everything regarding the program was in my safe. It is fireproof and locked."

"Is it?" Maggie asked. She turned and ran toward the burning building, scanning the ground in front of her as she went.

There.

On the sidewalk below the burning building was a hunk of metal, about three feet by four feet and a good six inches thick, with a combination lock on the front. The hinges on the side were twisted and ripped apart.

Katie. Shit.

Maggie turned back toward Beria, but saw several other limousines approaching, the flags of the Party and the Red Army flapping from the front fenders. The Politburo wasn't wasting any time. She ran forward again, hoping she could help defuse the situation before everything fell apart.

By the time she rejoined Beria, Nikita Khrushchev was jabbing his finger at the First Deputy Premier, with Marshal Zhukov by his side. "If you cannot maintain your own personal security, and the security of your headquarters—let alone keep our socialist allies abroad in line—how do you expect to continue in your position?" Khrushchev demanded.

Maggie reached out with her Empowerment to try to calm Khrushchev down—the man had a notorious temper—but found she couldn't sense the threads of his emotions. At all.

She quickly looked around—someone had a null generator going, she was sure of it, and the thought made her feel intensely vulnerable and jumpy. Yet in all the chaos—firefighters, NKVD and MGB men, Red Army officers, party officials, gawkers, and onlookers—she couldn't make anybody.

Meanwhile, Beria was pleading his case—assuming he still dealt from a position of strength. Maggie cringed inwardly. This wasn't going to end up well.

"Comrade Khrushchev, I promise you, all of this is a ruse. Yes, a ruse! There are counterrevolutionary elements within the NKVD and MGB who would seek to return the Motherland to its tsarist ways! All of this, I promise you, is part of an operation to flush out these elements, to bring them to the light of day! Even now, I have agents fanning out across the city, tracking them down and bringing them to justice!"

Khrushchev looked nonplussed at best, while Marshal Zhukov—the Soviet Union's preeminent World War II military hero—looked ready to haul off and punch Beria in the nose. "Comrade Beria, you will report to the Kremlin tomorrow at 9 a.m.—*sharp*—so that we may begin an inquiry into these events. And you will have proof of this operation, and results!"

"Of course, Comrade Khrushchev," Beria replied with a practiced smile, and Maggie knew then, even without her ability, that Beria would make his move then.

"Marshal Zhukov has already taken command of the East German situation, on the orders of Comrade Malenkov," Khrushchev continued. "The uprising will be put down immediately. You no longer have a role to play there, and will not impede this. Do you understand?"

Beria nodded, and Khrushchev turned on his heel and got back in his limousine, Zhukov in tow. The fact that Soviet policy had just been made, there on the street in front of a burning building, amazed Maggie. *Score one for MAJESTIC-12*, she thought. *They'll have a hard time getting another, though.*

As the Party and Red Army cars sped off, Maggie went to Beria's side. "Orders, Comrade?"

Grim-faced and seething inside—the null field was no longer active—Beria turned to Maggie. "We mobilize now. Tell Illyanov to get moving. We are all at the Kremlin by 8:30 tomorrow morning. All of us. Our time has come."

19.

June 17, 1953

It was a rare thing for Frank to feel good about his job. Everything about working for MAJESTIC-12 was, at best, morally gray, and always ended up as a collection of partial victories combined with sacrifice and stomach-churning worry.

So to watch thousands upon thousands of East Germans, camped out in Potsdamer Platz, with bonfires burning in the predawn light, singing and laughing and enjoying these tantalizing moments of promise and pride—it was enough to get him all teary-eyed.

"What is it, Franz?" Max said, wrapping his arm around Frank's shoulders. "We did it! We are here, now, finally standing up for ourselves. For the first time in my life!"

Frank nodded and gave the young man a half-hug. "It's beautiful, my friend. I just hope they listen to you. To us."

"Of course they will," Max said, raising his beer skyward. There was a lot of beer out there. "We are the proletariat! We are the workers and farmers and laborers. It is our government. They will listen to us!"

Frank's stomach shifted a little as he thought ahead to what might come. Communist rule in the Eastern Bloc hadn't really been tested before. For years after the war, people seemed satisfied with any government that would just get them some food, a roof, and a job. But that was eight years ago now. Maybe this was it. The start of something bigger. Maybe all the missions in Czechoslovakia, Poland, Syria, Guatemala, Egypt, China . . . maybe he and his fellow Variants really had made a difference. Maybe it all led up to this moment, where the people finally took matters into their own hands.

"Yes, Max," Frank said, clinking his bottle with Max's. "Maybe this is it. I hope it is."

Max gave Frank a full-on hug that squeezed the breath out of him, then went off to find others with whom to celebrate. Frank downed the remainder of his beer and went to go look for another one. But before he found one, his wallet began buzzing—four short bursts from the radio hidden inside it.

Four bursts. Rendezvous point ASAP.

Frank looked around immediately for signs of trouble, tamping down on his Enhancement to avoid unwanted commentary. A few snippets slipped through, though. *No change in police numbers. Only two obvious Stasi infiltrators in sight.* He half-expected another "kill them all" to come through, but nothing this time. It felt like the voices *wanted* to be heard, but also useful. Like they were on their best behavior.

Frank shook his head and slowly meandered toward the rendezvous point, a park on the corner of Charlottenstrasse and Krausenstrasse. He weaved around various groups of protesters and celebrants, finding a way to constantly check his back, to make sure he wasn't followed. It took a good twenty minutes to get there, but by the time he arrived, he was certain nobody had tailed him.

Danny was there, sitting alone by a fountain, away from revelers. Even dressed like a poor student, he somehow managed to stick out with nervous energy. Danny's head was on a swivel, and he checked his watch three times from when Frank saw him until he finally walked up and took a seat.

"This can't be good," Frank said in German.

"It's not," Danny replied in Russian; his German wasn't that great, and Frank knew he'd been using Russian and English to get by. "Flash message from West Berlin. Red Army and Volkspolizei are being mobilized outside the city. Soviet Army forces are in the vanguard. They're going to move against the protesters."

"Shit," Frank said, his heart sinking. "I thought the team in Moscow was going to handle that."

Danny shrugged. "They did. Put the squeeze on Beria. Might not be long for this world. But they put Zhukov in charge of the revolt here. He's not going to be subtle."

Georgi Zhukov was a military genius and a three-time Hero of the Soviet Union. He was also as much a true believer as anyone in the Soviet Union these days. He hated Beria with a passion, stemming from a little war profiteering Zhukov had done immediately after the fall of Berlin. Most Soviet commanders looted the place while the Party turned a blind eye, but Beria was gunning for him. Returning the favor by quashing the revolt would be a nice bit of revenge.

"We have to warn people," Frank surmised.

Danny's eyes widened. "No. Our orders are to get across to West Berlin immediately. I have our papers ready."

Frank took the forged documents Danny offered him, skimming through them absently while thinking of Max and Ernst and the rest of his work cohort. "Where's the extraction?"

"Chauseestrasse, over in Mitte. About a half hour walk." Danny got up. "Come on. We need to go. Now."

Frank rose and started following, but then grabbed Danny by the shoulder and pulled him back. "I'll meet you at the corner of Schlegelstrasse. Something I have to do first."

Danny fixed him with a hard look and switched to whispered English to drive his point home. "Don't you dare blow this, Frank. We have agents on the other side to cause a distraction and let us get through. If I have to, I'll leave you here."

"Then leave me here," Frank said simply. "I gotta do this. Go."

With a final glare, Danny turned and stalked off, while Frank took off at a sprint for Potsdamer Platz. It took a good twenty minutes for him to find one of his coworkers, the grizzled veteran Ernst, sitting by one of the fires.

"Young Franz! Come and have a beer!" Ernst said. "The radio says we're going to have forty thousand tomorrow. Can you imagine? Forty thousand!"

Of course, the American broadcasts would say that. They want these people to put their lives on the line. "Ernst, you have to listen to me. I don't have much time. You have to get our cohort out of here. The soldiers are coming."

Ernst looked at him with disbelief. "What soldiers? Are good Germans going to shoot at fellow Germans now? Bah. We're the people! We have a right to be heard, and that goes for soldiers too!"

Frank squatted down next to the man and looked him right in the eye. "There are Russian soldiers coming. You remember them back in '45, right? They hate Germans and they're going to put down this protest quickly and efficiently. They're going to shoot people. You need to find Max and the others, go home, lock the doors, and hide until this is all over. Do you hear me?"

"How do you know this?" Ernst said, suspicion growing. "You're not one of those Stasi bastards, are you?"

Frank shook his head. "No, just a regular bastard. I'm telling you, this will all go to shit tomorrow. They're coming with tanks and guns and God knows what, and we have to go now."

Ernst considered this, then took a gulp of beer and shook his head. "No. Fuck that. First Hitler, now the Party. Fuck them. Let them come. I'll stand right in front of that tank and tell them to go to hell."

Frank opened his mouth to argue some more, but saw the look in the man's eye and thought better of it. "Fine. But you find Max. He's got a baby boy and a wife. Tell him to get the hell home. This is real, Ernst. You're all in danger."

"*We* are all in danger," Ernst corrected.

Frank stood and put a hand on the man's shoulder. "No, Ernst. Just you. I have to go. For the love of God, tell Max to go home."

Before Ernst could say anything more, Frank took off at

a jog, heading north toward the extraction point—and a freedom he knew Ernst would never enjoy.

* * *

Maggie wished the Russians had more of an appreciation for coffee. Tea just wasn't cutting it.

She sat next to Beria once more in a limo driven by Illyanov, this time heading for the Kremlin. At least three cars trailed them, all filled with Variants—Champions of the Proletariat, ready to make their mark upon the world.

She'd long ago lost the words to describe feelings, but the feelings were there. Everything was coming to a head. An hour from now, they'd know whether the gambit would pay off, or if they'd all be arrested. Or executed on the spot.

The cars pulled into the plaza past the low, colorful outer buildings and into the secured area where mere proletarians dared not tread. There, Maggie saw dozens of Red Army soldiers staking out the entrances—Khrushchev, apparently, wasn't taking any chances. A Red Army colonel approached as they pulled up and got the door. "Good morning, Comrade Beria. They're waiting for you."

Beria got out and looked at his watch. "I am early, Comrade Colonel."

The colonel gave a tight-lipped smile. "So are they, it seems."

Maggie got out behind him and followed him into the building, where the corridors were lined with more and more soldiers. The rest of the Champions, led by Illyanov and Savrova, were barred from entering. That was fine— there were contingency plans for that. She checked her watch. *Twelve minutes.*

They walked through several ornate corridors and up marbled stairs until they reached the meeting room of the Central Committee of the Communist Party of the Soviet Union, the seat of power within the Kremlin. Maggie had never been there, never dreamed she'd see the place. As the doors opened, she was slightly disappointed to find a rather drab room filled with standard-issue metal chairs, plain tables, and wood paneling. To be fair, the Central Committee rarely met under Stalin, and Khrushchev had apparently done a bang-up job revitalizing it while Beria and the other princelings were busy with their own games.

There, seven old Russians in suits or military uniforms sat in a semicircle, with Malenkov in the center seat and Khrushchev and Zhukov on either side. In front of their desks was a lone chair. And no fewer than twenty armed guards stood stoically in the room. *Really subtle.*

Maggie closed her eyes at the door and concentrated, preparing to pull a great many emotional strings to get these clowns in line . . .

. . . but there were no strings to pull. Anywhere.

"Lavrentiy," she whispered beside Beria. "Null fields."

Beria stopped at the doorway and looked down at his hands for a long moment. Maggie figured he was trying to summon his own Enhancement and discovering, just as she had, it wouldn't do a damn bit of good.

"Recommendations?" he whispered back.

Maggie looked around, trying to spy the source of the null field. Was it Mikhail Tsakhia, the Mongolian Variant who could create such fields as part of his own Enhancement? He'd been left down in the square with the others, but perhaps he'd turned? Unlikely. And she couldn't see any overt display of any null generators.

Then she spotted one of the guards along the wall smirking at her. *Sorensen. Holy shit.*

"We need to go. Now. The Americans are helping them," she whispered.

Beria nodded. "Yanushkevich," he muttered, the code name of their immediate retreat operation, before addressing the Central Committee. "Comrades! I have forgotten a critical file in my car. Give me a moment and I'll go fetch it."

Khrushchev chuckled. "No need. We will have it brought to you."

"Ah, but Comrade, there is no one except those sitting

here who is even cleared to carry this information, let alone read it. I'll be but a moment."

Beria turned on his heel before anyone could say another word, and Maggie followed quickly behind. As they had predicted, it took the Central Committee a few seconds to realize what had happened, but by the time they were down the hall, Maggie could hear shouting, followed by boots clattering on the floor.

They were coming.

Maggie pulled a radio from the briefcase she carried, discarding the case onto the floor as they ran. "Boris! Yanushkevich!"

Beria ducked into a little-used stairwell and began clambering down the stairs, Maggie close behind. They were relying solely on Beria's memory at this point, and she caught a sharp pang of confusion on him as he paused before a door . . .

They were out of range.

"We're back," she said breathlessly. "Outside the null field."

Beria turned and smiled before kicking down the door. "Good."

And flames engulfed the Kremlin halls.

ACTION COPY

41

OFFICIAL USE ONLY

Control: 1334
Rec'd: JUNE 17, 1953
6 P.M.

FROM: MOSCOW

TO: Secretary of State

NO: 2843, JUNE 17, 6 P.M.

To be read only with the permission
of the Director of S/S.

1

CONFIDENTIAL

PRIORITY

EMBASSY PERSONNEL AND A NUMBER OF SOVIET
CITIZENS REPORTED THREE INCIDENTS OVER THE
PAST TWENTY-FOUR HOURS AT KEY LOCATIONS. AT
APPROXIMATELY 8 P.M. LAST NIGHT, THERE WAS AN
INCIDENT AT THE BOLSHOI THEATER INVOLVING
A PAIR OF VEHICLES INVOLVED IN SOME SORT
OF ACCIDENT NEAR THE SERVICE ENTRANCE.
BOTH VEHICLES, OF THE KIND USED BY SOVIET
OFFICIALS, WERE SAID TO BE HEAVILY DAMAGED,
AND SEVERAL NKVD OR MGB MEN WERE REPORTED
INJURED.

A HALF-HOUR LATER, AN EXPLOSION WAS WITNESSED
AT THE LUBYANKA BUILDING, HEADQUARTERS OF
NKVD, CENTERED ON A CORNER OFFICE ON THE
BUILDING'S THIRD FLOOR. NO INJURIES WERE
REPORTED. FIRST DEPUTY PREMIER BERIA WAS SEEN
IN CONVERSATION WITH CHAIRMAN KHRUSHCHEV
AND MARSHAL ZHUKOV AT THE SCENE.

THIS MORNING AT APPROXIMATELY 8:45 A.M.,
THERE WAS AN INCIDENT AT THE KREMLIN IN WHICH
SMOKE COULD BE SEEN RISING FROM ONE OF THE
BUILDINGS INSIDE THE WALLS. FIRE BRIGADES
RESPONDED, AS DID SEVERAL CONTINGENTS OF

XG

To be read only with the permission
of the Director of S/S.

PERMANENT
RECORD COPY • This copy must be returned to DC/R central files with notation of action taken.

OFFICIAL USE ONLY

UNLESS "UNCLASSIFIED"
REPRODUCTION FROM THIS
COPY IS PROHIBITED.

53

Action

EUR

Info

RMR

P

IES

UOP

E

OLI

DCL

OCB

USIA

CIA

POLICE AND RED ARMY PERSONNEL, AS WELL AS AT LEAST THREE AMBULANCES. SEVERAL CARS WERE SEEN LEAVING THE KREMLIN AT HIGH SPEED DURING THE INCIDENT.

SOVIET MEDIA REPORTED ONLY ON A GAS LEAK AT THE LUBYANKA BUILDING, AND MADE NO MENTION OF THE BOLSHOI OR THE KREMLIN. KHRUSHCHEV, MALENKOV, AND ZHUKOV WERE SEEN LEAVING THE KREMLIN IN SEPARATE VEHICLES. BERIA'S WHEREABOUTS REMAIN UNKNOWN. REPORTS ON THE PREVIEW PERFORMANCE OF THE BOLSHOI WERE NOT SEEN OR HEARD IN ANY MEDIA.

BOTH LUBYANKA AND KREMLIN ARE NOW GUARDED BY MASSIVE RED ARMY PRESENCE. WE ADVISE ANY AMERICANS IN THE CITY TO REPORT TO THE EMBASSY UNTIL FURTHER NOTICE.

BEAM

PA

20.

June 20, 1953

Despite having been in America for nearly four years, Ekaterina couldn't help but be amazed at the largesse Americans enjoyed—and how much they took it for granted. The U.S. Mission in West Berlin, a large, white-washed manor house in a leafy, genteel part of the city, had all the luxuries of home, from Coca-Cola in the commissary to some of the most comfortable beds she'd ever slept in, and yet just that morning she overheard the staff there complaining about the quality of the pancakes and bacon for breakfast and the weak coffee. Even the Berliners working there knew better, having seen their city rise from utter destruction just eight years prior.

She knew, intellectually, that the right to complain, to seek better things, was inherently American—and as far from the Russian mentality as could be. Russians made do with what they had. No matter who was in charge— the tsars, the Bolsheviks, the Party apparatus—Russians worked hard to get what they could and enjoyed what they managed to get without complaint. Who would listen, anyway? Certainly not the tsars, the Bolsheviks, the Party.

Yet Ekaterina looked on with disbelief as some minor embassy functionary demanded a word with the cook about that morning's breakfast, even as she tucked into hers with relish. One of the side effects of her Enhancement was a ravenous appetite, a condition shared with Boris. Their metabolisms skyrocketed after they became Variants, and both of them regularly ate meals that three normal people would have struggled to finish.

Boris. The look on his aged, wrinkled face haunted her. He *shot* her. Did he guess she could shrug it off? She fervently hoped that might be the case. If not, what did that say about him? About her? Would they ever see each other again? Would he die before that happened? He looked to be about eighty. His Enhancement kept him quick, of course, but when would his body give out? Perhaps, when all was said and done, she would try to find Cal and bring him to Russia, to undo the damage he'd done back in '48. As much as she hated Cal at times, she knew full well he was a good man, and if given the opportunity, he would indeed try his best to reach Boris and restore his youth.

But Cal was missing, and Boris was with Beria. And Beria was gone—somewhere.

"Join you, kiddo?"

Ekaterina looked up and saw Frank Lodge smiling down at her, a tray of food in his hands.

"It's a free country," she said with a tired smirk. "That is what you say, yes?"

"Yep, that's what we say," Frank said as he slid into a seat across from her. "Heard you saw your brother again."

Ekaterina felt her face grow red. "I don't wish to talk about it."

Frank nodded and started in on his pancakes. She hadn't see much of Danny and Frank since they'd arrived last night in West Berlin, courtesy of a diplomatic flight out of Leningrad and a somewhat nerve-wracking border crossing from East Berlin. Of course, she and Mrs. Stevens and Tim Sorensen had carried official-looking papers, but using those always made her nervous. She was Russian—she knew the value of identity papers more than any of them.

"So Leningrad was a bust?" Frank asked.

"What is a 'bust'?"

"Nothing happening. Couldn't get in."

"No, it was not a bust," Ekaterina said. "We saw that the Red Army had taken control of the Bekhterev Institute. We could not go in, but we could see the building had been severely damaged—another fire. Mrs. Stevens believes Beria's Variants took all their papers and studies and set the fire to cover their tracks."

Frank took a gulp of black coffee. "Yeah, but they have the other vortex."

"Maybe. It was kept in a basement much below the ground level. There were iron doors and locks and all different things protecting it. They bragged that it would take a month for anyone to break into the room where it is without the right keys and codes. So there is time, yet. I wish to find Beria. He is very dangerous."

"Tim said they used a code word in the Central Committee room. 'Yanushkevich.' That ring a bell?"

Ekaterina smiled slightly. "I thought you knew everything, Frank. It is a name. Nikolai Yanushkevich, one of the tsarist generals during the First World War. He was in charge when the Russian Army had its 'Great Retreat' from Poland. I think it is code for retreat."

"Makes sense. Burn everything and get the hell out of Dodge. We really stuck it to him. You and Tim did a fantastic job, by the way. Danny's giddy as a schoolgirl about all the records you got out of that safe."

"I am a schoolgirl. Or I should be. What is giddy?" she asked.

Frank chuckled. "Giddy. Happy, in a cute kind of way. Like when a girl likes a boy or gets a present or something."

Ekaterina thought about this for a moment. "That's not me."

"No, it's not," Frank agreed, looking a bit more somber. "Hey, question for you. Are your abilities changing? That's been a concern."

Ekaterina thought back to throwing the car halfway down the alley near the Bolshoi. "Yes, maybe I am getting stronger? But it is hard to say. I am also young. Growing up. Why?"

"Something Beria mentioned when I met with him, that's all," Frank said. He didn't seem very convincing, and quickly changed the subject. "What did you end up doing with our visitors?"

Ekaterina frowned. "I do not wish to talk about that either."

Frank nodded silently and focused on his food. The problem of the Soviet Variants was a profound one. Beria had done MAJESTIC-12 a massive favor by keeping his Variant program a secret from the rest of the Soviet government, but if the captured Variants were to be discovered by, say, the Red Army or other Party officials . . .

Ekaterina had pleaded with Mrs. Stevens and Sorensen to spare them. They nodded and consoled her. And then they didn't bring it up again. She hoped against hope that the three were somehow released or contained, but . . . that was unlikely.

The awkward silence was broken a few minutes later by Sorensen, who quickly stopped by their table, coffee in hand. "Meeting. Secure room. We got something," he said before rushing off. They quickly downed as much of their food as possible, and Ekaterina filled another plate with eggs, sausages, bacon, toast, and pancakes before heading up to the embassy's secure conference room, where Danny and the rest of the Variants were waiting for them.

"Got a cable from our man in Vladivostok," Danny said once the doors were closed. "A large contingent of high-ranking NKVD officers left the city about twelve hours ago in three different NKVD-flagged vehicles, along with a Red Army cargo truck. They apparently came in the night before from Chuguyevka, an airfield north of the city, and ended up taking over the local NKVD headquarters for the evening."

"Did they catch a glimpse of Beria?" Mrs. Stevens asked.

"No, but the report says all NKVD officers were summoned to headquarters before the caravan arrived, and stayed there all night. But it gets better," Danny said. "Four hours after the contingent left, an entire Red Army battalion roared into town and headed straight for the NKVD, setting up a perimeter and everything."

"That's our boy," Frank said. "Anything else?"

"Nope, that's it. But it's consistent with what I've been

sensing, that they've been heading east for the past three days. Vladivostok is as far east as east goes. So now they have to make a decision," Danny said, laying out a map of eastern Asia on the conference room table. "Thoughts?"

Everyone stood to get a look at it, but as had become habit, they waited for Mrs. Stevens to speak first. "He's not hiding, that's for sure," she said after a while. "Russia's a big place. If he wanted to hole up somewhere and hide, you don't go through Vladivostok to do that. You go to Siberia, somewhere you can set up shop with nobody caring. He's got a lot of Variants with him. He could have easily taken over a small town and built up a power base out there, or just waited until things cooled down. It's a huge country, and he went to a major population center instead."

"And then left," Sorensen noted.

Frank paced around the table. "So you have a traveling menagerie of at least a dozen Variants, some of the most powerful people on the planet, and you're not holing up anywhere—you're at the ass end of the Soviet Union. If you came in from Chuguyevka, that's, what, four hours north of the city? So they weren't heading back north. And you've got two major borders within a short drive from there—China and North Korea."

"Maybe he's going to hand everything off to Mao," Danny said. "Convince the chairman that Russia's fallen to rogue elements, and that the Chinese have to help him?"

"That's a tall order," Sorensen quipped.

"Beria does not ask for help," Ekaterina offered. "He is . . . pig-head. Stubborn."

"Arrogant," Frank added.

Mrs. Stevens nodded along and pointed again to the map. "And you don't need to go all the way to Vladivostok to get to China. You go through Kazakhstan or Mongolia. And you could've been there by yesterday."

"So he's going to Korea," Danny said. "But why? If you're trying to protect your Variants—the only real resource he has left—do you drag them into a war zone?"

"Maybe he's doing a deal with the North," Sorensen

said. "You know—we'll win your war for you, you give us a home for a while. Or maybe he thinks he can just take over or something."

"That's assuming his goal really is to just protect his Variants," Mrs. Stevens said. "It's a priority, sure, but again, if that's the sum total of his plan, he wouldn't have been seen. So there's something else up his sleeve, and yes, I think he's going to North Korea to do it, whatever it is."

Ekaterina studied the map and thought back to her time at the Bekhterev Institute, and the creepy man who could shoot flames from his hands and called her "daughter" in a very disturbing way. She was sure Beria was as sick as he was arrogant. He would not run and hide. He would run and do something else, but what could he do with three cars full of Variants and . . . .

"Excuse me," she said. "But do we know what's in the truck?"

Danny, Frank, and Mrs. Stevens traded looks around the table. "Red Army cargo truck," Mrs. Stevens said. "The Red Army isn't just going to up and give that to him."

Frank nodded. "Dan, maybe see if our man in Vladivostok can take a little drive north to Chuguyevka, see what that place looks like. Meanwhile . . ."

Danny finished Frank's sentence for him. "Pack your things. We're out of here in two hours. Move."

* * *

Night gently descended on the forested mountains around Songbul-sa, punctuated by the growing sounds of cicadas in the trees. Cal had just finished another meal with Hei Feng, and now walked slowly around the temple court-yard, with Kim in tow to translate and a couple guards keeping a respectful distance. Yamato and Padilla had joined them for dinner, then begged off on the walk.

Honestly, if it wasn't for the two guards shadowing each of them, weapons at the ready, Cal would've really enjoyed the stay. Well, that and missing his family. And failing in his mission. But Cal was always one to make the most of it, and while the Variants waited for the Reds to slip up and give them a window to escape—and maybe rescue those POWs before they were all killed in retaliation—he'd grown to appreciate the slower pace. Especially as his own pace had slowed.

Cal was very much feeling his real age—for the first time in years. In fact, he swore he felt older now. He should have been around fifty-seven, in a body that had seen a lot of miles and hard work and was getting a little arthritic before his Enhancement took hold. But today he felt—and looked—older than that, maybe early sixties. A little more gray, a little stiffer and achy. The thought worried him slightly, but given that he'd always kept himself younger and healthier than his real age, who was to say what his real age should be?

His captor noticed. "Your ability keeps you younger. And without it, you grow old," Hei Feng said through Kim. "Is that true?"

Cal smiled as they walked past some kind of statue or stele in the middle of the court yard. It wasn't the first time Black Wind had asked about their abilities, and he wasn't sure if the young Chinese was probing again or just being kind. "Well, seeing as we're not really on the same side, and with all due respect, I don't feel right talking about it."

Hei Feng nodded. "If you hold to our agreement, I may be able to let you slaughter some of the chickens we've gathered for food. Would that help?"

That sounded really, really good to Cal, and he was sorely tempted. But . . . "No, that's all right. Appreciate it, though."

"I understand. Your loyalty to your people is admirable, especially when . . . well, your people, Africans, they are not treated as well as they should be, yes?" Hei Feng asked.

"Nobody's ever treated as well as they should be, but yeah, we have a ways to go. But I've been a lot of places, and I can tell you that if you look different, no matter how it is that you look different, people gonna treat you different. Black folk in Africa, they don't like white folk much at all.

Understandable. Indian folk don't like Chinese folk. Arabs don't like Jews. The French, well, they don't like anybody. But America's home. And I think it'll get better, as long as we keep at it, keep trying to make a difference."

Hei Feng took all this in as Kim translated, then pondered it for several paces before replying. "And how do they feel about Chinese people?"

Cal could only shrug. "I don't rightly know. Most Chinese folks I know of tend to stick to their own kind in the cities. I don't think they have it as bad as black folk in the South, but I really don't know."

"I have no family left to speak of, and the farmers and peasants are treated as well as you can expect, I suppose," Kim translated. "Perhaps—what's that?"

Cal turned to look at the Korean, pretty sure that he wasn't translating anymore, and saw why a moment later when three Chinese Army jeeps sped into the tiny courtyard, filled with soldiers and at least three ranking officers.

"Friends of yours?" Cal muttered.

"No friend," Hei Feng replied—in English.

One of the officers, dressed to the nines with enough brass for a tuba, got out and marched straight toward Hei Feng, who saluted smartly. The officer began pointing and shouting, and soon soldiers were spreading out into the rest of the temple, while three of them trained their guns on Cal.

"He is here for you," Kim whispered. "You and your friends."

Cal raised his hand slowly. "I thought Hei was keeping this quiet."

Kim also raised his hands, out of caution if not solidarity. "He can be independent, but he still answers to people. Those people may have told his secret to someone else."

Padilla and Yamato were brought into the courtyard at gunpoint, hands on their heads, while the officer continued to shout at Hei Feng. "What's going on, boss?" Yamato asked.

"Think the vacation's over," Cal said.

Then the officer reached out and relieved Hei Feng of his sidearm and rifle, and Hei Feng raised his hands as well.

"Oh, shit," Cal said. "This is bad. Ricky, light 'em up. Time to go."

A moment later—nothing.

Cal turned to look at Yamato, who had a pained expression on his face. "It's not there."

"What do you mean, 'It's not there'?"

"I mean, it's like a null field or something. I can't call it up."

"But the Chinese don't have generators!" Cal hissed. "How the hell did—oh."

Cal had missed the face when the jeeps first drove into the courtyard, probably because it wasn't so different from the other Chinese and Korean faces he'd seen. But now, the person was unmistakable, the same one Cal had first seen in a European forest six years ago.

Mikhail Tsakhia, the original null-Variant, saw Cal looking over at him . . . and gave him a winning smile. Next to him, a human-shaped shadow coalesced from the darkness briefly, then disappeared again.

"What is it?" Padilla asked as they began to lead Hei Feng toward one of the jeeps.

Cal sighed. "We're in trouble."

21.

June 22, 1953

Lieutenant General Bill Harrison was on the short side, compact, and seemed to wear a permanent scowl. Surprisingly, it made him the perfect negotiator at the armistice talks with North Korea in the contested village of Panmunjom. Danny Wallace thought Harrison would make one hell of a poker player, though word was that the general was quite the upstanding Christian, and would probably frown on gambling.

He was certainly frowning at Danny at the moment.

"Commander Wallace, I recognize you have orders here from General Vandenberg. I know Hoyt. Good man. But what he's asking me to do is next to impossible," Harrison said from behind his desk at U.N. Command Headquarters. "Those Koreans, they notice *everything*. They're gonna notice new faces at the table. I don't care how good your Major Lodge is. I'm sure he's a damn fine negotiator, though nobody I know seems to have heard of him. We keep track of people in the Army, you know. We know the good ones."

"Yes, sir. Major Lodge has been on detached duty for some time," Danny responded, standing ramrod straight in his Navy whites, even though he stuck out like a sore thumb on the nearly all-Army base.

"And I can imagine to whence he's been detached," Harrison replied, carefully enunciating each word. "I'm well aware what happens to good military men on detached duty. And I remember when Hoyt was over at CIA. I can put two and two together just fine, Commander. But let me tell you, we are so close. *So close* to an agreement that could stop the fighting here and maybe get our boys home. If you and yours get in the way of that, I swear to God Almighty himself, you'll spend the rest of your days in Leavenworth."

"Sir, with respect," Danny began, "we're here because there's a chance that someone else may try to get in the way of that agreement. We want to prevent that from happening."

Harrison held up Vandenberg's orders again. "So I see. 'Rogue elements from the Soviet Union.' I didn't know the Soviets had rogue elements to begin with."

"It's a new development, sir."

"And I suppose you're not at liberty to tell me who or what these rogue elements are?"

It was all Danny could do to keep looking Harrison in the eye. "Sir, no, sir. I am not."

"And the rest of your people will be off doing something else, which you're also not at liberty to disclose."

"Correct, sir."

Harrison threw the paper down on the desk again. "I mean it, Commander. We're trying to stop a war here. If you mess this up with your antics, I'll have your head. I don't like saying it, but by God, I mean it."

Danny straightened up even further, so much so it felt like his spine would independently launch itself toward the ceiling. "Understood, sir."

"Have Lodge and this other person—Stevens, is it?— report to the staging area tomorrow at oh-seven-hundred. Dismissed."

Giving his best academy salute, Danny turned and walked out of the office, allowing his back to relax only when he left the building entirely. Outside, the rest of the Variants were waiting for him, all dressed in U.S. Army uniforms. Even Katie had been made a rather young-looking private, with a secretarial post as cover.

"Well?" Frank asked.

"You and Rose are reporting for duty with the delegation at 7 a.m. You remember how to spit-shine and polish, right?" Danny asked with a smirk.

"Like riding a bike. What about the rest of you?"

Danny pulled a map of the area from his pocket and unfolded it. "I'm getting the biggest concentration of Variant activity from somewhere in this direction," he said, drawing a line with his finger to the north and east. "I'm thinking they're near Kaesong. It's only seven or eight miles from Panmunjom, where they've been holding the talks. If they're going to disrupt things, it's a good staging area."

"What's the plan?" Sorensen asked.

"Russian observers," Danny said. "We still have some uniforms we can use, and the motor pool here has a couple Chinese jeeps to choose from."

"And the language barrier?" Frank asked. "Maybe I should come with you instead."

"No can do. You're the only one here with real military experience, and this is a high-protocol thing. And if shit happens, nobody's gonna listen to Rose here, sad to say."

Mrs. Stevens harrumphed at that, straightening out her uniform. "Well, you made me a major. Doesn't that count for something?"

Frank smiled at her apologetically. "Not when you're a woman, and not in a room full of generals. Sorry. In that room, a major is the one getting the coffee, man or woman."

Mrs. Stevens opened her mouth as if to say more, but thought better of it. Danny knew she'd quickly weigh all the angles before doing anything—which made her a good counterpoint to Frank's impulsiveness. Frank's plethora of talents, combined with Mrs. Stevens's genius and caution, should put them in position to handle anything that might threaten the armistice talks.

"Just remember, you two—you're there to observe, and only intervene if there's an absolute direct threat," Danny said. "And if things really go south, you make sure you save the North Korean delegation—and ideally, get seen doing it."

* * *

Maggie looked out the window from the back seat of the sedan at the pines and mountains surrounding the roadway. Here and there, signs of war were evident—a crater in an otherwise pristine farm field, a hulked-out tank by the side of the road, a series of graves marked by little more than piled rocks and bits of wood.

Next to her, Beria read through a series of documents in a plain folder provided by Chinese intelligence. It was a testament to Beria's charisma and manipulation, and the sway the Soviets still had over the Chinese and North Koreans, that they'd gotten the full cooperation of the officials in charge of the war—and the peace talks. By all accounts, they had complied with Beria's resource requests—demands, really—and also his admonition that they not communicate his presence in North Korea to either the Chinese or Soviet governments. They were on, he said, a most sensitive mission to uphold Communism against these heathens, and his actions could help bring the war to a rapid and victorious end.

That last part worried Maggie—and had a similar effect on the Koreans. It took quite a bit of emotional manipulation on Maggie's part to keep the government officials in Pyongyang compliant. But she was good. Very good, to the point where she could play a person's emotions like a violin, and she was getting to be quite the Mozart. The personalities of those she affected blurred together by now, remarkable only for a pang of fear here, an unusual bout of courage there, a little bit of extra resistance or a surprising degree of compliance.

It was easy. The sheep, it seemed, really wanted to be led by a shepherd.

Maggie thought she had ingratiated herself well into Beria's circle, but there were still things the former First Deputy Premier kept close to the vest—like the knowledge of other Variants in the Korean theater of war. She'd spent the last few days going out of her way to avoid being seen by Cal and Yamato, "until the time was right," according to Beria's orders. She wondered why she hadn't been told to give her former colleagues the recruitment pitch, but she knew it would be fruitless. Yamato was too young and headstrong; he'd have told her to go to hell just for the fun of it. And Cal . . .

She shifted uncomfortably in her seat as the pines began to give way to buildings and streets—they were entering the outskirts of Kaesong, a former capital of Korea and once a bustling center of commerce. The emotions lately were disconcerting. Maggie thought she'd become numb to her own emotions the more she played with those of others, but lately she'd fallen prey to pangs of regret and sadness that truly unnerved her. Cal was just another sheep in need of a shepherd, and yet she wished she could just send him back home to his wife and kid and let them live out a simple, peaceful, long—very long, in his case—life.

That just wasn't in the cards.

Beria knew Cal, of course, having held him prisoner in Kazakhstan four years ago, and they had a decent dossier on Yamato as well. The Koreans and Chinese gave up the Chinese Variant easily enough—he was a kineticist, focused on pushing things away, to the side, etc. Nobody was a hundred percent sure about the Latin guy, other than he was said to be an excellent shot. Maybe another kineticist, like the Black Wind guy.

Their caravan—now ten vehicles strong, including a full platoon of North Korean infantry—drove through the largely empty town and finally stopped at the site of a bombed-out factory complex. Beria apparently had extensive contacts within the Chinese and North Korean governments, because the area was already under guard by a squadron of soldiers, several of whom saluted crisply when they got out of the cars. A relatively undamaged building with a loading dock had already been prepared, and the cargo truck that had been with them since Chuguyevka backed up to it. Inside was Beria's biggest play yet, a Hail Mary like none other.

Beria stood with Maggie, watching the soldiers carefully place the large wooden crate onto a rolling pallet. "The more I think about it, Margaret, the more I realize just how important it is for things to have happened this way," Beria said quietly.

What a self-aggrandizing prick, Maggie thought. "What makes you say that, Comrade?"

"We tried to work within the power structure, to ease our way into positions of authority, so as to keep our blessings secret and ensure we were protected," Beria said. "We were fools. We are Empowered. The proletariat does not need to be coddled, nor should we coddle them. Each according to his ability—and we have such ability. It is only natural we should lead, and now we will."

Maggie nodded slowly. "A lot of people are going to die."

"There is no greater tool of revolution than death," Beria said simply. "Regrettable, but it is true. The world must be shocked out of its complacency, and we must take our positions as their Champions when that happens."

The crate was wheeled into the factory building, and the two Variants followed it inside. The future awaited.

* * *

Detlev Bronk ran a hand over his face, resisting the urge to check his watch. He knew it was well past midnight, and any greater precision on that account was unnecessary and likely depressing. But the work needed to be done. Vandenberg had been absolutely clear on that point, and with good reason—there was *something* new going on with the vortex.

Bronk looked up at the impossible fissure in space-time, swirling three feet off the ground like a milky whirlpool. The unnerving thing was, no matter which angle you looked at it from, the center of that vortex was always within line of sight. It was an utter paradox, a thing that modern physics simply could not explain. The greats in the field—given only enough information, and through subtle means—all agreed that the vortex should not be. The very few who were cleared to see it firsthand were uniformly confounded. Einstein himself grew visibly angry and agitated after watching it for just a few minutes.

The new sensors were doing their job. They continued to confirm a steadily increasing pattern of low-level radiation coming out of the thing, going in various directions, though mostly to the west and north. Tracing great circle routes on a globe found that many of the bursts were headed for Moscow, before suddenly shifting toward the Pacific.

What's more, the equipment was detecting even fainter, yet similar, patterns all around the vortex. They didn't seem to be coming *from* the phenomena, but were received nonetheless. They were coming from somewhere else, but were too faint and diffuse to triangulate.

"Dr. Bronk?"

Bronk looked up to see Kurt Schreiber at the door to his office, a large sheaf of papers and readouts in hand. In the days since his forced rehabilitation—during which time he had been under constant armed guard—Schreiber had reviewed reams of data and observations about the vortex, with an intensity that Bronk found utterly scary. The German had to be reminded to eat and sleep, and at one point had literally pissed himself because he'd forgotten to go to the bathroom in the midst of his work. He was absolutely nuts, completely certifiable. And yet Vandenberg insisted he be allowed to analyze the work, to seek out patterns that perhaps only his disjointed mind could see.

The excitement on the former Nazi's narrow, gaunt face was evidence he'd found something.

"It's about timing," Schreiber said, entering the office and dropping his papers all over Bronk's already cluttered desk. "The new patterns we're detecting. We needed to look at the timing. That's the key."

Plucking two separate wave patterns off the desk, Schreiber circled the time stamps above each. "This one came from the vortex yesterday at 2:37 a.m.," he said. "And *this* one was found in the radiation background at 2:38 a.m. Look at the patterns."

Bronk leaned in and put on his glasses. "They're different patterns, Schreiber."

"Not entirely!" Schreiber used his pen to circle similarities within the two patterns, snippets within the wavelength that looked similar. "There are pieces that are nearly exactly alike amidst the differences. It is like a call and a response. I've seen this in nearly every time stamp pairing I could find within the data."

"And how many was that?" Bronk asked tiredly.

"One hundred seventy-three."

That got Bronk's attention. "You went through all these and found a hundred and seventy-three pairings like this?"

"Of course. That is only over the past three days."

Call and . . . response. "My God. It's communication."

"Exactly!" Schreiber said, actually jumping in the air slightly in celebration. "Directionally, the vortex is sending these pulses to specific places, because the vectors are highly similar. Until recently, they were largely going east and north. Now, they're more concentrated toward the east. Where are our Variants now?"

Bronk frowned. "They're ours, not *yours*, doctor. And that's none of your business."

"Yes, yes, of course, fine. But it is easy for me to surmise that there is a large concentration of Variants at the other end of these pulses, and that these responses are coming from the Variants themselves."

He really, *really* wanted to dismiss the motion out of hand, but the sick feeling in his stomach told Bronk that Schreiber might be onto something. "None of our Variants have reported any kind of communication attempts with any intelligences that may or may not be inside that thing," Bronk countered.

"Do you control how you dream?" Schreiber asked. "Does your mind wander from time to time? Of course it does. The human mind generates electrical impulses that can be detected, does it not? If the beings from beyond the phenomena have gifted our Variants with Enhancements, they may also have implanted something in their minds as well."

"Like what?" Bronk demanded.

"I don't know, but if I were to speculate, I would say that these Enhancements may have come with a piece of the consciousness inside the vortex. Something that might respond appropriately to these communications."

Bronk looked at the wave patterns again and tried to ignore Schreiber's words. He couldn't. "Then it's possible this thing has an agenda," Bronk said quietly.

"I have no doubt it does," Schreiber replied.

After another minute or two of checking Schreiber's data, Bronk dismissed the German and picked up his secure line. He hoped Vandenberg was an early riser.

* * *

President Eisenhower looked over the two-page, hastily typewritten report in his private study in the White House residence, his first cup of morning coffee untouched and growing cold by his side. His face looked lean, tired—and it wasn't just because of the early hour.

"Gentlemen, I have to ask. How solid is this?"

Allen Dulles and Vandenberg traded a look. Dulles looked as disheveled as the President in a wrinkled suit and coffee-stained shirt, though Vandenberg, as always, looked ready for inspection in his dress uniform, the dark circles under his eyes the only evidence of the rude awakening he'd gotten hours earlier.

"Sir, it's a theory," Vandenberg said. "But it does confirm our suspicions that there's an intelligence behind this phenomena, given the wave patterns we've seen. None of our own Variants have reported any sort of communication, but there have been some slight alterations in the experience of their Enhancements. We can't say for certain they're related, but . . ." The Air Force general didn't need to say anything more.

"And Dr. Bronk and this Schreiber man think they have a way to stop the damn thing from transmitting?" the President asked.

"Yes, sir. It would work much the same way as the electronic jamming systems used in our secure conference rooms, but extended into the extremes of the electromagnetic spectrum so that these additional wavelengths would be affected," Vandenberg said. "I've worked with him on this project for years, sir. I think he can do it."

Eisenhower leaned back in his chair and nodded. "Do it. Now, Allen, we have to talk about our men in the field."

"Mr. President, this is a critical time. We have every reason to believe Lavrentiy Beria is in North Korea right now, and far too close to the armistice negotiations in Panmunjom for comfort. We have two teams going soon as it's daybreak over there—one to hunt down Beria and his people behind the lines, and the other to protect the talks."

"Unless they're already suborned and they're going to sabotage the talks," Eisenhower said. "That's a possibility, isn't it?"

Dulles could only shrug. "It's anybody's guess. Yes, possibly. But these agents have proven their loyalty time and again."

Eisenhower looked down at the rest of his briefing papers, including the black-and-white images of the MAJESTIC-12 Variants in the field. He remembered Danny Wallace from his initial briefing on the project. Smart, calm, collected, repeatedly honored for his work. By all accounts, a loyal officer.

"Okay, I need to make a call. Hoyt, get on the horn to Mountain Home and tell Bronk to shut that thing down. I don't care if they have to blackout the West Coast to do it," Eisenhower said. "Allen, head down to the mess and grab some breakfast. I'll see you downstairs in an hour."

The two men departed, leaving Eisenhower alone in his study, feeling the weight of his office acutely for the first time since he was sworn in. There were only a handful of people who knew what it was like—and only one who had faced such a decision before.

Eisenhower picked up his phone and dialed a number. It picked up on the third ring.

"Hello?"

"Hello, Bess. It's Ike. He up yet?"

"Oh, goodness. Hang on. I'll get him for you."

It took four minutes by Eisenhower's count before the phone came to life. "Well, hell, that didn't take long, Mr. President. Five months?"

Eisenhower smiled despite himself. "How are you, Harry?"

"I'm fine, Ike. Just fine," Harry Truman responded. "I didn't think we were on speaking terms after that election."

"Some things go beyond politics. This is one of them."

There were a few moments of silence on the other end of the phone. "This isn't a secure line, Ike. Not sure how much help I can be if this is what I think it is. This is about that special project, isn't it?"

Eisenhower drew a deep breath. "It is. I just need to know . . . well, I need to know about the people involved. The ones on the ground. There's a possibility that their, oh, hell, how do I say this? That their *blessings* may not be blessings after all. That they might turn."

"Have they wandered off the reservation?"

"No, not yet. But there's a chance they may have been influenced."

"And I assume they're hip deep in something somewhere you can't talk about?"

"Neck deep. I need to know if I can trust them."

Truman took a deep breath. "Ike, at the end of the day, they're *people*. They've been blessed and cursed in ways you and I can't begin to imagine. Some of them manage real well. Others don't."

"And?" Eisenhower said, his patience wearing thin.

"Look, Ike. We *use* them, and they agree to it. If they wanted to, they could easily slip the leash. With their abilities, some of them, they could literally do anything, and nobody could stop 'em. It's been five years since I approved that project. And in five years, they've been as patriotic as can be, most of them. Done everything we asked of 'em. The ones that didn't play ball, well, we took care of those. So you got the best of the best, Ike. Now, I can't say this influence or whatever is gonna affect them or not. We just don't know. But if they have any say about it, I think they'll pull through. Besides, can you even reach them right now?"

The President hadn't thought of that. "Some of them, yes. Others . . . no, I don't think so."

"Then you let them do their jobs and hope for the best. A lot of being President is like that."

Eisenhower chuckled. "All right. Thanks for that, Harry. Give my best to Bess."

"If you need another opinion, reach out to Roscoe Hillenkoetter. I think he's still up in New York, Third Naval District HQ."

"Will do. Thanks."

Eisenhower hung up the phone and downed his luke-warm coffee with one gulp. He'd need more before his day was done.

22.

June 22, 1953

Danny was beginning to second-guess not having Frank around, now that he was staring down the barrel of a dozen Chinese rifles.

They'd left the U.S. base just after midnight and made for the border—and for once, forward intel was right about a potential entry point between the lines. There was a crappy little road—little more than a wide deer trail—through no-man's-land that snaked through forests and mountains and was generally undetectable from above. They'd driven for maybe ten minutes at a time, then stopped for at least a half hour so Sorensen could invisibly scout ahead for signs of trouble. Sorensen had encountered a patrol about two miles in, but used a few grenades and a well-placed fire on a nearby hillside to distract them long enough for the jeep to get by unnoticed.

Dawn had made things more difficult, at least for Danny and Katie. They'd parked the jeep under a few low trees by the side of the road while Sorensen had scouted ahead at around 5 a.m., but Sorensen had failed to report back in time for them to hide from another patrol, commanded by a grim-looking Chinese officer who looked as hardened and battle-tested as Frank.

Danny had thought to hide, but there'd been no time, so their ruse was on. Once the scout had seen their jeep and rushed back to his companions—all on foot, likely a rearguard patrol—Danny and Katie had gotten out of the jeep and placed their weapons on the ground far from their feet. The patrol had rushed up, weapons at the ready. As expected, communication was a major problem.

"*Wǒ shì sūlián jūnguān! Wǒ shì sūlián jūnguān!*" Danny repeated, his hands still up. *I am a Soviet officer.* It made sense, of course, that a Russian speaker might not know a lot of Chinese, and Danny had memorized a few key phrases before they left. But it was still a tough row to hoe.

The officer—a lieutenant from his insignia—kept shouting in Chinese, a barrage of angry syllables that made zero sense to Danny. "*Wǒmen yào qù kāi chéng. Wǒ shì sūlián jūnguān. Ràng wǒmen tōngguò,*" he said, just about exhausting his vocabulary. *We are going to Kaesong. I am a Soviet officer. Let us pass.*

That's when the Chinese officer got on the radio, something Danny had fervently hoped to avoid. But before he could transmit, the group's sergeant stopped him, and another rapid-fire exchange took place. Finally, the sergeant turned to Danny. "I study engineering in Vladivostok," the sergeant said in halting Russian. "I talk Russian. You not be here."

Thank God. "Yes, Comrade, we know. We were part of the group that came in the other day and we were separated from the rest. We are heading toward Kaesong. Perhaps you can show us the way?" Danny asked in his best Russian.

The sergeant and lieutenant conferred again. "Papers, Comrade," the sergeant said finally.

"Of course, Comrade," Danny replied, handing over their forged documents, including a fake teletype from Beria himself authorizing their entry.

This prompted more conferring—the sergeant could read well enough. "This girl. Young. Why here?" the Chinese asked.

Danny put on his best smile. "Yes, she is a cadet in our academy. She is our best student, and is being given the opportunity to learn in the field this summer."

Danny turned to Katie, who gave the Chinese her best—and somewhat unconvincing—smile. *She really needs a break after this one*, Danny thought. *Maybe get her into school in Boise or something. Let her live a little.*

More discussion followed, and Danny wished he'd decided to throw in Chinese and Korean translations of their fake identities and orders. But if they were separated from their comrades, as Danny claimed, it would be a little too convenient for them to have a full suite of documents ready to go.

Finally, the lieutenant stared hard at them, then barked a single word. *"Xiūxí!"* Danny winced, expecting to be shot, but immediately the Chinese lowered their weapons and relaxed.

The sergeant handed their papers back, and unfolded a map. "You. Here. Kaesong there. Road." He traced a winding path across the map—the city was just ten miles away, give or take.

Danny smiled and nodded. "Thank you, Sergeant. You have been most helpful."

"Do you have food?"

This took Danny by surprise, and he looked at the squad of men around him with new eyes, seeing their sallow faces and baggy uniforms. "I'm sorry, Sergeant. We don't. Where are you based?"

"Kagok-ri. Here," the sergeant said, pointing to a dot on the map to the north. "No food. One week."

Christ. "When we get to Kaesong, I will personally make sure you're resupplied, Comrade," Danny said.

The sergeant translated, and several of the men broke out into smiles. Even the lieutenant seemed to relax slightly. They took a moment to shake hands and exchange comradely greetings, and then Danny and Katie hopped back in the jeep and took off down the road.

"Where's Tim?" Katie asked when they were out of earshot.

"Right here," came a disembodied voice from the back of the jeep. "I was up a tree just down the road from you. Nearly went with a bit of a distraction before you went and made friends."

"Glad you held off," Danny said. "Really don't want to leave a trail of bodies between here and Kaesong."

"Are you sure they are there?" Katie asked. "In Kaesong?"

Danny closed his eyes a moment and concentrated. "Yeah. They haven't moved since last night. Huge concentration there—fifteen in total. I'm hoping our people are with 'em."

"That's a long shot, boss," Sorensen said. "We've had no word from Cal and Rick."

Danny shrugged. "I don't sense any other Variants in the area. If they're alive, I think they'll be there."

* * *

Cal woke up to a swift kick in the ribs, courtesy of Maria Savrova, the Soviet Variant whom he met long ago in some godforsaken forest outside Prague. Savrova had already given Cal a demeaning pat on the head the other day, which meant she could now easily track his whereabouts—that was her Enhancement, the ability to track anybody in the world.

The kick was just for kicks.

"Get up," she said in Russian. "Let's go."

Cal knew enough of the language by now to catch her meaning, so he slowly, painfully got up off the cool concrete factory floor and nudged Yamato, who was still asleep. Padilla didn't seem to sleep much; he was already up, wide-eyed and worried. Hei Feng was slumped in a corner, and received another kick from Savrova to get him to his feet.

"How we doing, old man?" Yamato muttered as he stood, warily eyeing the North Korean guards nearby, their rifles at the ready—but not, at least, pointed at them.

Cal stretched and felt his bones shift a little. He was damn sure by now that he was getting worse, older than he should be. Back before he discovered he could harm, and not simply heal himself or others, Cal would age himself greatly in order to work his miracle. And after that, his body would eventually regress back to his real age. This, though, this was bad. "I've been better, you little whipper-snapper," Cal joked. "Gonna need me a fix if I'm gonna do anything useful."

Once everyone was up, Savrova and the guards led them into a different part of the factory, where a disused, rusting freight train car was sitting on equally rusted rails. There were several tracks here, each leading out from a train-sized hole in the wall. This was where they probably shipped from, or got raw materials from, back when this place was up and running, probably some twenty years ago.

Then a cadre of folks came in wearing Russian uniforms, and Cal froze.

"Aw, Maggie. No," he whispered.

She was walking right next to Lavrentiy Beria, in full NKVD uniform. Nobody had a gun on her. She even had her hair done up like Savrova's, and put on some makeup, too—things that she very rarely did back at Mountain Home. She looked composed.

"Please tell me she's doubling," Yamato whispered. "Otherwise, we're fucked."

Cal could only shrug, even as he tried to fight back a tear. "I sure hope so."

The prisoners were brought forward and forced to their knees, their hands on their heads, while the other Soviet Variants gathered around. Savrova, Tsakhia, and Illyanov were all there, and the Russian they'd taken to calling the Shadow Man was there too, though in his inky black, wispy form rather than in person. There were four others he didn't recognize, except maybe one who might have shown up in a surveillance photo he'd seen in some file long ago.

Maggie walked over to Cal. "Your Russian still weak?" she asked simply.

"Yeah," he replied bitterly. "Bet yours gotten all kinds of sharp lately, though."

A flash of something ran across her face a moment, which took Cal aback—she was never one for showing any kind of emotion, even briefly. But then she recovered and arched an eyebrow at him. "I've been asked to translate."

Cal looked her in the eye for a long moment, then shrugged. "Suit yourself."

Beria waved over the Chinese officer in charge and whispered something to him. A minute later, the guards cleared the huge, hangar-like room entirely, giving rifles to Maggie, Illyanov, and Beria. The rest of the Soviet Variants stepped closer, surrounding Cal and his fellow prisoners in a kind of semicircle.

"My friends," Beria began. "My fellow Empowered. Champions of the Proletariat. We have been together for a very long time now, and I am truly, deeply appreciative of all of your efforts and all you have done to further our true revolution—not the hollow, meaningless drudgery of Stalin and his cronies, but the real, the *only* revolution! The revolution in which the Empowered take their rightful place as the shepherds of the masses, the Champions of the Proletariat! Today is the day when we unleash the abilities granted to us, and grant them to so many more across the globe. Together, we shall help humanity rise up! Cast off their oppressors! We shall usher in an age of enlightenment! An era free from want! And all of you— yes, even you Americans—will have a beautiful role in this new future. You will indeed be the very cause of it!"

Cheers rose up from Soviets, but Cal could only roll his eyes. The man sure loved to hear himself talk. Maybe it was a Russian thing.

"Savrova, begin preparations," Beria ordered.

With two other Soviets by her side, Savrova entered the freight car from the side door and went inside. Meanwhile, Beria himself walked up to the four prisoners and addressed Cal directly in English. "I must ask you, Mr. Hooks, has your country improved its relations with your people?"

Cal knew full well what the Russian was talking about, but wasn't in the mood for chitchat. "What people? My fellow Americans?"

Beria just sighed. "Stubborn. They say many of your fellow Negroes are like this. And yet you live in a country that continues to enslave you. Not in chains, today. No, much more civilized. But you work harder for less money, and your prospects are limited by the same capitalist system that keeps you down."

"It'll get better," Cal said, looking the Russian in the eye. "Already has. Truman desegregated the Armed Forces. Parts of the country are downright pleasant now for black folk. The rest, well, we're working on it."

Beria motioned toward Tsakhia. "Here is a Mongol from the Russian steppe. He is our equal—not just in the Soviet Union, but here, with the Empowered. Your life, Mr. Hooks, could be so much better than it is. You can be an equal—more than an equal, with your gifts. There is a place for you with me, just as Miss Dubinsky has found."

Cal looked over to Maggie, who quite obviously decided not to meet his gaze. "That's all right, Mr. Beria. You go on ahead. I'm an American, come what may."

Beria gave Cal a small smile, then walked off.

"Hey, I don't get the recruitment speech?" Yamato said. "Come on."

Maggie eyed Yamato coldly. "He doesn't want you. Just Cal." She then knelt down next to Cal and looked him in the eye. "This isn't gonna end well, Cal. Come with us. For Sally. And Winston."

Cal's heart just about broke. "Aw, Miss Maggie. You ain't gotta do this. Help a fella out, what do you say?"

She smiled at him and got to her feet again. "I'm sorry. You're gonna die."

With that she walked off, and yet in that moment, Cal felt an incredible peace settle over him, as though the hand of God's grace, in that moment, had decided to reach in and heal his heart and make him whole. A tear finally escaped his eye, but one that was shed with joy and hope, not sadness or fear. This, he thought, was what the Lord wanted, and He was giving Cal a touch of heaven in what would surely be his last moments.

Cal looked over to Yamato, who was eyeing him strangely. "What the hell, old man? What's with that look?"

"I dunno . . . I just . . . It feels okay, you know? It's gonna be okay."

Yamato only snickered. "Sure, Pops. There's nothing okay about this at all."

They were interrupted by the pop of a rifle.

Cal turned and saw Illyanov—with his rifle trained on another Russian. There was a flurry of angry shouting, and Maggie was a part of it, her rifle trained on the Russians as well.

"Holy shit," Yamato breathed. "It's on! Let's go! I—wait. I still got nothing."

Cal turned to the young man. "That Mongol fella?"

"Dunno. I had a charge a second ago, but now nothing's working."

Another shot rang out, and this time one of the Soviets fell to the ground, clutching his leg, the result of Maggie's shot. The rest put their hands up, most of them looking downright pissed off as they were marched up into the freight car.

"Is Maggie flipping back now?" Yamato asked.

Then Illyanov walked over, and fixed Cal with a furious glare. "I should just kill you now," the now-old man said in rough English. "But you no heal me. You are old as well."

Sweet Jesus, does everybody here hate me now? Cal thought. "Well, you know what they say, Boris. Old age comes for us all." *Maggie, if you're really back, time to take care of this boy.*

Illyanov cried out and raised his rifle butt, striking Cal in the head.

Everything went dark.

* * *

The building was little more than a barn, though a particularly nice one with a very Asian flavor. The slightly curved, four-sided roof hung over a large, nearly empty space with simple floors and white-washed walls. The windows were open—Korea in late spring could get pretty hot—and the hum of conversation filled the room. There were two groups of folding chairs, well away from each other, with a long rectangular table between them. Several seats lined the sides of the table, which had pencils, paper, and pitchers of water at the ready.

It all seemed so very pedestrian. Frank expected a bunch of Madison Avenue types to come in, sit down, and start talking about the latest ad for Coca-Cola. But the room was full of military brass—Frank was one of the few there below the rank of colonel—and split into two very distinct groups. The first was American and South Korean, along with a smattering of Australian and British officials. The other was Chinese and North Korean. Aside from one or two brave souls who met in the middle to exchange pleasantries, the two clusters kept to themselves.

"I've never been to an armistice negotiation before," Mrs. Stevens said.

Frank looked over at her and smiled. She was visibly uncomfortable in the uniform, constantly adjusting her collar and pulling on her skirt, and she looked wide-eyed and worried the entire time. Of course, she was probably more worried about making a fool of herself than anything else; Frank knew she had multiple contingency plans in place should things take a turn.

"Major."

Frank turned and saw General Harrison; he saluted sharply, as did Mrs. Stevens—they'd spent an hour practicing last night. "General, sir."

"I assume you took a look at the perimeter already?"

"Yes, sir. All's well so far."

Harrison squinted a little at Frank. "I told Wallace this yesterday, and I'll tell you today. Whatever you got going, you make sure it doesn't affect this—what in God's name?"

The general's gaze wandered over Frank's shoulder to the entrance the North Korean representatives used. Lavrentiy Beria had just walked in.

"Rose?" Frank said.

She looked just as stunned as he felt. "Well, that narrows the contingencies down quite a bit," she said, reaching for the little notebook she kept handy to take notes and make plans.

"Major," the general said, "is that who I think it is? And were you expecting him?"

"Yes, it is, sir. And . . . well, this isn't what we expected, no." An ambush, sure. Some kind of sabotage. A diversion at the front. But walking right into the Panmunjom armistice talks? Not really.

"Sir, if you'll excuse me? Major Stevens, please feel free to answer the general's questions to the extent you can," Frank said before heading over toward the middle ground of the room. Mrs. Stevens would know just how much to tell the general. And Frank wanted a word.

Beria spotted him and walked over—they met at the far end of the table. "Major Lodge."

"First Deputy—wait. I'm sorry. *Mister* Beria," Frank said.

The Russian Variant squinted slightly before smiling. "Ah, yes, well. Temporary, I assure you."

"Man with a plan," Frank said. "What brings you to North Korea?"

"The same as you, Major. An end to this war."

"Somehow, I don't think we're on the same page when it comes to how to do that."

"Likely not. You remember Miss Dubinsky?"

Frank had been so focused on Beria that he hadn't seen Maggie behind and to the right. "Hard to forget. Heya, pal."

"Heya, Frank. Hats off to the team. Bang-up job in Moscow."

Frank couldn't help but smile. "And elsewhere."

Her eyebrows went up at that. "Oh, really? East Berlin?"

"Good beer there."

Shooting Frank a look, Beria walked off, leaving Frank face-to-face with Maggie. "We didn't know you were involved with that," she said.

Join them.

The dead man's voice slipped through Frank's mental defenses, and a deluge followed.

Join them. It makes sense. He's got something going. He's outthought you. Only way. Join them.

Frank closed his eyes a moment and shunted the voices back into the lockbox in his mind. When he opened them, Maggie was looking at him oddly.

"What was that?" she asked.

"Unwanted opinions. You're looking swell."

Maggie smiled. "The uniform's not flattering."

"Better than you think. Like Rita Hayworth on a USO tour."

"I was going for Garbo."

"Really?" Frank said. "You don't have the hair for it."

Maggie rolled her eyes. "But I got the chops. Left jacket pocket. See you later."

With that Maggie walked off and the crowd was asked to take their seats. Frank checked his pocket and, finding nothing, went to his assigned seat—front row, good sight-lines, and right next to Mrs. Stevens.

"Well?" she said as Frank sat down.

"Garbo."

"Really?"

"Yep."

"Anything else?"

Frank looked over to Beria, who had taken a front-row seat behind the North Korean negotiators. "Left jacket pocket."

* * *

The electrical hum coursing through the room was so loud, Detlev Bronk had to shout to be heard, and a few people on the team had managed to scrounge up earmuffs to protect their hearing. But after nonstop work for the past sixteen hours—starting before they even got the go-ahead from Washington—they were ready.

They were going to try to shut down the vortex.

The damn thing had been going absolutely crazy throughout the day, sending out pulse after pulse of low-level radiation, as if something inside it *knew* what they were up to. Likewise, the callbacks were increasing as well. Something was answering. More and more, Bronk felt that Schreiber was onto something big. Not bad for an insane Nazi.

The first order of business was to get the vortex into a smaller space—but the magnetic field generators that contained the phenomenon were massive, and not easily put on rollers. So Bronk had built a room *around* the vortex inside the hangar—a slapdash box about ten feet all around, the walls coated with layers of metal and mesh, all designed to keep radio signals from penetrating inside.

Then the jamming equipment had been brought in. They couldn't shut out the entire electromagnetic spectrum, so they'd decided to drown it out instead, concentrating on the wavelengths that the phenomenon seemed to prefer, but ideally sending along a massive influx of waves across the entire spectrum. That meant everything from microwave emitters to bright lights to no fewer than three dozen radios and four televisions, all tuned to different stations.

Bronk walked over to the jury-rigged control panel outside the box. Dozens of cables flowed out of it and down to the floor, and then into the box itself. The radiation detectors they'd used to ferret out the wavelength information were now tuned to the entire EM spectrum, as much as was possible, to see if any recognizable signals could escape.

With a last look around at his engineers, all of whom responded with nods, Bronk began flipping switches. Inside the box, the equipment came to life—and the noise was absolutely deafening.

Let's hope this works.

* * *

Cal woke up and felt, surprisingly . . . better.

Sure, his head hurt like hell from where Illyanov hit him, but a lot of his aches and pains were muted somehow, as if someone turned down the volume dial on his aging body's radio. And there were voices around him, speaking quietly, one at a time, in a couple different languages, it seemed. With all that, Cal figured he was still alive, which was a good start.

But then he opened his eyes and wondered if he'd gone blind.

"Rick?" Cal said. His words echoed slightly. "Rick, where you at?"

The sound of footsteps echoed, and Cal felt the thump of each step under him. He turned to see Rick Yamato holding a lit cigarette lighter. "I'm right here, Pops. Welcome back."

Cal looked around and saw metal walls and the silhouettes of a bunch of people, and figured he'd been thrown in the boxcar with . . . well, who else?

"The Russkies," Yamato said quietly. "Me, Miguel, Hei Feng, and most of the Soviet Variants. All stuck in here. And they're using null generators on us."

Cal slowly sat up. "Well, ain't that something. How's everybody feeling?"

"Pissed off," Yamato said with a grin, offering a hand to help Cal to his feet. "Seems like Beria turned the tables on 'em. Only ones not accounted for are Maggie and that speedy guy, Boris."

To Cal's surprise, his body wasn't protesting as much now. Maybe the null generators were having an effect on his aging—but then, that hadn't happened before during testing at Mountain Home or Area 51, either. "What else?" Cal asked.

Maria Savrova came over, rage on her face. "There is an atom bomb in here with us," she said in English.

"Come again?" Cal said, his heart starting to beat really fast.

"Beria has taken an atom bomb. He plans to detonate it—with us sitting here next to it," Savrova said.

"Why in God's name would he do that?" Cal asked.

The answer was terrifying.

* * *

Danny sped through the heart of Kaesong toward the concentration of Variants he had detected. There were two or three that had split off from the main group and were heading to the south and east, but he figured he'd best go with numbers for now. Besides, for whatever reason, his senses were growing fainter, not stronger, as they approached the city. Something was off, and he didn't know what.

He turned to Katie over in the passenger seat—and nearly ran off the road. A strange, ephemeral mist seemed to hang around her head, and it coalesced into the ghostly face of an old man, looking angrily at him. He glanced back at where Sorensen sat, still invisible, but saw the same mist where he should've been, and another face, this time a middle-aged Asian woman, glared back as well.

"Something's happening," Danny said. "Our Enhancements are changing."

Katie looked at him quizzically. "How do you know?"

"There's . . ."

Suddenly, the man's face hanging around Katie's head seemed to scream silently before dissolving into nothingness. The mist around Sorensen was gone by the time he turned his head. And suddenly, his senses grew much sharper, as if someone had finally fixed the rabbit ears on the television inside his head.

"Never mind," Danny said. "I'm getting Cal and Yamato up ahead. Maggie is heading to the southeast with two others. Assuming at least one of them may be Beria. Let's move."

Danny let his Enhancement guide him as he drove, and they soon pulled into an abandoned, bombed-out factory—surrounded by a couple dozen North Korean troops. Danny drove past the installation instead. "Ideas?" he asked.

"I'll recon and see what's there," Sorensen said as the jeep's rear lifted slightly, the telltale sign that he'd jumped off.

"I'll get close," Ekaterina said, sliding out of the jeep. "It is an old building. It looks like it will collapse at any moment. I will help it."

Danny waited a few minutes for everyone to get in place, then wheeled the jeep around and drove into the factory compound. Immediately, a half dozen soldiers leveled rifles at him, but he continued to drive ahead until he was no more than thirty feet from the building entrance before stopping on several rail tracks.

"*Wǒmen yào qù kāi chéng. Ràng wǒmen tōngguò,*" Danny ventured as an officer walked forward.

"I speak Russian," the officer replied. "I do not recognize you."

"I am here to join the others," Danny said. "Surely they told you I would be coming?"

The officer frowned deeply. "They did not tell me this. We did not expect anyone back here for two hours."

Somebody left for sure, then. "Well, where did they go?" Danny said. "Come now! I need to catch up to them."

The officer put his hand on his sidearm. "Step out of the vehicle."

Suddenly, there was a groaning, crumbling sound from above them, and Danny looked up to see the side of the corrugated metal building start to collapse downward. He took the opportunity to fling himself at the North Korean officer, tackling him to the pavement, and then rolled under the jeep as hundreds of pounds of metal crashed down on top of it.

From the darkness under the jeep, Danny could hear the sounds of men crying out, then gunfire, and then a massive snapping sound—and more screams. It took about five minutes for the ruckus to die down, and another three or four before light returned.

He rolled out to find Ekaterina and Sorensen standing over him. "No napping," Sorensen chided.

Danny got to his feet and looked around. Not only had the entire facade of the factory collapsed, but a massive steel girder, some thirty feet long, was on the ground about twenty feet away, with several inert bodies under it. "Baseball?" Danny asked.

"A bourgeoisie sport," Katie said. "But useful."

With the face of the building gone, Danny could see that the rail tracks continued into a large loading area inside. Sorensen handed him a Korean rifle, and together the three Variants ventured inside. Danny could sense all the Variants ahead, and it seemed like they were all inside the boxcar.

"Odd. Why—" Then his senses winked out. "Null generators," Danny said. "Find 'em. Move!"

They ran forward and fanned out around the boxcar, searching around the wheels and by the doors. The first two were easy to find and destroy, but Sorensen had to climb up on top of the car itself to find the third. Once that was off, Danny's senses roared back to life.

Katie crushed the now-dormant null generator in her hands, then went toward the chained and padlocked doors of the boxcar. But Danny rushed over and pulled her aside. "Give it a moment," he said, then shouted toward the boxcar itself. "All clear!"

The doors of the boxcar burst open, one of them flying across the loading area. Then, slowly, a large crate moved out of the boxcar . . .

. . . hovering in thin air.

"Well, that's new," Sorensen said from the top of the car.

The crate gently settled onto the concrete floor, and Danny could see that the top had already been removed.

Inside was the unmistakable shape of a bomb.

"Jesus," Danny breathed.

People began pouring out of the boxcar, including Yamato and Cal. The last time Danny had seen him, Cal was a hale thirty or so. Now, he looked close to his natural age. Danny rushed over and gave him a bear hug. "You all right?" he asked.

Cal returned the hug. "I'm okay. But we got a problem."

Danny turned and saw eight Soviet Variants, including Savrova and the Mongolian, staring at him. "Is this the problem?" Danny asked.

"Not sure. That bomb is the bigger problem," Cal said.

Savrova walked over to Danny. "We cannot disturb the bomb," she said. "Any attempts to disarm it or cut off the radio detonator will automatically engage the nuclear reaction."

Danny held up a hand. "Nuclear? This is an A-bomb?"

"Actually, it's a prototype H-bomb," Yamato said. "Our friends here say Beria diverted it from the Russian nuclear program he's been overseeing."

"And Beria has the radio detonator," Danny finished.

There were nods around the room, along with some quiet Russian translation.

"You all know where he's going?" Cal asked. "Come on, now. You know we gotta stop him."

"Panmunjom," Savrova said. "The armistice talks."

Danny glanced over at the bomb. "Okay, we need to go. Let's find vehicles. Move!"

The Russians looked at each other in confusion, even as one or two began to step forward, along with Hei Feng and Padilla. But Savrova wasn't one of them. "We are Soviets," she said. "We do not follow American orders."

Danny and Cal traded a look of disbelief. "Good Lord, there's a *bomb* here," Cal said. "Look, now I know you folks think we're the Devil's own, and honestly, we don't think too highly of you either. But Beria's done sold you out. So you can stay here and die, you can run and hope we take care of him, or you can actually do something about all this. It ain't about Russians and Americans no more. We got lives to save."

A few more Russians began walking forward, but there were still holdouts. "Look, we're in North Korea," Danny added. "When this is done and you wanna stay, it's not like we can stop you. But right now, for all our sake—for the sake of Variants everywhere and all these people who are gonna die—we gotta do this. Let's go."

At this, one of the Russians transformed into shadows and simply disappeared, which caused a murmur among the others. Finally, the holdouts looked over to Savrova, who finally gave a curt nod.

244 Michael J. Martinez

"Grab weapons from the guards outside," Danny said as the group surged forward toward the now-missing wall. "Find jeeps. Move it!"

They took off at a jog, though Danny stayed behind to keep pace with Cal, who was doing his best to move fast. "Well?"

"Beria is crazy," Cal said between breaths. "He'll do it, no doubt. Surprised he ain't done it already."

"Why?" Danny asked.

"You ain't gonna believe it."

23.

June 22, 1953

Something's different.

Frank looked around the room as one of the North Korean envoys droned on and the translator droned right along with him. Everyone looked rather sleepy as the heat of the day grew, and nobody seemed particularly bothered by anything.

And yet something happened in Frank's mind, like a balloon deflating. All of the voices he'd been holding back suddenly seemed to just . . . fade. When he dropped his concentration for a moment, all was silent.

"Rose," Frank whispered.

Mrs. Stevens looked at him wide-eyed. "Something happened," she said. "Hard to explain."

He looked over at Beria, who had stopped writing in his notebook, his pen in midair. The former First Deputy Premier was looking around furtively, and he seemed to catch Maggie's eye as well, who gave him an almost imperceptible shrug in return.

"Weird," Frank muttered. "Be ready."

After about an hour or so, the negotiators took a break. Beria closed his pen, stood up, and walked swiftly out of the building, Maggie and Illyanov in tow, causing some murmurs in his wake. Frank and Mrs. Stevens got up and followed.

Outside, amongst the guards from both sides and some of the other delegates, Beria was talking quietly and hastily with Maggie and Illyanov, but noticed Frank and immediately began walking over.

"What have you done?" Beria demanded.

Outline of an object in his left jacket pocket, too boxy to be a gun, one of the MGB men said in his head.

He's agitated. Something's not going to plan, General Davis added. *He's going to be unpredictable—be careful.*

Frank smiled slightly. It was kind of nice to have them back. "I didn't do anything, Comrade. What about you?"

"This is a trick," Beria said, his eyes narrowing. "Some sort of null generator."

"I feel fine," Frank countered. "How about you?"

Beria opened his palm and, immediately, a small flame rose above it. "Then what is it?"

"I don't know, but I feel better than I have in weeks," Frank said.

Mrs. Stevens stepped forward, putting herself between Frank and Beria. "Sir, maybe this is a good time to take a step back, think about what you're planning, whatever it is. You told Frank here that people's Enhancements had changed. Maybe they've changed again. Maybe not. But I think we should get a handle on it, your side and mine, before we do anything else."

Beria stared at her mutely, as if she were an animal in a zoo, then turned and stalked off, Maggie and Illyanov following him.

"I need to talk to General Harrison," Mrs. Stevens said. "This can't be good. You follow him."

Frank nodded and began walking off after Beria, who was heading for the jeeps on the North Korean side of the building. Before Beria got there, however, four other jeeps roared into the compound from the northwest, setting off all kinds of ruckus amongst the guards.

Danny. And . . . company?

Beria stopped in his tracks, then wheeled around and headed back toward the main building. *He's panicking*, said Dr. Koslov, a psychiatrist Frank had absorbed a few years back. *I don't think you should let him in there.*

Frank immediately moved to intercept him—but his path was suddenly blocked by Boris Illyanov, who had been walking behind Beria a second ago.

"Shit," Frank said. "Move your ass."

Illyanov just smiled and shook his head from side to side.

"Fine."

Legs, said a voice in Frank's mind. It was Yushchenko, the double-agent MGB man from back in '48.

Frank threw a punch, but kicked out his left leg while doing so. Illyanov easily dodged the fist, but hit Frank's leg as he tried to move around him, and ended up sprawled in the dirt. Frank immediately followed up with a sharp blow to the head, which put out Illyanov's lights for good.

He looked up to see several people in Russian uniforms running toward Beria—running *with* Danny and Cal and Yamato and a couple others Frank didn't recognize. In about a minute, they had Beria surrounded, and Frank rushed over to join them.

"Hand it over," Danny said in Russian, a rifle aimed at Beria.

By this time, the rest of the camp was in chaos, the Koreans not quite knowing what to do about this confrontation between people who all seemed to be Russian, and the Americans starting to back away and head for their vehicles.

"What is this?" Beria said, eyes shifting quickly from face to face. "Why have you joined with the imperialists?"

"You betrayed us," said Maria Savrova—Frank was surprised to see her, and doubly so that she'd confront him like this. "You said we would be at the vanguard of a new order! And you lied!"

Beria grew red. "Your sacrifice was a noble one! You were to fuel a new wave of Empowered across the world!"

"You never gave us the choice!" shouted another Variant, one Frank recognized from their initial surveillance activities in Moscow. "You would have killed us!"

Beria quickly reached into his left jacket pocket, even as he pulled out his sidearm with the other hand.

Here we go, Frank thought.

"Drop him, Mags."

* * *

"*You're looking swell,*" Frank said. Status report.

Maggie smiled. "The uniform's not flattering." Trouble brewing.

"*Better than you think. Like Rita Hayworth on a USO tour.*" I'm not buying it.

"*I was going for Garbo.*" Fake-double protocol in place.

"*Really?*" Frank said. "*You don't have the hair for it.*" Still not buying it.

Maggie rolled her eyes. "But I got the chops. Left jacket pocket. See you later." Double-agent confirmed. Check left jacket pocket. Will rejoin when appropriate.

With that Maggie walked off and the crowd was asked to take their seats. Frank checked his pocket and, finding nothing, went to his assigned seat—front row, good sightlines, and right next to Mrs. Stevens.

"*Well?*" Mrs. Stevens said as Frank sat down.

"*Garbo.*" She's still on our side.

"*Really?*"

"*Yep.*"

"*Oh, thank God. Anything else?*"

Frank looked over to Beria, who had taken a front-row seat behind the North Korean negotiators. "Left jacket pocket."

* * *

Immediately, Beria's eyes grew wide and his hands began to tremble, as if he'd seen the scariest fucking thing imaginable. Which, knowing Maggie, he probably had.

"It's over, Comrade," Maggie said, stepping forward. "You're really gonna want to give me that."

Beria began sobbing uncontrollably—but he still held his pistol in his right hand, and a small device in the other. "No!" he wailed. "We are so close! A new dawn for all the Empowered!"

Danny walked over to Maggie's side, sharing a small half-grin with her before turning to address Beria. "It's over, Comrade. Let it go."

"Never!"

Beria roared in agonized rage and lifted his gun, firing a shot toward Maggie. At the same time, he fumbled with the device in his hand . . .

. . . until a shot burst cleanly through his wrist, causing him to drop the detonator . . .

. . . which quickly flew away from him and landed several meters away.

Move. Now, came several voices in Frank's head.

Rushing forward, Frank hit Beria with a left cross that sent the Russian sprawling.

And then all was silent.

Frank turned to check on Maggie, only to see her kneeling on the ground, holding a prone Danny in her arms.

"Oh, shit." Frank rushed over and slid down next to them. "Move, let me see."

Maggie relented and Frank went to work. *Shot entered through left lung, between fifth and sixth ribs. Short range, likely reached his heart as well. Breathing shallow, pulse erratic. Emergency surgery needed stat.* If a disembodied voice could sound grim, this was very grim indeed.

"Get off him!" Frank shouted, pushing Maggie back. "I need a knife! Now! Cal, get over here!"

One of the Russians offered him a rather wicked-looking field knife, which he used to cut away Danny's uniform as Cal slid down next to him. "Oh, no. Oh, Danny, no."

"Give him as much as you can," Frank said.

Cal placed his hands on Danny's shoulders for several long moments as Frank began to make a ventral incision over Danny's heart.

"Frank."

Frank looked over at Cal—who hadn't aged.

"I can't get him, Frank. I think he's gone."

Agreed. Breathing and pulse have ceased.

Frank shoved Cal aside and prepared to pound the hell out of Danny's chest to try to revive him.

Then the world went dark.

* * *

Frank.

In the blackness, Frank could hear Danny's voice. "Don't go," he pleaded. It was all he could say.

I'm already gone. Just shut up and listen.

"What?"

They're not aliens or anything like that. The things beyond the vortex. They're people. People who have passed on. They latch on to the living, giving them abilities.

"Why?"

To get out. The A-bomb. It ripped a hole between the living and the dead. It made them want to come back. All of this, all of our Enhancements—all designed to keep us fighting each other. To build up to another bomb to release more of them.

Frank tried to look around in the darkness for Danny, but saw nothing. "What happened?"

I think they did something back at Mountain Home to keep them from communicating. They were trying to push us. They nearly succeeded with Beria. They wanted him to detonate the H-bomb with Variants at ground zero to open up another vortex.

Frank thought back to the voices, how insistent they were. "So what now?"

Tell them to keep a lid on the vortex. Tell the Russians too. We have to keep them out. You'll all still have your abilities, but we need to be careful now. Tell them, Frank.

"I will. I'll tell them."

Frank. I'm sorry. I tried to protect us.

"You did good, Dan. You really did." Frank wanted to cry, but somehow knew he had to keep Danny talking. "Stay with me, pal."

Tell the others. Be careful with their abilities. Tell them I tried. Tell—

Danny's voice was suddenly cut off. Frank screamed into the darkness, but could hear nothing.

24.

June 22, 1953

Hoyt Vandenberg received the sealed teletype from his aide and waited for him to close the door before opening it, as usual. The teletype itself was anything but.

The Air Force chief of staff read through it, smiling all the while, until he got to the end, which hit him like a truck and sent him staring off out his Pentagon window at the late night sky for a good ten minutes.

Danny Wallace had been the key to MAJESTIC-12, something Roscoe Hillenkoetter had recognized way back in 1945. Vandenberg and Hillenkoetter had convinced the powers that be—first the late James Forrestal, and then Harry Truman himself—that the Variants were indeed real, and that their abilities might be harnessed. And Wallace himself was their ace in the hole, with his ability to sense and track other Variants at great distances. Wallace put America ahead in a unique and frightening arms race.

And honestly, he was a good kid. He was a patriot, yes, but he genuinely cared about the Variants placed under his command. Compared to them, he was supposed to be the weak link—the tracker who really ought to just get out of the way once the quarry was found. He never did. He'd stuck by his people right until the very end.

Finally, Vandenberg picked up the phone and dialed a special number. It picked up on the third ring.

"Yes?"

"Mr. President, reporting in on MAJESTIC, sir."

There was a short pause; Vandenberg imagined Eisenhower was shooing a bunch of people out of the White House residence. "All right, Hoyt. Go ahead."

"Our people have captured Lavrentiy Beria in Panmunjom and kept him from detonating an H-bomb nearby," Vandenberg said simply.

This time, the pause was a little longer. To be fair, it was a lot to take in. "Jesus Christ. Whose bomb?"

"Our person on the inside said Beria diverted it from the Soviet Union's weapons program while he was still running it. This was not, repeat, not an official Soviet mission. It was all Beria."

"And where's that rogue bomb now?" the President demanded.

"Took some doing, but it's been defused and disarmed. The nuclear material has been destroyed," Vandenberg said. "Also, sir, I have to inform you. We lost Subject-1."

There was a loud exhale on the other end of the line. "That puts a huge dent in the program, Hoyt."

"Yes, it does, sir. He was a good man."

"What about that thing in Idaho?"

Vandenberg reached over and pulled out another teletype he'd received an hour before. "No clear signals have been recorded. We believe the jamming worked."

"You believe," Eisenhower repeated, an edge in his voice. "You're not sure?"

"Mr. President, I'm not sure about any of it. But as far as we can tell, yes. Our people reported there was some kind of shift in their abilities, hard to define."

"Where are they now? And what about the other Russian Variants?"

"Given the situation with the armistice talks, outright capture of any Russian Variants was deemed inadvisable. We had a couple defect. The rest have retreated back into North Korean territory. Our people say only a couple of them seem to want to head back to Russia. Apparently, Beria turned on them. The defectors and our people are back at U.N. Headquarters."

"All right. Seems like they did a fine job."

"Yes, sir, they did. Great work."

"That doesn't change my decision," Eisenhower said.

Vandenberg felt his face go red, and it wasn't just from the pain he felt from shifting in his seat. "Mr. President, once again, I urge you to reconsider. These people are Americans. Patriots. We've asked them for the impossible, and they've done it time and again. At great sacrifice."

"I know, Hoyt. Really, I do," Eisenhower said gently. "And I know you've gotten to know some of them over the years. I'm sure they're fine people. But I have an entire country of fine people to think about."

Vandenberg wanted to say more, but he'd tried to make his case earlier, and failed. "Understood, Mr. President. I'll send out the orders first thing in the morning."

"Thank you, Hoyt. Have a good night."

The general hung up the phone and sat in silence, staring at the calendar on his wall. June 30th was circled—his retirement date. He supposed he was grateful to have made it that far—the docs were getting increasingly gloomy with his prognosis—but he still desperately wished to go out on his own terms. He'd fought the Nazis, helped create both the United States Air Force *and* the Central Intelligence Agency. His public legacy was assured.

And yet.

* * *

When Frank opened his eyes again, he was in a tent. From the open flap, he could see it was night outside.

"There he is." Cal smiled down at him. He was looking younger and healthier now, which Frank took as a good sign.

"What happened?" Frank asked. He felt as though his head was floating three feet from his body.

Cal exhaled sharply. "Oh, boy. Where to start? Beria had an H-bomb and we stopped him, so that's good."

"Danny's gone."

"Yes, Frank, he is. We brought his body back. Gonna send him home proper, full honors."

Frank sat up a little and felt his head swim.

"Beria. How'd we do that?"

Cal brightened up a little at this. "Couple of our new friends. The one Danny and I were after, his name's Miguel, he's a sharpshooter. Can't miss from any distance no matter what. He shot Beria in the wrist. Then our other new friend, Chinese fella named Hei Feng, used his Enhancement to get the detonator away."

Frank nodded. "Where's Beria now?"

"We got him," Cal assured him. "Rosie made sure the American brass was all cleared out by the time we caught up with him, so only the Reds know we have him—and the Russian Variants who didn't defect are making sure Beria's involvement stays under wraps. We have him bound, gagged, drugged up to his gills, and sitting with three null generators."

With a thin-lipped smile, Frank swung his legs out onto the floor and sat up completely, then waited for the room to stop spinning. "We got defectors, then?"

"Some, but we got another problem."

Cal's tone got Frank focused fast. "What now?"

Cal held out a teletype. "Came in while you were out."

It had just one word on it:

NIGHTINGALE

"Holy shit."

Cal nodded. "Yeah. At least somebody still loves us."

NIGHTINGALE was a code word Danny had developed back in '49, after the Variants had been mistakenly implicated in the death of James Forrestal, Truman's first defense secretary. Frank had hoped never to see it.

"Who sent it?" Frank asked.

"Hell if I know."

"Are we sure this is real?" Frank said. "Did we get any other orders?"

Cal handed over two other teletypes, both with a lot more words on them. "Yeah. All Variants are to report to Mountain Home immediately. Drop what you're doing and go back. Specifically, we're to bring back Beria and any defectors, too. Other one is the report Rosie and I filed."

Frank scanned the teletypes several times. "Well, shit."

Cal got up and offered Frank a hand, pulling him up and steadying him. "Maggie's gone already. She just up and left. She gonna take care of herself just fine. The others, I think they need to hear this from you."

Frank got his bearings well enough to start heading for the tent flaps. "Why me?"

"'Cause Danny's not here, and you're next up. Simple as that. We took over one of the officers' quarters. Everybody's in there."

The two left the tent and, with Cal leading the way, started walking. "They'll listen to you, Cal. You know that."

Cal shook his head sadly. "Frank, I'm an old Negro man, and fact is nobody listens to an old Negro man as much as they will a white fella with authority like you. Ain't right, but it's how it is. Come on."

They walked the rest of the way in silence. Cal was right—it wasn't fair. Frank hadn't really given much thought at all to black people until he met Cal. After all this, though, he couldn't imagine *not* listening to the man. Cal was committed, upstanding, and smarter than he ever gave himself credit for. Whether it was Prague, Syria, Guatemala, even here—Cal was their north star. If Cal had reservations about something, Frank listened. More people needed to, skin color be damned.

They entered the officer's quarters to find it packed with people—Mrs. Stevens, Ekaterina, Yamato, Sorensen for starters. Cal introduced Frank to Hei Feng—who seemed grateful somebody could actually talk to him in Mandarin—as well as Miguel Padilla, a Venezuelan enlisted man who was part of the multinational force. And there were four Russians there, too, Mikhail Tsakhia among them. Illyanov and Savrova weren't, however, and Frank didn't know the other three, but greeted them warmly nonetheless.

"Okay, folks, settle down," Cal said. Despite what he'd said to Frank earlier, everybody immediately stopped chatting and looked up expectantly. "I think Frank here should explain exactly what's going on before we decide anything. Frank?"

Frank thought he might start by talking about Danny, and what he'd heard in the darkness. But that seemed like a tall order right now, and they had more pressing things to consider. "Okay. Let's talk about NIGHTINGALE. We need to be clear on exactly what this means. When Danny came up with this code word, he said it was our worst-case scenario. He'd given it to a couple of folks higher up in the MAJESTIC program, folks he thought he could trust. I didn't agree with that then, but looks like he was right.

"The long and short of it is this: the government is shutting down MAJESTIC-12."

There were murmurs around the room as the words were translated and opinions made. Worries lined the faces of everyone there.

"Furthermore," Frank continued, "we just got orders to drop everything and return to Mountain Home. All of us. We have four days to comply. Now, I can't say for certain—none of us can—but if we follow these orders, there may be a chance that they're going to keep us there. Permanently. Mrs. Stevens worked through any number of scenarios, and the chance of them just letting us walk away and return to normal life . . . well, it isn't high. For our own safety and freedom, I think we have to assume that we'll be locked up for good when we get back. We weren't exactly at liberty in this program, after all—there's always been elements in the government who've wanted us thrown in a hole and forgotten. And the government is now aware that a Variant tried to detonate an H-bomb and scuttle the armistice talks. That's not gonna help our case.

"So I want you—each one of you—to think carefully about what you do next. There's a chance that this is overblown, that maybe they're just gonna pull us out of the field and keep studying us or whatever, and that things won't change too much. I personally don't feel that's realistic. Truman nearly locked us away in '49—that's why we developed NIGHTINGALE. I think we need to take it seriously."

There was more murmuring, which Frank let go until silence reigned again. Finally, Sorensen raised his hand. "So if we don't follow orders, what do we do?"

"Well, you'll be AWOL. If you try to go back to the United States, you'll run the risk of being arrested—and then you'll definitely be thrown in a hole and forgotten. I mean, you're all trained up pretty well. I have no doubt you could get back into the country without being noticed. But if you try to reach out to your families or in any way try to go back to your normal lives, I got ten bucks that says they'll find you inside of a week. So if you do decide to disobey orders, your lives will be changed forever. Period," Frank said.

"So that's it?" Yamato asked from the back of the room. "Just walk away from everything?"

"Yeah, that's it," Frank answered. "Get an alias and the papers to back it up. Spend some time moving around, don't get rooted right away. In a couple years, maybe you can pick a spot to try to settle down. Maybe Mexico or an island somewhere. Don't try to send a letter or tell anyone from your old life where you are. When we thought of NIGHTINGALE, we came up with some ideas for staying in touch with each other that should work—we'll use classified ads with code words in the newspapers. We can brief you up on it if you want. But yeah, otherwise, you drop everything and everyone and go find a new life, because the old one will be gone."

Ekaterina looked like she was on the verge of tears—Frank felt for her, having her second home in four years ripped away from her—but managed to speak up. "What about the other Variants who aren't here?"

"Whatever guardian angel sent us this likely sent it along to the others as well. I know Zippy Silverman was in on it, and one or two others. We can only hope that the word's gotten out. I know we'll keep an ear to the ground in case we hear about anybody getting into trouble." Frank looked around for other questions, but most everyone was just sitting there, taking it all in. "Cal, anything to add?"

Cal looked surprised, but stepped forward anyway. Frank didn't like putting him on the spot, but he knew Cal would offer something good—and he wasn't disappointed. "I guess I'll just say that if you do decide to head off on your own, you really ought to keep your Enhancements to yourself. I'm sure it'd be mighty tempting to use 'em to set yourself up—and you got your training aside from that, too. But this ain't a movie. It ain't a comic book. International jewel thieves get caught. And there ain't no such thing as superheroes. You stay true to yourselves, make sure you can look at yourselves in the mirror in the morning. Maybe we got sold up the river, I don't know. But two wrongs don't make a right. Be smart about it, is all."

Frank smiled a little at that. "Listen to the man. He's right. Don't be dumb. And if I see any caped crusaders in the news, I'll personally come and kick your ass." That got some chuckles in the room, as intended. "You have four days to decide. If you do end up going back, all I ask is that you give the rest of us the four full days to get clear before you check in with Washington."

After listening to one of his countrymen translate, Tsakhia stood up and addressed Frank in Russian. "What will you do?"

Frank turned to the rest of the crowd and spoke in English. "Mikhail here wants to know what I'm doing, and that's fair, since I'm the one doing all the goddamn talking. I'm out. I have a few things I need to do, but I'm not heading back."

"And what about Beria?" another Russian asked in English.

Frank just smiled. "Worry about yourself. Comrade Beria will see justice. Anybody else?" There was nothing but silence. "Okay. Let me or Cal or Rose know what you end up deciding to do, and if you're out, we'll let you in on our message system. Good luck."

The group immediately started talking amongst themselves again, and Frank took the opportunity to head outside for some air. Cal and Mrs. Stevens followed. "Good job in there, Frank," Mrs. Stevens said. "I think you handled that well."

Frank looked at them both and smiled. "I just realized I don't know if you're going to bail out or not. I just assumed."

Cal chuckled. "Frank, first thing I did when I got that teletype was commandeer a line back home. Sally and I set up our own little code a while back. She's on the road to Calgary by now. Winston has an open plane ticket. We gonna be fine."

Frank clapped him on the shoulder. "You're a helluva spy, Cal."

"Yes, sir, I am," he replied. "What about you, Rosie?"

Mrs. Stevens gave a sad little smile. "I have twenty-three contingency plans in place for NIGHTINGALE. Eight of them are applicable now. I just . . . I had always hoped . . ."

She started to cry a little, and Cal enveloped her in a hug. "I know. I know," Cal said. "But we knew this was coming. That's why we planned. Hope for the best, prepare for the worst."

Mrs. Stevens returned the hug for a healthy while before disengaging herself, only to hug Frank as well. "I can tell you're heading out soon," she told him after the hug. "Good luck. Stay in touch. Be safe!"

"I will. Maybe after a decade or so, we'll get together again for a little reunion. Somewhere nice. Cuba, maybe."

Mrs. Stevens nodded and wiped away her tears with her hand. "I'd like that. I'll keep an eye out. You two . . . you take care of yourselves, you hear me?"

"Yes, ma'am," Cal said.

After looking around and straightening her uniform, Mrs. Stevens gave them an awkward smile and headed back inside with the other Variants—undoubtedly to mother-hen them until each of them left. They were in good hands.

Frank extended his hand to Cal. "Mr. Hooks, proud to have served with you. It's been an honor."

Cal ignored Frank's hand and gave him a hug instead. "You're a good man, Frank. You stay that way, you hear?"

"Yes, sir."

Cal put his hands on Frank's shoulders. "Good luck."

The two men then walked off into the Korean night, but in different directions.

* * *

Detlev Bronk stared at the stacks of teletypes on his desk, having read them several times over. First the one from Washington, closing down MAJESTIC-12 and telling him to keep the electronic jammers on indefinitely and to confine all Variants at Mountain Home to quarters, under armed guard. The second, also from Washington, was a copy of the orders sent to the Variants in the field, telling them to come home. Of course, they'd be immediately detained if they did.

The third ensured they wouldn't come home. It simply said NIGHTINGALE. Danny had confided in him years ago what that meant.

Finally, the fourth one. Bronk picked it up and read it through again. He had no idea who had sent it, but his money was on either Rose Stevens or Frank Lodge. It reported that Danny Wallace had died in the line of duty, which saddened Bronk greatly. Danny was a good man, one who always advocated for his kind while still loyal to the United States—a massive balancing act if there ever was one.

It also gave a brief rundown on what Beria had done and why—and a theory as to the source of the vortex itself and the intelligences behind it. Or within it. Beyond it. Whatever.

It made keeping the jammers up and running seem perfectly reasonable indeed. As for the rest . . .

Bronk got up from his desk and headed toward the hangar and the newly constructed "black box" which now housed the vortex. The first thing he'd do would be to send Kurt Schreiber as far away as possible. St. Elizabeths Hospital in D.C. would be perfect—they had plenty of rubber rooms there. Let the bastard rant and rave to his heart's content.

After that, he figured he'd gather his engineers and get to work on a more permanent solution to keep the vortex from ever communicating with anyone ever again.

As for the Variants . . .

25

June 27, 1953

T he night sky blended into the calm waters of the Black
Sea, making it difficult to see where one stopped and
the other began. But it was an excellent view, one that
had drawn Nikita Khrushchev to the sleepy little Georgian
town of Pitsunda years ago. One of the benefits of his position was a vacation dacha, and he had chosen this one as
an escape from Stalin's overbearing madness—and yet,
at the same time, to curry favor with the old Georgian as
well.

Perhaps, one day soon, his colleagues would move their
vacation homes here to curry favor with *him*.

But there were matters to manage first—one of which
had shown up at his door not twenty minutes past.

"I cannot forget what I have seen," Khrushchev said to
his visitor as they stood sipping vodka on the back bal-
cony of the dacha. "I saw Lavrentiy Beria somehow produce flames out of nothingness. We have yet to be able to
penetrate the basement vaults of his Leningrad institute.
And now you come here and tell me all this. What am I to
believe? You are not even Russian!"

The man next to him smiled. "How do you know this,
Comrade?" he said in an impeccable Leningrad accent,
his Red Army colonel's uniform perfect in every regard,
right down to the shine on his shoes. The visitor lacked
the roundness of many Russian faces, yes, but that was not
a universal trait.

"Your teeth, Comrade," Khrushchev said. "They are
too perfect, and you do not have the aristocratic bearing

of someone who has known comfort enough in the Soviet Union to enjoy fine dentistry."

The visitor chuckled. "You're good. So why invite me in for a drink?"

"Because you brought me such a fine gift. And I would like to know why."

They turned around to see Lavrentiy Beria, bound and gagged and unconscious, dumped unceremoniously on the floor of Khrushchev's study. The strange visitor had stored the former secret police chief in the trunk of his car, and had also provided photographs and documentation of the weapon Beria had somehow commandeered. That, of course, would result in months of investigations and interrogations before they had the truth of it, but given Beria's involvement in the Soviet nuclear program, it was not beyond the realm of possibility that he might have diverted a weapon away from the military into his own hands. It would be a masterstroke of bureaucracy, of course, but Khrushchev knew the Soviets were getting quite good at putting the Red in "red tape."

"People with Beria's abilities should not place themselves in positions of power," the visitor said. "Indeed, perhaps they should not be trusted at all."

Khrushchev nodded. "We recovered some files from the Lubyanka and the Behkterev Institute, enough to know of these individuals. Should we find them, they will be taken care of. But what of the others outside the Motherland? It is likely America has some."

At this, Khrushchev saw a flicker of anger on the visitor's face. "America, Comrade, has similarly ended its involvement with such people," the visitor said. "Like you, they will be hunting down these people whenever possible."

"People like you?"

The visitor paused, giving Khrushchev a sidelong look, before taking another sip of vodka. "As I said, Comrade, you're good."

Khrushchev smiled. Of course he was good. He'd survived Stalin's purges and had placed himself in command of the Party—and soon, he figured, the country. And he'd done so by understanding people, by reading the signs. He could come off as a smiling, pleasant, fat buffoon at times. That was intentional. "We could, of course, continue to use these people as Beria had used them," Khrushchev ventured. "There is value in such abilities."

"If you can find them," the visitor said. "After the Korea incident, those on both sides agreed that the world might be better off if they kept to the shadows. Yes, you may yet have one or two show up and ask to serve the Motherland once more, and if you search, you may find one or two others. But between Beria's program and the Americans', they will be very, very hard to track down."

"And perhaps that is best," Khrushchev said. "Though of course we will still look. And what of the phenomenon you described?"

The visitor downed the rest of his drink and placed his glass on the railing. "I suggest, Comrade, in the strongest terms, that you keep the phenomenon buried deep. The Americans have discovered it emits low levels of electromagnetic radiation. You should assemble electronic jammers and shielding to keep it from doing so."

Khrushchev nodded; next to Beria was a stack of folders on this subject as well. "You have given me an advantage. I'll ask again: Why?"

With a sigh, the visitor turned to look Khrushchev in the eye. "I know you're going to continue to oppose America and the West. I know you will fight these stupid proxy wars in Asia and the Middle East, Africa, South America. I know that peace is unlikely. But I hope that even as you do this, you will still *want* peace. Of all the leaders fighting for Stalin's scraps, I see you as the best of many bad choices." The visitor smirked at this. "So perhaps, Comrade, you'll do better than Stalin did, or Beria would have. I hope I'm not wrong."

The visitor turned to leave, but stopped at the door leading inside. "If you do revive Beria's program, or decide to try to affect the phenomenon in any way, we'll know about it. And we'll put an end to it."

"Who will? The Americans?"

"No, Comrade," the visitor said. "People like me."

With that the visitor walked back into the house and flipped a switch on a small device—a null generator, Khrushchev remembered. He then leaned in and spoke to Beria in English, even though the latter remained unconscious, and then walked out of the room and out the front door of the house.

Khrushchev smiled and finished his own drink. They'd recovered many more files than he let on, of course. And he would try to find a way, someday, to bring Frank Lodge and his friends into the fold.

* * *

"What do you mean, *gone*?"

Allen Dulles blanched as the President stared daggers at him from across the Oval Office desk.

"Sir, the Variants have disobeyed orders and are officially AWOL," Dulles responded, summoning as much calm as he could. "The Variants in place in Asia all simply up and left, while the ones still at Mountain Home have escaped. Meanwhile, we have Soviet media reporting Beria's arrest, with new photos."

Eisenhower threw his briefing folder onto his desk with an angry slap. "What the hell kind of operation were we running here?"

"Mr. President, the Variants in Idaho weren't being held as prisoners. They were given base housing according to family status and time of service, and they had as much right to come and go as anybody else on base. Yes, they were being constantly watched and tailed, but . . . well, we trained them well. Even without their Enhancements, they were among the most effective covert operatives in the world. Slipping away from some Air Force M.P.s would be child's play. As for the ones in the field, well, sir, they're spies. It's what they do best."

"But how did they *know*?" Eisenhower asked. "When I ordered MAJESTIC-12 rolled up and shelved, part of that plan was to hold all those people. I saw the plans Truman and Hillenkoetter drew up. They were good ones. This shouldn't have happened. Were they tipped off?"

Dulles's mind flashed back to the one-word teletype that appeared on his desk the morning after Eisenhower's order. He didn't know who sent it, but he could assume why. "We can't say for certain. It's possible that sympathetic elements within the MAJESTIC-12 oversight committee may have done that, yes, but I don't know for sure. Remember, some of their Enhancements may have contributed to their escape as well."

Eisenhower grimaced as he picked up the folder and leafed through it again. "So what are we doing about it?"

"I have teams looking for them now," Dulles said. "Overseas, all CIA stations are on alert. Here, I went with the U.S. Marshals and Secret Service to begin a search."

"Good. Keep Hoover out of it," Eisenhower said. "Last thing we need is for him to stick his nose into this." Eisenhower flipped through the summary pages on each of the Variants missing—which was all of them. "We're not gonna find 'em, are we." It wasn't a question.

"Not likely, sir. Between their Enhancements and their training . . . not likely at all."

"And how likely is it they'll be coming back for us? Revenge against the government, all that?"

Dulles could only shrug. "Hard to say. We have full contingency plans to recapture or eliminate each and every one of them should we ever come across them again. We know their strengths and weaknesses. But they know *we* know. We might get one or two, but we estimate that most of them will simply vanish, try to live out their lives. We'll redirect the remaining MAJESTIC-12 resources toward finding them, but I think we'd have to get awful lucky."

Eisenhower stood and buttoned his suit jacket; he had some Boy Scouts coming in for a photo in a minute or two. "That's not good enough, Allen."

"I know, sir."

With a grimace, Eisenhower motioned the CIA director

to the door. "Clean it up as best we can. If any of them ever shows their face anywhere in the world, I want to know about it ASAP."

Dulles gathered his things and stood. "Understood, Mr. President. But . . ."

Eisenhower relented slightly. "I know. Truman should've never let them out. But it is what it is. Thank you."

Dulles nodded and left the room, striding past a veritable platoon of Boy Scouts waiting to visit the President. He'd follow his orders to the letter, of course, and knew the United States would spend millions of dollars searching for their wayward Variants, and others.

But without Subject-1, it would be a wild goose chase. A big one. And maybe that wasn't necessarily a bad thing at all.

41

Action
SS

Info

FROM: MOSCOW

TO: Secretary of State

NO: 3007, DECEMBER 24, 3 P.M.

Control: 2453
Rec'd: DECEMBER 24, 1953
3 P.M.

To be read only with the permission of the Director of S/S.

This Document Must Be Returned to Kr/R
Central
Files

SECRET

PRIORITY

FINAL DISPOSITION OF BERIA CASE BROUGHT NO
SURPRISES. DESCRIPTION OF SUMMARY COURT
PROCEEDINGS ACCORDANCE LAW DECEMBER 1, 1934
ADDED NO NEW FACTUAL OR OTHER INFORMATION
CONCERNING REAL BACKGROUND AND CAUSE OF
BERIA CASE. IT IS STILL EMBASSY'S VIEW THAT
ESSENCE OF CASE FROM BEGINNING WAS ROLE
OF SECRET POLICE IN SOVIET DICTATORSHIP
FOLLOWING STALIN'S DEATH AND THAT DECISION
FOR WHATEVER REASON OF MALENKOV AND HIS
ASSOCIATES TO SUBORDINATE POLICE TO PARTY
WAS DIRECT CAUSE BERIA'S DOWNFALL. FROM ALL
ACCOUNTS FINAL LIQUIDATION BERIA AND HIS
IMMEDIATE ASSOCIATES HAS BEEN GREETED BY
COMPLETE INDIFFERENCE AND POSSIBLY SECRET
PLEASURE BY SOVIET POPULATION AND THERE HAVE
BEEN NO SIGNS OF ANXIETY OR APPREHENSION
WHICH ACCOMPANIED SIMILAR PHENOMENA
DURING STALINIST PURGES IN THIRTIES. INDEED,
ALL PUBLISHED MATERIAL IN LAST WEEK HAS
EMPHASIZED THAT CASE WAS CLOSED AND SOUGHT
TO CREATE IMPRESSION THAT IT WAS NOT A
BEGINNING BUT AN END. HOWEVER, SHOULD NEED
ARISE IN FUTURE UNDISCLOSED "EVIDENCE" IN
BERIA CASE COULD BE CONVENIENTLY USED FOR
IMPLICATING ALMOST ANYBODY IN SOVIET REGIME.

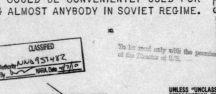

53

Action

EUR

Info
RMR

P
IES
UOP
E
OLI
DCL

OCB
USIA
CIA

OFFICIAL USE ONLY

PRESENCE OF TWO LEADING REGULAR ARMY MEMBERS ON SPECIAL PANEL SUPREME COURT (ONE OF WHOM MARSHAL KONEV) WHILE NOT UNUSUAL IN CASES OF TREASON IS PROBABLY REFLECTION ROLE OF ARMY IN AFFAIR. OTHER MEMBERSHIP OF COURT APPEARS TO REVEAL DESIRE TO INVOLVE IN RESPONSIBILITY REPRESENTATIVES OF CHIEF INSTITUTIONS SOVIET UNION.

THE REGIME IN THIS CASE MADE A DEFINITELY HALF-HEARTED ATTEMPT TO CONSTRUCT A CONVINCING CASE AGAINST BERIA POSSIBLY DUE TO EXTREMELY TROUBLESOME CONSEQUENCES OF "PROVING" THAT BERIA HAD BEEN AN AGENT OF FOREIGN IMPERIALISM WHILE HE WAS WORKING HAND-IN-GLOVE IN POLITBURO WITH PRESENT LEADERSHIP. INDEED, IN READING MATERIAL OF PAST WEEK IT IS DOUBTFUL IF PRESENT LEADERSHIP WISHED SOVIET POPULATION REALLY TO BELIEVE MOST OF THESE CHARGES AGAINST BERIA.

THERE IS OF COURSE ELEMENTARY JUSTICE IN FATE OF BERIA AND HIS GPU ASSOCIATES BUT IT WOULD HAVE BEEN MORE FITTING IF RETRIBUTION HAD BEEN METED OUT BY HIS VICTIMS RATHER THAN HIS ACCOMPLICES. APART FROM POLITICAL SIGNIFICANCE OF BERIA CASE WHICH IS OF COURSE IMPORTANT, ENTIRE PROCEEDINGS GO TO CONFIRM OBVIOUS FACT THAT STALIN'S SUCCESSORS HAVE NO GREATER SEMBLANCE OF MORALITY OR REGARD FOR TRUTH THAN HAD STALIN HIMSELF.

BOHLEN

741.11/10-357

PA

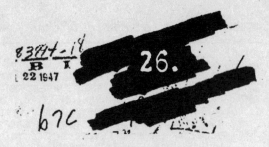

26.

January 12, 1954

Hoyt Vandenberg sat in an easy chair in his robe, pajamas, and slippers, with a pillow underneath him that wasn't helping one whit, and tried to focus on the newspaper as he drank a cup of tepid tea. An intravenous unit hung from a stand next to him, slowly dripping chemicals into his bloodstream that might—just might—stem the tide of cancer inside him. It was a long shot, and if the latest round of therapy didn't work, the folks here at Walter Reed would begin a round of "palliative care."

What a pleasant-sounding death sentence that was.

They were already doing everything they could to make him comfortable, knowing that it was likely this would be the last room he ever slept in. There was a sitting area with his chair and a couch and coffee table, and the bed on the other wall was made up with quilts and blankets taken from home. His wife and family were already in and out, trying to give the place homey touches—yesterday, they had put up some photographs on the wall and on the nightstand next to his bed. But while he appreciated the effort, Vandenberg knew that this was the ultimate in window dressing. He had months, on the outside. Weeks if his body wasn't in the mood to cooperate.

The phone rang, and while he desperately wished it would go away, he relented and picked it up on the fourth ring. "Vandenberg," he said curtly.

"General, this is Calvin Hooks. You remember me?"

Vandenberg smiled, despite himself. "Of course, Mr. Hooks. I hope you're well."

"I am, thanks. Took a little bit, but I got me and Sally all settled in nicely."

"I suppose asking where would be counterproductive," Vandenberg said.

There was a gentle chuckle on the other end of the line. "Let's just say it's nice and quiet, and the folks here don't care much about the color of my skin. I fit in just fine. And I'm not calling from there anyway. Just in case."

Caribbean, maybe. Or up in Canada somewhere. Hooks wasn't much for languages. "Well, that's smart. And I'm glad to hear it. You deserve a break. What can I do for you?"

"Well, General, I wanted to see if you wanted some help."

Vandenberg's heart started to beat a little faster. "With what?"

"Heard you were laid up some. Heard the docs aren't being optimistic. Might be something I can do."

Vandenberg's mind raced as he recalled Cal's file. "I didn't think you could do that."

"There's things I can't cure, sure. But I can roll back your age a bit. Give you a little more time. Figure it's the least I can do for the heads-up you gave us."

"I don't know what you're talking about, Mr. Hooks," Vandenberg said, his smile growing a little wider even as his voice took on a tone of warning.

"Right. You didn't do anything. Still want to thank you for it."

Vandenberg tried desperately to quash the growing hope inside him. "How much time?"

He could envision Cal shrugging as he spoke. "Can't rightly say. Months. Years. Depends on how healthy you want to look, how many questions you want them doctors to ask you."

"But how would you get here?"

"Well, I thought about that, sir," Cal said. "There's places, nice and small, where I can come over without too much trouble. Then just take a bus into Washington. You'd have to set up a visitor pass for me, of course. Find me a name I could work with."

"Sounds dangerous."

"Oh, ain't too bad. Lord knows I've been through worse. I can come through farm country first, take on a little juice from the livestock. Not too much trouble, really."

Vandenberg couldn't find any words for several long moments. It was, without a doubt, the kindest, most generous thing anybody had ever offered him, and any doubts he had about providing the MAJESTIC-12 people with the bug-out code were immediately erased. He worked with the program from the very beginning, since Roscoe Hillenkoetter came to him in 1945 with news of strange vortexes and superpowered people. But they were, in the end, *good* people, he'd found. Or at least Cal Hooks was, and that was more than enough.

"That's a mighty kind offer, Mr. Hooks," Vandenberg said, his voice cracking. "Mighty kind. But . . . much as I want to, I can't let you do that."

"But, sir—"

"No. Please," Vandenberg pleaded. "You know they're gonna be looking for you. I know you have some fine skills, Mr. Hooks. I figure you might even get in here and be able to do it. But getting out is another story. And they'll notice my miraculous recovery. There'll be questions, and there'll only be so much I can do now that I'm retired."

"I know the risks, General," Cal said, protest in his voice.

"I know you do, son. I know you do. And . . ." Vandenberg paused to fight back the tears that were nonetheless coming through. "And I know what kind of man you are. You've earned your peace and quiet. Don't jeopardize that. You go have a good life now, you read me?"

There was a pause on the other end of the phone. "I might just come anyway."

"Then I'm gonna put out an alert on you," Vandenberg said, steel entering his voice. "*Please*. Don't tempt me. I can't have more time, knowing you could end up in prison for the rest of your life. Just . . . go on now. Thank you. Really. But you just let me be. Go enjoy yourself. Be with your family."

"Sir, really, I can—"

Vandenberg didn't wait for Cal to finish, instead replacing the phone on the cradle. Only then did he allow himself to break down.

* * *

January 21, 1954

Frank walked through the McClellan Gate, an ornate red sandstone archway with an inscription in yellow-gold: "Rest On Embalmed And Sainted Dead Dear As The Blood Ye Gave No Impious Footsteps Here Shall Tread The Herbage Of Your Grave." Frank thought it overwrought and maudlin, but it was built while the memory of the Civil War was still fresh, and the folks back then seemed to be a more florid bunch to begin with.

He took a left and began walking, past rows and rows of simple white stone markers and leafless trees, looking at the paper in his hand. After about five minutes, he found what he was looking for.

IN MEMORY OF

DANIEL J. WALLACE

MISSOURI

MEDAL OF HONOR

COMMANDER

US NAVY

WORLD WAR II

MAR 3 1920

JUNE 23 1953

Frank shoved the paper back in his pocket, then folded his hands and stared down at the stone, at the dead winter grass, at the little American flag placed there by some school kids or ladies' group or whatever. He thought maybe he should say a prayer, but after all he'd experienced, it seemed the entire notion of heaven and hell was just . . . off.

Maybe Danny was in that other place, on the other side of the white light. Maybe not. Frank knew only that he didn't know, and he'd never know until it was his time.

"Heya, Frank."

He turned and smiled slightly as Maggie walked over. She was dressed in a long dark coat and a blue dress, heels, a hat, the whole nine yards. She even had those little formal white gloves ladies sometimes wore, and her red hair was done up nice. She really did look like Rita Hayworth when she wanted to.

"Garbo. I always liked that one," Frank said. *Garbo* was a perfect code word for a fake-double agent. The more obvious reference was the Greta Garbo picture, *The Two-Faced Woman*, and talking about Greta Garbo in most circumstances was pretty benign and easy to work into conversation.

The other reference, though, was far more interesting—and known only to spooks. Juan Pujol García was a Spaniard who went to work spying on the British on behalf of the Nazis—except he was really working for the British. He did so well in his double role that he got the Iron Cross from Germany. And his code name during the war was *Garbo*.

"You doubted me?" Maggie teased.

Frank just smiled. "Always. Why didn't you work it in at the Lubyanka? We got the SATCHMO all-clear from Washington. Big and brassy. Could've wrapped it up then and there."

Maggie grimaced a little at that. "I figured you were doing SATCHMO. But I didn't know where Beria was keeping his nuke. I needed more time. Tried to work Garbo in there, but you were way too spooked. And then you threw a chair through the fucking window and jumped. If you had just waited a few more minutes . . ."

"I'm not the most patient guy," Frank said. "Glad you got my message. You didn't give us a chance to catch up before you got out of Dodge. What have you been up to?"

Maggie shrugged. "Laying low, moving around a bit.

Staying out of trouble. Well, there was that weekend in Atlantic City. A girl's gotta have fun."

"I don't even want to know," Frank said. "What about long term? What'cha gonna do with your life?"

"Honestly? No idea. For now, just gonna find a small, quiet corner of the world, not a lot of people. Somewhere to hunker down a while and sort things out. You?"

Frank shoved his hands in his pockets and took out his cigarettes and a lighter. "Gonna travel some. I still got all these languages in my head, might as well put 'em to use. Probably just do what I did back before Danny found me. Job to job, place to place, just see what a world without all this spy crap looks like."

They both grew silent at Danny's name and looked down at his final resting place. "He was a good guy," Maggie said finally. "Fought for us every step of the way. Really thought it would work, that we'd do our time and then be left alone."

"Maybe if he were still around. Now? I mean, we were dangerous before. Now, one of us tried to nuke Korea, and the rest of us know way too much. Danny's gone, Vandenberg's retired and doesn't have much time left." Frank lit his cigarette and took a long drag. "Nobody left to speak for us. We did the right thing."

Maggie reached over, took Frank's cigarette, and took a drag of her own. "We should've left years ago. But, it is what it is." She handed the butt back to him. "How are the others?"

Frank smiled. "Cal's fine. He had plans in place for him and his family. Rose ended up in Switzerland, doing something with physics there, of all things, and she took Ekaterina with her, working to get her officially adopted. Sorensen just moved to Winnipeg and just made contact with his family to get them up there."

"Not smart," Maggie said.

"I helped him work it out, don't worry," Frank replied. "And Yamato's off God knows where. I'm trying to keep my ear to the ground for the others."

She looked at him quizzically. "Why? It's a risk."

"Because he'd want me to," Frank said, nodding at Danny's tombstone.

They both stared at the grave for a while, until Maggie broke the silence. "All right. I'm off. See you around."

"Maggie."

She turned around, but Frank was at a loss for words. Of all the experts who'd inhabited his head for all those years, nobody had any idea of what to say next. "Wait . . . yeah. I, uh . . ."

Maggie smiled, turned back and gave him a peck on the cheek. "Trust me, I'm the last girl you'd want around. Go find someone nice."

That wasn't what Frank had in mind, which he figured she already knew, but the gesture was oddly comforting. "If I need to reach you . . ." he said finally.

This time, she turned and kept walking.

"Don't," she said.

"Which parts of this are real?"

When one writes historical fantasies, that's a completely valid question, and my excellent editor, Cory Allyn, had to ask that a few times over the course of our work on the MAJESTIC-12 books. History is full of noteworthy characters and unusual circumstances, so you might be surprised as to what's real, and what's not. (*Editor's note: in a series full of superheroes and supernatural occurrences, the sections I originally noted as least plausible were usually the ones that stuck closest to actual history!*)

The MAJESTIC-12 books are historical fantasy (or, perhaps, historical science fiction), but they're not necessarily alternate history, because at the end of the day, I wanted to make sure the general course of history wouldn't need to change as a result of the Variants' existence. Consider the MJ-12 program as more of a secret history that leans on existing events and individuals to help inform the story.

This series hews close to history because . . . I really couldn't make this stuff up if I tried. There was plenty to mine throughout the Cold War, a period in the history of espionage that was about as Wild West as you could possibly imagine. When the emergence of superpowered agents seems almost rational in comparison, how could you *not* run with it?

That said, I certainly took my liberties here and there over the course of the trilogy. The first book, *MJ-12: Inception*, had a looser connection to real historical events, but was closely intertwined with real conspiracy-theory lore. The infamous "Truman memo" ordering the creation of Operation Majestic Twelve—which is a very "real" document you can find quite easily with a quick Google search, but is widely considered by historical scholars to be utterly fake—was dated September 24, 1947, and has long been used by UFO enthusiasts as proof of the "Roswell incident." I decided early on to leverage the MJ-12 myth for this series, so the memo was a major touchpoint. In doing so, I moved the establishment of Area 51 forward a bit to 1948—in real life, it was established as a secret CIA aircraft-testing facility in 1955.

The real-life inauguration of Czechoslovakian President Klement Gottwald in June 1948 served as another touchpoint in that first book, even if the event simply provided a reasonable excuse for the new MJ-12 agents to rendezvous with their potential double agent.

The MJ-12 UFO mythos also informed a huge number of characters in the books—Roscoe Hillenkoetter, Hoyt Vandenberg, James Forrestal, the Dulles brothers, Harry S. Truman, and Dwight D. Eisenhower, just to name a few. Forrestal's mysterious death in 1949 became a key plot point in *MJ-12: Shadows*; similarly, that sad event became a rallying cry for real-life conspiracy theorists who claim that he was murdered to cover up the existence of extraterrestrial life.

As the series continued, I shifted away from MAJESTIC-12 conspiracy lore and more toward historical fact. The utter chaos in Syria in 1949, for example, played a huge role in *MJ-12: Shadows*. There were three coups in Syria that year, the first sponsored by the CIA and the other two well out of the agency's control. Not only did these events come with an immense amount of drama— the burglary of Miles Copeland's home in Damascus actually happened—but they felt, to me, like an object lesson in what happens when the United States tries to covertly meddle in other nations' affairs.

The first successful nuclear test by the Soviet Union in 1949 was the other major touchpoint in *Shadows*. Again, those events in Kazakhstan gave me an immense amount of material to work with, right down to the structures on site and the people involved. Yes, I did play around with some of the details—Laverentiy Beria *was* actually the political director of the USSR's nuclear effort, for example, but it's highly unlikely he exercised such a direct role in such a critical military project.

Beria, as you've just read, was one of the movers and shakers in the Soviet Union in the waning days of Stalin's rule, and had a good shot at replacing him as Premier after his death in 1953. There are those who claim Beria played a, shall we say, *active* role in Stalin's demise; while this hasn't been proven, Beria's reputation as a murderous bastard makes the theory plausible, at the very least. Indeed, Beria was responsible for the deaths of millions of innocents in the post-war Soviet Union, and did much to further, and benefit from, the culture of fear under Stalin.

That interregnum period between Stalin's death and Khrushchev's consolidation of power is very lightly covered in American history lessons, but the uncertainty and fear felt by the Soviets can't be understated, and Beria's eventual purge and execution were ultimately a key turning point in history; had he successfully taken control of the country, the Soviet Union would've gone down an even darker path. Khrushchev was no saint, but the glimmers of reform during his rule would never have occurred without him. I would argue that if Beria had won the day, there might still be a Soviet Union today, complete with an ongoing Cold War and nuclear tensions.

While the Kremlin's internal power struggle made the perfect backdrop for *Endgame*, there were obviously major liberties taken, and not just Beria's superhuman abilities. Beria never meddled in the armistice talks in Korea, for example, and certainly did not travel there to do so. His control over the USSR's nuclear arsenal had waned considerably by 1953 as well. However, the workers' protests in East Berlin actually did serve to undermine his credibility as head of the Soviet Union's spying and secret police organizations, and really were used by Khrushchev and others against him.

In the end, I think there are some very interesting things to be learned from the Cold War, especially in today's geo-political climate. It's been nearly thirty years since the end of the Cold War, more than fifty years since the heyday of the CIA's cowboy covert actions, and more than sixty years since McCarthyism nearly put a stranglehold on individual liberties in America.

But the lessons from these events, and their application to modern American life, I'll leave to you to determine.

Acknowledgments

Now I'm six books into a career I didn't really believe I'd have a decade ago, and there are so many excellent people who have helped make this a reality. Naming everyone who has made a positive impact on my career as an author would be an entire extra chapter of this book, and likely interesting only to me. So to all those fellow authors who have lifted me up and made me a part of an excellent, welcoming community within science fiction and fantasy, know that your generosity means more to me than I could ever say.

And to all of the people who have steadily bought my books, reviewed them, told others about them, come to conventions to see me and get books signed, interacted with me online and likewise helped lift me up, I see you and deeply appreciate your time and your enthusiasm.

As we wrap up the MAJESTIC-12 series, I want to thank everyone at Night Shade Books, former and current, who helped bring all my novels thus far to bookshelves. Cory Allyn has been my editor for five novels now, and has been an excellent editor and collaborator in making these works better than they would've been. Richard "Shecky" Shealy is still, and likely will always be, the best copyeditor an author could ask for, given that enforcing continuity over three books is exponentially more difficult than a single novel. Jason Katzman, Ross Lockhart, and Jeremy Lassen are also to thank for making all this a reality.

There are also plenty of family and friends and coworkers who have supported me throughout my authorial career, giving me the encouragement and support I need to keep going. I want to give a special thanks to Linda Johnson, the absolute best boss I've had in more than a quarter-century of being in the workforce. Her unwavering support at work—and in life—is a big reason why I can write books and you get to read them.

This book is dedicated to Sara Megibow (at long last!), my agent and my friend. She is a tireless advocate of my work, and greets my ideas with just the right mix of enthusiasm and grounding. I'm proud and humbled to have someone like her in my corner.

Finally, as always, none of this would be nearly as much fun without my wife, Kate, and daughter, Anna. Thank you both for all your love and support and patience.

Here's to the next adventure.

Michael J. Martinez
March 2018

Also Available
from Michael
J. Martinez and
Night Shade Books

A TEAM OF SUPERHUMAN SPIES NAVIGATE DANGEROUS GLOBAL ESPIONAGE IN THE SEQUEL TO THE PARANORMAL HISTORICAL THRILLER *MJ-12: INCEPTION*.

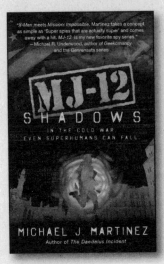

"*X-Men* meets *Mission: Impossible*. Martinez takes a concept as simple as a hit. 'Super spies that are actually super' and comes away with a hit. MJ-12 is my new favorite spy series."
—Michael R. Underwood, author of *Geekomancy* and the *Genrenauts* series

MJ-12: SHADOWS
Book Two of the
MAJESTIC-12 Series
Michael J. Martinez
978-1-59780-926-9
Mass Market / $7.99

"So good, in fact, that it makes you wonder why all sequels can't be this good . . . a fun, inventive, action-packed exploration of super spies operating in the shadows of history, and an almost perfect sequel."—*Fantasy Faction*, 10/10

It's 1949, and the Cold War is heating up across the world. For the United States, the key to winning might be Variants—once ordinary US citizens, now imbued with strange paranormal abilities and corralled into covert service by the government's top secret MAJESTIC-12 program.

Some Variants are testing the murky international waters in Syria, while others are back at home, fighting to stay ahead of a political power struggle in Washington. And back at Area 51, the operation's headquarters, the next wave of recruits is anxiously awaiting their first mission. All the while, dangerous figures flit among the shadows and it's unclear whether they are threatening to expose the Variants for what they are . . . or to completely destroy them. Are they working for the Soviet Union, or something far worse?

© Anna Martinez

About the Author

Michael J. Martinez is the author of the MAJESTIC-12 series of Cold War spy-fi novels and the *Daedalus* trilogy of Napoleonic-era space opera books. In addition, his short stories have appeared in *Cthulhu Fhtagn!*, *Unidentified Funny Objects 4*, *The Endless Ages Anthology* for *Vampire: The Masquerade*, *Geeky Giving*, and as part of the *Pathfinder* web fiction collection on Paizo.com. He's a member of the Science Fiction & Fantasy Writers of America and International Thriller Writers. He and his family recently relocated to the Los Angeles area, where the people are chill and the weather is not.